Amy Tolnitch

A Lost Touch of Innocence

Jewel Imprint: Amethyst
Medallion Press, Inc.
Printed in USA

(continued)

A LOST TOUCH OF PARADISE:

"Fans of Fairy Tales, Historical, and Paranormal Romances will find a new author to add to their shopping lists . . .

With a blend of fairy tale, medieval, and highland romance, Amy Tolnitch was able to reach out and grab this reader from the opening scene; a witch burning. Brilliant characterization, stunning descriptive ability and a truly romantic hero; A LOST TOUCH OF PARADISE has it all."

—Romance Designs

DEDICATION:

For Styrling, always.

Published 2007 by Medallion Press, Inc.

The MEDALLION PRESS LOGO
is a registered trademark of Medallion Press, Inc.

Typeset in Adobe Garamond Pro
Printed in the United States of America
10-digit ISBN: 1-9338360-9-1
13-digit ISBN: 978-1933836-09-6

10 9 8 7 6 5 4 3 2 1
First Edition

ACKNOWLEDGEMENTS:

Many thanks to my family and agent for their continued belief in me. Also, thanks to the team at Medallion Press for doing such a great job. As always, my critique partner, Mary Lennox, provided invaluable input on this book. I couldn't have written the horse scenes without the help of my friends at Summertree Farm, who have shown endless patience with this fledgling rider. Finally, thanks to the readers who thought that Piers deserved his very own story. I hope you like it.

Chapter I

"W icked girl," the Abbess of Kerwick hissed. "How dare you befoul the walls of God's house with your unclean presence?"

"I did nothing wrong," Giselle insisted, her voice catching. She stood facing the Abbess in the courtyard of Kerwick Abbey, a gray drizzle of rain dampening her threadbare woolen bliaut, adding to her deepening misery. Though she knew it was likely useless, she turned to the Bishop of Ravenswood, her gaze pleading. "I had naught to do with Sister Anne choking. Please believe me."

The Bishop's gaze was empty of warmth, as it ever had been when he deigned to look at her. "It was inevitable that your dam's tainted blood would reveal itself."

Giselle reared back, her hand pressed to her throat. "But—"

"Silence," the Abbess snarled, before she slapped Giselle's cheek. "Your place is not to question."

Giselle instinctively moved her hand to cradle her burning cheek, though she scarcely felt the pain. Behind the Abbess and the Bishop, a group of nuns stood watching. As Giselle looked from one to another, each dropped her gaze. Sister Alice, who had patiently taught her about herbs and healing. Sister Elena, from whom she'd learned so much about embroidering the beautiful tapestries that helped keep the abbey going. Her chest ached when Sister Cecilia refused to look her in the eye. Sister Cecilia, one she'd called friend, one with whom she'd sometimes lowered the guard on her thoughts and emotions the Abbess had studiously whipped into her. Disgust and shame choked her. They were like a line of brainless, timid sheep, hovering over one who'd been judged unworthy of the herd.

She searched the crowd for Sister Gertrude, but the older nun was not there. No doubt the Abbess had sent her on some task, making sure Giselle had no defender, she thought with a rare burst of defiance.

The Bishop's eyes bored into hers with hard contempt. "Gather your things."

Giselle sucked in a breath. She was to leave? Simply to be thrown out? Fear coursed through her.

"Quickly," he barked.

"But, where shall I go?" Her voice wavered but she held his gaze, finding somewhere deep inside the strength to do so, and not bow her head in submission as she'd been taught. "Please, no. I belong here."

"I have tried to see to your welfare, guide you to a life of grace, but you failed me. Failed all of us." His

2

condemnation rose in volume, his booming voice sounding as if he spoke with the Lord's own conviction and approval. "You have hidden a vile, unholy nature."

He glared at her with such naked hatred that Giselle took a step back. "You are no longer my problem." He waved a hand and Giselle found her arm snagged roughly in a strange man's grasp. "Take her to collect her belongings," the Bishop ordered. Another man came up beside her and the Bishop handed him a sealed packet.

"No," Giselle cried and tried to pull free. She ended up sprawled in the muck, peering up at the Bishop through the strengthening rain. "Please."

"Begone," he said in a cold, flat voice. "Your presence offends all of us."

"Wait," Giselle cried as a man yanked her up and dragged her away. "Where are you sending me?"

No one answered, but she caught the briefest glance of cruel satisfaction on the Bishop's face.

Within less time than it took her to say the Pater Noster, Giselle found herself clinging to the mane of a skinny old palfrey as they rode away from the gates of Kerwick Abbey, her small bundle of possessions tied behind her.

Kerwick Abbey. Her home for thirteen years, nearly all she remembered.

She looked back at the high gray walls, the ivy-covered gates, the old stone chapel, and wanted to weep. The peace and rhythm of each day, the sense of belonging to a place, a group of women apart from the world was all she knew.

A lone figure moved into the courtyard, barely visible through the rain, and Giselle's heart wept.

Sister Gertrude, who had been more a mother to Giselle than the birth mother she could scarcely remember.

Tears blurred Giselle's vision.

The only life she had ever known was gone, the only love she could recall swallowed by growing distance and teardrops from the sky. All of it, gone.

And she had no idea what awaited her on the outside.

❧ ❧ ❧

Piers Veuxfort, indulged younger brother of the Earl of Hawksdown, stroked a hand up Clarise's soft belly. She gave a purr of pleasure. He grinned and continued his lazy exploration of her body. By the saints, the woman's appetite for bed sport nearly exceeded his own. Twice they'd joined, and from the sounds and scent of her, Clarise was ready again.

"Piers," she said over a moan. "Do not tease me so." Even as she spoke the words, she jumped at the stroke of his fingers.

"Ah, Clarise, you know I would never tease you without making sure your desires were satisfied." He positioned himself between her pale thighs.

"Piers!" a voice shouted, just before a fist crashed

against the door.

"Go away," he called back, and slid Clarise up onto his own thighs.

Her eyes widened.

More banging ensued. "Piers, let the girl be!" his Uncle Gifford hollered.

Piers groaned and dropped his head. Damn Gifford for knowing him so well. "I am busy," he yelled over laughter. "Where is Saraid?"

"Welcoming *your* visitors," Gifford responded.

Reluctantly, Piers put Clarise aside and got up from the bed. "You'd best get dressed," he told her. "Gifford is not likely to go away."

Clarise laughed and swung her legs to the floor. "Nay." She quickly drew on her plain chemise and bliaut, and braided her hair in one long plait before opening the door.

Gifford stood there with a wide grin. "Good day to you, Clarise. My, do you not have the glow of health about you this day."

Piers coughed and shot Gifford a chiding look, which his uncle naturally ignored.

"Thank you, my lord," Clarise said, and sauntered past him.

"I believe Adela is seeking your aid in the kitchen," Gifford told her.

"Aye, I expect she is." Clarise continued down the corridor.

Piers let out a breath and pulled on clothing. Clarise

would no doubt get a swat for her absence, but he knew she didn't care. Just as he knew he was not the only one to lure Clarise from her duties. "Who are these visitors? Is it about that stallion I inquired after?"

Gifford shrugged. "Not sure. Saraid sent me off to find you."

Piers ran his fingers through his hair and led Gifford down the curved steps toward the great hall. His mind was already on what foals he could breed if the Earl of Carbonneaux was willing to sell him his Arab stallion. Rumor was the horse was completely unmanageable, but that had never bothered Piers before. He was adept at gentling skittish creatures.

When he entered the hall, he found a group of four awaiting him. Three appeared to be guards and a fourth wore a hooded cloak that concealed his face. Piers sighed. Not about the stallion then, he thought. "Hawis," he called out, winking at the older servant. "Fetch me a drink, if you please. I've fair worn myself to a nub this day."

Hawis rolled her eyes, but went for ale.

He glanced back at the group and thought he saw the cloaked figure stiffen, but shrugged off the thought. After gratefully accepting a cup and taking a long swallow, he asked, "Now, what have we here?"

A sharp-featured man handed him a sealed packet. Piers frowned. Was that a smirk on the man's face?

His confusion deepened when he broke the seal and saw the top sheet of parchment was a letter from the

Bishop of Ravenswood. As the unbelievable import of the Bishop's written lines slowly invaded Piers's mind, the man pushed the hooded figure in his direction.

"The Bishop said to tell you the wench be your problem now," the man said and gave the figure a second, and decidedly malicious shove.

It, or rather she, Piers's muddled brain corrected, fell onto her knees with a soft cry.

"By Saint George's sword, what is this about?" Piers demanded. He glanced at Gifford, who merely raised his palms before taking a gulp of ale from his ever-present jug. Beside him, Saraid's mouth was flat with concern.

The man's smirk deepened, as if he knew a secret, one Piers instinctively knew he would not like. "The girl is your responsibility now."

Piers tossed the letter aside and studied the document beneath. God in heaven, what had his sire done?

My dear friend, Annora,

Please be advised of my kindest regards. Your news is sorrowful, indeed. It would please me greatly to betroth my son, Piers, to your sweet Giselle. Please come to Falcon's Craig. I shall see to the welfare of you both.

Fondly,

William, Earl of Hawksdown

Shock thudded through him as he reached down to pull back the kneeling girl's hood.

For a moment, Piers couldn't catch a breath. An angel stared back him with beautiful turquoise eyes.

Her hair reminded him of spun silver, her face a smooth, creamy expanse of perfection. He blinked.

And took in the girl's expression of distaste.

"Who are you?" he demanded, his voice coming out much harsher than he'd intended. A damned betrothal was absolutely the last thing he needed at the moment, Piers thought with an inward curse.

The girl slowly stood, her gaze never leaving his. Her lips were pressed tightly together and she stared at him as if she'd just swallowed a piece of rancid meat. "I am Giselle," she said and lowered her gaze.

"Your surname?"

She shook her head.

Piers glanced at his father's letter. Its meaning was clear. But Piers was sure this Annora and her daughter had never come to Falcon's Craig. Certainly, he had not heard of his father's intent before this moment. "Where do you come from?"

"Kerwick Abbey."

Piers closed his eyes. Even better, he thought, barely resisting the urge to howl in denial. A girl fresh out of the nunnery. He opened his eyes to find Gifford holding the girl's arm and frowning at him.

"For God's sake, Piers," his uncle said. "Can you not see the girl is near dead on her feet?"

As if on cue, Giselle swayed against Gifford.

"We can sort all this out later," Gifford added. "I will see her to the rose chamber."

Piers nodded, too stunned by events to come up with words. The leader of the girl's small band gave him a taunting look. "We'll be takin' our leave now, my lord."

"Not just yet," Piers answered. "Hawis will bring food and drink. I have some questions for you."

The man shrugged. "Don't know nothin' to tell, my lord."

Piers watched Gifford guide the girl out of the hall, Saraid following. The girl did seem weary. Probably had developed a weak constitution with all that praying, he mused sourly with another twinge of dismay.

After the men accepted a cup of ale from Hawis, Piers crossed his arms and studied his visitors. Beneath the grime of travel, they were all fairly well dressed, their tunics free of holes or tears, their boots sturdy. They also were apparently well fed as none reached for the plate of meat and bread Hawis set on a nearby trestle table.

"Who is this girl?" Piers asked the leader.

"Like she said, her name's Giselle."

"Why did the Bishop order you to bring her here?"

Something flashed in the man's eyes before he shook his head. "You'll have to take that up with the Bishop, my lord. I just do as I'm told."

"Is she a nun?"

The leader shrugged. "I told you. We don't know nothin' about her."

"I think you do," Piers said in a cold voice as he took a step toward the men. Something inside him roiled with anger. "Why did she leave the convent?" He fixed the leader with a hard stare.

The man sighed. "I don't know."

"I heard," another of the group began, then halted at a glare from his leader.

"What?" Piers demanded.

The man took a long drink of ale. "Heard a rumour the wench did something to offend the Abbess. Don't know what it was though."

Piers rolled his eyes. "Miss a prayer time? Speak without being asked a question?"

The man slid the others a sideways glance.

No, Piers thought. It was nothing so simple as that.

The leader put down his cup and lifted his hands, palms up. "We do not know any more, my lord. Truly."

His gaze seemed honest this time, and Piers reluctantly nodded. "You are free to go."

The men filed out of the hall, obviously eager to leave Falcon's Craig, their package delivered.

What kind of package was she? Piers wondered as he stared after them.

One you are apparently beholden to marry, his inner voice mocked.

Piers cursed and went to find his brother Cain.

 ⭠ ⭠ ⭠

Giselle was so exhausted she was barely aware of where

she was going. Over the last three days, she'd done little but grip her palfrey's thankfully full mane as they sped across the countryside. Her escorts were so anxious to get rid of her they barely stopped at all during the day, only when nightfall forced them to halt.

Dear Lord, aid me, she silently prayed.

The man at her side kept a firm grip on her arm, as if he sensed just how close to collapse she was. Three days with naught but an occasional bite of food, plain water, little rest, and no chance to wash had left her feeling much like a shattered piece of pottery.

"Here we are," the man said in a cheerful tone as he guided her into a large chamber. A woman walked in behind them.

"I . . . thank you," Giselle managed to say. She fumbled with the ties of her mantle.

"Saraid, my sweet, can you aid the poor girl?"

The woman stepped in front of Giselle. She looked like the kind of woman who could have a warm smile, but her lips were pressed together and her blue eyes were vaguely disapproving.

Giselle tried to summon a smile but found it beyond her.

Saraid reached for the ties and quickly undid them, sweeping Giselle's mantle off and hanging it from a hook on the wall.

Giselle rubbed her arms, feeling exposed and uncertain.

"Are you hungry?" Saraid asked.

"I . . . yes, I am, my lady," Giselle told her.

"Gifford," Saraid said.

"Aye?"

Giselle glanced at him. He was studying her in between drinks from his jug. She looked away and wrapped her arms around her waist. *Dear Lord, help me*, she thought. *What am I to do?*

Saraid pointed to a fireplace. "Build up the fire. The girl is clearly chilled."

"Thank you, my lady," Giselle murmured.

Saraid gave her a short nod and left.

As Gifford stacked kindling in the fireplace, he said over his shoulder, "Rest, child."

Giselle looked around and finally saw the bed, really saw it. She gasped and hesitantly walked over to touch the coverlet. Never had she seen such luxury. Rich, rose-colored velvety hangings encircled the bed, which was covered with the same material. The mattress was easily three times the size of the thin pallet she'd had at Kerwick.

She pulled back the edge of the coverlet and found smooth linen sheets. *I've landed in heaven*, she thought, then revised her conclusion recalling the man her escorts had gleefully informed her she was to marry.

Even in her innocence, she sensed he'd come straight from a woman's bed. And made no secret of it. The sight of him had startled her so much she was glad to be hidden under the hood of her mantle. He had burst into

12

the hall with a gleam in his golden brown eyes, his stride sure, a cocksure grin on his face that revealed dimples bracketing his mouth.

She was sure he had no problem persuading any woman he targeted into his bed.

Marry such a man? Giselle sat on the bed and watched the flames spark to life. Her belly clenched in protest of such a fate.

"There," Gifford said as he straightened. "That should be better."

"The chamber is beautiful," Giselle told him.

"Aye." He gestured to a wooden shutter. "That window overlooks the rose garden, and the other the sea. You should be comfortable."

"Thank you. I am very weary."

"Slip into bed, then, and take your ease. Someone will be here soon with food and drink." He eyed her with a curious expression, but didn't say more.

She was so tired she could only nod as he turned and left, pulling the door shut behind him. Though Giselle only wanted to crawl under the soft covers, close her eyes, and pretend her life hadn't just been turned inside out, habit took her to her knees.

She said her prayers by rote, the familiar pattern soothing. After she finished, she remained kneeling. "Dear Lord, show me the path back to your service. I pray to you, aid me." She swiped a tear from her eye. "Please take me back."

Stifling a sob, she rose and slid under the covers. Though her stomach grumbled and ached with hunger, she couldn't keep her eyes open and slowly succumbed to exhaustion.

❦ ❦ ❦

Piers stomped into Cain's solar and found him with his very pregnant wife, Amice, who was perched on his lap. The two of them were locked in a passionate kiss. "Cease," Piers said as he entered the room. "I've need of you."

Far too slowly for Piers's comfort, his brother ended the kiss, and stared at his wife with a besotted expression which, on any other day, would have Piers cheering in thanks.

"Cain," he barked.

His brother shifted Amice on his lap and looked at Piers. "Has someone attacked the castle?"

"No, of course not."

"Then why the great urgency?"

Piers scowled. " 'Tis a disaster."

"What is wrong, Piers?" Amice asked.

"Unbelievable," Piers said as he paced across the room. "A . . . girl just arrived."

"Normally, that would be glad tidings to you," Cain observed.

Piers gritted his teeth. "Not just a girl, but one who is apparently my betrothed."

Both Cain and Amice gazed back at him with expressions of astonishment. Cain started laughing and shook his head. "You jest, surely. You are not betrothed."

Piers shoved the documents at him. "Close enough. To a nun, no less," he finished on a roar.

Amice stared at him as if he'd lost his mind, which about summed up how he felt at the moment.

"This cannot be true," Cain said as he smoothed out the parchment. "The Bishop of Ravenswood? What has he to do with the girl?"

"She comes from Kerwick Abbey," Piers answered. "He would be their overlord."

Unable to remain still, Piers paced back and forth while Cain read.

The door to the solar flew open and Gifford blew in, followed closely by Cain's adopted daughter Olive. Both had an excited light in their eyes.

Piers groaned. "Give me that jug, old man."

For once, Gifford handed it over, and Piers gratefully took a slug of ale.

"I knew nothing of a betrothal," Cain finally said. "Gifford?"

"William never mentioned it. And Ismena," Gifford shrugged, "mayhap didn't know."

Olive danced over to Cain and Amice and squeezed onto Cain's knee. She looked at Piers. "It is about time you stopped wenching and found a nice woman to marry."

Piers tossed back another drink. "You are not

supposed to know anything about that."

Olive grinned. "I am eight years old now, not a baby. Besides, *everyone* knows."

Gifford chuckled and Piers shot him a disgusted look, which, typically, passed right over his uncle.

Piers stopped pacing as a thought occurred to him. "Mayhap the document is a ruse for the Bishop to get rid of the girl."

"I do not know, Piers," Cain said. "The signature looks to be Father's."

"But why? Why agree to this? Who is this Annora? I have never heard the name. And why not tell anyone about it? Why do I find out now?"

Cain shook his head. " 'Tis a mystery."

Amice whispered something to him, and he nodded.

Piers emptied the jug and handed it back to Gifford. "What in Hades am I going to do?" He stared at his brother and saw a flash of humor in Cain's gaze.

"Marry her, I suppose," Cain said.

"The girl is a pretty piece," Gifford offered.

"Are you both mad? Did you not hear what I said? She is a nun, or nearly so. What would I do with a woman like that?"

Cain grinned. "What you usually do, I imagine."

"You are not helping," Piers snapped. Inside him, something stirred to life before he could stamp it down. The dark being that had invaded him during his and Gifford's adventure on the magical island of Parraba. With what was becoming habit, Piers shoved the whoreson's essence back into the recesses of his mind. The fact that it was becoming more difficult to control did not escape him.

"Talk to the girl," Amice said. "She must know the answers to your questions."

Gifford patted Piers on the back. "The girl is resting from her journey. Poor thing was done in."

Piers clenched his jaw. How could this be happening? Of all the women in the world, how could fate send him a timid girl who'd spent her life undoubtedly listening to admonitions against anything remotely enjoyable? He recalled the disapproving expression on her face, and blew out a breath. "I shall be out riding while the girl sleeps." Ignoring the sympathy in Amice's eyes, he strode out of the solar.

🐎 🦎 🐎

Giselle woke slowly, instinctively clinging to the warmth and comfort of her bed. *No, I want to sleep,* she thought. *I do not want to face whatever lies ahead.* But she was not used to excessive sleep or idleness and opened her eyes.

Only to shriek in terror at what she saw.

A huge animal gazed back at her. Thick brown fur covered its body and head. When it yawned, it displayed big, sharp teeth.

And it was resting its head on the mattress.

Giselle slowly slid her body up to the head of the bed and curled into a protective ball. "Go away," she said, her voice shaking. "Praise God, please deliver me," she prayed. She eyed the partially open door, but knew she'd never make it in time.

Instead, the beast launched itself onto the bed with a heavy thump and sat back on its haunches looking at her.

At the same time Giselle screamed, the door swung open and a young woman ran in.

"Save me," Giselle implored.

The woman laughed and grabbed hold of the beast's fur. "Go on now, Guinevere. You are scaring our guest."

"Guinevere?"

"Aye. Olive named her. The child has a fascination with the old legends."

Rather than exit the chamber, as Giselle prayed it would, the dog merely retreated to the center of the floor and plopped down with a satisfied snort.

"Guinevere," the woman suddenly exclaimed. "You bad dog, you've eaten all of the lady's food."

Giselle followed her gaze to a scattering of crumbs on the floor.

The dog gave out a clearly unrepentant snort.

"Can you . . . can you get rid of it?" Giselle asked.

"Surely you are not frightened by Guinevere. She is far too lazy to threaten anyone."

"I am not accustomed to dogs."

"Well," the woman tilted her head, "as you can see,

18

this one is naught but a nuisance."

From the floor, a snore sounded and Giselle found she could take an even breath.

"I am Nona," the woman announced. "Lady Amice bid me attend you."

Giselle blinked. "Attend me?"

"Aye." Nona moved closer and clucked. "Poor thing, you are nearly in rags. We shall have to remedy that at once."

Giselle glanced down at her bliaut. Nona was right, the bliaut was poor and worn, but Giselle knew of nothing else. She squared her shoulders. "It serves. Vanity is the mark of a loose woman."

Nona burst out laughing. "Oh, my lady, the things you say. And look at your hair. 'Tis filthy."

On that, Giselle had to agree. While true baths were, of course, forbidden at Kerwick, she'd always done her best to clean herself each day. Now she was so dirty she itched.

"A bath. I shall return anon, my lady."

Giselle opened her mouth to refuse, but before she could utter a word, Nona was gone.

Leaving her with the hound of the unlikely name Guinevere.

The dog awoke and with what Giselle thought looked like a gleeful look, jumped back on the bed.

Giselle went back to praying. She shut her eyes, wishing she had the courage to retrieve her rosary. At least she could die with the comfort of smooth agate beads in her hands.

When nothing happened, Giselle cracked one eye open. The dog gazed at her unblinkingly. "Go away," she tried again.

The dog whined.

Giselle scooted tight up against the headboard and took up fistfuls of the sheets. "I do not have any food. You ate it already."

The dog tilted its head as if it were actually considering her words.

Giselle's legs were beginning to cramp from her curled position, and she slowly stretched out, praying the dog would remain still. Giselle swung her legs over the side of the bed, but before she could escape, the dog moved until it sat down close to her and put its head on her shoulder.

Hesitantly, Giselle reached out a hand and patted the dog. Guinevere gave out a long sigh, and Giselle released a shaky breath.

You are no longer at Kerwick, Giselle told herself. *You must adjust to new things.* The thought sent a deep sense of unease surging through her belly.

A soft knock at the door preceded another woman's appearance. Giselle stared at her. She was strikingly beautiful, with dark hair and big dark eyes. She was also very pregnant, the fine, blue wool of her bliaut stretched over her rounded stomach.

Giselle felt like a bedraggled orphan next to her. It struck her that she *was* exactly that.

"Welcome to Falcon's Craig," the woman said. "I am Lady Amice."

"I . . . thank you, my lady. I am Giselle."

"Guinevere seems to have taken a liking to you." Lady Amice laughed when the dog licked Giselle's cheek. She sat on a stool before the fire. "Are you feeling refreshed? Gifford said you were most fatigued from your journey."

Memories of her travel from Kerwick blended in Giselle's mind to a harrowing blur. She looked down and pulled a loose thread from her bliaut. " 'Twas a difficult trip, my lady. I am not practiced in travel."

"You were sequestered at Kerwick Abbey," Lady Amice guessed.

"Aye, my lady." Safe, she added to herself.

"How long did you live at Kerwick?"

"Most of my life. I was but seven years of age when I came to the abbey."

"What of your family?"

"I had only my mother, who died." And a father who would never acknowledge her or the fact that he once bedded a woman, she thought.

"Did you enjoy life at the abbey?" Lady Amice's voice clearly evinced her doubt.

"It is . . . was my home." Giselle smiled. "It is my greatest desire to be a nun."

For a moment, Lady Amice appeared discomfited.

"But, I understand you are promised to marry."

"I—" Giselle cut off when the door opened once more. Nona sailed in carrying a stack of cloths. Behind her streamed a line of servants, some carrying a wooden tub and others buckets of water. Like a swarm of industrious bees, they descended upon the chamber and within a few minutes set up a steaming bath and departed, but for Nona.

"Come on now, afore the water cools," Nona said with a bright smile.

Lady Amice stood and arched her back, rubbing her belly. "Would you like aid, Lady Giselle?"

Giselle opened her eyes wide in horror. "No, no," she stuttered. She thought to correct Lady Amice's address to her, but couldn't find the words. Giselle knew little of her background, but no one had ever suggested she was of the nobility.

"Very well. Nona can see to you then. Please join us in the hall later. We can all become better acquainted." She turned and left.

"I can take care of my own needs," Giselle told Nona.

"Oh, my lady, 'tis kind of you to offer but that is why I am here. Let's get you out of those dirty clothes." Nona took Giselle's arm and pulled her up.

Giselle was so startled she did not have a chance to protest before Nona began unlacing her gown.

"Tsk, tsk," Nona said. "I do not think we can salvage this one, my lady. 'Tis good you and Lady Amice are of a similar size."

Giselle pulled away. "Nona, I appreciate your willingness to assist me, but I assure you I am well-used to taking care of myself."

Nona ignored her and continued her unlacing. " 'Tis no wonder with you being trapped in that nunnery." She shook her head. "You will find things at Falcon's Craig are much different."

When Nona stripped off her bliaut, Giselle crossed her arms. There was no way she could bare herself to another.

"My, your chemise is little better," Nona said. "Best give that to me to burn as well."

The maid began pulling up the hem and Giselle pushed it down.

"Is something wrong, my lady?" Nona asked, peering up at her.

" 'Tis a sin to display my body."

Nona giggled. "You are not displaying anything, my lady. You are simply taking a bath. Asides," she added with a wink, "sometimes 'tis a pleasurable thing indeed to show the beauty of your body, particularly when the one eyeing it is a braw man."

Giselle flushed. "I could never do such."

"Oh, methinks you could if it was the right man. Mayhap like the young lord." Nona sighed, then shook herself. "Now, come, we mustn't waste this fine bath."

Realizing the maid was not going to give up, Giselle

walked over to the barrel, faced away from Nona and quickly removed her chemise, splashing into the water as quickly as she could.

Nona poured water over Giselle's head and began massaging in soap. "You have lovely hair, my lady. Such an unusual color."

"My mother's was the same."

"Ah, she must have been a beautiful woman as well."

Giselle felt a lurch in her chest. Some days, she could barely remember her mother, just a vague picture of pale hair and a warm, loving smile. She knew she should not allow herself to enjoy the bath or the kneading of Nona's fingers against her scalp, but it was impossible.

Nona handed her a cake of soap and a small cloth.

Giselle sniffed and smelled the scent of lavender.

"Lavender is Lady Amice's favorite scent. The earl brings in that fine soap for her."

I must be dreaming, Giselle thought. A dream filled with luxury she had never envisioned. The soap was soft in her hand, the water warm and soothing, and her hair felt cleaner than it had ever been.

The dream ended when Nona said, "Stand up so I can rinse your hair."

Giselle swallowed, realizing she had no choice. Heat stung her face as she slowly stood in the tub. As water cascaded over her head, she heard Nona saying, "You have a lovely body, my lady. You should be proud of it."

Giselle pretended not to hear her.

Nona giggled again. "I am sure the young lord will favor it. He is a man known to have a great . . . *appreciation* for women." She dumped another pail of water over Giselle's head, saving her from answering. The very thought of any man even seeing her naked body was terrifying enough. Her mind would not dare think of what Nona was suggesting.

"There, all done."

Giselle opened her eyes as Nona handed her a drying cloth.

Within a few minutes, Giselle was gowned in fabric softer and more colorful than anything she had seen in her life. Nona combed her hair out to dry in front of the fire and gave a satisfied nod. "Much better, my lady."

"Thank you, Nona."

"Can I do aught else for you, my lady?"

Giselle's stomach rumbled, and she made a face. "Could you perhaps bring me a piece of bread?" She glanced at Guinevere, happily sleeping on the floor, her belly full with Giselle's food.

"Of course, my lady. And I will send some men to remove the tub." With a burst of energy, Nona breezed out of the chamber.

Giselle fingered the soft wool of her blue bliaut. Guilt assailed her. Such finery was not for her. A woman needed no fine possessions to belong to God. She put her face in her hands. *Dear Lord, I feel so adrift*, she thought. *I do not wish to marry anyone but You. Particularly, not a man who clearly doesn't want me, and apparently spends a great deal of time indulging his pleasures.* She groaned aloud.

And felt a furry nose press against her lap. Guinevere gazed up at her with liquid eyes, as if she sensed Giselle's distress. She rubbed the dog's head. "I must find a way back to where I belong," she told her. "Not Kerwick."

Giselle caught back a sob, thinking of Sister Gertrude. "There is no place for me there anymore. But perhaps another nunnery. Surely there is a refuge somewhere."

Without coin? her inner voice asked. She had been fortunate to be permitted to stay at Kerwick, thanks to the Bishop. He would not aid her now, she realized with a pinch of hurt.

Her shoulders slumped in defeat. "I must find a way back into God's service," she whispered. "Surely He will help me find a way."

Though she said the words, her faith in them had been shaken and no number of prayers would ease her soul.

The Bishop's men had told her she was betrothed. If it was true, even she knew the weight such an agreement carried.

It was no less than a sentence to matrimony.

Her chest hitched and a sob escaped. *Have faith*, she told herself. *God's will is far more powerful than any betrothal.*

But a heavy sense of foreboding settled firmly into her heart, and no amount of faith could dislodge it.

Chapter
II

P iers galloped across the countryside outside the
castle walls, wishing he could just keep going.
"Betrothed," he snarled in disgust. He was so
angry with his "father" he could scarcely think. *Would
that the old man were still alive so I could swear at him*,
Piers thought.

"Damn you, Father," he yelled into the wind instead.
And damn his faithless mother for not telling anyone of
the agreement if she knew of it.

The girl's face popped into his mind. With her pale
hair and skin, her turquoise eyes had stood out sharply,
eyes that clearly evinced her disapproval of him. No
doubt the wench was probably immersed in prayers to
God for deliverance from the punishment of having to
marry him.

He nearly laughed when he envisioned her reaction
to the man he'd become after the Isle of Parraba. Slowing
the horse, he imagined their conversation. *Well, my lady
it appears that I have a bit of a problem. You see, Gifford*

and I spent some time on an island filled with magic. Unfortunately, some of the magic spilled into me, and now I find I have a very unwelcome, very noxious presence of another man inside me. His name is Eikki. And I have not yet discovered a way to banish him.

She would undoubtedly faint in abject horror of the very idea of magic. Probably see it as the devil's work.

Piers thought she might have a point in that.

A voice hissed inside him. *The wench is a beauty. Use her as you will. She cannot deny you.*

"Shut up," Piers told the voice. Yes, the girl was a beauty but he'd never before resorted to rape and wasn't about to start now. It *would* be rape. He had no doubt of that.

The irony of his predicament swamped him. He, who had become accustomed to women seeking him out, eagerly lying with him, was now bound to the one woman who would run screaming in revulsion at the prospect.

There has to be a way out of this, he told himself as he turned his mount back toward Falcon's Craig. *I will talk to the girl and figure out a way to send her back.*

The voice inside him laughed in mocking glee.

🐎　🐎　🐎

Piers stopped in the buttery and grabbed a jug of wine before making his way to the rose chamber. He felt like burying his face in a barrel before having to deal with

28

the girl Giselle.

He climbed up curved steps to the rose chamber, gathered his resolve, and knocked.

No one answered.

Surely, the girl had awoken by now, he thought. It had been hours. He slowly pushed open the door.

A shaggy bundle of fur plowed into his legs, nearly making him drop the jug.

"Guinevere," Giselle called out.

The dog gave him a look, then returned to the girl's side.

"My lord," she said, dropping her gaze.

Piers took another drink. Damn, she was even more beautiful than he remembered. Her pale hair fell around her in shimmering waves, her generously curved body draped by one of Amice's pretty gowns. When his sight stopped at her breasts, he had to take another long drink of wine. They were so full they strained the fabric, clearly revealing her ample endowments. Despite her ethereal looks, this was no body of a nun.

"Lady Giselle," he began when he found his voice.

She did not look up. "You should not be in my chamber."

Piers rolled his eyes. "We must talk."

She glanced up at him from under thick lashes, improbably dark against her pale skin.

"What do you know of this . . . agreement between our parents?" he asked.

Giselle turned a shade paler, but did not answer. She looks like a child, Piers thought, despite her breasts. A timid, frightened child. The idea of marrying the girl was beyond absurd.

"Why have I not heard of this before today?" he asked her.

"I do not know, my lord."

"Did *you* know of it?" *Stand up and look at me*, he wanted to shout.

"Nay. I knew naught until I left Kerwick."

"You must have carried the letter with you when you came to the abbey," he said, suspicions swirling in his mind.

"Letter? Mayhap. I . . . I remember the Abbess looking at what I had brought with me. She must have taken it. I have never seen any letter."

"Neither the Abbess nor the Bishop ever told you of it?"

"Nay." She looked up then and he saw a trace of defiance in her gaze. "Perhaps they thought it best to ignore it as they know of my wish to take my vows."

"Why have you not taken them yet?"

Uncertainty shadowed her face. "The Abbess did not feel I was ready."

Piers leaned against the doorway, surprised at her answer. "What of your parents?"

Giselle looked away again. "My mother died when I was seven."

"And your father?"

30

A tremor shook her shoulders before she said, in an undertone, "I do not know of him."

"You do not know who he is or do not know where he is?"

"Both, my lord."

Piers frowned. Who was this girl? "How did you come to be in the nunnery?"

She shrugged. "I do not remember, my lord. I was so young. I remember my mother dying and being alone, but I cannot say how I came to Kerwick."

Something was not right about her story, Piers thought. Or missing. "Why did you leave?"

The girl began crying, tears flowing down her smooth cheeks like rainfall.

Piers briefly closed his eyes. *By Saint George's sword, what am I to do with this girl?* "You wish to become a nun?"

She nodded through her tears.

"I shall think on this." Could it be the document was created by the Bishop as a way to get rid of the girl? But why? The girl seemed perfectly suited to be a nun. "You remember naught of your mother contacting my sire?"

"No, my lord."

"You never traveled to Falcon's Craig?"

"Not that I remember."

Piers studied her. Even as a green lad, he was sure he would have remembered if a girl as beautiful as Giselle had visited Falcon's Craig. "We will talk more after I have considered this matter."

"Thank you, my lord."

Giselle watched Lord Veuxfort leave with a feeling of relief. She sensed he was not entirely satisfied with her answers, but she had no others to give him. She did not understand it herself. Why would her mother have sought to betroth her to a noble man? Why would the earl have agreed?

He does seem kind, she told herself.

And, as Nona would say, he was indeed a braw man. His presence had filled her chamber with masculine energy. She shivered, and told herself to forget how broad his shoulders were, how finely hewn his features, how his beautiful brown eyes drew her in.

"I am a fool," she told the dog. "The first man I've ever met who is not a priest, and my mind is spinning with thoughts I should not have."

Remember the rules, she told herself.

One: Your only purpose is to serve God.

Two: Unless necessary for a task or in prayer, your voice should remain silent.

Three: Idleness is a sin.

Four: Your body must be a pure reflection of God's grace.

Five: Honor God by imbibing simple food and drink.

On number six, she got stuck. She looked at Guinevere in panic. "I cannot remember number six!" The dog gave a sniff.

"No, wait. Six: To flaunt your body is an offense against God."

32

Seven: To covet possessions is against God's will.

Eight: Hard work is a tribute to God's greatness.

Nine: The only purpose of fornication is to bear children.

Ten: Obey and submit to those in authority.

Eleven: Displays of emotion are coarse and vulgar.

Twelve: You must resist temptation, for it is the work of the devil.

At once, she felt better. Lord Veuxfort had said he would think on her wish to take her vows. Perhaps he could devise a way to aid her. Clearly, he wanted the marriage no more than she. They could simply forget their parents' apparent agreement and she could go her way. *Where?* her inner voice asked. She pushed back the twinge of pain the thought evoked and patted Guinevere's head.

She'd thought she was wanted at Kerwick, but that had turned out to be a lie. It was clear to her now the nuns, other than Sister Gertrude, had tolerated her as long as she produced the embroidered tapestries they sold, and did as they bade her.

She should have never tried to warn Sister Anne, never let anyone know that sometimes she "saw" things. The Abbess had condemned her "sight" as the work of the devil, no doubt inherited from her disreputable mother.

Though the people at Falcon's Craig had been surprisingly hospitable to her, it was clear she wasn't wanted here either. Why would she be? A girl with no dowry, no skills in running a household, and who didn't even know her ancestry?

What should she do? Giselle wondered. Where should she go? *I cannot marry,* she thought. *I will not marry.* "I belong to God," she told Guinevere. "No one else."

And deep in her heart, she knew that God wanted her.

Giselle spent most of the remainder of the day in prayer. On the morrow, she would have to find the chapel, though today she had no desire to leave her chamber.

Unfortunately, her stomach felt otherwise. Despite the chunk of bread she'd earlier eaten, her belly cramped with hunger. Lady Amice had asked her to come to the hall for supper, she recalled.

She bit her lip in indecision. As much as she hated the idea of appearing before all of the strangers likely to gather in the hall, it would be rude to ignore Lady Amice's invitation.

Her stomach gave a loud rumble. Guinevere batted her head against Giselle's shoulder as if to say, "Come on."

"Poor Guinevere, you are probably hungry too." Giselle stood and rubbed the small of her back. "You will have to lead the way," she told the dog and opened the door.

Either Guinevere actually understood Giselle or just followed the scent of food, but within a few minutes, Giselle followed the dog across a patch of grass and into a large stone structure.

When she entered, she paused and gaped at the scene. The hall was immense, a vast, columned space filled with treotle tables and a large dais where she spotted the man whose face had interrupted her prayerful thoughts too many times this day. Though she knew from her escort he was a younger brother, he looked every inch as if he were born to rule Falcon's Craig, at ease in his exalted position.

She looked around and saw candles along the white-washed walls cast lambent light over the room. A fire burned cheerfully in a fireplace set into the wall near the dais.

And there was food and drink everywhere, either being carried about by servants or resting upon the white-clothed tables.

Giselle just stood there and took it in. Guinevere abandoned her to seek out scraps.

Gradually, Giselle became aware of the stares and whispers directed her way and fought a flush. She made herself take a step forward and saw with relief that Gifford approached.

"Good evening, Lady Giselle," he said with a welcoming smile. "Are you feeling more refreshed?"

"Aye."

He took her arm and led her to the dais. Along with Lady Amice, Piers, and Saraid sat another man Giselle assumed must be the earl. There were two empty spots at the table.

When they reached the dais, the man next to Lady Amice stood. He looked much like Piers, but with piercing blue eyes. "Welcome to our home, Lady Giselle," he said, his voice cool and composed. "I am the Earl of

Hawksdown."

Giselle dropped a curtsey. "Thank you, my lord, for your kind welcome. You have a beautiful home."

"Come now," Gifford said, pulling her along. "You must be hungry. I know I am."

Saraid looked at him, her expression filled with affection. "You are always hungry."

"Aye. And thirsty," Gifford said as he settled Giselle in between him and Piers. He poured wine into a cup and filled the cup in front of Giselle.

Piers laughed at something the earl said, and Giselle turned to look at him. She drew in a shaky breath. The man was handsome when he was not smiling, but with the smile he was much more than that. A strange flutter swept through her belly that Giselle told herself was merely hunger. An appealing face and form is not the substance of a man, she chided herself.

She broke off a piece of bread and cut a chunk of cheese.

"Ah, here we are," Gifford said, glancing behind him. "You must try this, Lady Giselle," he said as he dropped chunks of meat onto her trencher. "Adela does a superb preparation of our lamb."

Giselle slowly chewed a bite of bread and stared at the meat. It did look wonderful. "I cannot, uh, do not eat meat."

She sensed Piers turn and stare at her, but Giselle could not seem to take her eyes off of the forbidden food. It smelled delicious, of some kind of spice she didn't recognize.

"God's wounds," Gifford said with a snort. "Probably half-starved you in that nunnery."

She looked up to find Gifford rolling his eyes.

"Eat, my lady," he urged.

With effort, Giselle ignored the lamb and took a bite of cheese.

Gifford pushed a cup in Giselle's direction. When she didn't pick it up, Gifford snorted again. "Do not tell me you cannot drink wine either?"

"I have never tried it."

"Well, it is past time you did."

Giselle looked at him and saw understanding mixed with determination in his gaze. Slowly, Giselle reached out and took the cup, trying a small sip. The Abbess had always claimed wine led a person to foolishness, but Giselle knew the Abbess herself regularly drank wine with her meals. The liquid trickled down Giselle's throat and hit her stomach with a hint of warmth.

She braved a look at Piers. Behind him a serving woman stood balancing a platter on her hip. She looked at Piers with familiarity and leaned down to whisper something in his ear. The movement brought her partially exposed breasts down to his eye level and Giselle saw him grin.

She took another sip of wine.

As the woman sauntered off, she heard Piers say to Lady Amice, "I notice your hair is still a bit damp."

The earl shot him a look, which Piers ignored. "And

37

I swear I smell lavender," he added.

"No doubt, the two of them have been in the bath-house again," Gifford said with a chuckle. "They spend so much time in there, I can hardly find the place available for myself."

"Oh?" the earl said with a raised brow. "I seem to remember interrupting you two just yesterday."

As the import of their teasing sunk in, Giselle flushed and took a big gulp of wine. How could they casually speak of . . . she couldn't say the word, even to herself.

Apparently undeterred by her presence, Piers laughed again. "Perhaps I shall have to see to constructing a second bathhouse as the one seems particularly popular."

The earl leaned forward and put his arm around Lady Amice's shoulders. "I have heard that the Earl of Carbonneaux has a private bathing room near his chamber with warm and cold water piped in."

Giselle blinked. Surely, he was mistaken. She couldn't imagine such a thing was possible.

"Hmm." Piers stroked his chin. "Now, that would be a fine thing indeed." He turned to Giselle with a challenging look. "What do you think, my lady?"

Giselle felt the others' scrutiny as she gazed into Piers's eyes. A sudden vision of being with him in such a place sprang into her mind. Warm, fragrant water. Soft candlelight. The comfort of his strong arms around her. Her mouth went dry as stone and she gulped some wine. "It would be useful, I suppose," she managed to say.

"Aye." Something flickered in his eyes and Giselle looked away.

"Well, if you figure this out, I want one too," Gifford said. "An old man should be allowed his comforts."

"Do not forget the old woman you are married to," Saraid said.

Gifford put his hand over hers. "You are not old, my jewel. Your beauty and grace still outshine the sun itself."

Saraid giggled.

Giselle knew she should stay until the Lord Veuxfort and his wife left the table, but she suddenly found she could not bear another moment. The hall was too loud, too crowded, too everything. "I pray you will excuse me, my lord," she said to the earl. "I find I am still weary from my travels, and 'tis nearly Compline."

The earl gave her a long look, then nodded. "Of course, my lady."

"I shall escort you," Piers said as he rose. A faint shadow of disapproval crossed his features before his expression blanked.

"Thank you, my lord."

As they walked toward Giselle's chamber, she struggled to find something to say to break the awkward silence. "Have . . . have you had the opportunity to consider our earlier discussion, my lord?"

"Not as yet," he replied, gesturing for her to precede him up the steep steps to her chamber.

As Giselle passed him, her body brushed against his and she paused, startled at the sensation. She found herself looking up at Piers's face only inches from hers.

His eyes flared and he rested his big hand against her back.

Giselle felt as if she were a rabbit caught in a snare. She licked her lips, then immediately regretted it when his gaze traveled to her mouth.

He slowly smiled, and Giselle felt the force of it clear down to her toes.

"You are determined to become a nun?" he asked quietly.

"I . . . yes. That life is all I have ever known."

He nodded. "Watch yourself, my lady. These stairs are steep and narrow."

Giselle swallowed and began climbing. She sensed him behind her, close enough to touch if she reached back, and smelled the warm, woodsy scent of him. *Dear Lord, I beg you for your aid*, she silently prayed.

Piers frowned as he followed Giselle. Damned if Gifford wasn't right again—the girl *was* a beauty, particularly when her expression wasn't fearful or disapproving. Still, she claimed to be committed to God. What a coil this was.

There was no other solution—he would have to find a way to send her back to Kerwick.

As soon as possible, he thought, given his body's response to her nearness. He'd come perilously close to

40

kissing the girl, far too tempted by her lush mouth so close to his.

The presence inside him stirred to life and lust coursed through him. *You needn't stop at a kiss,* the inner voice purred. *Take the pretty virgin and seize your pleasure.*

Piers gritted his teeth. He heard a murmur of sound from Giselle and realized the girl was already praying.

Leave her to God, he told himself. *Leave her to God.*

ୡ ୡ ୡ

"What do you think of the girl, Cain?" Gifford asked.

"I am not sure."

" 'Tis obvious she has been very sheltered from life," Amice offered.

Saraid let out a snort of disgust. "Aye, and no doubt reared on rules made up by hypocritical priests who judge others who don't follow the same rigid code."

Gifford put a hand on her shoulder.

"I fear you may be right," Cain said. From Gifford, he knew some of Saraid's past and she had good reason not to trust the church. "But I am not sure what to do about it."

"Such a girl is not for Piers," Saraid said with a frown. "He deserves better."

Amice turned to Cain. "There is no signed betrothal agreement, and Giselle claims she wishes to become a nun."

"Aye," Cain answered, idly stroking her hand as he

spoke. "I do not understand why she has not already taken her vows, though. Apparently, she knew nothing of her mother's request."

"Why did she leave the abbey at all?" Saraid asked. "There is something wrong here."

"I agree. I am thinking we should contact this Bishop of Ravenswood," Cain said.

"Do you think 'tis in truth my brother's letter?" Gifford asked.

Cain exchanged a glance with Amice. Only she knew of the secret chamber where the journals of the Earls of Hawksdown were kept. They had gone there soon after Giselle's arrival and found his father's reference to the betrothal. But he could not share that with Gifford. "As I said before, it looks like Father's signature. There is no evidence it is not a legitimate betrothal agreement, though not in the typical sense."

"A betrothal to which the girl brings nothing," Saraid commented.

"So it appears."

"Pah," Saraid said. "Just deliver the girl back to the nunnery. Piers need not be bound by an old agreement no one knew existed."

Gifford sighed. "I would like to agree with you, beloved, but a betrothal is not a matter to treat lightly. And 'tis clear that for some reason, the girl is not wanted at Kerwick."

"We cannot simply abandon her to the fates," Amice said.

Cain's face softened as he gazed at his wife, still thanking God each day he was lucky enough to have won her heart back. "I will not force Piers to put duty before his happiness."

"Good boy." Gifford beamed his approval.

"Aye. I learned the folly of that course." He took Amice's hand. "And nearly lost everything that mattered."

She smiled her love back at him.

Cain chuckled. "The decision is up to Piers, but I cannot help but find a bit of humor in the situation. To find my brother bound to a pious girl who devotes herself to prayer is a strange match, indeed."

Amice squeezed his hand. "We do not know the girl well yet. A nun's life is all she has known."

Cain's smile faded. "Aye, and that is what concerns me."

🐾 🐾 🐾

After Lord Veuxfort left, Giselle refused Nona's offer of assistance and gently pressed the door to her chamber shut. She tried to flood her mind and body with calm, to find the serenity she desperately needed.

It didn't work.

Though she knew she should begin her evening prayers, the sight of the sun setting over the sea drew her. She stood at the window, captivated by the glow of fading sunlight dancing over the waves. Perhaps tomorrow she would venture down to the shore, she thought. Feel the water that looked so soft and welcoming wash over her hands.

As she stared out over the sea, her vision gradually blurred and shifted. Too weary to fight it, Giselle let the vision sweep her into its depths.

She was running across a lush, green valley. Two flaxen-haired children, a girl and a boy, bobbed and weaved ahead of her, shrieking with delight at the chase. The sun shone down from a clear blue sky, the fragrance of wild roses sweet in the air. When she caught up with the children, she gathered them close and laughed with them, her heart light and happy.

Strong arms came from behind her and pulled her against a hard chest. Comfort and love spilled though her, and she tilted her head back to see him.

She couldn't see his face.

Giselle blinked and sank to the floor. "No," she whispered. The woman in her vision could not have been her. That life was for another woman, was another's dream.

She clasped her hands together and bent her head, but the prayers refused to come. Instead, for the first time in many years, she yearned for her mother. Longed for someone to guide her, someone who loved her. Despite what the Abbess and the Bishop had said, Giselle knew her mother had loved her. She remembered that much at least.

A tear trickled down her cheek.

For a moment, she'd felt such joy, such completeness. She could still feel the man's warm arms around her, still hear the children's laughter.

Guinevere pushed the door open and trotted over to nudge Giselle's shoulder.

Giselle buried her face in the dog's shaggy fur.

❧ ❧ ❧

Aldrik Durand, Bishop of Ravenswood, sat in his shadowy solar at Kindlemere Castle with a cup of wine in one hand and a message from his guardsman in the other. His men had delivered the girl to Falcon's Craig. Aldrik let out a sigh of relief and sipped his wine.

"You saw to the girl?" Donninc asked.

"Aye." Aldrik's lips tightened. "I should have sent her away years ago."

Donninc raised a brow. "I often wondered why you did not. You held a simple way to rid yourself of the . . . embarrassment."

Aldrik scowled. It was the same question he'd asked himself time and time again, ever since he'd found the girl at Kerwick, looking so much like her mother it was as if the past had returned to taunt him. "She possessed skills useful to the abbey."

His visitor said nothing. He didn't need to. Aldrik knew his words for the weak excuse they were.

"We all must atone for our sins," Donninc said. "In

this life or the next."

"I paid for the girl for fourteen years. 'Tis atonement enough." Aldrik shot back a drink of wine. Despite its quality, the wine tasted sour on his tongue.

"Does she know?"

Aldrik refilled his cup. It seemed he could not drink enough this eve, his usual satisfaction at presiding over such a grand holding as Kindlemere escaping him. "Nay. Do you take me for a fool? The girl knows nothing, nor shall she. She will spend the rest of her days well wed on the remote edge of nowhere."

"She has her mother's looks."

Aldrik put his cup down with a thunk. "Enough of the girl. She is gone."

Instead, Donninc leaned closer. "What of the girl's strange ability? Do you not worry that—"

"No," Aldrik snapped. Before he could catch it, he crossed himself. The Abbess had claimed the girl foretold that Sister Anne would choke on a piece of stale bread. And so the nun had. "It was mere chance. The girl undoubtedly had seen Sister Anne eat, and knew how quickly the cow stuffed food into her mouth."

"I heard a story once, from a man who had been on crusade. He claimed to have met a woman who could see into the heart of a person simply by tracing the lines on his hand."

"Peasant superstitions."

"It would be interesting though, if it were true."

"Enough!" Aldrik stood. "The girl is gone, with whatever devil's taint she carries with her. I never want to hear mention of her again." He walked to the doorway of the solar, picking up the jug of wine on the way.

"I will never have to look upon her again," he proclaimed. Never have to look upon a face so familiar, a face that had teased, beguiled, and ultimately hated him for what he'd done to her.

"I often wondered why you did not see that the girl suffered an . . . accident."

Aldrik paused. "Even I have my limits, Donninc."

Donninc chuckled. "As you say."

Aldrik frowned as he left the solar. Perhaps he should have gotten rid of the girl. But, no, he thought. She posed no threat to him. He'd seen to it she knew nothing of her true background.

And now, settled into the isolated north, she never would.

Chapter III

After a restless night filled with alarming dreams of Piers Veuxfort, Giselle rose early. She splashed water on her face, and drew on the gown she had worn the evening before.

Even as she told herself to hasten to the chapel, she pulled back the wooden shutters to look at the sea. The sky was just beginning to lighten, casting gold onto the smooth surface of the water. Giselle gazed at it in wonder. *Here is proof of God's majesty*, she thought.

The sea stretched out endlessly, like a shining platter of blue. Gentle waves lapped against the shore below. Giselle drew in a deep breath of salty air. The sight and sounds of the sea soothed her restlessness. *There is something so peaceful about it*, she thought, reluctantly turning from the sight.

After making her way out of the tower, Giselle hailed a passing laundress and obtained directions to the chapel, a two-story stone building near the great hall. She managed to keep Guinevere from following her and entered. For the first time since leaving Kerwick, she felt at ease.

At the front of the chapel sat an ornately carved altar bearing a golden cross beneath a colored glass window. The ceiling arched high overhead. Only a single candle burned, leaving most of the chapel in darkness.

Her footsteps echoed on the stone as she made her way to the altar and dropped to her knees. As she began her morning prayers, she heard a rustle of movement and glanced up.

A man moved out of the shadows carrying a brace of lit candles. He wore a plain, black robe loosely belted around his waist. "Good morrow, child."

Giselle rose to her feet. "Good morrow."

"I am Father Michael," he said with a gentle smile. "You must be our new guest."

"Aye, Father. I am called Giselle."

"Welcome to God's house." He gestured to a long bench. "Come, sit with me and tell me of yourself."

Hesitantly, she sat on the bench and clasped her hands. "Perhaps we should pray together first. 'Tis Matins."

"Ah, a pious woman."

"Until I came to Falcon's Craig, I lived at Kerwick Abbey."

The priest frowned. "Under the Abbess Maud?"

"Aye, Father."

"Poor thing," he said. "The Abbess is a strict woman."

Giselle thought back to the hours she'd spent on her

knees praying for forgiveness for the smallest of mistakes, and the many times she'd been denied food in order to purify her spirit. "She is a devout lady."

"Hmm. And now you are at Falcon's Craig. How did that come to pass?"

" 'Tis a long story, Father, but it appears I am betrothed to Piers Veuxfort."

The priest's eyes widened, then he slapped his thigh and laughed. "You will have quite a time of it with that one."

"I want no part of it." Giselle bowed her head. "I wish to be a nun. I wish to go back or . . . to another convent." For a moment, the contrast between her lush chamber at Falcon's Craig and the spare cell she'd shared with Sister Gertrude spilled into her mind, but she stamped it down, reminding herself she had no need of comforts.

"Ah. Sometimes, the Lord guides us in ways we would not have expected."

Giselle fought back tears. "I cannot imagine that God wishes me to marry." She glanced around and realized the chapel was still empty. "Do you not perform mass in the morning?"

"Of course, but not so early."

"I am accustomed to beginning my day with prayer."

"I imagine the Abbess demanded much of that."

"At Matins, Laud, Prime, Terce, Sext, Nones, Vespers, and Compline."

"Prayer is good for the soul, true, but you are not in

the nunnery any more. You need not follow their strictures. I believe that twice a day is enough for our Lord."

Giselle was shocked.

Father Michael smiled at her look of astonishment. "You will find that the earl does not expect such expansive devotion."

"And you agree?"

"I do, indeed. 'Tis why I never sought to join an order. There is time for prayer and time for living."

Giselle had a difficult time envisioning what to do with that much time to herself.

"You are a young woman," he continued. "It is a time to enjoy life, not bury yourself in continuous prayer."

"I find great solace in it, Father."

"And so you should. So you should. Would that all at Falcon's Craig were of like mind."

"Does . . . Lord Veuxfort attend mass?"

"You mean Piers? Not often, though I am sure he shares our beliefs."

"What of the rest of the family?"

"There are some that do, particularly the earl and ofttimes his uncle. Unfortunately, I have not been able to persuade the Lady Saraid as of yet, and Lady Amice, well, that is another matter."

"What do you mean?" Giselle could scarcely believe it. Not attend mass? She had always been taught that to ignore devotion to God was to put your very soul in peril.

Father Michael leaned closer and winked. "'Tis a well-known secret that Lady Amice follows the ancient ways."

Giselle felt the blood drain from her face. "She is pagan?"

"Aye."

"Dear Lord." What was this place she found herself in? A priest who urged her away from prayer, people who did not attend mass, and this, the lady of the castle a pagan? Giselle fingered her rosary in apprehension. Had she put her own soul in jeopardy by coming to such a place? The Abbess's oft-repeated words rang in her mind. *You must fight the taint of your blood by strict devotion to God.*

"Do not worry, child. Lady Amice is a good woman."

She had thought the same until this discovery. "If you will excuse me, Father, I feel the need to pray for the Lord's guidance. This has all been very unsettling to me."

He squeezed her shoulder. "Surrender to God's will, child."

She nodded and knelt once more before the altar. In a few minutes, she heard Father Michael depart, leaving the chapel in shadowy light. God's will, he'd said. She gazed up at the cross and shivered.

"What is your will, Lord?" she whispered. "Show me."

The chapel remained silent, as if God were watching but revealing nothing.

She bent her head to pray.

Piers awoke with a start. He brushed hair back from his sweaty forehead. The sheets were twisted around him and damp with sweat.

"Damn." He sat up and rested his face in his hands. The dream was so vivid in his mind he knew Eikki had a hand in creating it. Cursed creature. He winced as he recalled his dream.

It was as if another had taken full control of him. A man without mercy, without any emotion but the determination to slake his own desires. Scenes flickered through Piers' mind. Giselle, tied to a bed, her eyes wide in stark terror. Laughter that was his own and yet not. His face mirrored in her eyes—a hard, hungry gaze, lips curled in lustful anticipation.

He had taken her without a care for her cries of pain, her pleas. Taken her ruthlessly, driving into her, innocent body until he found his release. A release sweetened by the taking of her maidenhead, and her futile attempts at resistance.

And even now, even as the thought that he might be capable of such brutality sickened him, a part of him was aroused by the memory of all that sweet purity surrounding him.

"Sick bastard," he cursed, and rose to splash water over his face. "Leave me be."

As he drew on his clothes, he realized this presence was not going anywhere simply because Piers willed it.

He needed aid.

How he hated having to admit what his stupid reck-lessness had wrought. "Do not venture into the depths of the cave," Iosobal had told them. "Even I do not know what lies within."

But no, he had shrugged off her warnings. Curiosity drew him further and further in, certain he would find something wondrous. Indeed, he had. The cave was a beautiful, exotic place, with crystals adorning the walls, soaring ceilings, and crystalline pools of still water.

And beneath it all, a deep sense of something mystical, apart from the world in which he lived.

He'd known the moment he plucked the dark purple crystal from its gold chalice he'd made a grave mistake. Freed something that should never be released.

It was too late now.

So, what to do? He pulled on his boots, consid-ering possibilities. Perhaps Father Michael could help. No, whatever Eikki was, he was not the devil, that much Piers was sure of.

Beyond that, Piers wasn't sure what Eikki was. Spirit? A product of dark magic? Piers's own mind going slowly mad?

He rejected the last. Eikki was real, if unseen.

Iosobal was the only magical being he'd ever known. Would she aid him or view it all as just punishment for disobeying her order?

Deal with Giselle first, he told himself. *Then, see to your own soul.*

ⰻ   ⰻ   ⰻ

Giselle's stomach rumblings finally drove her from her prayers. She walked out of the chapel with a lightened heart, sure God would see to her welfare. As if to confirm her thoughts, sun shone down from a bright blue sky, the air holding the warm brush of spring.

She walked into the great hall and up to the dais, pasting a slight smile on her face and endeavoring to keep her gaze from seeking out Piers. When she reached the table, she heard Gifford say, "I am telling you, I saw the damned wraith last eve." He shot back a drink of ale. "She was watching," he hissed, his face red.

Saraid put a hand on his arm. "I did not see anyone."

Gifford looked around. When he saw Giselle, his expression eased and he smiled. "Good morrow, Giselle. Where have you been?"

Giselle sat. "In the chapel, of course."

"Hrump. While you are at all that prayer, say one that will banish ghosts."

Giselle blinked. "Ghosts?"

"Aye."

Piers slid her a look. "Have you never seen a ghost, Giselle?"

"I . . . nay. Ghosts do not exist."

Lady Amice gave her a knowing smile. "Aye, they do." She turned to Gifford. "Muriel is gone, Uncle Gifford. You know that."

"Then we have been invaded by another one," he grumbled. "Probably going to be just as much trouble."

Giselle decided to have some wine. How could they calmly sit there discussing ghosts of all things, as if there was no question of their existence? Were the inhabitants of Falcon's Craig mad?

"Lady Giselle," the earl said. "Please excuse my uncle's . . . opinions. He has an eccentric nature."

"Aye, and glad of it," Gifford responded. "Still does not change what I saw."

"Well, it has been a bit dull around here with Muriel gone," Piers said as he stabbed a chunk of cheese.

Cain rolled his eyes. "I, for one, am quite happy she has departed."

Even the earl believed this? Giselle thought in amazement. "Who is Muriel?" she found herself asking.

Piers answered her. "Muriel was a troublesome ghost who refused to leave Falcon's Craig. Well, until Amice managed to figure out why, and helped her reunite with the ghost of the man she loved." He put his hands on the table, and leaned close. " 'Twas quite a touching sight to see."

Giselle opened her mouth but no words came out. Surely, they jested, she thought with increasing misgivings.

"Enough of this talk," Lady Amice said. "Clearly, this is disturbing to Giselle."

"Aye," Giselle managed to utter, thinking that disturbing was far too mild a term. She felt as if she had been thrown into another world, so far from her life at Kerwick as to defy description. She clutched a handful of her bliaut in her fist, determined not to reveal the panic she felt.

Piers rose in a fluid motion. "Cain, I would like a private word with you," he said, his tone somber.

The earl lifted a brow and nodded. "Amice, can you see to our guest?"

"Of course." Lady Amice ran a fingertip down the earl's cheek, and he smiled before he kissed her.

"Lady Giselle," Piers said with a cool nod.

She took another sip of wine. In a few moments, the table was empty but for her and Lady Amice. Saraid had excused herself to tend to some matter with Gifford following, but Giselle sensed enough of Saraid's censure to know her task was a pretext to leave Giselle's presence.

Perhaps I remind her of her sin in abandoning the church, Giselle thought crossly.

Lady Amice gazed at her with a pensive expression. Giselle fought the urge to squirm on her seat and kept her expression blank. *To be serene in the face of chaos is a tribute to God's greatness*, she told herself. "Lady Amice, I am unaccustomed to being idle. Is there something I can do to aid you?"

The lady quirked a smile. "I do not suppose you know aught of expelling ghosts."

Giselle paled. "Nay, I—"

"I was jesting. I am not convinced Gifford saw what

he believes he did."

"Oh." Giselle glanced down, then back to Amice. "I have some skill with a thread."

"Come, let us walk." Lady Amice put a hand on her round belly. "I feel if I remain in one place for too long, I may be anchored there."

Giselle moved forward and took Lady Amice's arm to help her up. With the touch, her mind filled with the vision of a tiny baby girl, with blue eyes like her father's and her mother's dark hair. She swayed and blinked.

Lady Amice gazed at her with concern. "Are you well?"

Giselle swallowed.

"You did not eat." Lady Amice took a cloth and piled in some cheese and bread, folding the edges. "Take this with you."

"Thank you, my lady." Giselle glanced at Amice's stomach. "When is she due to arrive?"

"She?"

"The babe."

"Very soon. Why do you say *she*? How do you know?"

It occurred to Giselle that Lady Amice did not question her prediction. "I . . . it is just that if I were to bear a babe, I would wish for a girl."

"Hmm." The lady looked unconvinced. "I imagine my lord would like the babe to be a boy."

Giselle frowned. "If he cares for you, he should love any child you bear, boy or girl."

She realized her tone had been unduly harsh when

Amice touched her shoulder. "And I believe he shall."

Giselle followed Lady Amice out of the hall and up into a sunlit solar. Guinevere padded along behind her. Rush mats covered the floor and a fire warmed the room, though one window opening was unshuttered to let in the breeze. Giselle went to stand at the window while Lady Amice sat heavily upon a stool. Guinevere discovered a patch of sun and plopped down as if she'd put down roots.

"If you do indeed have skill with a thread, I would be pleased. I do not," Lady Amice admitted with a wry laugh. She pointed to a basket. "That is an example of my work."

Giselle pulled out a large piece of linen and unrolled it. She clamped a hand over her mouth to stifle her laughter. Strands of gold thread were sewn into the material in an apparent attempt to depict something. She turned the piece first one way and then the other but could not recognize what that something might be.

" 'Tis pathetic, is it not? I keep trying, then ripping out the threads. I fear the linen is too worked over to be of any use."

Lady Amice sounded so forlorn that Giselle's spark of laughter died. "I embroidered many tapestries for the Abbess to sell," she said, "but . . . they all depicted religious scenes." She cautioned a look at Lady Amice, and found her smiling.

"Not one honoring the Goddess Eostre?" she asked,

her eyes twinkling.

"Nay." Giselle bit her lip, oddly reluctant to offend the lady by condemning her pagan views.

"Ah, well, I suppose the Goddess Eostre shall have to wait. You say the Abbess sold your work?"

Giselle nodded. "The income helped the abbey to buy what we could not produce ourselves."

Lady Amice lifted a brow. "You must be very talented."

Pride is a sin, Giselle reminded herself. "So it was said."

"Would you consider making a tapestry in honor of my . . . first child?" A trace of sorrow flickered over her face, and Giselle wondered if the lady had miscarried. It was common enough, but Giselle could not imagine being with child at all, let alone grasp the pain a woman must feel when losing one.

"Of course, my lady. 'Twould be my privilege. What would you like it to be?"

Lady Amice tilted her head and stared out the window. "Something warm and beautiful, with rich colors displaying the bounty of nature around us."

Giselle sat on a stool and began picking out the threads. It was no use. Lady Amice was right, the fabric had just been too worked over. She sorted through the basket and found another bundle of fabric, this one a long length of white linen. "Perfect," she said, half to herself.

"What shall you do if you do not marry Piers?" Lady Amice suddenly asked.

Giselle stilled. It was as if the lady had peered into

her thoughts and cut to her core. "I would take my vows, my lady," she whispered.

"Do you not want children?"

"I . . ." Giselle found she couldn't answer. She had believed her life neatly mapped out, her future clearly set, one that did not include a husband or children. With the thought of a babe, a strange, warm feeling bubbled inside her, and for a moment, she was back in her vision. "I have never thought about such, my lady."

"Well, perhaps 'tis time you did." Lady Amice stood and arched her back. "Oh, but I wish the babe would come. My back plagues me every moment."

"I could make you an ointment to rub into your skin."

"My, you are a clever woman." Lady Amice put her hand over her mouth as she yawned. "If naught else, you could earn your own livelihood with your skills."

Giselle stared at her, a tight kernel of an idea taking root. Earn her own livelihood? Make her own way? It was inconceivable. Wasn't it?

"I am going to lie down for a bit. Do not stay shut up in here too long. 'Tis a lovely day."

"Aye, my lady."

Lady Amice stopped at the door. "And do not forget to eat," she added in a knowing voice. "I would not wish you to become . . . lightheaded again."

After she left, Giselle stared at the door. Did Lady Amice sense what had happened was more than a combination of lack of food and a chance assumption? She swallowed, fear suddenly tightening her throat.

You must be more careful, she told herself. *Keep your secrets hidden, where they cannot hurt you.*

🦎 🦎 🦎

"I cannot marry her," Piers said baldly.

Cain eyed him with clear concern. "Is it the girl you object to or the idea of marriage?"

"Both." Piers made a fist. "You have an heir well on the way. Asides, I have little to offer a bride."

"You have your name."

Piers gave him a baleful look.

"I would grant you Styrling Castle."

"Nay. Truly, I do not want it. I am happy to raise horses and," he grinned, "keep the ladies of the castle pleasured when the spirit moves me."

"Are you?"

For a moment, Piers hesitated, the question raising a yearning buried deep inside him. He shoved it away. "Very. And as for the girl . . ." He stretched out his arms. "She has made it clear she has no interest in pressing marriage. Why the woman would wish to return to a nunnery is beyond my comprehension, but it seems she is intent on doing so."

Cain rolled a quill in his fingers. "Though the Bishop sent her away."

Piers frowned. "This whole business does not feel right."

"I agree."

"I think I should send a message to the Bishop of Ravenswood. I have a right to learn why he sent her from Kerwick, why she has not taken her vows, and why he kept Father's letter all this time."

"I have already taken that step."

Piers blinked, then smiled. "My thanks."

"I also asked him to recommend another nunnery if Kerwick will not accept her return."

"Surely there is a place for her."

Cain gave a faint smile. "With enough coin, there should be."

"I will pay the fee."

"It is not necessary. Falcon's Craig has enough wealth."

Bitterness left a sour taste in Piers's mouth. Though he loved his brother, a part of him could not help being resentful that he was beholden to Cain for everything. He knew he was fortunate—most men in his position had to choose to fight or to join the church. He had nothing against a good battle, but it would be tiresome to do naught but move from one enemy to another. "I will see to it. The last sale of horses I made to the Earl of Whitbourne should cover the cost of one nun." His mouth turned down.

"Is there aught else amiss, Piers?" Cain gazed at him steadily. "Of late, you seem not quite yourself."

Piers crushed the urge to howl in sheer anguish. *If you only knew how right you are*, he wanted to say. But no, Cain shouldered enough burdens, had done enough for Piers. He would not thrust this dilemma upon his brother's shoulders as well. Particularly not when the birth of his child was imminent. "I am fine."

And as he turned to leave, he almost believed it until the sound of soft laughter echoed in his mind.

ᖗ ᖗ ᖗ

Hours into sketching a design for Lady Amice's tapestry, a ray of sunlight spilled across the parchment and Giselle glanced up to look out the window. A slight breeze brought the scents of Falcon's Craig to her nose: salt, the inescapable odor of animals, and the fragrant scent of flowers and lush grass. She stood and walked over to the window.

It overlooked part of the bailey. Below, people walked to and fro carrying bundles and leading horses, all of the activity punctuated by calls back and forth. She smoothed her hands over her skirts and took in the busy scene.

She didn't think she could ever become accustomed to the noise and frenzy of activity. Life at Kerwick had been hard, but quiet, the slow rhythm of the days blending into each other. She could spend most of a day without hearing another's voice.

Her heart ached with the loss. Suddenly, she felt as if the solar walls closed in on her with nowhere to go.

"Dear Lord, why am I here?" she whispered.

He did not answer.

She put away her sketches and descended the stairs. The chapel beckoned her like a small anchor in a roiling sea. As she made her way across the bailey, however, she spied a low-walled garden.

Perhaps there would be some arnica there, she thought, remembering Lady Amice's discomfort. When she passed through the gate, she paused and smiled in pleasure. Someone had taken great care with the garden.

Grassy walkways spread out in a labyrinthine pattern, edged by apple and pear trees. Raised beds held so many herbs and flowers, Giselle could scarcely take it all in. As she moved into the garden, she smelled lavender. Deep into the garden she saw a squat stone structure. No doubt the well-loved bathhouse, she thought, wrinkling her nose.

She stopped at an overgrown bed of sage, betony, and wormwood. Birdsong filled the air, and as she dropped to her knees and put her hands on the damp soil, the burdensome pressure on her shoulders eased.

The soothing familiarity of weeding washed over her, the fragrant air soft against her cheeks. When she glanced up, it took her a moment to realize a face was staring back at her. Giselle shrieked and fell back on her bottom.

She heard giggling before a young girl hopped into view. The child stared at her with big brown eyes, a small sprite with a mop of brown curls.

"Hello," she said, stopping to give Guinevere a pat.

Giselle stood and tried to dust off her skirts. "Hello to you."

"I am Olive," the girl said. "You must be the one who is going to marry Piers."

"Do you mean Lord Veuxfort?" Giselle was shocked at the girl's familiarity.

Olive made a face. "He does not have a title. He is just Father's younger brother."

"I see." Giselle crinkled her brow. "Your father—"

"The earl. Well," Olive said with a shrug, "he is not my father by birth, but he rescued me when my mother was killed." She beamed Giselle a smile. "I like to call him Lancelot."

Giselle's lips quirked. "Ah, yes, you are the one who named Guinevere."

Olive nodded. "When are you going to marry Piers? I love weddings." She rubbed her belly. " 'Tis always the best food."

"I am not sure that is going to happen, Olive. I have devoted myself to God."

The child's eyes grew wide. "Why would you do such a thing if you do not have to? You do not get to wear pretty clothes and you have to pray all the time. Father told me you cannot even eat meat!" she finished in a horrified voice.

Giselle crushed a bunch of weeds in her fist. "You

are just a child. You do not understand. There is great peace in leading a simple life devoted to the Lord."

"Sounds dull as dirt."

"I . . . well, 'tis true, the life of a nun is not exciting, but there are other, richer rewards."

Olive wrinkled her nose. "I do not understand. Asides, all the women want Uncle Piers."

"I am not like other women." Giselle stepped around her and headed for a planting of chamomile. The girl followed, trailed by Guinevere.

"What did you do at the convent?"

Giselle realized with an inward sigh that the solitude she'd so briefly enjoyed had ended. "Prayed, of course. I also embroidered tapestries and helped the sisters with other tasks."

"How old were you when you went there? Did you always want to be a nun?"

"You ask a lot of questions."

"Aye, Uncle Gifford says the same." Apparently undeterred by Giselle's comment, Olive said, "Well?"

Giselle sighed. "I was seven years of age. It is the only life I have ever really known."

Olive appeared to consider that for a moment. "Did you get to play with the other girls?"

Giselle stared at her, realizing the very idea was foreign to her. "There . . . there were no other girls my age. And I was too busy to play."

"Uncle Piers knows how to play," Olive assured her.

"I am sure he does."

Olive hopped close, her eyes gleaming. "I am not supposed to know about this, but I overheard Clarise in the kitchen. She says Uncle Piers is built like a stallion, and knows very well how to use the gifts God has given him."

Giselle felt a flush start at her toes and creep up her body to burn her face. Good Lord, how was she to respond to that? She was appalled by the child's casual words. Wasn't she?

Surely, God would not force her to marry such a man. A stallion? Her mind filled with imaginings. Though she'd never seen a man's member, the Abbess had talked enough about how fortunate Giselle was to escape having her body used by a man. Like her mother, she thought with an inward cringe of shame.

"As I told you, I have committed myself to the Lord. I am not going to marry anyone but Him."

Olive sniffed. "Are you hungry?"

Momentarily perplexed by the change of subject, Giselle finally said, "Aye."

"Let us go to the kitchen. Adela always has something for me." Olive reached out and took Giselle's hand, tugging her toward the gate. "Come, Guinevere. Food."

The dog bounded ahead with energy Giselle had never seen her exhibit.

"I shall have to think of a way to change your mind, Lady Giselle," Olive murmured as they walked. "You are far too beautiful to waste away in a nunnery."

Giselle opened her mouth to correct the girl, but never got the chance. Her vision blurred, then faded completely. Another scene slowly spilled into her mind.

She was running through the forest. The crunch of another's footsteps on dry leaves grew closer and she raced ahead, terror lodged in her throat. Shadows and mist shrouded the trees, making it impossible to discern her direction.

"Giselle!" a man's voice yelled.

Her foot caught on a root, and she stumbled, coming up hard against the rough bark of a tree. Her lungs burned, and she panted for breath, desperate to escape from the man chasing her.

"Giselle, stop!" he called again.

She paused and tried to catch her breath. The voice sounded like Piers. But, no, that couldn't be right. Why would he be chasing her through the forest? She turned and tried to peer through the dense growth.

A sliver of moonlight penetrated the leafy canopy and she saw a man's face. Piers's face.

She took a step forward, the image blurring, then clearing once more. Another face stared back at her, his lips curled in anticipation. Dark hair spilled over his shoulders, his face carved into sharp planes and hollows, his black eyes glowing, seeking her.

"Giselle," he said. "Come to me now."

Horror swamped her, freezing her in place as he plowed through the woods, his dark gaze never leaving her. Deep inside she knew evil stalked her.

"No!" she screamed, and fled into the night.

Giselle looked up to find Olive's small face staring down at her with concern. "Are you all right, my lady?" the child asked, gripping Giselle's hand tightly in hers.

"Aye." Giselle realized she was lying on the ground, and pushed herself into a sitting position. Her head spun, and her stomach felt queasy.

"What happened? Are you ill?"

"I am fine," she assured Olive and managed a smile. "I am still weak from my travels, and I have not eaten well today." She stood and dusted off her skirt with her free hand. "Let us go to the kitchen."

Olive bit her lip, then nodded.

Giselle let out a breath and let the child lead her forward.

Chapter
IV

Clarise is most distressed over the news of your impending marriage," Madoch said as he walked next to Piers toward the training grounds.

Piers eyed his friend. With his blond hair, hard build, and sleepy blue eyes, Madoch seldom went without a woman in his bed. "I am sure you were able to console her."

Madoch grinned. "I gave it my best."

"And I do not intend to marry Giselle."

"Why not? She's a fetching wench."

Piers frowned. "She has spent nearly her entire life in a nunnery. Can you imagine me being shackled to a woman like that?"

"You can pray together," Madoch said, chuckling.

"That is not exactly what I have in mind for a bride. Asides, we have already taken steps to see her settled in another nunnery."

"Well, then, I suppose I shall have to look for someone other than the fair Clarise to keep me company."

Madoch let out a long sigh.

"I doubt you will have to look far." Piers stopped and withdrew his sword. "Why have you never married, Madoch?"

Madoch gave him a look of horror. "Commit to one woman? Deprive all the rest of my considerable talents? Surely not."

Piers rolled his eyes.

"Despite my substantial charm and manly form, I am landless. I have little to offer a bride."

"You could become seneschal of Styrling Castle. Talbot is getting old."

"Too much responsibility, but thank you. Now," Madoch said as he withdrew his sword. "Let's see if you have improved enough to beat me."

Piers grinned and brought his sword up.

Giselle watched Piers and another man slash and hack at each other across the training field, wondering how she had allowed Olive to talk her into witnessing this. Piers's expression was taut and hard as he thrust his blade at his opponent's neck. Sweat dripped down his face as he dodged a thrust from the other man.

Dear God in heaven, she thought. The men fought as if they were the greatest of enemies, snarling and snapping at each other.

"Is that all you have, you lazy whoreson?" Piers called out.

The other man grunted and attacked, narrowly missing

Piers's shoulder. "You fight like a wench," he told Piers.

Piers whirled and arced his sword up. Metal whined when the two blades met. Braced against each other, Piers and his opponent shoved and growled at each other. "Yield," Piers shouted.

The other man smiled. "I yield," he said. "For today."

Piers lowered his sword.

Olive started clapping and Piers turned. For a moment, his gaze snagged on Giselle's and she fought the urge to step back. The cold intent in his eyes made Giselle feel as if she were a wounded sparrowhawk about to be gobbled up by a predatory falcon.

"Uncle Piers, that was very well done," Olive said.

Piers's expression cleared and he gave Olive a smile. "Why, thank you, Olive. And Lady Giselle. How nice to find you admiring my swordplay."

Giselle's mouth opened and closed. Admiring? She squared her shoulders. "I cannot admire such a violent display. 'Tis an affront to God." She knew she sounded stiff and judgmental, but she couldn't help it. She had listened to the Abbess rail against the sinful violence of men too many times.

Beside Piers, the other man gave a snort and murmured, "I see what you mean."

Giselle stiffened. It didn't take the sight to know Piers had been speaking of her in less than a flattering way. *It doesn't matter*, she told herself.

Piers marched over to Giselle, an angry look on his

face. "An affront to God? Did the pope himself not call upon good Christian men to kill as many of the foul infidels as possible?" he snarled, his lips curled with derision.

Olive took her hand and gave Piers a stern look.

"I . . . I have never understood the pope's reasoning," Giselle said. "The Lord instructs us not to kill."

Piers laughed. "Does He? I have never had the privilege of speaking to God, myself."

Giselle's lips tightened and she bit her lip. *Do not offend this man*, she told herself. *He holds the key to your freedom.*

"How do you think we defend what is ours, Lady Giselle? With prayer? 'Tis a man's skill in battle which allows him to protect his holdings and his people." He frowned. "And now that apparently includes *you*."

The way he said it made it clear he wished otherwise. Giselle dropped her gaze, stamping down her anger with the ease of long practice. "Forgive me, my lord," Giselle said as she took a step back, Olive clinging to her hand. "I know only what I have been taught."

"Mayhap it is time for you to open your eyes to the world outside your precious nunnery. The real world. The one in which you now reside."

"You know of my wish to return to a nunnery, my lord. 'Tis where I belong."

"Aye, that much is clear," he said.

"I do not think Lady Giselle should go to live with nuns," Olive said. "She is too pretty to hide away like

74

that. Do you not think so, Uncle Piers?"

Giselle inwardly cringed. She lifted her gaze to find Piers studying her. " 'Tis the lady's wish, Olive," he said.

Though she had no interest in Piers, Giselle was perversely disappointed he didn't respond to Olive's question about her appearance. *Vanity and pride have no place in God's service*, she told herself sternly.

"Though 'tis indeed a shame to see such beauty closed away," Piers added.

Giselle blinked. She loosened Olive's hold and smoothed down her skirts. "If you will excuse me, my lord, 'tis almost None.

He lifted a brow. "Off to the chapel?"

"Of course."

"Of course." He shook his head and turned away.

Giselle fled.

❧ ❧ ❧

Olive crossed her arms and frowned at Piers. "Do you not like Lady Giselle?"

He tousled her hair. "I do not know her." *Nor do I want to*, he thought, remembering her tight expression of disapproval.

"She seems nice."

"Olive, do not become attached to the woman. She will not be here long."

"Are you not going to marry her?"

"Nay."

Olive stuck out her chin. "Why not? She *is* very pretty."

"Aye, but she is committed to her God."

"I like going to mass."

"That is because Father Michael always has a treat for you. And you do not go to the chapel seven times a day."

"But—"

Piers raised a hand. "Olive, you do not understand. Marriage is forever. The two people involved should at the least be compatible. And Lady Giselle is assuredly *not* well-suited to me. I will not enter into such a barren union."

"Then who will you marry?"

"Mayhap no one. Now, come," he said, draping an arm around her shoulder. "I have built up a thirst. Madoch?"

"Aye."

"What think you of breeding Tyjs to Skye? She is in season."

Madoch fell into step beside Piers and Olive. " 'Twould be a good match. Tyjs has the strength and power, but Skye has an elegance about her."

Piers focused on his horses and told himself to put the problem of Lady Giselle from his mind. He had no doubt the woman was even now on her knees praying to God to deliver her from such a place of brutality. He had nothing against prayer, of course, but for Giselle it was an obsession and he suspected a well-ingrained way to hide from life. If she knew some of the thoughts that had wound through his brain during training, she would have fainted in horror.

Eikki was always there, just below the surface, like a snake coiled and ready to spring. *Take him*, Eikki's voice had urged. *Spill his blood. Win the fight.*

You'll not overcome me, you bastard, Piers thought. *I am stronger than you.*

Eikki laughed. *Not strong enough.*

Piers gritted his teeth and shoved the presence down deep.

Lady Giselle was welcome to her prayers. He had his own problems to deal with.

I am betrothed to pure innocence, and I harbor a demon inside me, he thought. *A demon who would use Lady Giselle as a slave to slake his every desire. Pray her prayers bear fruit.* He could hold Eikki back for now, but Eikki increasingly crept into Piers's thoughts.

An innocent such as Giselle would be devoured by such a being.

❧   ❧   ❧

A sennight later, Piers stood in Cain's solar in shock.

Cain gave him a grave look and passed over the piece of vellum. " 'Tis not the answer I expected."

Amice sat on a nearby stool rubbing her belly and

looking worried.

"I do not understand this." Piers looked down at the Bishop of Ravenswood's letter. "Not only does he refuse to take her back at Kerwick, he says there is no place in the church for Giselle at all."

"It does not make sense," Cain agreed. "I offered to pay for her to go to another abbey. Usually, the church is eager to accept coin."

Piers crumpled the vellum in his fist. "He offers no reason."

"No. Most curious."

"What could Giselle possibly have done to warrant such treatment? All the woman does is pray!"

"Obviously, she somehow managed to offend the Bishop."

Piers scoffed. "How? Most of the time the girl acts like a scared rabbit. I cannot imagine how she could bring herself to offend anyone."

Cain shrugged. "Mayhap she disagreed with some of the Abbess's teachings. Whatever happened, 'tis clear she is no longer welcome in a nunnery."

"Hell." Piers eyes lit with an idea. "We could send her to Italy. Surely there is a nunnery close to your villa."

"The Bishop of Ravenswood has a long reach, Piers. I doubt they would take her." Cain gave Piers a sympathetic look.

"I have to try, Cain. By Saint George's sword, I cannot be saddled with such a woman."

"There is a small abbey not far from Villa Delphino. I know little about it."

Piers felt a glimmer of hope. "Send a message to the Abbess. Mayhap if we offer enough coin, she will accept Giselle."

"Nay," Amice spoke up. "I have heard of that place. 'Tis said to be a poor, mean abbey, with only a few older nuns in residence. You cannot send Giselle there."

"There must be *something* I can do!" Piers paced across the floor. "Perhaps if I go to visit the Bishop myself."

" 'Tis a thought. If naught else, you could discover why he put Giselle out of Kerwick."

"I think you should talk to Giselle, Piers," Amice counseled. "And do not frown and bluster at the poor girl. She has as little a say in this as you."

Piers sighed. "I will try, but 'tis difficult to engage Lady Giselle in conversation. She has spent most of the past sennight closing herself off in either your solar or the chapel."

Amice stood and stretched. "She is not comfortable here yet."

"I very much doubt she shall ever be," Piers muttered. He tossed the vellum atop Cain's worktable and strode from the room.

Cain put his arms around his wife. "What do you think of this?"

" 'Tis a difficult situation. I feel sorry for Giselle, but . . ." Amice shook her head and leaned into him.

"I want Piers to find what we have."

Amice patted his hand, and turned her face to his with a smile. " 'Tis a rare thing to find that kind of love."

Cain smiled back at her. "Aye, I am a lucky man."

"Yes, you are." Amice covered her yawn. "And one with a very weary wife."

He smoothed his hand down her belly and felt movement. "Our son is anxious to make his appearance."

"Perhaps the babe will be a girl."

"A girl who looks like her mother would be a treasure." The thought of it brought a rush of warmth to Cain's chest. Dear Lord, he was a fortunate man. Even after all this time, he still woke up each morn scarcely believing he had found the sense to win Amice's heart a second time.

"I wonder," Amice began then stopped.

"What is it, sweet?"

"A small thing. Giselle . . . she seemed to know the babe would be a girl."

"How could she?"

"What if she has some special ability? Could be a reason for the church to turn against her."

Cain groaned and rested his chin on Amice's head.

She laughed. "You married a woman who can talk to ghosts. And think of the woman Lugh married."

"I try not to. I am thankful for your talent, particularly since you were able to rid me of Muriel, but what I have heard of Iosobal goes beyond my imaginings."

"Giselle said if she ever had a child, she would wish

for a girl. Perhaps that is all it was."

"I hope so. Do not mention anything to Piers. He has enough to worry about, without wondering if his betrothed has the sight too."

"Does Piers seem . . . different to you?"

"How?"

"I do not know exactly. It is just a feeling. Sometimes he seems harder, darker than usual."

"Aye, I know what you mean. I questioned him about it. 'Tis no doubt the strain of this betrothal hanging over him."

"He may have to marry her, Cain."

Cain tightened his grip on her. "I know, love. I know."

෩ ෩ ෩

Piers found Giselle in the chapel. She knelt in front of the altar, a circle of sunlight surrounding her, her silvery blond hair gleaming. No one else was about. He could hear the whisper of her voice, and for some reason, it sent a chill down his spine. No doubt Eikki's reaction to being within a house of God, he thought with resentment.

What could this woman possibly have done to the Bishop of Ravenswood? She was like an angel kneeling there, pure and apart from others. Far apart from him and the man he had become after Parraba. He was almost hesitant to intrude, but the words of the Bishop's letter rang in his mind.

"Lady Giselle," he said.

She straightened and glanced back.

"I need to speak with you."

She bent her head briefly, then crossed herself and stood.

"Walk with me," he said.

"Have you news, my lord?" she asked softly.

"Aye." They walked out into the sunlight and Piers turned toward the garden. He didn't say anything more until they walked through the gate into the garden. *The girl is your responsibility now*, the Bishop's letter had said. *She is not welcome in the church.*

Giselle stopped and gazed at him, her hands clasped tightly together, her expression wary.

"I am confused, my lady."

"Confused?"

"Aye. Very." Do not frown, he reminded himself. "The earl sent a letter to the Bishop of Ravenswood requesting either you return to Kerwick or be permitted to enter another nunnery. We offered to pay for your entrance, of course."

Her gaze brightened.

"He refused our requests."

Her shoulders shook and she looked away.

"Why, Giselle?"

She fluttered her hands, but did not answer.

"Why would the Bishop refuse to aid you?"

"I . . . I do not know."

Piers narrowed his eyes. "Did he force you to leave Kerwick Abbey?"

Her throat worked, then she slowly nodded. She still didn't look at him.

She is like Avalon, he realized, remember the mare he'd owned several years ago. Whatever had befallen the horse before she arrived at Falcon's Craig, it had so affected her it had taken Piers two years to gain the horse's trust enough to ride her. But he could not simply put Giselle in a stall and leave her to become accustomed to her new home. "What happened, Giselle? I want to help you, but I do not understand this. Why is the Bishop so determined to deny you your wishes?"

When she turned to look at him, her eyes were so bleak his heart softened. "He has always hated me," she said slowly.

"For what reason?" Piers furrowed his brow in puzzlement.

She let out a long sigh and bowed her head. "Because I remind him of my mother."

"He knew her?"

"Aye." She lifted her gaze. "You should know that I am illegitimate. My father is the Bishop, though he shall never admit to it."

Piers blinked. "Your father? But, how? How do you know this?"

A bitter smile crossed her lips. "He told me once. 'Twas a mistake, but apparently I look very much like my mother. He was . . . angry to find me at Kerwick."

"I see." Actually, he didn't at all, but he couldn't think of how to respond to this surprising revelation. Illegitimate. All at once, he wanted to laugh out loud.

" 'Tis another reason why marriage between us would not suit," she said.

Piers opened his mouth, then snapped it shut. He was half tempted to tell her of his own mixed parentage, but thought better of it. "You are not at fault for the circumstances of your birth."

"I am sorry to be a burden to you, my lord."

Well, hell. He felt as if anything he could say would be like striking an already whipped dog. "Perhaps we can find another nunnery for you."

The hope that bloomed on her face made him silently curse.

"I am sorry, Giselle. I do not know where. I fear the Bishop would interfere. He is a powerful man."

"Aye, I know." Her face crumpled and her eyes gleamed with tears. "Then, what am I to do?" She asked the question so softly he realized it was as much to herself as to him.

And he had no earthly idea what to answer.

❧   ❧   ❧

Piers peeked around the door to Gifford's workroom, making sure there was no suspicious smoke before entering,

When his enthusiastic quest to find the answer to life's mysteries took his fancy, Gifford frequently ended up combining just the right ingredients to create havoc.

Piers walked in to find his uncle industriously mixing something in a stone bowl. "What are you doing?"

Gifford paused and took a swig from his ever-present jug. "I am making a potion," he announced.

"A potion? Does Saraid not satisfy your needs?"

"Not *that* kind of potion. Asides, Saraid is perfect in every way. I'm a lucky bastard to have found her and lured her away from Parraba."

Piers grinned. "I am glad for you, Gifford."

His uncle snorted. "Now, we need to see to *you*."

Oh no, Piers thought. "Can you can concoct a potion to make the Bishop of Ravenswood change his mind?" He settled on a stool and reached for Gifford's jug.

"Won't take her back, eh?"

"Nay. Nor will he allow her to enter another nunnery."

"Just as well." Gifford wrinkled his nose. "No place for a beautiful young woman."

"Gifford, you do not understand. Living the life of a nun is all Giselle knows. 'Tis what she wants."

His uncle peered at him over the bowl. "How is she to know what she wants? She has only been away from the abbey for a few weeks."

"She appears quite certain."

"Hmph." Gifford shook some kind of pink powder into the bowl.

"Saraid does not appear to approve of Giselle."

" 'Course not. Saraid, bless her sweet soul, has no use for the church, though she worships God in her own way. The priest at Sturbridge, damn him three ways to hell, put the blame of her mistreatment squarely on Saraid's shoulders. He would do nothing to aid her." Gifford scowled. "Always told her God intended her to submit to her husband, no matter how cruelly he treated her." He took a mallet and pounded on a pink stone.

"I need to find a way to get rid of her, Gifford." Piers took a long drink of ale.

"It does not sound as if that is going to happen, boy. Give the girl a chance. Perhaps she shall surprise you." Gifford beamed at him. "With the help of my special potion."

"Which is what, exactly?"

"Why, a love potion, of course."

Piers rolled his eyes. "Gifford, really."

"You are going to have to marry her, Piers. There's nothing for it. 'Tis what William agreed, and the girl has nowhere else to go."

"Damn." The ale tasted sour in his mouth. *Marry her and put her away*, Eikki whispered. *Take your pleasure of her when you wish. Shut up*, Piers told him.

"Try a taste of this," Gifford said, holding out a spoonful of liquid.

"You first."

Gifford chuckled and slurped down the liquid. He tilted his head to the side. "Needs a bit more honey."

"What have you put in that?"

"Oh, this and that. Do not worry." Gifford gave him a sideways look. "I helped Cain."

"I am not sure that your 'elixir' had much to do with it. He was already in love with Amice."

"Well, there is no harm in it."

"Are you sure?"

Gifford drew himself up straight. "Aye."

"I cannot imagine falling in love with Giselle, Gifford. And I am sure she has no interest in loving any man, particularly me."

"Poor first impression you made, coming straight from Clarise."

Piers sighed. "I make no excuses. 'Tis my life, and I happen to enjoy two things—horses and women."

"Do you not remember Laila's prediction?"

Piers inwardly groaned. "I do not believe anyone can see into the future."

"She said you shall discover a great love. And," Gifford paused and gave him a sharp look, "that she will not be at all what you expected."

"Aye, and something about uncovering what lies deepest in my heart." Piers waved a hand. "Gypsy fortune telling."

"You would never have expected a woman like Lady Giselle."

Piers barked out a laugh. "Nay, that much is true. For the rest . . ." He shrugged, but he wondered. Had

Laila seen a window into his future? A great love? With Lady Giselle? He could not fathom it. "Perhaps I could just install her at Styrling. She would have a place to live and as much time as she wished to spend on her knees in the chapel."

"You cannot simply ignore the betrothal."

Piers groaned and took another drink. "Then you'd best finish that potion, Gifford. It looks as if I am going to need it."

❧   ❧   ❧

After Piers left, Giselle was too distraught to do anything but sink down into the grass and stare at nothing. Eventually, Guinevere found her and settled in next to her. Giselle put her hand on the dog's head and fought the impulse to sob into her fur.

Forgive me Lord, but how I hate the Bishop of Ravenswood, she thought. She had never understood why her beautiful mother would have ever considered such a man. Glutted with power, bloated with too much food and drink, he had always reminded Giselle of a fat snake, his beady brown eyes ever watchful and conniving.

Over the years at Kerwick, Giselle had seen him many times. More often than she could count, he had looked at her with revulsion in his narrow gaze, letting her know without words he considered her tainted.

And typically, after each of his visits, the Abbess decided

Giselle had committed some unnamed offense, requiring her to fast and scrub the floors until her hands bled.

She had never understood why he had persuaded the Abbess to change her status from unpaid servant to novice, but thanks to the Abbess's contemptuous explanation, Giselle knew he had.

You are the spawn of a conniving whore, he had told her. *The only way to save your soul is to devote yourself to God's service.*

But now he denied her even that. Dear Lord, how she wished she could seek Sister Gertrude's counsel, but she had no way to reach her friend.

Tears trickled down her cheeks, and she bent her head to press against Guinevere.

Dear God, please aid me, she silently prayed. *Deliver me from this place.*

At the sound of a cough, she looked up. Piers stood there, arms crossed, his mouth set in grim purpose.

Giselle wiped her face and stood. "My lord?" Her legs trembled and she sought Guinevere with one hand, the other clutching her skirt.

For a moment, he said nothing.

He has come to a decision, Giselle thought. She felt as if she waited on the edge of a precipice, mere steps from plunging into a vast abyss.

"I will honor my father's wishes," he finally said, speaking the words as if they were torn from his throat.

No, Giselle wanted to scream. *I do not want to*

marry. She swallowed and tried to harness her whirling thoughts into calm. Think, she told herself. "You . . . wish to marry me?"

He scowled. "Nay. I will not lie to you. Though I do not know you well, what I do know does not bode well for us."

"Surely, you can find a nunnery somewhere to take me. Anywhere."

His scowl deepened. "I know of no place. And I cannot in good conscience just send you off somewhere that may be harsher than Kerwick."

"I was content at Kerwick," she protested, stamping down the memories of being cold and hungry. "The Abbess could be very strict, but others were kind to me. I loved Sister Gertrude. She was like—"

"And though we both may wish otherwise, the fact remains that your mother sought out a betrothal and my father agreed."

"But—" Her mind cast about wildly for another solution. Marry him? Her legs shook so much they could barely hold her upright. "There must be some place I can go."

A glimmer of sympathy lit his gaze. "Where?"

Giselle opened her mouth but she couldn't find any words. He was right. She was alone, her only family the nuns who had shunned her. Even if Sister Gertrude wanted to aid Giselle, the nun had no way to do so. Her thoughts turned to marriage and she dropped her gaze, feeling sick to her stomach. She could not help but pick up from the servants that Piers devoted a considerable amount of his time lying with different women, all of whom seemed eager to oblige him. He would expect her to do the same. She cringed inside. She could not do it.

"There is no other option. We shall marry."

It struck her, really struck her that he spoke true. The prospect of it made fear spiral through her veins. Someplace deep inside her she grabbed onto a scrap of courage, and slowly lifted her head. "I never thought to marry."

"Aye, I realize that."

Giselle sucked in a breath. "I am not prepared to be a wife in all ways."

His gaze turned wary. "What are you saying?"

She held on to the scrap of courage with everything she had. "I shall . . . submit to you once to seal the marriage. Once only."

An odd light came into his gaze that sent a shiver down Giselle's spine. "You would deny your husband?"

Giselle gripped her skirt. "You must understand—"

He barked out a laugh. "That you expect me to marry you, see to your welfare, but bar me from your bed?"

Put that way, it did sound terribly selfish, Giselle thought. But then her mind turned to the alternative and she inwardly cringed.

"Then I shall take my pleasure elsewhere."

Continue his wenching in front of her while she resided at Falcon's Craig as his wife? Dear Lord, what kind of man was she to be bound to? "You—"

He stepped closer and raked his gaze down her body. "I am a man, with a man's needs. If you refuse to oblige me, I shall find others who will." He gave her a slight smile. "I can assure you it will not be a problem."

"You would make a fool of me that way? No honorable man would do such a thing."

"Oh? And would an honorable woman refuse her husband? Does your God not command you to be fruitful and multiply?"

Giselle gulped. She knew he had a point, but she just couldn't envision lying with him at all, let alone on a regular basis. Her rules spilled through her mind. *Your body must be a pure reflection of God's grace. The only purpose of fornication is to bear children. You must resist temptation, for it is the work of the devil.* "I cannot change who I am," she finally said, lifting her chin.

"Your duty as my wife shall be to obey me in all things."

Obey. How she'd grown to hate that word. Obey your superiors. Obey when the Abbess locks you in a bare cell for days with only a few pieces of stale bread and water. Obey by never speaking what is on your mind, never showing how you feel. "I am not a dog you can command to heel," she snapped.

His gaze darkened and his lips twisted in a mockery of a smile. "My wife shall be under my command. If I wish, I can send you to another estate and do whatever I please. The truth is, my lady," he said taking her arm in a solid grip, "you have no rights other than those I deign to grant you."

"You cannot expect me to abandon the teachings of a lifetime simply because you decree it," she cried.

His hold on her arm tightened, and he bent close enough she saw his brown eyes darken with shadows that deepened her fears. "I expect you to do as I bid," he said coldly. " 'Tis the way of the world."

Giselle tried to pull free, but his strength far exceeded hers. "A world I want no part of."

His smile deepened into a strange and chilling expression rife with the certainty of his power and position. "Unfortunately for both of us, it appears you have no choice." He stroked a finger over her cheek. It was not a caress, but a mark of possession. "Are you not curious about what can happen between a man and a woman, Giselle?"

"Leave me be," she whispered.

"It seems I cannot. We will marry."

No. The thought rang through her mind, and filled her with anger. "I release you from the betrothal."

" 'Twas your mother's wish we marry. Do you grant no importance to that?"

"My mother did not know what I . . ." Giselle gulped, "have learned of you."

His gaze stabbed into her in accusation. "Oh? And what is that?" His hold on her arm tightened. "What is it you believe you have learned?"

Giselle's cheeks flamed. "That you devote your life to

. . . pleasures of the flesh, and little else," she whispered.

"I see. The little nun does not deem me worthy of her." His voice was so filled with mockery Giselle's temper snapped.

"Nay." She managed to draw in a breath, at the same time appalled by her speech and relieved to be finally speaking the truth. "As I said, I release you."

He dropped her arm, his expression shuttered. "And what shall you do, little nun?" he asked smoothly. "Subsist on prayer?"

"I . . . I shall find my own way." Giselle whirled and stomped away. Such rage consumed her that she felt as if she would erupt with it. Thank the Lord Piers had shown the kind of man he really was before she found herself bound and enslaved to him. She could only imagine what their marriage would be like. He would no doubt find it perfectly within his rights to tie her to his bed to await his pleasure. *God will show me the way,* she told herself. *With faith, all things are possible, even as impossible as they may seem.*

∽ ∽ ∽

Piers stared at Giselle's retreating form and cursed inside. *Damn you, Eikki.*

The presence chuckled. *You merely told her the truth. We cannot accept such defiance.*

There is no "we", Piers told him.

There is now.

Piers imagined a small room and slammed the door shut. Eikki's voice ceased for the moment, thank God. Piers had not intended to sound so harsh, but with his shock and disappointment at Giselle's condition to their marriage, Eikki had crept in.

She had deemed him unworthy, idle but for indulging himself in activities she clearly disapproved of. He grimaced. No, he was not responsible for Falcon's Craig, though he had been for a long time during Cain's absence. And he was not a powerful earl, but only the younger brother of one.

Damn her, he thought, glaring at her back. Without giving herself a chance to know anything about him, she had judged him and found him wanting.

Still . . . she had released him.

He forced a grin onto his face and took a deep breath. *I am free*, he told himself, as relief spilled through him. *I am free.*

🐌 🐌 🐌

Giselle gathered up her few possessions and stuffed them into a leather bag, so angry she could barely see. She looked around to make sure she'd packed everything, and hoisted the bag. The sooner she was on her way the better, she thought. She could not bear to stay another moment.

The door swung open and Nona entered. She halted at the sight of Giselle's bag. "My lady?"

"I am leaving. Thank you for your assistance to me."

Nona's face paled. "But, why? To where do you go?"

Giselle walked forward, carrying the bag. "I am not sure." *Some place where I shall be valued for myself,* she thought. "I cannot marry Piers Veuxfort," she told Nona, her mouth turning down. " 'Tis clear to me now."

"But, but, my lady, you cannot just go off by yourself."

"Aye, I can." Resolve filled Giselle's veins, almost enough to overcome the terror she felt at what she was about to do. She glanced down at Guinevere, who stared up at her as if she understood. Tears stung her eyes when she realized how much she would miss her furry friend.

"Please, Lady Giselle, let me find Lady Amice."

"There is no need to trouble her." Giselle bent down and hugged Guinevere, forcing her tears back. "Stay," she said softly.

"My lady, please," Nona said. "It cannot be as bad as that."

"Oh, but it is," Giselle said. "Farewell, Nona." The maid opened her mouth to protest, but Giselle ignored her. She made her way down the steps and entered the bailey, glancing around her, hoping she did not come across the earl or his lady. Determinedly, she put one foot in front of the other, refusing to think of anything but the cold expression in Piers's eyes when he announced he intended to treat her no differently than a well-kept hound.

He was mad, or playing a cruel game with her. Either way, she knew there was no one to turn to in this place.

She was nearly to the gatehouse when she spotted Olive from the corner of her eye. The child ran over to her, with her awkward hopping gait.

"Lady Giselle!" she called out.

Giselle paused and waited for her.

Olive pointed to the bag. "What is that?"

"All I own."

The child's eyes widened. "You are . . . leaving?"

"Aye." Giselle managed to give the child a smile. "I have enjoyed meeting you."

"No, my lady. You cannot leave Falcon's Craig." Olive's face darkened. "You have no idea of what may await you outside."

"You are right, Olive. And I have decided it's time for me to learn about those things." She reached out and squeezed the child's thin shoulder. "Farewell."

Before Olive could protest further, Giselle gathered her courage and walked out of the gatehouse.

Chapter
V

C ain sat in his chamber, Amice propped between his outstretched legs on a window seat, filled with a sense of peaceful joy he'd never thought to find. As he kneaded Amice's shoulders, she let out soft sighs of contentment.

She splayed a hand across her stomach. "I vow, I feel like an overgrown sow these days. One with a very active child in my belly."

"Perhaps the babe shall come soon."

"I hope so."

The door crashed open, and Gifford barreled in, followed closely by Olive. "Cain," his uncle shouted.

"What is it?" Cain frowned at the interruption.

"The girl is gone."

Amice straightened and swung her feet onto the floor. "Giselle?"

Olive hopped up and down. "She left. I saw it myself."

Cain exchanged a glance with his wife. "Unaccompanied?"

"Aye," Olive said, her small face crinkled with worry. "I tried to tell her not to go, but she would not listen."

"We'd better find Piers," Cain said as he rose.

They found his brother in the hall, swilling wine, with Clarise hovering nearby. At their entry, Piers lifted his cup. "Join me!" he called. "I am celebrating my freedom."

"Freedom?" Cain asked, surprised to find Piers well on his way to becoming sotted.

"Aye." Piers grinned. "Lady Giselle has released me from the betrothal." He tossed back a long drink of wine. "I am a free man."

"What did you say to her?" Amice asked, her voiced edged with concern.

" 'Told the girl I would marry her. Couldn't think of anything else to do." Piers shook his head. "She wants no part of a real marriage."

Cain considered his words. "Ah, I understand."

Gifford swiped Piers's jug and took a drink. "Could have given the girl time."

Piers shrugged. "She was most adamant about her feelings on the matter. And about *me*."

"She is gone, Piers," Cain told him.

"Gone?" Piers blinked up at him.

"Aye."

"Well, that did not take long," Piers muttered.

"Alone," Cain added.

"But, that is foolish."

"Go after her," Gifford urged.

Piers stared at Gifford as if he were mad, then his mouth turned down. " 'Twas the lady's decision to refuse me and leave."

"She is an innocent," Gifford argued.

"Damn," Piers said, with a sideways glance at Clarise. "A man cannot even get sotted in peace."

Cain rolled his eyes. "You must go right away, Piers. The girl cannot have gotten too far on foot."

"I shall go after the reckless little nun, do not worry. But I say Godspeed to the woman."

ఆ   ఆ   ఆ

For the first time in her life, Giselle found herself alone. It was both a strange and heady feeling. She walked on a path for a time, then veered off toward some woods, avoiding the village. She felt as if she embarked on a grand quest, and reminded herself over and over again that God would protect her, show her the way.

As she walked, she came up with a plan. After she put some distance between her and Falcon's Craig, she would seek out a village and inquire about the nearest abbey. No one knew her. Other than her brief visit to Falcon's Craig, she had not been outside Kerwick Abbey since she was a child.

She would simply give the Abbess a different name and come up with a story to explain her lack of possessions. She would be a widow, she decided. One on a pilgrimage.

Thou shall not lie. The thought of doing just that made her cringe, but what else could she do? Surely God could forgive her this once.

As she walked into the dense growth of trees, she considered how she might persuade an abbey to take her in. She had no coin, but she did possess some skills. Would her tapestries expose her? Surely not. Many women had such talents.

She kept walking throughout the day, considering how she might find a place in an abbey. Most women paid well for the sanctuary an abbey offered. Even widows. She should have demanded that Piers give her coin, she thought in disgust. But she'd been far too angry to bear his presence for a moment longer. Lost in her thoughts, she didn't realize for a moment that she'd entered a clearing.

"What have we here?" a man's voice asked.

Giselle stopped and met a flat brown gaze. She looked around and saw four men, all gazing at her with open interest. They were roughly dressed, their mounts tethered nearby. The one who had addressed her gave her a big grin and rose to his feet. He was huge, towering over her as he ran his narrowed gaze over her body.

She took a step back and eyed the horses, her heart sinking. Even if she could free one, her skills at riding were so poor the men could easily catch up with her. "I am on my way to a nunnery," she said.

The man laughed. "There is no nunnery in these

parts, girl."

Before she could think what to do, the men circled her. One tugged off her wimple and touched her hair. Giselle pulled free and glared at him. "Do not touch me."

He gave her a look that sent a cold shiver of terror down her spine.

Dear Lord, aid me, she silently prayed. She turned to the man who had first spoken. "I shall be on my way now."

"Oh, no. Stay for a bit." He pointed to a fire, over which roasted a fat hare. "Surely, you are hungry."

In fact, she was far past hungry, but as good as the hare smelled, it did not tempt her. "I recently ate," she lied, wincing as she did so.

The man picked at his teeth. "I really must insist," he told her. He nodded at one of his companions, who immediately seized Giselle's arm in a hard grip.

She tried to yank free, but it was like pulling against iron. "Let me go!"

"Not just yet."

Another of the man grabbed her other arm, and within a few horrible moments, Giselle found herself on the ground, gazing up at a man's leering face. She was so terrified she could barely take it in. The man pulled up his tunic and unbelted his braies.

"No!" she screamed, her heart thumping in her chest. "Release me! I am a nun!" She heaved against the hands holding her down, but it was no use. They were too strong and there were too many of them. "Let me go!"

In response, the man shoved up her skirts and dropped his braies, giving Giselle her first look at a man's member. She gagged at the sight, whimpering in fear.

Dear God, save me, she prayed. *Save me!*

The man gave her a cold smile and said, "I have never taken a nun."

Oh, God, he was going to put that thing . . . Giselle's vision blurred, and she closed her eyes, praying with everything within her.

"Leave the girl be," a man's voice suddenly shouted.

Giselle cracked her eyes open. She gasped in shock. The man striding into the clearing made the others look short and scrawny. His face drew her astonished gaze. Scars marred his bold features, and his eyes blazed blue flame. He held a long, shining sword in one large hand.

The men holding her arms released her and rushed toward him, their daggers drawn. Giselle couldn't move, frozen in horror and disbelief as the new arrival calmly dispatched two men, leaving them crumpled on the ground in a wash of blood. Within moments, the two others met the same fate, leaving Giselle staring at her savior over the fallen bodies.

"Are you all right, lass?" he asked in a rumbling voice.

Giselle let out a shriek and pulled her skirts down. She tried to stand, but her legs refused to obey and she landed hard on the ground.

"Do not be afraid," he said, drawing closer. "I will

not hurt you." He reached down a hand.

Giselle looked up into his scarred face, then down at the big, calloused hand reaching for hers. The same hand that had just sent four men to their deaths without a qualm. No, not men, she told herself. Foul, would be ravagers of an innocent woman. She slowly put her hand in his, and he lifted her to her feet. "Thank you," she whispered. "Those men, they . . ."

"I ken what they were about." He scowled, drawing his visage into a fearsome mask.

Giselle swayed, but managed to catch herself.

"You are safe now. You should return to your home."

Giselle started to shake, and before she could stop it, tears spilled from her eyes. "I do not have one."

He peered at her gown, and tilted his head, studying her. "Those are not the garments of a peasant. Where did you come from?"

Sobs choked her and she couldn't bring herself to speak.

The man let out a long sigh. "Come with me." He turned, then stopped and returned his gaze to hers. "I am called Padruig."

"Gi . . . Giselle," she sputtered. She forced herself to look away as they passed the bodies of her attackers. Padruig stopped before a massive black horse. "You can ride one of the others."

Ride? She could barely walk. Giselle eyed the other horses.

"*Can* you ride?"

A fragment of courage rallied inside her and Giselle nodded. "Not well though."

He inspected the horses and drew one forward. "Get on this one. I will hold the reins."

Giselle shot him a thankful look, then tried to mount. Her legs felt boneless, and she was trembling so badly it took her four tries, but eventually she made it onto the horse's back. "My . . . my bag," she said, remembering she'd left it on the ground.

Padruig fetched it and tied it on the saddle behind her. He untethered the other horses.

"What of them?" she asked.

"They shall follow." He leapt onto his mount, and took hold of her reins.

Giselle closed her eyes and prayed.

ঙ্গ   ঙ্গ   ঙ্গ

Piers stood in the bailey nursing a throbbing head and wondering how in the world he'd allowed his uncle to talk him into this. In fact, it had taken Gifford very little effort. Piers had not yet drunk enough to forget all sense of responsibility.

Damn the girl, he thought. What had she been thinking to set off on her own? She knew nothing of the world, he reminded himself. Nothing of the dangers that lay outside the walls of Kerwick Abbey and Falcon's Craig.

She was thinking of escaping you and your evil twin, his inner voice reminded him. He frowned.

Olive walked toward him across the bailey, pulling on the hand of a young boy. Piers knew him. The boy worked in the stables; Milo was his name. "Uncle Piers!" Olive called out.

He softened his expression. It was a fortunate day for all of them when Cain found Olive and brought her back to Falcon's Craig. The child could soften a heart of granite with her sweet smile.

She hopped to a stop before him, hauling the boy to stand next to her. "I have exactly who you need to find Lady Giselle," she announced.

The boy shuffled his feet.

"Milo? How can you aid me?"

"He can track *anything*, Uncle Piers. Tell him, Milo."

Milo's face reddened, but he nodded. " 'Tis true, my lord. My sire taught me."

Piers rocked back on his heels. "Well, then, I suppose you must come along."

Olive beamed her approval.

"Find yourself a horse. We leave soon."

Milo nodded and scampered off toward the stables.

"You *will* bring her back, won't you?" Olive asked.

He tousled her hair. "Aye."

Gifford emerged into the bailey, wearing a coat of mail that was far too big for him and clutching a jug of ale. A scabbard slapped against his thigh, and Gifford marched along as if he were the king himself deigning to pay Falcon's Craig a visit. Saraid walked behind him, wearing her common expression of bemusement mixed with affection. Gifford barreled to a stop next to Piers and grinned.

"What on earth are you doing?"

"Going with you, boy."

"Gifford, 'tis not necessary." Piers looked closer. "Where did you get that mail?"

Gifford waved a hand and took a swig of ale. "Doesn't matter. I am ready to go."

Behind him, Saraid rolled her eyes.

Without turning, Gifford reached back and took her hand. "I saw that, my sweet."

"Do not bother trying to talk him out of it," Saraid advised Piers as she came to Gifford's side. The old fool is convinced he is the only one to look after Lady Giselle once you find her."

"I can see to the lady."

"With the charm you seem to have lost of late?" Gifford asked. "Nay, I shall go."

Wonderful, Piers thought. Now, he had a young boy and his uncle to contend with as he searched for his wayward betrothed. What next?

She should be punished for fleeing you. 'Twill not take much effort to bring the timid wench to heel. She is yours to do with as you please. Eikki hissed, and an image bloomed in Piers's mind—one of Giselle, naked and trembling, her head bowed, her silvery hair cloaking her body in silken strands.

"Piers," Gifford said, frowning at him. "Did you not hear me?"

Piers shook off Eikki's thoughts and put his mind to the task at hand. By Saint George's sword, he must find a way to rid himself of this increasingly invasive companion. "I am sorry, Uncle. I was thinking of how best to find Lady Giselle."

"Humph," Gifford snorted.

Piers stared toward the stables from where Milo led a horse, followed by another stable hand leading Piers's mount. "If we are lucky, Milo can find her trail." He looked down, and saw that the dog, Guinevere, sat on his other side, staring up at him as if she actually knew what they were about. "You too?" he asked.

The dog thumped her tail on the ground.

"Let us be away. I would find Lady Giselle afore the sun sets."

Gifford grunted and toddled off to the stable, hollering, "Halden! I need a horse, man!"

Saraid let out a sigh. "See that he does not come to any harm."

Piers patted her shoulder. "I shall. Do not worry, my lady. We are taking a score of guards with us."

She stared after Gifford, currently being heaved atop a horse with Halden's aid. "He fancies himself some kind of romantic hero, you know."

"Aye." He smiled at her. "And he is, would you not agree?"

Saraid's expression turned soft. "Aye, that he is."

"We shall return anon, my lady."

"What shall you do with the girl when you find her?"

A damn good question, Piers thought. Giselle's words curled through his mind. *I will submit to you once.* He scowled. Submit, as if he were some kind of conqueror come to demand his spoils. Could he change her mind? He'd certainly been with enough women to learn how to bring them their own pleasure, in fact prided himself on the fact. Still, he could only envision Giselle cowering from him. She would do everything in her power to deny herself pleasure if only to prove to herself she was still worthy of being a nun.

"I do not know," he finally said to Saraid. "I do not know."

&⁊ &⁊ &⁊

Giselle periodically opened her eyes as they traveled, but could see little in the deepening shadows but the solid form of her rescuer's back and the pale glint of his blond hair. She felt as if they had ridden for days, her bottom sore and her legs cramped and achy.

Images of her attack whirled through her mind over and over again, and she barely suppressed a sob. If not for the massive warrior leading her, she would have been at the men's mercy. Her throat closed and she found it hard to draw a breath.

She'd never even imagined men like that existed. She could still see the leer on the man's face as he dropped his braies and shoved her legs apart. *Dear Lord, thank you*, she prayed. *Thank you for sending Padruig to me in time.*

But who was the man leading her? She shivered in the cooling air, wondering what she'd fallen into this time. At least she was gone from Falcon's Craig and the overbearing knave she'd been nearly trapped into marrying.

No doubt he had not even noted her absence.

Gradually, out of the shadows she made out a low, stone dwelling. Padruig's horse snorted and quickened his pace. They emerged into a small valley, rimmed by thick growths of trees. No one else appeared, and the place was dark.

"Is this your home?" Giselle managed to ask. Her throat was so dry she rasped the question.

"Aye," Padruig replied without turning around. He led them to a long structure and dismounted.

Giselle tried to get off the horse, but felt herself falling instead. Strong arms caught her just before she hit the ground. She jolted at the contact, but Padruig said nothing. He grunted and carried her into his dwelling. "Thank you," she said and deposited her onto a chair.

He bent and stirred some embers to life, then added more wood until a good fire burned. "Be at ease, my lady. I must see to the horses."

Giselle sat and stared into the fire. Absolute quiet enveloped her. She scooted a little closer to the flames, craving their warmth, and listened for Padruig's returning footsteps. Dear Lord, she felt as if every bone in her body ached. What she wouldn't give for a warm bath, she thought, then chided herself. The luxury of Falcon's Craig was behind her, she told herself as she straightened her shoulders. She was responsible for her own destiny. The very idea brought tears of fear to her eyes.

Lost in her efforts to shore up her flagging courage, she started when Padruig asked, "Are you hungry?"

He loomed over her, and Giselle had to remind herself that the man had saved her. "Aye."

She heard movements, then the glow of candlelight filled the room.

Padruig thrust a cup into her hand. Hesitantly, Giselle took it and cautioned a sip. She blinked. Even with her small experience, she realized the wine was a fine one, even better than that at Falcon's Craig. *Who is this man?* she wondered as she looked about his home.

"You've a fine dwelling," she said, taking it in. She sat in a surprisingly large chamber, the living area occupying one side, a kitchen nestled on the other side, separated by a long, oak table.

"Thank you," Padruig replied as he lit another fire in the kitchen. Both fireplaces vented to the outside, leaving the interior clear of smoke.

Another chair rested on the wooden floor next to her,

with a tapestry spread over the floor beneath. Trunks and pegs lined one wall and a set of stone steps climbed up another wall. Hung tapestries of hunting and battle scenes kept the chill air from seeping in through the stone walls. It was so comfortable and warm Giselle found herself simply sitting in the chair, sipping wine and gazing into the fire.

For the first time since she'd left Falcon's Craig, her fears and anger at her circumstance drained away. Despite Padruig's obvious skill with his sword, or perhaps because of it, she felt safe here. She gulped a swallow of wine, remembering her contemptuous words to Piers after witnessing his sword training. *How do you think we protect what is ours?* he had asked. She now understood far better than she ever wanted to what he meant.

After a bit, Padruig clomped back across the floor and thrust a bowl and spoon at her.

She peered into the bowl and breathed in the scent of spices.

" 'Tis stew, with bits of venison." He took the other chair and began to eat.

Meat, she thought as her stomach rumbled. She gazed at Padruig, who calmly spooned the concoction into his mouth. "Eat," he said.

She took a spoonful, chewing slowly. Her eyes opened wide. Perhaps it was in part due to her hunger, but the stew was very tasty. *I am not in a position to refuse food, even if I would never have been permitted to eat it at*

Kerwick Abbey, she told herself.

In her mind, she heard Father Michael. *You are not in the nunnery anymore. You need not follow their strictures.* She settled down and proceeded to eat, enjoying the stew more than she had anything else in a very long time.

Padruig finished, set aside his bowl and picked up a cup. "What was a girl like you doing in the forest alone?" he asked.

A piece of venison stuck in her throat and she swallowed some wine. " 'Tis a long story, I fear."

He leaned back and crossed his arms with a faint smile. "I have the time to listen."

The smile transformed his face. Though the scars remained clearly visible, Giselle could see that at one time he must have been a fine-looking man, with his broad shoulders, clear blue eyes, and pale hair. Giselle sensed she could trust him.

She took a last bite of her stew and set it aside, sucking in a deep breath. "I am not sure how to begin."

"I daresay 'tis best to begin at the beginning, lass."

Even his voice was oddly comforting, like a smooth, accented rumble. "I spent most of my life within Kerwick Abbey, studying to become a nun."

He lifted a brow. "A pretty young lass like you, a nun?"

" 'Tis what I have always wanted."

"Is it, now?"

"Aye." She dropped her gaze. "It is what I know, my lord."

"Just Padruig. Why did you leave?"

She lifted her head and stared at him. *What would he do if she told him?* she wondered. Scowl at her in revulsion just before he tossed her out of his home into the cold? No, she thought as she gazed into his eyes. Not this man. Something told her he had seen too much to be shocked with her tale.

"Lass?" He leaned forward. "Why did you leave the abbey?"

She sighed and picked up her cup of wine. "They threw me out. I . . . sometimes, I can see things. Things that haven't happened yet."

He slowly nodded. "You have the sight."

"Aye. When I tried to warn one of the sisters to take more care with her food, she ignored me and ended up choking so badly she could barely draw a breath. They blamed me for it. They *all* blamed me."

For a moment, he was silent, then said, "Kerwick Abbey is a fair distance from here."

Giselle took a strengthening sip of wine. "The Bishop had me escorted to Falcon's Craig Castle, where I discovered that long ago my mother had arranged for me to marry the earl's brother." Her mouth turned down.

"I see." Padruig fixed her with a curious gaze. "'Twould seem to be a good solution, lass. Falcon's Craig is a fine holding. And I have heard the earl is a fair man."

"Perhaps so, but I . . ." She flushed and ducked her head. "I do not wish to marry. I wish . . ."

He chuckled. "You are afraid to lie with a man."

Her face warmed further and she nodded jerkily. "Terrified," she whispered, scarcely believing she was confessing to a virtual stranger. A strange man with whom she was presently alone.

When he reached out and patted her leg, she jumped. "It can be a wondrous thing, lass."

She eyed him doubtfully. "The earl's brother does not want me. He is not the type of man to cleave to one woman."

"He refuses to marry you?"

"Nay but . . ."

His face sobered. "What else shall you do? You are a gently born girl, 'tis obvious."

"I have skills," she said, remembering Lady Amice's comment.

"You think to work a trade?"

"The abbey earned much coin from my tapestries. I thought to offer my skills to another nunnery to take me in."

"How would you explain your past?" he asked gently.

"I would make up a story." Her shoulders slumped. "I am not a very good liar, I fear."

" 'Tis a hard thing to live a lie, lass."

Something in his tone made her gaze at him more closely. "How did you come to live here?"

His face closed and he shook his head. "We are speaking of you."

She bit her lip and cast about for an idea. "Perhaps if I went to a town and offered my services to a tradesman."

"Giselle, you cannot simply set off across the countryside in the hopes of finding a hospitable town and a tradesman willing to take you in. You have seen what can happen to a woman traveling alone."

"Perhaps, you could escort me? I have nothing to offer you, but I vow I would find a way to repay you."

He stood and picked up his bowl. "I cannot," he said slowly.

Her spirits plummeted and she fought the sting of tears. "What shall I do?"

"If the young lord is that reluctant to marry, perhaps he will see you settled elsewhere."

"He threatened to send me to another estate."

"Would that be such a bad thing?"

She shrugged helplessly. "I no longer know, it seems. The life I thought I had has been stripped from me. I know not what to do."

He rested a heavy hand on her shoulder. "You need not figure that out this eve. The day has been an eventful one. Take your sleep and we shall discuss this in the morning."

A tear leaked out of her eye. "Thank you."

"Up the steps is the bedchamber."

For a moment, Giselle froze. Surely he did not mean . . .?

"You may sleep there. I shall stay down here by the fire."

"Oh." She gazed up at him. "You need not give up your bed. I shall be fine here." She was so exhausted she could sleep on frozen ground if that was all that was to be had.

"I am not such a selfish knave as that, lass. Take the bedchamber."

She rose stiffly to her feet, amazed once more at how he dwarfed her. "I do not know how to thank you."

" 'Tis no need." He gathered up their bowls and walked to the kitchen.

As Giselle made her way up the steps, she paused and turned. "Good night."

"Sleep well, lass. Everything will appear clearer in the morn."

She wanted to believe him, but could not see how anything would ever appear clear again. As she snuggled into a soft bed piled with blankets and furs, she pondered what to do. Weariness crept over her and she blinked, striving to keep her eyes open.

Perhaps Padruig was right, she thought with a spark of hope. Piers was clearly anxious to get rid of her. Surely, he could be persuaded to provide an escort to a nearby town and enough coin for her to survive while she found a place to ply her craft. He would be free to resume the life he enjoyed, and she . . . She sighed. *Dear Lord, what am I to do? It is as if your house is closed to me. What is your will?*

The only sound was the wind rattling a shutter overhead.

❧   ❧   ❧

Despite Milo's talents, Piers could find no trace of Giselle. It was as if the girl had sprouted wings and simply flown away.

He reined in his horse several leagues from Falcon's Craig and gazed around him at the empty countryside. Gifford pulled up next to him.

" 'Twill be dark soon," Gifford said, his usually affable face drawn into lines of concern.

"Milo," Piers called.

The boy rode up and shook his head. "I am sorry, my lord. I truly thought she headed in this direction, but I must have been mistaken."

Where could the girl be? Piers wondered. Perhaps she found a traveler willing to take her along, he thought. She could be anywhere by now.

"We should return to Falcon's Craig," his uncle advised. "We can search for Giselle again at first light."

Even though his head ached, and his legs were stiff from hours of riding, Piers was hesitant to abandon the search. What if Giselle was lost? She'd taken very little with her, according to Olive.

"Piers," Gifford said. "We cannot find the girl in the dark."

Piers took a last look around them and reluctantly nodded. "Very well. We go back." As they rode, he found himself silently uttering a prayer that Giselle's beloved

God was taking care of her.

Heaven knew, she was completely incapable of doing so herself.

He surely did not want to marry her, but at the same time her complete discontent over the idea rankled. *What did you expect?* his inner voice asked. *That she would take one look at your handsome face and forget fourteen years of training at Kerwick Abbey?* With not a small bit of chagrin, he realized a part of him had thought exactly that.

Arrogant simpkin, he chided himself.

Guilt bore down on him like a solid boulder wedged onto his shoulders. He should never have said the things he'd said to her. No wonder she'd panicked and fled.

Damn you, Eikki, he thought.

For once the being remained silent. Perhaps even he realized they'd driven an innocent girl into peril.

🐇 🐇 🐇

Giselle awoke to the sounds of birds shrilling their greetings, with a faint morning sun spilling in through the cracks overhead to light her chamber. The bed was so comfortable she was loath to leave, tempted to crawl beneath the warm covers and remain.

Sounds from below reminded her this was not her home, not her bedchamber, only a temporary refuge thanks to the generous kindness of a stranger.

She got up and stretched, unsurprised to find her

limbs still ached from the day before. She smoothed her bliaut as best she could and headed down the steps.

"Good morn, my lady," Padruig said as he fed bits of meat to a large, gray animal with patches of white on its chest.

Giselle paused at the bottom of the steps. "What is that?"

The animal cocked its head toward her voice, and Giselle inched back up a step.

"His name is Cai," Padruig said.

"Is that a . . . dog?"

Padruig stood and ruffled the beast's fur. "Nay. Cai would be offended to be called such. He is a gray wolf."

A wolf. Giselle backed up another step. Guinevere was one thing, but a wolf? Dear Lord, what if the thing attacked?

Cai yawned, revealing a truly impressive array of sharp teeth.

"Come and break your fast," Padruig told her, gesturing toward the table, where a platter of bread and cheese sat next to a jug and two cups.

"I—" Her eyes widened as the wolf trotted over to her. She shrieked and fell back onto the steps. The wolf just stared at her as if he was wondering what was wrong with her.

Padruig chuckled. "He wilnae hurt you lass."

"Are . . . are you sure?" She gazed into the wolf's round eyes and tried to stamp down her fear.

"Yes. Cai has been with me for a long time."

Giselle gathered her courage and stood. The wolf followed her to the table. When she gratefully sat on a stool, he sat on the floor beside her, looking up. "What does he want?"

Padruig took another stool. "Food, as always."

She cut off a chunk of cheese and dropped it. The wolf snapped it up in one bite and moved closer to her stool. Fighting the urge to moan in sheer panic, she pointed at the jug. "May I have something to drink?"

"Of course." Padruig poured her a cup and slid it across the table.

Giselle took a deep drink of wine, ignoring her inner voice that whispered perhaps she was becoming a bit too fond of the drink. " 'Tis an unusual pet."

Padruig munched on a piece of bread. "Aye." He gazed at her, and Giselle sensed what he was about to say. Her appetite fled. "I have given much thought to your situation, lass."

"As have I," she murmured, sipping wine.

"I do not see any option but to return you to Falcon's Craig."

Her stomach clenched.

"If the life of a nun is closed to you, then you have no choice but to take a husband. The earl's brother may not be the kind of man you might have chosen, but," he shrugged and took a drink, "you will no doubt be well cared for at Falcon's Craig."

Giselle stared down at the table, feeling as if the un-breakable strands of a rope net closed around her. "I know you are right, but . . ." She buried her face in her hands. Padruig *was* right, of course. And Piers *was* a young, exceedingly handsome man, with family and wealth. At times he'd shown her kindness. The Bishop could have delivered her to far worse. Still, the scrap of independence she'd never been able to completely quash wailed in resentment that she had no choice in the matter.

"I shall see you to Falcon's Craig this morn."

She lifted her gaze to his, and the sympathy in his eyes nearly broke her resolve not to crumble into tears.

"Eat, lass. 'Tis likely your betrothed is already searching for you."

"I doubt that." She grimaced and sipped more wine. "More likely, he is celebrating being rid of me with a woman in his bed."

Padruig grinned. "Well, if he is as you say, at least you will gain a husband experienced in such matters."

Giselle wrinkled her nose. "I would prefer he were well-versed in prayer."

"You'll not find that outside a monastery."

"Nay, I suppose not."

"I shall ready the horses. Eat something, lass. We have a bit of a ways to travel."

Giselle gave him a glum look as he left the cottage. She jerked when Cai put his head in her lap. Dear Lord, she felt so numb, she could not even be afraid of the fact that a wolf who undoubtedly outweighed her was presently resting his shaggy head on her in the hopes of catching a morsel of food. She tried to eat a piece of bread, but it tasted like sawdust in her mouth and she gave up, giving the rest to Cai, who happily lay down and ate it.

Back to Falcon's Craig, she thought with an inward shudder. But, back to what?

Chapter VI

The moment Piers walked into the misty clearing the next morn, his gut clenched in dread. Four bodies lay in a bloody heap on the ground. There was no sign of Giselle.

"Dear Lord," Gifford cried as he dismounted.

Piers turned one of the roughly dressed bodies over with his boot. He didn't recognize the man. He gazed at the other bodies and fear curled in his gut. "Cut down by a sword, each one," he told Gifford. "It doesn't look as if there was much of a fight."

"My lord," one of the guards called out.

"Aye?" He turned.

Rauf held a piece of white fabric in his hand. The edges fluttered in the slight breeze.

Piers walked to where Rauf stood and held out his hand. He took the material and studied it in growing dread. "This is a piece of a wimple."

Gifford peered over his shoulder and gasped. "There is blood on it."

Piers looked down. The grass was crushed and scraped away in spots. His blood chilled. What had befallen Giselle, if, in fact, she had been here? He cringed with guilt at the fear the men had ravaged her. Or that someone else had taken her. *Do not think about that now,* he told himself. *Just find the girl.* "Milo?" he called.

The boy scampered over. "Aye, my lord?"

"Have you found anything?"

Milo nodded quickly, his eyes beaming. He held out a scrap of blue wool. "I found this snagged on a branch."

"Show me where." Piers followed the boy to an area beyond the clearing, hope and dread roiling in his belly.

Milo pointed toward the ground, but Piers couldn't see anything.

"What is it?"

"The horses went this way."

Piers still couldn't see any sign, but he had no choice except to trust the boy. "Lead on, Milo." He mounted, and the troop followed Milo into the woods. "Can you tell how many horses trod this way?"

Milo was bent over double studying the ground. "More than two."

"How many riders?"

The boy shook his head. "The tracks are too faint to tell."

In silence they followed Milo as he led them through the woods. Even Gifford refrained from comment, as if he shared Piers's concern over where the trail would lead.

Milo stopped and dropped to his knees, craning his head around, sifting leaves through his fingers. He frowned. "They veered off here."

"Which way?"

The boy sniffed a handful of leaves. Guinevere joined him, wagging her tail as if it were a game. Suddenly, she lifted her head, barked, and took off through the woods.

Piers stared after her, wondering.

"No doubt caught the scent of a hare," Gifford said.

"Perhaps." They heard more barking in the distance.

Milo put his ear to the ground and slowly nodded. "Horses approach, my lord."

Piers drew his sword and the guards followed suit. Even Gifford managed to get his sword out of the scabbard without injuring himself. The guards moved out into the trees, circling Piers, Gifford, and Milo.

Guinevere's barking grew closer. Piers peered through the mist and saw the vague outline of a horse and rider. As they neared, he saw it was a man atop an immense black horse. Another shape traveled behind him, but Piers could not make it out. "Be ready, men," he ordered.

The moment Giselle spotted Guinevere, she realized Padruig's prediction had been accurate. The realization that someone cared enough to search for her held no comfort. It only made the fact she was returning to Falcon's

Craig and a frightening future all the more real.

She rode behind Padruig, feeling much as if she were riding to the gallows. As they neared the clearing where she'd been attacked, she began trembling from head to foot, suddenly unable to force the horrifying images from her mind. The horse danced beneath her, and Padruig turned. She couldn't keep the fear from her eyes.

"You wilnae come to harm, lass," he said, understanding the source of her alarm.

The rumble of his voice calmed her, and she took a deep breath. But just as she managed to shove the memories to the back of her mind, she looked ahead and saw a sight that brought a new shiver of trepidation into her veins.

"They wear the blue and silver of Falcon's Craig," Padruig said over his shoulder.

Giselle just stared. In the center of a group of guards, Piers sat atop his horse, his sword drawn, and his expression hard. "Who goes there?" he called out.

"A friend," Padruig yelled back. He stopped his horse with a murmured command and turned in the saddle. "Who is that?"

Giselle's lips were so dry she could barely speak. "Piers Veuxfort. My betrothed."

Padruig grinned. "I told you he would be looking for you."

"But, why?"

"Perhaps you should ask him." Padruig turned and

urged his horse forward. When they reached the group from Falcon's Craig, Padruig moved his horse aside, and Giselle found herself looking into Piers's surprised gaze.

For a moment, no one spoke. Relief slowly spilled over Piers's face and the warmth in his gaze held Giselle fast. She licked her lips and his eyes dropped to her mouth in a way that brought a tingling to her body.

"Lady Giselle, thank the Lord we found you," Gifford called out. "Are you well?"

The spell broken, Giselle turned to Gifford. She couldn't help but smile at his appearance. Wearing a coat of mail clearly designed for a man much larger, his white hair in spiky disarray around his smiling face, he held a sword in one hand and a jug in the other. "Aye," she said, and nodded at Padruig. "Thanks to Padruig."

Piers frowned, though he sheathed his sword. He ran his gaze over Padruig, suspicion stamped on his features. "Who are you?"

"As the lady said, I am called Padruig." He gestured toward the clearing. "I came across the lass when she was in need."

"You are the one who killed those men?"

"Aye."

Piers nodded. "You have my thanks. If you would accompany me to Falcon's Craig, I shall see you rewarded."

He had yet to address a word to her, and Giselle felt her annoyance rise.

"I need no reward." Padruig glanced at Giselle and gave

her a supportive look. " 'Twas my honor to aid the lass."

"You are a Scot?"

"Aye."

"Of which clan?"

Giselle saw Padruig stiffen. "I have no clan." His voice was harsh and cold.

Piers studied him for a moment, then apparently decided to let the matter alone. Giselle was puzzled. From what she knew of the Scots, which was admittedly very little, she thought their clans were all-important, how they defined themselves.

"Giselle." Piers looked at her, but the warmth was gone. "Are you able to ride to Falcon's Craig?"

Why? she wanted to yell. *What difference does it make to you where I go?* But years of suppressing her emotions made her lower her eyes and nod. "Yes."

"Then, let us go. I have no wish to linger further in these woods."

Padruig sidled his horse close to hers. "Do you wish me to accompany you back to the castle?" The reluctance on his face was visible.

Giselle swallowed. Over the past day, she had come to view the big, scarred man as her protector. "I . . . that would please me."

He grunted. "Very well, lass."

"To Falcon's Craig," Piers called and urged his horse ahead. He did not look back once at Giselle.

She gritted her teeth, half tempted to stay where

she was to see how long it would take for him to notice she didn't follow in his wake. Guinevere yipped and bounded ahead.

"Giselle?" Padruig asked.

She sighed and urged her horse on. Some of the guards fell in behind them, and the horses picked up speed. Giselle focused on remaining atop her mount, trying to ignore the ache that settled firmly in her bottom and legs. Piers rode ahead, laughing with Gifford as if he were on a task no more important than exercising his horse.

What did you expect? she asked herself. *You put conditions on the marriage that you knew he could not accept. You fled from him.* Her mood darkened, and she considered what he might do with her now. Send her away, no doubt. She tried to tell herself that would be for the best, but the moment of warmth in his gaze refused to leave her.

Remember Rule Number Twelve, she reminded herself. *You must resist temptation, for it is the work of the devil.*

And even Giselle in her innocence recognized that, for her, temptation came in the unlikely form of Piers Veuxfort.

❧   ❧   ❧

The Bishop of Ravenswood glared at the man he'd sent to Falcon's Craig. "What do you mean, the wench is not yet wed?"

"There has been no marriage." The man eyed Aldrik's ewer of wine and licked his lips, but Aldrik ignored him.

"Why?"

The man shrugged. "The servants say the girl still seeks a nunnery."

Aldrik frowned. "I know that much. But I have seen to it that she shall not find one. Is there a problem with this Piers Veuxfort?"

"Not that I could ascertain." The man chuckled. "He is quite popular with the wenches in the castle."

That brought a smile to Aldrik's face. Perfect, he thought. A husband to use Giselle well. But first, he needed to marry the girl. He crossed to a table and scrawled a letter. "Return to Falcon's Craig. Remind the earl that I expect the marriage to take place at once. I sent the girl to Falcon's Craig to be wed, by God, and that is what shall occur."

"I will see to it, your grace."

"Good. Bring word to me when the deed is done."

The man nodded and turned to leave.

"Joseph."

Joseph turned back. "When I say done, I mean completely," Aldrik said. He scowled and went over to a locked trunk. "I would not be surprised if Giselle tried to avoid the marriage bed. Do whatever you can to ensure Piers Veuxfort takes her. I do not want to have to deal with the girl again."

"What do you want me to do?"

Aldrik unlocked the trunk and reached around the bottom until he located a small vial of powder. He pressed it into Joseph's hands. "Put this in the girl's drink on her wedding day." He slowly smiled. "She will be like a bitch in heat."

"What is it?" Joseph's gaze was alight with interest.

"Something very rare. Aldrik pulled another cloth-wrapped object from the trunk and thrust it into Joseph's hands. "Take this as a gift to the newly wedded couple. 'Twill give you an innocent reason to visit Falcon's Craig." Asides, the gift amused him. It had once graced a prominent place within Kindlemere Castle before he'd replaced it as he had many things that once belonged to the St. Germain family.

"Now, go." Aldrik dismissed Joseph with a wave of his hand.

After Joseph left, Aldrik poured himself a cup of wine and stared at the burning fire. Memories crept into his mind, long buried memories that even after all these years had the power to bring him shame over his weakness.

He remembered vividly the day he'd spotted Giselle at Kerwick Abbey. It had been like gazing upon a ghost of his past, a horrific reminder of a time he wished he could erase from his memory. There she stood in the garden, her face the very picture of young, beautiful innocence, yet her lush body so similar to the one who'd brought about his fall from grace.

He swallowed some wine. It didn't matter anymore, he told himself. Giselle was gone, as was her mother, a true daughter of Eve if ever there was one. Just like her daughter, she had resembled an angel, but within dwelled a foul temptress.

His hand shook as he set down his cup. His manhood throbbed, but he would do nothing to ease it. Instead, he embraced the discomfort, turned it into strength. He was a man of God, above his flesh.

And he had well reaped the worldly rewards for such devotion.

🐎 🐎 🐎

Upon their arrival at Falcon's Craig, Giselle murmured something about a headache and fled to her chamber. Piers barely acknowledged her. Throughout the ride back to the castle, he'd been much the same, ignoring her but for an occasional glance. If not for the solid presence of Padruig riding beside her, Giselle wasn't sure how she would have withstood it.

When she entered her chamber, she found Nona waiting for her. "Oh, my lady, thank God you have returned. We were all so worried for you." She drew Giselle down onto the window seat, clucking at the dirt stains on Giselle's bliaut.

"It was not the journey I had envisioned," Giselle

said wearily.

"Poor thing," Nona said as she unplaited Giselle's hair. "I've called for a bath for you."

"Thank you, Nona."

"Who is that fearsome looking man who accompanied you?" Nona whispered. She shivered. "Hawis said his face was so terrible, it hurt to look at it."

How odd, Giselle thought. She felt the same at first, but she barely noticed the scars any more. "He is called Padruig. He saved me from horrible men who . . ." She couldn't bear to say it.

Nona clapped a hand to her chest, her eyes wide. "Well, you are safely returned." At a knock at the door, she opened it and ushered in a troop of servants carting a bathing tub and buckets of steaming water.

Giselle closed her eyes and leaned her head against the stone wall. She felt Nona shake her shoulder, and realized she'd fallen asleep "Let's get you into the bath, my lady. Then you can rest."

Giselle was too tired to protest when Nona propped her up and stripped off her clothing. She stumbled to the tub, and sank into the water, letting out a hum of pleasure as the warm water seeped into her aching limbs.

By the time Nona rinsed her hair, Giselle was blinking hard to keep her eyes open. Nona wrapped her in drying cloths and sat her in front of the fire. "Are you hungry, my lady?" she asked.

"Nay. I am too weary to be hungry." She stared into

the fire wondering what would happen to her now that she was back at Falcon's Craig.

Nona put a hand on her shoulder. "Rest, my lady. I shall have the tub removed later."

"Thank you, Nona."

"It will be all right, you shall see. Once you marry, everything will be better."

Giselle didn't bother correcting her as she slid into bed. She turned toward the wall and closed her eyes.

🦎 🦎 🦎

"Lady Amice?"

Amice looked up to find the man called Padruig. She set aside the stack of linens she was counting. "Padruig, I have not had the chance to thank you for your service to Giselle." It struck her that the man reminded her a bit of Lugh MacKeir, though his face was so marked it was difficult to note anything else.

" 'Twas my pleasure." His face darkened. "That band meant the poor lass ill."

"But you stopped them."

"Aye."

Amice let out a sigh. She'd not wanted to ask, but feared Giselle had not emerged unscathed from the attack. "Is there aught I can do for you?"

He shifted his feet. " 'Tis a matter of some . . . delicacy I wish to speak with you about."

Oh, no, Amice thought. *Surely, he is not going to ask for Giselle.* "Pray, go on," she said.

"It concerns the Lady Giselle."

"She is betrothed to Piers."

His gaze froze for a moment, then he smiled. "I am not after Giselle for myself, my lady."

"Oh."

"While she was at my home, we talked of the matter of her marriage."

Was that a flush she saw on Padruig's face? "I know Giselle is not eager for marriage. Her life in the nunnery has not prepared her well for a woman's life outside of one."

"Aye. She is a tender lass. I thought as the lady of the castle, you might speak to her, reassure her."

Gradually, it dawned on her what the man was saying. "You are referring to—"

"The bedding, aye." He gave her an uncomfortable look. "She is mighty frightened of the act, my lady."

"I see." Amice folded a piece of linen. " 'Tis not a surprise, given her past. I shall talk with her about it."

"Thank you, my lady."

It was obvious this big, scarred man cared for Giselle. Amice found herself wondering just what had transpired between them. She could not have envisioned a more unlikely pair to so quickly have formed a bond. "What else did she tell you? Giselle has not been with us for long, and has been very reticent to talk of herself."

Padruig appeared to consider her question. "Naught

of import, my lady. She does not wish to marry, but I imagine you are aware of that."

"Aye." Amice shook her head. "Her arrival was as much a shock to us as it was to her."

"Is the lad willing to marry her?"

A good question, Amice thought. She once would have said yes without reservation, but Piers's behavior of late had become more unpredictable. "I believe so," she finally said. "Do not worry for Giselle. The earl will see that she is provided for."

"Good." He turned to go.

"Will you stay and have supper with us?"

"Nay, my lady. I'd best be on my way afore darkness falls."

"You are welcome to stay the night."

"My thanks, but I have matters to attend to at home."

Amice studied him. Padruig was a mystery, appearing out of nowhere to, thankfully, save Giselle. A Scot, by his accent, but according to Piers, one who claimed no clan, no roots. "Where do you live?"

"Beyond the forest."

"You are a Scot."

"Aye. I was born in the Highlands."

"Have you family there?"

Padruig's eyes flickered, but his expression remained blank. "No. I have no one." He bowed. "I shall take my leave, my lady. Please give Lady Giselle my farewell."

Amice watched him go, wondering yet again who

the man really was. The babe kicked hard in her belly and she put her hand over the spot, forgetting about the mystery of Padruig at the prospect of soon holding her child. "Soon, little one. Soon I shall hold you in my arms." She smiled. Sometimes, she could scarcely believe how perfect her life had become. She had Cain, who had finally learned to shed his demons for love of her, a rarely boring family surrounding her, and very soon a child to love.

Aye, life could not be more perfect.

Chapter VII

Much later in the afternoon, Giselle slowly woke. Guinevere lay sprawled on the bed beside her snoring softly, her legs twitching in a dream chase. For a moment, Giselle just lay there watching the sunlight pick up dust motes in the air.

If only she could fly away that easily, she thought. Fly to a distant place of peace and serenity, where each day blended into the next with ease.

And without an infuriating, confusing man to whom, it appeared, she had no choice but to marry.

The door swung open and Nona bounced in, a bright smile on her face. "Oh good, my lady. You are awake."

Guinevere lifted her head, and her tail thumped on the bed.

"Aye." Giselle climbed out of bed and winced at the ache in her legs.

Nona set down a jug and a cup. "Would you care for something to drink?"

Why not? Giselle thought as she curled onto the

139

window seat. "Thank you."

After Nona handed her a cup of wine, she passed her a folded piece of parchment. "The Scot asked me to give this to you before he left."

"Padruig is gone?"

"Aye, my lady." Nona shivered. "Such a . . . strange looking man. You must have been terribly worried to be alone with him."

Giselle took a sip of wine and looked up at her, struck by the realization that she had never been in any fear of Padruig at all. "He was very kind to me."

"Well, I know he saw to your welfare, but I cannot say I am sorry he is gone."

But, I am, Giselle thought with a hollow twinge. Something about Padruig was so solid, so clearly evincing an inner strength that, for a brief time, his presence gave her the illusory sense of being safe and secure. She unfolded the parchment.

Lady Giselle, he wrote. *I cannot stay at Falcon's Craig, but know that I would offer you what aid I can. If you have need of me, send word. Your friend and ally. Padruig.*

Giselle felt tears sting her eyes. Would that God had seen fit to betroth her to a man with Padruig's understanding, his easy acceptance. Even as her mind completed the thought, she realized its lie. The tiny part of her heart that didn't belong to the Lord still craved love, and she knew she would never feel that way toward Padruig. Unfortunately, she couldn't imagine developing those feelings for Piers either. She sighed and gazed out her window at the sea.

"May I help you dress for supper?" Nona asked.

"I would prefer to stay in my chamber this eve," Giselle murmured.

Nona clucked and patted her shoulder. "Of course. You must rest and regain your strength. You will want to appear your best for the wedding."

"Wedding?" Giselle snapped a look at her.

"Well, aye. Now that you are back, you will be wedding the young lord." Nona beamed her a smile. "A fortunate girl you are, indeed."

Giselle just stared at her blankly.

"Poor thing, you *are* weary. I shall see food is sent to you anon."

Giselle couldn't summon a single sound of thanks. The word wedding sunk into her mind like a large, cold chunk of granite. She laid her head against the stone, staring out at the placid, glittering water and seeing nothing but that instant of warmth in Piers's gaze, wishing she could have captured the moment.

But it was clear she would never be more than an unwanted burden to him.

Perhaps it was all someone like her deserved.

⚝ ⚝ ⚝

Giselle had just finished choking down a few bites of food when there was another tap of the door. "Enter," she called, hoping it was simply Nona checking on her.

Instead, Lady Amice walked in. "Giselle, how are you feeling? Nona said you were still too fatigued to come down for supper."

"I—"

"But I have a feeling that is not the whole of it," Lady Amice continued as she sat on a stool.

"My lady, all of this . . . has been most unsettling to me."

Lady Amice sent her a gentle smile. "Aye, I realize that. Your Padruig seems to be a fine man, though. You are most fortunate it was he who found you."

"Yes, I am."

"He spoke to me of your concerns about your marriage to Piers. I thought perhaps it would help to talk to another woman about it."

Giselle tried in vain to calm her suddenly racing heart.

"Do you know aught of what happens between man and wife?" Lady Amice asked.

Giselle gulped some wine and shook her head. "My lady, as you know, I spent most of my life at Kerwick Abbey. I never expected to marry."

Lady Amice's smile widened into one filled with knowledge and mystery. "Marriage can be a wondrous thing. And Piers is a fine man."

"I . . . I do not know him, my lady." Giselle's voice came out in a whisper, and she felt the burn of tears at the backs of her eyes.

"Piers is a good man."

Giselle merely stared at her and sipped more wine. "It is more than that, my lady. You do not understand. God demands more of me than to give in to . . . temptation."

"Temptation can be a good thing. Have you ever seen a man? All of him?"

"I . . ." Giselle started to shake her head, then realized she had seen the part Lady Amice undoubtedly referred to. She started to tremble. "In the forest, the men, one of the men let down his braies. It was horrible."

Lady Amice's expression changed to concern. "You must not equate that . . . whoreson's treatment with the loving intentions of your husband."

"He did not . . . Giselle dimly realized she should be shocked at Lady Amice's language, but thought her description more than apt. "Padruig slew him before he could," she gulped, "do more."

"Thank God." Lady Amice rose and patted her on the shoulder. "You must trust Piers in this matter. Joining with your husband can be a very pleasurable experience, Giselle."

Giselle couldn't help it, a hysterical giggle burst from her throat. "I have heard Piers has much experience in the matter."

"Aye." Lady Amice gave a soft laugh. "That he does, indeed. And now, 'tis to your benefit."

"Benefit?" Giselle sobered. "I cannot see it that way, my lady."

Lady Amice sighed. "I understand this is difficult for you, Giselle, given your background, but you are to be wed. The joining of a man and woman's bodies is part of that." She winked. "At times, the very best part."

"Is it not a sin to seek pleasure in mating? Is not our purpose to create life, no more?" Giselle fingered her rosary.

"That is what you have been taught?"

"Aye." Giselle's chin came up. "That is all I know, my lady. That is all I am allowed to believe."

"You are embarking on a new future."

"I am sorry, my lady, but I cannot change everything I believe in the span of a few days."

"I have a feeling Piers is just the man to change your mind," Lady Amice said with a last pat on Giselle's shoulder. "Trust in him, Giselle."

Trust? Giselle thought as Lady Amice shut the door behind her. How was she to trust a man she scarcely knew, a man who was only reluctantly wedding her because he didn't know what else to do with her? A man who had coolly informed her that, once wed, she was his property to deal with as he saw fit.

You were born of wickedness, the Abbess had ofttimes told her. Perhaps it was as simple as that. No matter how many prayers she said, maybe to be bound to a man who would never love her was her true penance.

Giselle dropped her head into her hands and gripped the smooth stones of her rosary tight. If this truly was

God's will, she had no choice but to accept it, yet deep inside, her heart cried out at the unfairness of it all.

Lady Amice could not understand Giselle's dilemma. Amice glowed with anticipation of holding her babe conceived in love.

Giselle blinked as images tumbled into her mind like pebbles scattered by a raging current.

Lady Amice lay upon tangled, sweat-soaked sheets, her beautiful brown eyes glazed with pain. Red splotches marred her beautiful face, and her fists clutched the sheets so tightly her knuckles were white. "Aid me," she pleaded to a woman Giselle had never seen. "Save my babe."

The woman shook her head in sorrow.

"Do something," Lady Amice ordered, just before she shrieked in pain. Lines of sweat streamed down her cheeks.

"There is nothing more I can do. The babe will not come."

"Damn you," Lady Amice cursed. "My babe will come."

A servant tried to press a cup of wine to Lady Amice's lips but she batted it away. "Get the earl," she said over a short breath. "Now."

The servant fled the room.

Silence descended over the chamber, the woman, apparently the midwife, peering between Lady Amice's splayed legs, her expression resigned. With a great whoosh of breath, Lady Amice fell silent. Her eyes filled with helpless tears.

Giselle had not seen the final outcome of her vision, but dread coiled in her belly and the stark expression of agony in Lady Amice's eyes bored into her.

Both the lady and the babe were fated to die.

Dear Lord, what more could happen? she wondered, catching her breath on a sob. Have I so offended you, Lord? Am I truly so tainted, so foul inside that I have brought all of this upon myself? Upon a woman who has been nothing but kind to me, despite her devotion to the old gods and goddesses, instead of you, the one true God?

There was no answer. There never had been.

🐌 🐌 🐌

"Do you, Lady Giselle," Father Michael paused and glanced down at Giselle's frozen face, "freely give your body to Piers Veuxfort in holy matrimony?"

Dear Lord, how was this happening? She looked at Piers from beneath her lashes. He stared straight ahead, his expression one of a man facing certain doom. She recognized the look, sure her face appeared the same.

"Giselle?" Father Michael murmured.

In her mind, Giselle saw the metal bars of a cell slam shut. "I do," she whispered.

"And I receive it," Piers clipped.

"And do you, Piers Veuxfort, freely give your body to Lady Giselle in holy matrimony?"

"I do."

Giselle swallowed and forced the words out. "And I receive it."

Father Michael took their hands. "I bestow the blessing of the Lord upon this union. May your life together be long and fruitful."

He squeezed Giselle's hand, but she barely felt it, as if all of this were happening to someone else. Piers said not a word, but guided her into the chapel, where they took seats in front for the mass.

As Father Michael performed mass, Giselle tried to find comfort in the rhythm and words of the service, but for the first time in her life, could not. She couldn't think of anything but the fact that she was now married to Piers Veuxfort, a man who wanted her no more than she wanted him.

He sat close enough beside her that she could smell his scent, feel the warmth of his body. She stared down at his long fingers and shivered. Would he want to consummate the marriage right away? Though she wasn't entirely sure what that meant, everything inside her recoiled from the idea.

Please, Lord, help me get through this, she silently prayed as Father Michael droned on. *Give me strength*.

Piers gave his bride a sideways glance and grimaced. The girl was near to trembling, her face downcast, her hands gripped tightly around a rosary. He was surprised she hadn't dissolved into tears by now.

God, what a tragic farce this was, he thought. He felt as if he were attending his own funeral, instead of a wedding. He half-listened to Father Michael finishing the mass and wondered how he was going to get through the wedding feast, let alone deal with the girl afterward.

A virgin, Eikki whispered. *Just think of it. All of that beautiful innocence yours to plunder.*

Shut up, Piers thought with a frown. He stood and took Giselle's arm. When they turned, a sea of faces studied them. Piers tried to paste a light smile to his face, but knew he'd failed completely when he met his brother's gaze.

Of all people, Cain knew the price one could pay for following duty. His own path had led him into marriage with a perverse adulteress, after which he'd closed himself off so well it was nothing short of a miracle he'd come to his senses in time to avoid losing Amice. Amice stood to his side looking only slightly less somber than her husband.

"Come, Giselle," Piers said.

The girl didn't respond, but began walking at his side.

Piers wanted to groan aloud as they led the wedding guests into the great hall. He seated Giselle, then gratefully took his own seat and filled his cup to the brim with wine.

Gifford slapped him on the back. "I never thought I would live to see the day you were wed, boy." He and Saraid took seats along the table. "A true vision of loveliness you are, Lady Giselle."

"Thank you, my lord," she answered in a subdued voice.

Piers poured her wine as the others found their seats. A group of musicians picked up a song and servants carried in platters of food. "You are recovered from your journey?" he asked.

Her face flushed pink. "Aye."

She probably thought he was asking her if she was well enough to bed, Piers thought. Clarise bent around him and set a platter of fish in a wine sauce on the table, sending him a warm smile. He saw Giselle stiffen at the woman's friendly manner.

And then, to Piers's surprise, Giselle looked directly at him. "Thank you for coming to search for me. And for . . ." She waved a hand. "I know 'twas not your wish."

"We are wed now, Giselle. We shall have to find a way to make it work."

"You . . . will you . . ." her voice trailed off to nothing and she took a deep drink of wine.

He knew what she was asking. "Aye," he said softly.

Fear flitted across her features.

Could it be simple fear that made her fight against the marriage? he wondered. Had someone told her things to make her afraid of what happened between a man and a woman? He leaned close, finding his gaze caught by her full lips. "Do not be afraid, Giselle. I can be a gentle lover, and I am not without skill in bringing a woman pleasure."

Her face paled and she swayed on her stool. "I . . .

you should not be speaking thus to me."

"Why not? You are my wife."

Her hand shook as she brought the cup of wine to her mouth. "I know nothing of such things, my lord."

"You will." He smiled at her and saw her cheeks heat once more. "And you shall enjoy it. I shall make sure of that." A surge of optimism spiraled through him as he gazed at her. Gifford was right—she was indeed a vision of loveliness. An angel with the body of a temptress.

"The only purpose of such is to conceive a child," she said, a trace of defiance in her voice.

"Is that what you have been taught?"

"Of course."

"They lied," he said calmly, taking a bite of the fish. He grinned at the expression of shock on Giselle's face.

"The Abbess herself told me. *Many* times."

"She knew nothing of the joy a man and a woman can take in each other, clearly." Piers found he was gaining no little enjoyment from holding a discussion about mating with his timid bride.

"Piers!" Gifford called out. "Cease drooling over your bride and pass me that platter of mushrooms."

Piers slid over the platter, and noticed Giselle had barely eaten a bite from their trencher. "Are you not hungry?" he asked her.

"Nay." She clutched her cup to her as if it were a shield. "I would like to be excused, my lord, if you please."

Amice stood and came up beside them. "I shall

show Giselle to your chambers."

"Thank you," Piers said. He looked at Giselle. "I shall join you anon."

Somehow, Giselle managed to stand on legs that felt filled with water instead of bones and tissue. She followed Lady Amice out of the hall and across a section of the bailey to another tower. They climbed up curved steps and emerged into a narrow corridor.

Amice put her hand to the small of her back and stretched. "I truly hope the babe decides to make her arrival soon."

The memory of Giselle's vision slammed through her mind. She'd been so immersed in the disastrous turn of her own life she'd briefly forgotten what she'd foreseen. Should she warn Lady Amice to take care? No, Giselle decided. Look at what her effort to protect Sister had wrought. But she would do what she could to change the course of her vision. "Do you feel well, Lady Amice?"

"Aye, but for the fact that I feel like a bloated sow." She pushed open a door and walked in.

Giselle followed slowly, swamped with such nervousness she could barely hold it in. The chamber was large, with two shuttered windows like the ones in her chamber. Her former chamber, she thought with a lump of dread. A bed piled with blankets occupied the center of the room. Trunks lined one wall and pegs another, with two chairs and a fireplace in a corner. It was a fine chamber, she thought.

The door opened and Nona danced in, her eyes alight. "My lady, your husband sent me to aid you."

Lady Amice leaned down. "Be happy, Giselle. Allow yourself to be happy as I am."

Giselle watched her leave the chamber, thinking of the gulf of difference between them. It was clear Lady Amice deeply loved the earl, and his love for her was a palpable thing. Giselle had been driven into marriage to a man who'd made no secret of the fact he did not view her with any favor.

"My lady, we should hurry," Nona said as she tugged at the lacings on Giselle's bliaut. "I do not think the lord shall wait long."

"What . . . what are you doing?"

Nona cocked her head. "Why, aiding you in disrobing, my lady."

Giselle wildly looked around the room, her gaze landing on the wide bed. "But I have nothing else to wear."

Nona kept unlacing. "Why would you wish to wear anything?"

Dread and fear pooled into a hard lump in Giselle's belly. Chills rolled over her body, and she felt frozen, unable to say or do anything while Nona quickly divested her of her bliaut, undertunic, and hose. When she reached for Giselle's chemise, she jolted back to herself. "Nay. I shall keep this on."

Nona winked. "Not for long, I expect."

Giselle fought back a moan

"Sit, my lady, and I shall brush out your hair."

Dear Lord, aid me, Giselle silently prayed as she sat. She was trembling so much she could barely raise her cup of wine.

"You have such lovely hair, my lady."

"Thank you."

Nona stood back and nodded. "There. You are ready."

Ready? Giselle wanted to crumple to the floor and howl her pain. Rule number eleven, she reminded herself. *Displays of emotion are coarse and vulgar. Serenity is a tribute to God.*

"Thank you, Nona."

The maid smiled and winked. "Enjoy your evening, my lady."

With a thump of wood, the door closed, leaving Giselle in the chamber with only her churning thoughts for company. *Dear God, how am I to get through this night?*

The murmur of voices came from outside the door, and Giselle leapt to her feet. Would he bring others? Panic seized her and she jumped into the bed, drawing the blankets up to her chin and closing her eyes.

She began saying the prayers of the rosary, her mouth moving in a soft whisper. "Hail Mary, full of grace, the Lord is with thee; blessed art thou among women, and blessed is the fruit of thy womb, Jesus. Holy Mary, Mother of God, pray for us sinners, now and at the hour of our death."

The door opened.

"Glory be to the Father, and to the Son, and to the Holy Spirit. As it was in the beginning, is now, and ever shall be, world without end. Amen."

Piers stood in the doorway, and felt the day's events crash down on him. His wife lay in bed like some kind of sacrificial maiden of old, clutching her rosary, eyes tightly closed, whispering prayers. He briefly considered returning to the hall and drinking wine until he passed out under the table, but knew he couldn't.

He pulled the door closed and set the ewer of wine on the table. As he poked the fire and added wood, he heard Giselle's whispering cease and sensed her watching him.

What did she think he was going to do? Leap upon her like a starving animal? Without turning, he stripped off his tunic and undershirt, hanging each on a peg. A soft gasp from the bed told him Giselle watched.

He sat in a chair and tugged off his boots and hose.

Another gasp came from the bed.

A spark of mischief lit his blood, and he removed his braies, tossing them onto the floor and stretching.

Absolute silence.

He turned toward the bed.

Giselle's eyes were huge in her face, and even in the dim light he could see her red cheeks.

As he walked closer, she let out a little shriek and scooted farther across the bed away from him. When she did, he noticed she still wore her chemise. Unfortunately, he also noticed how her hair gleamed in the firelight. The blanket had slid down, revealing the swell of her breasts under the thin linen. His body responded immediately, and Giselle's eyes widened even more.

"Giselle," he said as he slid into the bed.

Her throat worked. "My lord?"

"We are wed now." He leaned up against the head-board and studied her. By Saint George's sword, the girl was trembling so much the bed shook with it.

"Aye, my lord."

"You have my leave to call me Piers."

"Uh, very well."

Take her, Eikki's voice urged. *Order her to remove her chemise. Spread the wench's legs and have her.*

Piers slammed his mental door shut tight. "Giselle, do you have any idea what is going to happen?"

She clutched her rosary so tightly her knuckles were white. "Nay, but I suspect it has something to do with," she pointed, "that."

That being his manhood, which was rapidly coming to the realization that bedding Giselle was not going to be an easy matter. "Yes. I will put myself inside you, between your legs."

Giselle made a keening sound.

He reached out and touched her hair.

She flinched.

"I am told it hurts a bit for a woman the first time, but that shall fade."

"You cannot mean to . . . Oh, my God."

"You have never touched yourself there?"

She reddened and shook her head violently. "Of course not."

"Let me guess. 'Twould be a sin?"

"Aye."

He leaned over her. "Pleasure is not a sin, Giselle."

She gazed up at him with horror in her eyes. "My lord, Piers, I . . . I do not think I can do this. And it *would* be a sin for one such as I."

"We must." He stroked a finger down her cheek. "But not tonight. I will give you time to become accustomed to the idea. And to me."

She blinked. "Thank you. You are . . . kind."

He drew the blanket up over his body and slid down to lie on the bed. "Sleep, Giselle."

For a moment, she looked at him as if she couldn't quite believe he was not going to pounce on her. The ache in his groin made Piers not quite believe it either.

It is your right, Eikki hissed.

And it would be the same as rape, Piers told him.

You are weak. The wench is yours to do with as you wish.

Giselle turned her back to him and snuggled into the bed.

Piers let out a breath. *Nay, I am strong. That is why I shall give her time.*

You could give the little nun years, and she will still not come to you willingly. Best to make her understand her place tonight.

If you are that in need of bedsport, why not leave me and find another man to aggravate?

'Tis not so easy.

Piers shoved Eikki back into the recesses of his mind and closed his eyes, intent on finding his own sleep. The scent of warm woman laced with a hint of lavender came to his nose, and he gritted his teeth. The truly pathetic thing was that he did want Giselle. Her innocent beauty drew him, fascinated him. Even her pious judgments could not quite quell his lust for her.

But he just couldn't do it. Not tonight, when she gazed at him with such fear, like a child facing a painful punishment. He gazed at the fire for a long time, hearing the slow sound of Giselle's even breathing, and wondering what he had done to deserve this—a wife who made it clear she wanted no part of him, and an insidious presence determined to turn him to darkness.

He was tempted to leave the chamber and seek out Clarise, but despite his earlier threats brought on by that demon, Eikki, he wasn't ready to dishonor Giselle in that way.

Deal with her as you did with Avalon, he told himself as his eyes blinked closed. *Gentle her step by step, until she turns to you.* Well, perhaps a bit faster than he'd worked with the mare. He knew he could not last two years without a woman.

But still . . . the same method may work. He fell asleep plotting his approach on the morrow.

Chapter
VIII

G iselle awoke slowly, so comfortable she instinctively sought to remain in slumber. Warm, so delightfully warm, she thought, and snuggled deeper into the . . . With dawning horror, she realized where she was and why she felt surrounded by heat.

She lay sprawled halfway atop her husband's naked body, her chemise scrunched up around her waist and her legs entwined with his larger ones. One of her hands was splayed over his bare chest, with her cheek resting next to it.

His warmth and strength seeped into her and for a wild moment, Giselle wished she had the courage to smooth her hand over his muscled chest, trace the dips and planes of his skin. *Dear Lord, what should she do?* She wished the bed would simply swallow her up whole.

Slowly, holding her breath, she eased away from him, head, then hand, then legs. She was nearly free when she felt a tug and realized a section of her hair was trapped beneath his shoulder.

She pulled, but nothing moved. Piers let out a soft snore and Giselle renewed her efforts. She tilted his shoulder up and yanked her hair free, losing several strands in the process. With a grunt, Piers turned on his side away from her.

For several moments, Giselle just stared. She'd been so terrified last night she'd barely registered what a truly magnificent body the man possessed. Wide shoulders narrowed to taut buttocks and powerfully built thighs. Rule number twelve, she reminded herself. *You must resist temptations of the flesh, for they are the work of the devil.*

She scooted out of the bed, praying he did not awaken. At least he did not know where she had ended up over the night. Heat flared in her cheeks as she took a bliaut out of one of the trunks.

Her hands were so clumsy she could barely pull the lacings shut. She quickly bound her hair in one long plait, slid on her hose and shoes from the night before and slipped out of the chamber, closing the door behind her.

When the door shut, she let out a long sigh of relief and started toward the chapel.

Piers cracked his eyes open when Giselle fled the chamber. He couldn't believe it when he awoke to find her draped over him like a soft, warm blanket of silk. His hands had itched to slide her chemise up further, to run his hands over the tips of the full breasts pressed against his chest.

No doubt she'd been shocked and mortified to find herself in such a position. Probably even now fleeing into the chapel to beg God for forgiveness.

He smiled as he jumped out of bed. Whatever his bride convinced herself of during her waking hours, it appeared her slumbering self thought otherwise. For the first time, he found himself wondering if perhaps the marriage wasn't as hopeless as it seemed.

Perhaps he should forbid her the chemise this evening, he thought. Now, that would be interesting.

He splashed water on his face and reconsidered. If he awoke with Giselle's lush, naked body cloaking him, there was no way in heaven he wouldn't touch her.

So, take her, the now familiar voice inside him pressed. *Imagine touching all that sweet flesh, burying your rod into her tight body.*

Even as Piers inwardly condemned Eikki's coarseness, the image took hold of his mind, and his sex hardened. *You are becoming tiresome, Eikki. The same refrain over and over. Can you not be more original than that?*

I know what I want. What we want.

There is no "we."

The mocking echo of laughter spilled through Piers's mind. He groaned and quickly dressed, suddenly anxious to leave the bedchamber and lingering scent of Giselle. At the door, he paused, fingering his dagger.

Should he mark the sheets to show others he and Giselle had consummated the marriage? He shook his head and decided there was no need. After all, she brought no dowry to the marriage he needed to protect. Apparently, no one else wanted the girl.

And, if there was no consummation, he still potentially had a way out. As did Giselle. The thought did not bring him the measure of comfort he'd expected.

🦎 🦎 🦎

"Lady Giselle, I am surprised to see you so early this morn."

Giselle looked up from her prayers to find the kindly face of Father Michael gazing down at her. "I must not miss my devotions, Father."

He sat next to her. "You did not manage to drag that new husband of yours to chapel, I see."

"Nay." Giselle stared at her clasped hands, reluctant to tell the priest she'd run from the bedchamber before Piers had woken.

"Are you well, child?"

Her gaze flew to his, and she flushed. "Yes. I am fine."

He smiled and patted her shoulder. "Good. I have heard that sometimes for women the act can be difficult at first. I am pleased to learn Piers took good care of you."

"Father, I—"

"Do not be embarrassed, Giselle. I may be a priest, but I live out in the world. The people of Falcon's Craig

161

know they can speak to me of anything."

Giselle had no idea what to say. Should she confess to Father Michael?

"Ah, and it would be a fine thing for Lord Cain and Lady Amice's child to have another child close in age to play with."

"I am not sure that will happen, Father," Giselle whispered.

"Oh, one can never tell. You are a young, healthy woman, and Piers is a robust man. At least that is what I am told," he finished with a chuckle.

Giselle couldn't imagine how she'd come to be having this conversation with a man of the church. She'd come to the chapel to find surcease for her soul, not advice on lying with her husband. "Father, I was taught that the only purpose of . . . of fornication is to bring more of God's children into the world. My body must be a pure reflection of God's grace."

The priest laughed. "By the saints, the things they taught you at Kerwick. No wonder the Abbess is always in such a bad humor."

"Do you not agree?"

His mirth faded. "Nay, my lady. Not at all. I have studied the words of the Lord long and hard, and I have not found such admonitions from him."

Giselle's mouth dropped open. "But, that is . . . is blasphemous."

"Is it?" He lifted a brow. "I have spent many, many

years studying the greatness of God, and His messages to us. What do you think is the most important of God's teachings?"

"Obedience, I suppose. To obey Him in all things."

"Nay. 'Tis love."

"The Abbess never said anything about love, Father."

He snorted. "Think about it, Giselle. Think of all the ways God has shown His love for us, how His son gave His life so we might see the error of our ways. Love, Giselle. That is the foundation of the church."

"Love for God, perhaps, but that is a pure love, not a . . . a physical one."

" 'Tis part of love between a man and woman. God does not disapprove of that. He created us."

"But you . . ." Giselle flushed.

"I am a priest. I have devoted myself completely to God."

"Which is what I long to do."

"Perhaps. But God has not willed that to happen in your life. He has another purpose for you."

"You sound so certain, Father. I cannot see it as clearly. I have spent my life dedicated to God, in a place of purity."

"You may still serve Him, Giselle, but in a different way."

She frowned. "I do not understand."

Father Michael rose with a sigh. "You are wed now. Cleave to your husband."

"I am sorry, Father, but I do not think I can ever love Piers Veuxfort." The memory of his warm skin against hers floated across her mind, and she clenched her rosary.

Father Michael patted her shoulder. "I shall pray that you find the guidance you seek."

"Thank you, Father." As he walked away, she bent her head and began to pray. *Please, Lord, show me the way of Your will. Help me to be strong and hold to Your teachings.*

And dear Lord, please, oh please, lead me not into temptation.

❧ ❧ ❧

Piers stomped down to the great hall to find something to eat. And drink, particularly drink. Giselle was nowhere to be seen, though Cain, Amice, Gifford, and Saraid all sat on the dais.

"No doubt praying yet again to God to deliver her from the horror of marriage to me," he muttered to himself.

"Where is your lady wife?" Gifford asked. "Still abed from enduring your attentions, I wager." Saraid poked him in the side, but he ignored her.

Piers sat and eagerly poured a cup of wine. "Hardly." He scowled into the cup.

"I saw her heading toward the chapel earlier," Amice said.

Piers glanced up in time to see her exchange a worried

look with Cain. The sympathy he saw in their eyes soured his mood further. "Piers," Cain began, then paused, obviously considering his words. "Is all well?"

"Of course. How could it not be? I have wed a beautiful woman, my horses await, and I have my loving family surrounding me." He cut off a piece of cheese and popped it in his mouth, somehow managing to affect a light humor, despite the deep discontent swirling in his gut.

Cain held his gaze for a moment, then nodded.

"And I am giving the girl time to adjust to the idea of being married," Piers told Gifford.

Saraid's lips tightened. "She has no idea how fortunate she is."

Piers smiled at her. "Thank you. Perhaps you could do me the favor of reminding Giselle of that fact." His smile faded. "If she ever emerges from her prayers."

He looked into four pairs of eyes, all holding expressions of sympathy, and found he could not sit for another moment. He grabbed up a cup and stood. "I am going to see to the horses."

Before he could leave, Gifford slipped a vial of liquid into his hand.

"Gifford, what have you done now?" Cain asked, his voice wary.

Gifford sighed loudly. "Boy has never learned to trust in the wisdom of his elder," he told Saraid.

Piers held the vial up to the light. It was a muddy green color. He took out the stopper and cautiously took a sniff, then wrinkled his nose. "What on earth did you put in this?"

Gifford fluttered his hands. "Oh, a bit of this and that. The taste is better than it would seem from the smell."

"What is it supposed to do?" Amice asked, peering around her husband at the vial.

" 'Tis a love potion," Gifford responded proudly. "I found the recipe for it in one of my old books."

Cain rolled his eyes.

Gifford pointed at him. "Do not be so quick to dismiss my potions. *You* finally pulled your head out of your arse long enough to go after the woman you loved."

Amice giggled.

"He has a point in that, Cain," Piers commented, and tucked the vial into his tunic. "Well, I am willing to take any aid available." Before the concerned looks of his family members made his spirits sink even lower, he left the hall.

Gifford chuckled as Piers left. "Poor boy. I am thinking this is God's way of teaching him a lesson."

"By binding him to a woman who only cares about her God?" Saraid asked.

He patted her hand. "By binding him to a woman who will not simply fall into his bed when he snaps his fingers. Piers has too long sought the company of the wrong kind of women."

"You've a point, Gifford, but I hate to see him in such a marriage," Cain said with a frown. "I had a loveless marriage. 'Twas naught but misery."

"Luce was no Giselle," Gifford reminded him. "God rest her soul, Luce was a conniving, deceitful bitch who never cared for anyone but herself."

Cain gave a snort of disgust.

"But Giselle, now there is a complex woman."

"She must feel very discomfited, to find herself suddenly cast out from the only home she's ever known and married within the span of a few weeks," Amice said, absently rubbing her belly.

"Aye, and that will make her cling even harder to what she knows. The church," Saraid said with a frown.

"For now," Gifford agreed. "Still, I am thinking that once the girl accepts her change in circumstance, it will be very interesting to see what she does." His eyes gleamed. "I would wager on Piers in the end."

"I hope you are right, Uncle," Cain said. "I would not see my brother spend the rest of his life in such a cold union."

Gifford stood and stretched. "Speaking of cold, I am feeling a bit chilled this morn. My dove, what say you to joining me in the bathhouse?"

Saraid shook her head, but she was laughing. "Did we not visit there yesterday?"

"I cannot recall." Gifford gave an exaggerated shiver. "Come, my sweet. These old bones need warmth."

She stood and took his hand. With a jaunty wave, Gifford led her out of the hall.

Cain turned to Amice. "I am looking forward to the day when you and I can spend that kind of time in the bathhouse."

She smiled. "Soon, my love." She jumped and her eyes widened.

"What is it?"

Instead of answering, she took his hand and put it on her belly.

By the saints, what an incredible feeling, Cain thought as he felt the babe kick. The very idea that a small being waited within Amice's body to enter the world filled him with wonder. "What does that feel like?"

"Like I am filled with a very active little person who is anxious to meet us."

"Have I told you yet today how much I love you?"

Her lips pursed and her eyes shone with laughter. "You have not."

"Ah, but I do," he said as he kissed her. "Madly, utterly and always."

"Mmm, I do like the sound of that."

"My lord?"

Cain looked up to find his usher, Alfred, waiting with a strange man standing behind him. "What is it, Alfred?"

"This man," Alfred said, motioning "arrives from the Bishop of Ravenswood."

The Bishop of Ravenswood, Cain thought with distaste. The man responsible for leading Piers into what was appearing more each day to be a disastrous marriage and who had treated Giselle so deplorably. "What do you want?" he asked, his tone cool.

The man moved forward and placed a bundle on the table. "Greetings, my lord. I am Joseph, in service to the Bishop of Ravenswood. The Bishop bade me deliver this to Falcon's Craig as a gift to your brother and his future bride."

Cain glanced at the cloth, but didn't touch it. "Lady Giselle and my brother are wed."

An odd look crossed the man's face and he clasped his hands together. "Very good, my lord."

Amice unwrapped the bundle. "Oh, 'tis lovely," she said.

Cain saw that she was right. The gift was a delicately engraved cross inlaid with garnets and pearls. "A fine gift. You may present it this eve."

Joseph nodded. "Thank you, my lord."

"I wonder, though," Cain continued, "why the Bishop would send such a valuable gift to a woman he so thoroughly rejected from the nunnery." He fixed the man with a hard stare.

Not one hint of expression crossed the man's face. "I know naught of that, my lord. My master simply charged me with a task."

There was something furtive about the man, but Cain couldn't quite determine what it was. Perhaps it was as he claimed and he was simply a messenger. "You are welcome to Falcon's Craig. If you are hungry, you shall no doubt find something in the kitchen."

Joseph bowed. "Thank you, my lord."

"Alfred shall show you the direction."

After the men left, Amice ran her hand over the cross. "Giselle will be pleased with this."

"Aye." He put his arm around her shoulders and pulled her close. "I am surprised the Bishop would send such a gift."

She shrugged. "Perhaps he feels some measure of remorse over his actions toward Giselle."

"I doubt it."

"Well, it is a fine gift."

"Giselle will probably hang it on the wall over their bed, so she can continue to pray while Piers attempts to persuade her to consummate the marriage," Cain said with a wry chuckle.

Amice giggled. "Perhaps I should talk to her again."

Cain rested his chin on her head. "I think we should let the two of them try to work things out. Piers surely has never had any trouble luring women into his bed before."

"But none of them wanted to be a nun."

"Nay." Cain sighed. "I wish there was something I could do to aid Piers in this."

Amice patted his arm. " 'Tis early in the marriage. The girl has had her life turned upside down."

"Aye." He sighed again. "And continues to spend nearly all of her time in the chapel."

"Why not have Father Michael talk to her? He is a reasonable man."

"Good idea." He pressed a kiss to her forehead. "I believe I shall do that."

Amice yawned. "And I am going to take a nap."

With a last kiss, Cain went off to find Father Michael.

❧   ❧   ❧

Comforted by her morning prayers, Giselle emerged into the morning sunshine loath to head back indoors. She heard the neigh of a horse and followed the sound to the stable area. After her ride back to Falcon's Craig, she realized she needed to find a way to improve her riding skills.

As she drew closer, she heard men shouting and high-pitched neighs. Curious, she walked further and entered the stable. The interior was dim, the air scented with hay and horse. A big, gray beast stuck its head out, its liquid gaze studying Giselle. She smoothed a hand over its velvety neck.

"Be ye looking for Piers, my lady?" a voice asked.

She started and looked around. A man came out of one of the stalls, his pitchfork full of straw and dung. He gestured over his shoulder. "He be out back."

"Oh. Uh, thank you." She bit her lip, uncertain what to do. Most assuredly, she was not seeking Piers, but she imagined he would be the person to talk to about which horse would be best to practice her riding on.

The man shot her a gap-toothed grin. "Miss your new husband already, do ye?"

Giselle flushed, which only made the man chuckle.

"I'm sure he'll be pleased to see his comely new wife, my lady."

Now, that she very much doubted, but she didn't correct the man. "Ah, well, then pray excuse me." She continued through the stable, nodding to other men who labored on cleaning stalls. When she left the stable, for a moment she shielded her eyes from the bright sun.

"She's ready," a male voice announced.

As her eyes adjusted to the sunlight, she saw the speaker was Madoch. He stood next to Piers and another man. Within the paddock in front of them, a beautiful bay-colored horse trotted back and forth, her tail high in the air.

"Aye," she heard Piers say. "I would say Skye is more than ready."

What are they talking about? Giselle wondered as she walked closer. Ready for what? She paused behind the men, feeling as if she were intruding. Out of the corner of her eye, she saw a groom lead a big black horse toward the paddock. His coat shone in the sun as he pranced along, his big feet striking the earth with soft thuds.

The closer the black horse got to the paddock, the more agitated the horse already inside became, running in circles and tossing its head. "Easy, Skye," Piers called.

The groom led the black horse inside the paddock

and set him free.

And Giselle gasped, her gaze caught on an enormous protrusion from the black horse's lower body. Oh, my God, she thought, her face heating. She looked away, and found herself gazing into the mocking eyes of her husband.

"Lady Giselle," he said.

While every inch of her wanted to flee, somehow she managed to stifle the urge and calmly walk up next to Piers.

"What brings you to the stable?" he asked, his gaze once more focused on the two horses circling each other in the paddock.

"I . . . I thought I should try to improve my riding."

He glanced at her. "I will be happy to teach you."

"Oh. You need not bother yourself. If you will show me which horse would be suitable for me, I can practice on my own."

" 'Twould be safer to take lessons. I will take care of it."

Well, there was no way to politely refuse, she thought. "Thank you."

"She is close," Madoch said.

"Close to what?" Giselle asked, eyeing the two horses.

Piers slid her an intense look. "Breeding."

Heat washed up over her face again, and Giselle found her gaze fastened on the black horse, gradually realizing just what hung from his body. "Dear Lord, the poor mare," she murmured.

Piers looked at the mare and then back at Giselle. His eyes gleamed and he barked a laugh. "Poor mare? Look at her, Giselle."

Giselle looked, then immediately wished she had not. The mare had turned so her rump faced the stallion. Her tail was lifted to the side, and, oh my God, Giselle thought. The mare stood planted on her back feet, and a slit in her body under her tail opened and closed, with a whitish liquid dripping from it.

"Go on, Tyjs," one of the men called out. "Enjoy yourself."

"She is not running away, Giselle," Piers said softly. "She wants this too. Skye knows this is what she is made to do."

Giselle looked up to find Piers far too close, his gaze passing over her in a way that brought a tingling heat to her skin. Her mouth went dry, and she felt lightheaded. "She is an animal."

Piers slowly smiled at her and her legs turned to pottage. "So are we."

"There he goes," Madoch said.

As much as Giselle desperately wished she were anywhere but standing next to Piers while two horses mated, she couldn't help but watch. The stallion let out a loud neigh and reared up, covering the mare and plunging that huge appendage into her body.

"Look at her eyes, Giselle. She is enjoying having

him take her," Piers said, his tone challenging.

God in heaven, she could not bear it another moment. Giselle turned and ran back through the stable, her heart pounding, her body awash with embarrassment and something else she refused to name.

        🐇   🐇   🐇

"She lasted longer than I thought she would," Madoch commented.

"Aye," Piers agreed as he watched Tyjs finish covering Skye. Damned if the big black beast didn't look like he was smiling, Piers thought.

"Maybe this will give the girl an idea or two."

Piers grunted, but couldn't dispel the images that leapt into his mind. By St. George's sword, he could clearly envision it in his mind—Giselle on her knees, her soft, round bottom in the air, her legs spread, poised for him just as Skye had poised for Tyjs. His rod hardened at the picture his mind drew, and he silently cursed his ill fortune. The only thing that would bring his wife to her knees was prayer.

"Piers?"

"Just thinking."

Madoch grinned. "I can guess your thoughts, I imagine."

"Would that women were as easily managed as horses."

"Aye. 'Tis but one of the reasons I remain unwed."

"But not idle," Rauf commented. "You seemed quite
. . . interested in the new girl from the village last eve."

"Ah." Madoch braced his hands on the fence. "The
fair Caterin. There are few events like a wedding to bring
a woman to thoughts of having a man."

"Caterin?" Piers asked.

"She is newly arrived at Falcon's Craig," Madoch
told him. "I am surprised you did not notice her. A
comely wench, with tits the size of ripe melons," he said,
gesturing with his hands.

Piers groaned. "I have been busy."

Madoch slapped him on the back. "You are newly
wed, man. You should be busy with your new bride."

"Who is no doubt fleeing into the chapel as we
speak," Piers muttered.

Madoch chuckled. "Perhaps you should join her."

Piers frowned. "See to Skye and Tyjs."

"Where are you going?"

"To find my bride," Piers snarled and stalked off.

∾ ∾ ∾

Giselle knew she was being cowardly, but she was so
overcome by what she'd just witnessed that her feet instinctively sped toward the chapel. She breathed a sigh
of relief when she saw it was empty.

The very last thing she needed at the moment was another talk with Father Michael about what he thought she

should be doing with her husband in the marriage bed.

She shuddered as she dropped to her knees in front of the altar. The image of Skye, positioned and obviously ready for Tyjs was absolutely the most raw and elemental thing she'd ever seen. And the most arousing, she thought in shame.

She clasped her hands and began to pray. "Dear Lord, forgive me for I have sinned. Again. I pray to you to guide me back into Your grace. Help me to be strong against temptation. Help me to rise above the stain of my origins to live in the light of Your path."

The sunlight streaming in through the stained glass window overhead cast ribbons of blue, red, and gold light onto the stone floor where she knelt. She gazed up at the depiction of Mary with the baby Jesus, and desperately sought the calm peace she always found in prayer.

Today, it eluded her.

A shuffle of feet against the stone reached her ears, and she peered around a massive wooden bench, then immediately shrank back again. Piers stood in the entrance to the chapel, a grim expression on his face, his arms crossed.

"Giselle?" he called.

She tucked her body under the bench and didn't answer. Dear Lord, she was a coward, but she couldn't possibly face him after watching the horses mate. *Calm*, she told herself. *Serene*. Her heart pounded and her hands were damp.

His footsteps approached her hiding place. "Giselle, are you in here?"

She held her breath.

Piers gazed around the chapel, but saw no one. Where had the girl gone? By Saint George's sword, he felt in an ill temper. Watching Skye and Tyjs mate with Giselle standing next to him had been a severe blow to his self-control.

So, give it up, Eikki's voice cajoled. *Find the girl and claim your rights.*

"Cease," he muttered.

Eikki laughed. *You want to. I can feel it.*

"Aye, I do indeed, but I cannot stomach bedding a woman who all the while prays to God for deliverance." He was going mad, Piers decided. Having a conversation with an invisible presence while bathed in the holy light of the chapel.

Just imagine all the soft skin, yours for the taking. Imagine how she will look on her knees for you, those full breasts in your hands. Imagine spreading her legs, stroking your hand over the quivering folds of her body, preparing her to take you inside.

The hell of it was Piers could vividly imagine just that. He threw back his head and groaned. "Get out of my head, you vile creature." He turned and tromped back toward the chapel door. Damn, he thought. It was probably a good thing Giselle hadn't been in the chapel. Between the horses and Eikki's seductive urgings, he was holding onto what remained of his honor by a tight thread.

He left the chapel, slamming the door shut.

Giselle lay trembling under the bench. *Dear Lord in heaven, what was all that about? Who had Piers been speaking to?*

She drew a shaky breath, and stared at nothing. One thing was abundantly clear—whoever he was talking to the subject had been her. Slowly, she slid from her hiding place and stood, looking around the chapel.

It was as empty as when she'd arrived.

She sank down onto the bench and put her face in her hands. Had she married a madman who heard voices in his head? Dear God, how she longed for Sister Gertrude's counsel. If only she could return to Kerwick.

But no, she realized with a lurch in her chest. The fact was that she would probably never see Sister Gertrude again.

"Lady Giselle?" a voice asked. "Is there something amiss?"

She lifted her head and stared into Father Michael's kindly gaze. "Hello, Father. Nay, it is just that this is a . . . troubled time for me."

"You should speak to your husband of your concerns, my child. Seek his advice and guidance."

From which man? she wondered, her nerves on the edge of unraveling.

"Come, my lady. 'Tis time for dinner."

Giselle's stomach rumbled at his words, and she rose. She could not stay hidden away in the chapel all day. No, she *would* not. She straightened her shoulders. Though she had not wanted any of this, the truth was that Falcon's Craig was now her home. It was time she faced it.

Father Michael took her arm and patted it. "All will be well in time, child."

"Are you a seer also, Father?" she asked with a forced smile. Would that her affliction provided her with a vision of her future, she thought, shying away from the idea that perhaps it already had.

He returned her smile as they walked out of the chapel. "No seer, my lady, but a priest who has gained a certain measure of wisdom over my years here at Falcon's Craig."

As much as she wished Father Michael was right, she had her doubts, particularly after hearing Piers argue with an unseen person. One with whom he was obviously discussing bedding her, of all things. However, with the ease of long practice, she hid her emotions behind a mild look and strolled with Father Michael toward the great hall.

When they entered, Giselle was glad for his steady presence beside her. From the doorway, she sensed Piers's gaze on her, and it was all she could do not to walk right back out again. *No, Giselle*, she told herself. *You must begin to face your new circumstances. You must face the fact that, for good or ill, you are now wed.*

She walked to the dais, taking a seat next to Piers, who sat next to Gifford and Saraid. Lady Amice and the earl were absent.

He studied her for a long moment. Somehow, Giselle made herself stare back at him.

"Where have you been?" he asked as a servant filled their cups.

"I . . . nowhere in particular," she lied. "Simply exploring the castle."

"Where?"

Giselle bit her lip and reached for her cup. It is a sin to lie, she thought, but then pushed the admonition away. *Forgive me, Lord, but I cannot tell him the truth.* "As I said, nowhere in particular. Why?"

"I thought to find you back in the chapel. You reacted most strongly to the sight of Skye and Tyjs."

Was that a glimmer of humor she saw in his gaze? She sipped some wine. "I have never seen the like, my lord. You must forgive my reaction."

"Did they teach you to speak like that in the nunnery?"

"My lord?"

"To speak without revealing anything about yourself?"

Giselle opened her mouth to protest his description, but found herself unable to do so. "Aye. I suppose they did."

He winked at her. "I would like you to speak plainly."

"Oh."

"That shocked you this morning."

Giselle tried to swallow, but failed. "Yes, of course."

" 'Tis a part of life here at Falcon's Craig. And a big part of what I do." His eyes twinkled. "When I am not about ravishing the womenfolk, that is."

Giselle felt her face flame. By the heavens, the man had beautiful eyes, wide and golden brown. "You . . . you breed horses?"

"Aye. You shall be surprised, no doubt, to learn I am quite good at it. Nobles from all across England purchase my foals." His faintly mocking tone reminded Giselle that she had accused him of doing nothing but chasing women.

"I see there is more to you than first appears."

"I am thinking I can say the same of you, my lady."

Giselle reached for a piece of cheese to give herself something to do other than to continue gazing into his warm eyes. She jolted when he placed his hand atop hers.

"Perhaps we shall discover a common ground in time," he murmured.

Giselle started to respond, but abruptly her vision blurred. No, she thought. Not now. But there was no controlling her "gift."

The vision flashed across her mind, leaving only traces of images, feelings in its wake. Piers. A horse. A cry of alarm. A shout of pain.

"Giselle?"

She blinked at him.

"Are you well? You looked very pale a moment ago."

"She needs to eat," Gifford piped in from down the

table. He turned and motioned to a servant. "Give her some of that fine roasted beef."

As the servant hastened to do Gifford's bidding, Giselle felt the curious eyes of the others at the dais upon her. "I am fine. Gifford is right—I am hungry."

"You need to eat more. You are far too thin," Piers said.

Thin? Giselle thought with an inner laugh. At Kerwick, the Abbess was forever chastising her for eating too much. *Gluttony is a sin* was a phrase she had heard many, many times.

Before she realized what was happening, Piers held a chunk of beef in his fingers.

"Girl don't eat meat," Gifford said. "Should, though."

He wanted her to take the meat from his fingers? Giselle wondered. A mixture of panic and something she very much suspected was excitement spilled through her veins. "The girl does now," she said, and plucked the meat from Piers's fingers with her mouth.

A slow smile of approval spread across his face, and Giselle had to remind herself to chew.

"So, the little nun is not beyond trying new things," Piers commented, his teasing expression taking the bite from his words.

"Not entirely, it seems."

Piers stabbed another piece of beef and laid it on her trencher.

"My lord—"

"Piers," he said.

"Uh, I—"

"I wish you to call me Piers. Can you grant me that boon?"

"Piers, then." Giselle abruptly realized that using his given name leant an air of intimacy to their conversation. "What are you doing after dinner?"

"Do you have need of me?"

"I, uh, no. I am simply curious."

"Damn fool is going to see if he can break his neck," Gifford grumbled.

Piers gave his uncle a disgruntled look, which Gifford ignored. " 'Tis part of what I do." He turned back to Giselle. "I have acquired a new horse who needs training."

"Thing's a demon, not a horse," Gifford offered.

"Do you not have grooms able to do the task?" Giselle asked.

"None as skilled as myself."

Giselle sipped wine and tried to figure out a way to warn him without rousing suspicion. "I thought perhaps we could commence my riding lessons."

"Of course. Come to the stable with me. 'Twill not take long for me to ride Angel."

"Angel? That is the horse's name?"

Piers smiled, and Giselle's stomach fluttered. "Aye. I suspect 'tis the former owner's attempt at a jest."

"Why not have someone else ride him today?"

"The girl shows good sense, Piers." Gifford said.

"You are going to end up in the dirt."

" 'Twill not be the first time."

Giselle bit her lip.

Piers leaned close. "Are you concerned for me, lady wife?"

"I . . . Giselle gazed into his eyes and momentarily lost the ability to speak. "I just have a bad feeling about this Angel," she finally managed to say, wincing inside at the mention of her "feeling."

"No doubt due to your inexperience with horses. But I am touched by your concern."

What more could she do? Giselle thought. Aside from revealing the fact she'd had a vision of him being hurt, there seemed to be no way to dissuade him. She looked away. He would probably not believe her anyway, she reasoned. And she would have exposed herself for naught.

The memory of the Abbess's hard look of condemnation washed through her mind, and she suppressed a shiver. *No*, she thought. She would simply pray that Piers remained safe. That would have to suffice.

Chapter
IX

P iers marched off to the stable with Giselle in tow. For the first time since he'd seen her, her lush mouth pursed in disapproval, he had a tiny shred of hope that perhaps their marriage had a chance.

"Goin' to try Angel?" Michel, one of the grooms, asked as they walked into the stable.

"Aye," Piers responded. "Today is the day Angel learns some manners."

Michel smiled. "Good luck to you."

" 'Tis a matter of skill, Michel," he said with a grin. He turned to Giselle, who had remained silent since they left the hall. "When I finish, I thought to put you on Etain," he told her, gesturing to a stall. "She is a good, solid girl."

Giselle followed the direction of his arm, and Etain stuck her white head out to nudge Giselle's shoulder. Giselle laughed and stroked the horse. "She is sweet."

He moved next to her, fascinated by the sound of her laughter. It struck him that he had never heard her laugh before. "The one next to her is Angel."

At the sound of his name, the improbably named Angel put his head over the stall door with a snort.

"He is beautiful," Giselle said, but didn't move to touch him.

"Aye, that he is. Once he is trained, I intend to breed him to one of my mares."

Giselle flushed and looked away.

Piers quickly saddled Angel and led him out of the stall.

"He seems quite calm," Giselle commented, her brow furrowed.

"He is until someone tries to get on his back," Michel said.

Piers led the horse into a fenced area next to the stable. Giselle stood with Michel, watching, her turquoise eyes glowing with concern.

If he ended up eating dirt, it was worth it to evoke this change in attitude from his bride, Piers thought with an inward smile. He walked the horse around the pen, then stopped next to Giselle and Michel.

"Be ready for 'im," Michel advised.

"Are you sure this is a good idea?" Giselle asked quietly. "You could be hurt."

Piers laughed. "Nay." He launched himself atop Angel.

The moment he landed in the saddle, the horse bolted. Piers immediately turned Angel in a circle, but it barely slowed him down. He turned him in a tighter circle. "Cease, you stubborn beast!" he shouted.

Angel responded by bucking and fighting the bit, tossing his head and speeding up once more.

"You'll have to do better than that," Piers yelled at him, yanking the horse's head around until his nose was nearly at Piers's boot.

Angel bucked again, then reared and bolted to the far side of the pen.

"He doesn't lack for energy," Michel called.

Piers was too busy trying to regain control of the horse to answer. He turned Angel in a tight circle at the fence, only to be bucked again. "Damn horse," Piers cursed.

Angel spun to the right and dropped down, before launching forward.

Piers lost a stirrup, but clung to the horse's back. At a cry of dismay, he glanced up to find Giselle staring at him with stark fear in her eyes, her face drained of color.

Angel spun again and bucked. Distracted by Giselle's expression, Piers cursed as he felt his body fly off the horse. He landed hard on the dirt.

Giselle screamed, and he looked up to see Angel rear over him. He rolled, barely escaping the horse's hooves. Michel ran into the ring and chased Angel away from him.

"Are you all right?" Michel asked, bending over his form.

By the saints, it hurt to breathe. Piers slowly pushed himself into a sitting position. Pain lanced through his chest. "Think I might have cracked a rib or two," he said lightly.

Michel reached down a hand and helped Piers to his feet. Though he forced a smile to his face, his body throbbed with pain. "Not sure anybody's going to be able to ride that beast," Michel said as they walked toward the gate to the ring.

"Not unless he decides to allow them, I fear," Piers answered, biting back a groan. "Well, my lady," he said as they neared Giselle. "It appears your feeling was a valid one."

She looked down before meeting his gaze. "Are you injured?" she asked in an undertone.

Piers thought of denying it, but decided he might make more progress with his bride if she thought he needed tending. He groaned and rubbed his chest. "Aye, my ribs, I think."

"Can you make it your chamber?"

He groaned again. "Aye, with aid."

Within a few minutes, Piers found himself installed in his chamber, and miracle of all miracles, being fussed over by his wife. He sat on a stool, suppressing a grin.

"I need a length of cloth," she muttered as she pulled clothing from his trunk. "And some arnica."

The door crashed open and Piers looked at his brother. "What happened?" Cain asked. "Are you hurt?"

"Angel happened," Piers said dryly. "Is your lady wife about? Giselle needs some supplies."

"She is in the solar."

"Pray, remain where you are," Giselle told Piers with

a frown. "I shall return anon." She bustled out of the chamber.

Cain lifted a brow. "*Are* you hurt?"

Piers sighed. "Aye. Michel, see if you can find some wine. I feel like I just ate a large clump of dirt."

Michel exited.

" 'Tis my ribs," he told Cain. "Cracked, most likely." His eyes twinkled. "My lady wife is tending me."

"You are fortunate your injuries are not worse."

"To be honest, they feel fairly bad at the moment," Piers said, trying but failing to draw in a deep breath.

"That horse is unmanageable."

Piers nodded. "I have to agree. Not sure what to do with him, though. No one would want to buy the beast."

"Perhaps you should put him down."

" 'Tis a thought." Piers winced. "Nay, I cannot kill him. As long as no one tries to ride him, he is easy to handle."

Giselle burst back through the door carrying a basket, Amice close behind her. "What happened?" Amice asked as she waddled into the chamber.

"Just as Giselle predicted," Piers told her.

Amice tightened her lips, and exchanged a glance with Cain. "Do you need aid?" she asked Giselle.

"Aye. We need to get his tunic off."

Well, this should be interesting, Piers thought. Unfortunately, pain overshadowed his enjoyment over having Giselle actually touch him. By the time they succeeded in removing his tunic and undershirt, a sheen of sweat covered his forehead. "Damn beast," he said.

Michel strode in with a jug of wine.

"Thank you, Michel," Piers said, gratefully accepting a cup.

Giselle knelt before him with a pot in her hand. Piers saw her tremble, and bit back a smile. He remained completely still while she spread some kind of balm over his skin. By Saint George's sword, it was a good thing Cain and Amice remained. The innocent touch of Giselle's hand was sending quite a different message to his mind and his body.

He sniffed. "What is this?"

"Arnica. 'Twill help the bruising." She shook out a length of linen and began wrapping it around his ribs.

Amice put her hand on Cain's arm. "Well, love, it appears we are not needed here. Lady Giselle clearly knows what she is about."

Piers grinned at her. "Go on. I am in good hands."

Giselle stiffened, but continued binding his ribs. After Amice and Cain left, Piers took a sip of wine. Giselle was so close he could smell her scent—lavender and warm woman. He told his body to calm, but the command had no effect.

Finally, she drew the fabric taut and tucked it in.

"Thank you, Giselle," he said, taking her chin in his hand.

"You are welcome, my lor . . . uh . . . Piers. You should rest now."

"Sit with me," he said, gesturing to the other stool. "Have some wine."

Giselle looked around the chamber as if she sought an escape path. "I need . . ." She flushed. "I shall return in a moment."

After she left, Piers allowed himself to smile. Off to the garderobe, no doubt. While he waited, he found himself staring at an empty cup. The opportunity was there, but should he take it? With an inward shrug, he slowly rose and made his way to a trunk along the wall. Stifling a groan, he bent and retrieved the vial Gifford had given him. Just a small bit, he thought, and splashed the liquid into Giselle's cup before adding wine from the jug. He couldn't imagine a mixture of herbs and honey would soften the lady's heart, but who knew?

By the time Giselle returned, he was seated on the window seat, leaning against the cool stone. "Join me," he said, patting the wide stone seat.

Hesitantly, she collected her cup and sat beside him. "How did you know?"

She took a gulp of wine and looked out over the sea.

"Giselle. Look at me."

Slowly, she shifted her gaze to his. Damn, but the woman had beautiful eyes, he thought. They reminded him of the sea on a bright, sunny day. Troubled eyes, however, at the moment. "How did you know?" he asked again.

She licked her lips.

Those lips would tempt the most devout of priests, Piers thought as he shifted on the window seat. But even if he could persuade the woman to yield to him, he was in little condition to do much about it.

" 'Twas just a feeling, naught more," she finally said.

"Do you often have these kinds of feelings?"

She shrugged and sipped more wine. "Sometimes."

"I shall be sure to listen to you the next time," he said, smiling at her.

For a moment, she appeared shocked, but then she nodded. "What shall you do with the horse?"

"I still think that with time and the right rider, Angel could be a fine mount. I cannot sell him the way he is."

"Perhaps—"

"What? Speak your mind, my lady."

"Well, perhaps he does not like men," she offered.

Piers started. "I had not thought of that. Still, there is not a woman I would risk on him. Amice is a fine rider, but she is nearly ready to give birth."

A flash of concern crossed Giselle's face.

"Have you a *feeling* about Amice?"

"Do you mock me, my lord?"

"Piers," he corrected. "After today, why would I mock you?"

Again, she looked surprised. "I . . . nay. Childbirth is always a perilous matter, though."

"But well worth it, do you not agree?"

"I have never given it much thought."

"Surely you desire children."

She flushed and looked down. "I never thought to be in a position to bear children."

"Now you are. Well, almost," he added with a chuckle.

Her flush deepened. "I thank you for your patience."

"Were my ribs not paining me, I am not sure just how much patience I could summon."

"You are in pain? You should lie abed."

" 'Tis not too bad. I am accounted a good lover, you know," he said carefully, watching for her response.

"So I have heard."

She sounded so irked that he laughed aloud. Ignoring the pain in his ribs, he leaned close. "I am looking forward to showing you."

Giselle's mouth opened and closed, but no words emerged.

"Aye. One day soon you shall lie in that bed with me, drawing pleasure from my touch, learning how to grant me the same—"

"My lord, please." She shot off the window seat. "I have been taught 'tis wrong to seek such pleasure."

"I know. And it will be my great privilege to show you just how wrong such teachings are."

Giselle's throat worked and she gulped a big drink of wine. "You should rest now," she said, backing up. "I have . . ."

"Prayers to recite?"

"Uh, yes." She set down her cup. "Many."

Piers chuckled as she whirled and escaped their chamber. "One of these days, you shall stay, little nun," he murmured. By the saints, he could not wait for the day when Giselle succumbed to her body's natural urgings, the day she sighed his name as she found her release.

So, do not wait, a voice inside him hissed.

Not this again, Piers thought. *I am not exactly at full strength at the moment.*

A weak excuse, Eikki jeered.

"Go away," Piers said, thinking perhaps a nap was in order.

She belongs to you.

Piers lay down and closed his eyes. The thought of taking Giselle with this thing inside him, sharing the experience was beyond distasteful. What if he lost control and Eikki took over?

The idea was too bleak to contemplate.

You want her. Her innocence draws you.

Well, Eikki had a point in that, Piers thought. Knowing he would be the first to awaken her desires was a heady feeling. But still, he would prefer to do so by himself.

Eikki laughed. *Oh, I shall be here with you, do not doubt that. Here when you drive yourself between her soft thighs, here when you break through her maidenhead to possess her.*

Piers slammed Eikki back. *Dear Lord, what am I to do?* he wondered.

195

Amice could communicate with ghosts. Perhaps she could do something with the spirit of Eikki. Before he ended up taking Giselle in a way that would forever turn her away from him, and with good reason.

He would have to admit his foolishness and beg for aid. He had no other recourse.

෴෴ ෴෴ ෴෴

Giselle stared in disbelief at the man holding out a cloth-wrapped object. "What did you say?" she asked, certain she had not heard aright.

"My lady, 'tis a gift from the Bishop of Ravenswood in honor of your marriage." The man bowed and set the object on the table in front of her.

"You jest."

The man appeared puzzled by her comment. "Nay. The Bishop himself instructed me to deliver this gift to you and your husband. I have also sent a special ewer of wine to your chamber."

Giselle looked down at the bundle and felt her throat close. Why would the Bishop send her gifts? Was it possible he felt some remorse for his actions?

"What is it?" Gifford called over.

Slowly, Giselle pulled the object close and un-wrapped its red silk covering, all the while feeling the curious stares of the others in the hall, and strangely wishing Piers had felt well enough to join her for the evening meal.

" 'Tis beautiful, is it not?" Lady Amice asked.

As Giselle stared at the ornate cross, it suddenly became clear to her just why the Bishop had sent the gift. It was a reminder to her of who she was, of why it was so important for her to cleave to the Lord.

The memory of the day she'd first encountered the Bishop flooded her mind. His expression of shock slowly turning to revulsion. *You were born of sin and avarice*, he had told her. *Spend the rest of your days in penitence and perhaps you may save your condemned soul from the devil.*

"Giselle?" Amice asked.

She shook off the memories. "Aye, my lady, the cross is beautiful indeed." She looked at the Bishop's messenger, wondering how much he knew of her. His face revealed nothing but polite deference. "Pray convey my thanks to your master," she said coolly.

He nodded and backed away.

"Is there a note with the cross?" the earl asked.

"Nay," Giselle answered.

"Odd."

Giselle carefully rewrapped the cross. What could she possibly say? Odd was not the word she would choose. Cunning, perhaps, like a powerful spider who never made a move without the idea of furthering his own cause.

The only reason she knew anything about him was Sister Gertrude. From her, she'd learned the Bishop was the younger son of an impoverished earl. He had excelled in rising in the church, so much so the king had granted him a wealthy castle.

Why would such an ambitious man have risked being discovered breaking his vow of abstinence? She had never understood it, and had never had the chance to ask her mother about what had happened.

It doesn't matter anymore, Giselle, she told herself. *He has no control over you now.*

"Oh!" Lady Amice exclaimed.

The earl immediately looked concerned. "Is it the babe?"

"I . . . oh!" she said again, leaning against him, her eyes wide. "I think so."

"Is she kicking?" Saraid asked.

"No, it is not that. Oh, my," Lady Amice said on a long breath.

Fear curdled in Giselle's belly. "Perhaps you should send for the midwife," she told the earl.

For a moment he froze in clear panic. "Hawis!" he yelled.

Hawis bustled toward the dais.

"Fetch the midwife." The earl's face split into a wide grin. "We are going to have a babe."

Hawis beamed a smile, then whirled and sped out of the hall.

The earl jumped up and swept Lady Amice into his arms.

She giggled. "I am not ill."

He gazed down at her with such raw devotion Giselle caught her breath. In one instant, she couldn't help but wonder what it would be like to be loved like that, and in the next, her heart wrenched at the possibility her vision of Amice might come true.

What could she do? She had skills at healing, true, but surely the midwife knew her business.

"Cease your dithering and get Amice to comfort," Gifford boomed. "I've a grand-niece coming!"

Amice laughed again as the earl bore her off. Saraid rose and followed them. "I shall stay with you until the midwife comes," she told Amice.

Giselle was left with only Gifford for company.

"And now we wait," he said, refilling his cup and then hers. "If I know my nephew, he will be hovering over poor Amice until she throws him out."

"He appears to be very devoted to her."

"Aye." Gifford gave a snort. "Wasn't always so, at least not that a body could see. The damn fool almost lost her." He eyed Giselle in a way that made her want to squirm on her stool. "Until Muriel, God rest her troublesome soul, brought Cain and Amice back together, Cain thought only of *duty*. Duty to Falcon's Craig and to the family."

He said the word as if it were a curse. "Duty is not a bad thing," she said.

"Aye, you are of the same ilk, only your duty is to God."

Surely, he could not be criticizing her devotion to God? That would be blasphemous.

He shook a finger at her. "Do not look at me like that. There is nothing wrong with worshiping God, of course."

"I . . . I fear I do not understand."

" 'Tis simple." He took a long drink of ale. "Duty is not living."

"I—"

"I can see you still do not understand. Would that you had been here when Muriel was still haunting us."

Giselle decided another sip of wine was in order. "You truly believe in ghosts?"

He chuckled. "I do, indeed. I saw the shade with my own eyes, as did many others." He leaned near her. "In the end, however, Muriel served a purpose. She aided my stubborn nephew to open his eyes and his heart."

She finally understood. " 'Tis not the same."

"Is it not?"

"Nay." Giselle rose and took up the cross.

He didn't say another word, but simply watched her go. The truth was, he didn't need to and he clearly knew it.

❧ ❧ ❧

In the middle of the night, Giselle suddenly awoke. Dear Lord, what was wrong with her? she wondered. Her stomach rolled, and she jumped out of bed, managing to reach the chamber pot just in time to retch.

She knelt on the floor and wiped her mouth. Perhaps her body was so unused to eating meat it had made her sick, she thought, but then dismissed the idea, remembering the delicious stew she'd eaten at Padruig's dwelling.

"Giselle?" Piers asked, leaning his head over the bed. "Are you all right?"

The sound of his voice sent a spiral of heat through her to explode in her woman's place. She stifled a gasp. Her body itched, actually itched and she felt as if her woman's place was swollen, throbbing, desperate for . . . *Dear God, preserve me*, she silently prayed.

"Giselle?" Piers swung his legs over the side of the bed.

Her mouth went dry. Even in the dim light of the dying fire, she could see his man part. It was huge, jutting out from his loins.

She knew she should look away, but her body inched closer. What would it feel like to have him inside her? she wondered. Her body clenched in response to the thought.

No, she told herself. *Resist temptation.* "I . . . my stomach is queasy."

Piers glanced down with an odd look, as if he were surprised to find his body in such a state. Slowly, he lifted his gaze to hers. "Come back to bed," he said, his voice flowing over her skin like warm honey.

"I—"

He smiled and reached out a hand. "Come to bed."

Her body convulsed inside, already anticipating what

he clearly intended. She stood and clenched the folds of her chemise. *Run, Giselle*, her inner voice screamed. She took a step toward Piers instead.

"You are injured," she said, appalled at the husky sound of her voice.

"Thanks to your care, I am feeling much better."

She took another step.

"Come to me, Giselle," he cajoled.

Lead me not into temptation, she recited to herself. It had no effect. Her body had taken over her mind, and she quivered with the realization she wanted him to take her, to show her what his gaze promised. But just as she started to close the remaining distance between them, a loud banging on the door rang through the chamber.

"Lady Giselle!" a voice called.

She whirled and edged the door open to find the earl standing there. The anguished expression on his face told her at once her vision of Lady Amice was coming true.

"Can you help?" he asked, his voice raw.

"I can try," she said, rushing over to pull a bliaut from a trunk. Hastily, she laced it on and thrust her feet into a pair of slippers.

"What is happening?" Piers asked, coming to his feet.

Giselle cautioned a glance at him, relieved to find he'd pulled a sheet around his body.

" 'Tis Amice. The labor is not," the earl's throat worked, "not going well."

"Go, Giselle," Piers told her. "Cain, what can I do!"

The earl ran a hand over his face. "I do not know."

Giselle laid a hand on his arm. "I am ready, my lord."

They rushed down the stairs and into another tower. Giselle held her skirts up to match the earl's rapid pace, all the while praying they were not too late. When they entered the chamber where Lady Amice lay, it was just as Giselle had foreseen it.

Several candles illuminated the scene. Amice lay on a tangle of sheets, her legs splayed open. The pungent smell of sweat filled the air, and blood stained the sheets. To one side of the bed, an older woman stood, grim resignation stamped on her features.

"Amice!" the earl hollered, running to her side.

She opened her eyes, and reached a hand to stroke his face.

Giselle cautiously approached the bed. "What is wrong?" she asked the midwife.

The woman shook her head. "The babe will not come."

"Giselle." Amice's voice was so faint Giselle barely heard her. "Can you aid me?"

There had been women, from time to time, who had sought the aid of the nuns in childbirth. Giselle had assisted Sister Alice many times with the women as most of the nuns would have no part in such an intimate event. She looked into Amice's eyes, clouded with pain and fear and nodded.

She pushed the sheet back over Amice's legs and barely stifled a cry of dismay. The problem was immediately clear. Instead of the babe's head, she was looking at her buttocks.

The midwife moved close and peered down at Giselle. "Nothing can be done," she said.

All at once, Giselle was back at the abbey. Sister Alice had once faced the same dilemma. Giselle stared down at her hands. "I need to turn the babe," she told Amice.

Amice's eyes flared with hope.

"It will hurt," Giselle told her.

"I care not. Save my babe."

Giselle quickly washed her hands and gently touched the baby's buttocks. As she inched the babe around, Amice screamed. Giselle paused.

"No!" Amice shouted. "Do it."

Though in truth it happened quickly, it seemed hours before Giselle managed to shift the babe into the right position. Throughout, she felt the anguished gaze of the earl upon her, her ears ringing with the sounds of Amice's moans and shrieks. As soon as Giselle turned the babe, she shot out into Giselle's hands.

The midwife handed her a wet cloth and Giselle wiped out the tiny infant's mouth, gently pressing on her chest.

The babe let out a piercing cry.

Giselle smiled. Tears flowed down both Amice's and the earl's faces as the earl stepped forward.

Thankfully, the midwife sprang into action, cutting the umbilical cord and cleansing the babe before wrapping her in a piece of linen. Giselle simply knelt at the side of the bed, unable to move, the wonder of what she'd done overcoming her completely.

The earl put a hand on her shoulder. "Thank you."

Giselle looked at him, and then at Amice, who cradled her babe. Her face was radiant as she gazed down upon her child.

"You are most welcome, my lord."

Chapter
X

iers found Cain in the great hall, slumped in a chair with a beatific expression on his face.

"Cain?" he asked as he took a seat. "Is all well?'

His brother shook himself and beamed a smile. "Aye, thank the Lord. And thanks to your lady wife."

"You have a child?" Piers shifted on his stool. Damned if his rod hadn't developed a mind of its own this eve. He was so hard he ached, but knew the brief moment of possibly sating his desires was no doubt gone.

"Aye. A daughter with her mother's beauty."

Piers clapped a hand on his brother's shoulder. "Congratulations. Amice is well?"

Cain nodded. He took a long sip of ale. " 'Twas a close thing, Piers. I have never been so terrified of anything in all my days. Amice was so exhausted she fell asleep not long after the babe came."

"Giselle?"

"Saved both my wife and my child." Cain's gaze turned a dark blue. "Giselle, thank God, has such small

206

hands she was able to turn the babe." He shuddered. "I shall never forget the sight, Giselle so determined, Amice so resolute even though she screamed in agony."

"I am surprised Giselle would know of such things." And that she would willingly participate in the product of an act she refused to consider, he thought, though for an instant before Cain's interruption, he'd thought perhaps she might.

"Aye. But thank the Lord, she did." Cain rose. "I am off to find my bed for a few hours." He picked up his cup and left Piers alone in the hall.

As he pondered the events of the night, and the uncomfortable state of his arousal, he suddenly felt two hands massaging his shoulders. He jolted and snapped his head around, some part of him hoping the hands belonged to Giselle, even though his rational mind knew she would not touch him in such a way.

Clarise stood there, her ample breasts nearly exposed, her lips curved in a provocative smile.

" 'Tis early for you to be out of bed," he commented, trying but utterly failing to squelch the desire to lay her on the table and take her right there.

Her gaze dropped to his braies, and she licked her lips.

Piers barely bit back a groan.

"I was lonely," she said. Before he could anticipate what she was about, her hand was inside his braies and around his rod.

This time, he couldn't control his moan. Dear Lord, he craved a woman so badly he shook with it.

Clarise stroked the length of him and let out a sound of appreciation. "Your wife does not leave you satisfied," she said, clearly pleased with the fact.

Stop her, his inner voice shouted. *You are wed.* But his body craved release, no *demanded* it. He was so damn close, Clarise's hand pumping him with the skill of long practice. "Not quite," he managed to hiss, bucking against her hand.

"Let me help you," she said, pulling up her skirts and straddling his lap.

Take her, Eikki cried. *Bury yourself in her now. She wants it. You want it.*

Even though every inch of his body screamed at him to do it, Piers hesitated. He gazed into Clarise's plain brown eyes and saw Giselle's gaze of clear turquoise. With strength he didn't know he possessed, and had surely never made use of, he shook his head. "Nay," he whispered.

Clarise pulled the top of her gown down, exposing her breasts. She lifted them in her hands. "Aye. Take me, Piers."

He closed his eyes, sweat beading his brown. "I am wed," he said softly, as much to remind himself as to refuse Clarise.

She laughed and slipped her hand into his braies again. "Your body does not care," she said in a triumphant tone.

She is right, Eikki hissed. *Think of how good it will feel to sink into her body, find your pleasure.*

Piers groaned. "I am injured, Clarise."

"I will do most of the work. You need not worry."

He pushed Clarise off his lap. She stood over him, nearly naked and held out a hand.

Piers took it, but simply squeezed it gently. "I am sorry, Clarise. Cover yourself. I shall see you back to the kitchen."

They left the hall together, never seeing the figure hidden in the shadows.

Giselle clamped a hand over her mouth to keep herself from screaming. How could she have considered for one moment mating with Piers Veuxfort? She watched him leave with the woman who had so brazenly displayed her breasts, had touched him.

And he had welcomed it. She could see it in his face, hear it in his moans.

He was doing exactly what he'd threatened, what she'd feared. Even his cracked ribs did not deter him.

I am a man, with a man's needs. If you refuse to oblige me, then I shall find others who will, he'd told her that day in the garden.

It was obvious that he was doing just that.

🐇 🐇 🐇

Padruig sat before a low fire, Cai happily slumbering at his feet. He liked the hours before dawn, the silence. Though he had long lost his ability to find peace, the stillness of the pre-dawn soothed his restless soul.

He found himself wondering how Giselle fared. Had she wed the Earl of Hawksdown's brother? Was she able to accept marriage, and not a life in God's service?

There was something about her angelic look of innocence that had touched his heart, a part of him he'd thought beyond feeling much of anything at all. He simply moved through each day, doing his best to ensure his survival but little else.

Cai was the first living thing he'd allowed into his life since he left the Highlands.

He leaned his head back and closed his eyes, his mind swelling with memories, some bittersweet, some just painful.

Perhaps soon he would pay a visit to Falcon's Craig, he thought. Make sure Giselle was adjusting to her new life.

And what if she is not? his inner voice mocked. *What shall you do about it?*

He sighed. The girl would be fine. He'd done what he could for her.

⑪ ⑪ ⑪

Giselle awoke, unsurprised to find herself alone but for Guinevere who slept curled on the floor. Her husband had no doubt found a quiet corner somewhere to be with that slatternly woman.

She splashed water on her face, refusing to think of it. *It is all for the good*, she told herself, stamping back the ache of pain and shame. *If he sates his desires elsewhere, he will not bother me.*

After drawing on fresh clothes, she flung open the shutters on the window overlooking the sea. Sun rose high above the water, glowing orange and yellow. The sea appeared calm today, the waves lapping softly at the shore.

She had yet to feel the sea, she realized. "Come, Guinevere," she said.

The dog lifted her head but didn't otherwise move.

"Come, you lazy thing," Giselle said, patting her thigh. "We are going to explore this morn."

Guinevere stood and shook herself all over before bounding over to Giselle and licking her hand.

Within a few minutes, Giselle made her way out of a doorway set into the east curtain wall, and began winding down the rocky path toward the shore, Guinevere trailing behind. She stepped onto the sand, and smiled at the pillowy sensation under her feet.

The sea appeared endless, a vast, shimmering glide of blue. She shaded her eyes, gazing into the distance. For a moment, she thought she spied an isle, but when she blinked the speck was gone.

"Lady Giselle!" a child's voice called.

Giselle turned to find Olive skipping across the sand,

a bright smile on her face. Guinevere ran to meet the child, dancing and yipping in circles around her. "Good morn," Giselle said as Olive hopped to a stop.

"Are you going for a swim?" Olive asked.

"I . . ." Giselle paused and looked at the water. "I do not know how."

" 'Tis not deep here. We can walk in the water."

I am not afraid, Giselle told herself, walking closer to the edge of the sea. She stripped off her shoes while Olive did the same. The child took Giselle's hand and pulled her into the gentle waves.

"Oh!" Giselle exclaimed, rocking back and forth as a wave came in and the sand beneath her feet shifted.

Olive giggled.

" 'Tis a strange feeling," Giselle said, gripping Olive's hand.

"You shall get used to it." Olive laughed as Guinevere plunged in, splashing both of them with cool water. Olive let go of Giselle's hand and hopped forward, scooping up handfuls of water and tossing them at Guinevere.

The dog barked and splashed through the water.

With wet sand oozing between her toes, cool water lapping over her legs, and sun warming the air, Giselle's sense of disquiet eased. She breathed in the salty air and put her hands in the water, spreading her fingers so the waves washed through her hands. She glanced up just in time to see Olive, a triumphant look on her face, splash water over her.

Giselle laughed and splashed her back. In an instant, the battle was engaged, and water flew through the air, soaking them both to the skin. Giselle shrieked when Olive splashed water straight at her face.

As she aimed her counter attack, a big wave washed over her. She lost her footing and ended up sitting in the water, still laughing. Guinevere bounded over and gave her face a long lick.

Olive stood, arms crossed, her light laughter filling the air. "Do you concede, my lady?"

"Aye." Giselle struggled to her feet and wrung water from her hair.

They trudged out of the surf and collapsed on the warm sand, Guinevere panting beside them. Giselle let out a breath. " 'Tis a fine morn," she said, realizing she truly meant it, despite what she'd seen of her husband the eve before. Today, with the splendor of the sea spread out before her, a peaceful feeling stole over her.

"Father told me you saved Lady Amice and the babe."

Giselle looked at Olive, who was gazing at her in wonder. "I suppose I did. Have you seen the babe?"

Olive's gaze turned mischievous. "Aye, I snuck in to peek at her." She wrinkled her nose. "Father says she has Lady Amice's beauty, but I cannot see it."

Giselle chuckled and squeezed Olive's shoulder. " 'Tis difficult to see in a newborn babe, but perhaps in time."

"I am glad to have a sister, no matter what she looks like."

The back of Giselle's throat stung at Olive's earnest

words, thinking how different her life might be if she had a sister or brother or any kind of family.

"I am going to help take care of her. When you have a babe, I shall help you too."

Giselle's mouth opened. "I . . . uh . . ." Dear heavens, what was she to say? She could not possibly explain her reluctance to share her husband's bed with the child.

Olive shrugged. "Father always says he is surprised Piers has not already fathered a hundred children, but perhaps the women know how to not conceive."

Well, and what was she to respond to that? "I know little of such things."

Olive popped up. "Uncle Piers is most knowledge-able. He can teach you. I am going to see if Adela has any fresh bread made." With a bright smile, the child turned and skipped down the beach.

He can teach you. With Olive's assurance, the memory of how close she'd come to allowing Piers to do just that crashed into her mind. She shivered and put her hand on Guinevere's soggy fur.

What had come over her? She had never felt such desire in her life, never even close. It was as if she were under a spell, as if she'd lost control of who she was. She must have drunk too much wine, she decided. She would be more careful in the future.

She gripped Guinevere tightly and gazed sightlessly over the sea. *Forgive me, Father for I have sinned*, she said to herself. *I was weak, and nearly yielded to temptation.*

Help me to be strong, Lord, and live in your grace.

Though the prayers rolled through her by rote, all she could see was the hunger in her husband's eyes, the seduction of him saying, "Come to me."

And, God aid her, she still wanted to do that very thing.

🦎 🦎 🦎

Piers rocked back on his heels, astounded by what he'd witnessed. It seemed another woman had replaced his pious, reserved wife. A woman capable of laughing and playing, clearly enjoying cavorting in the sea with Olive.

He watched her as she slowly made her way back into the castle. Her wet bliaut clung to the curves of her body, her hair a loose banner of gleaming, pale silk down her back. In his mind, he saw her emerge from the sea, her naked body glistening with water droplets, a setting sun outlining her in gold. He would lay her down on the soft sand and pleasure her until she cried out, until the last bit of her control succumbed to her body's demands. And then he would take her. Gently at first, but then hard, the way he truly wanted to.

He fisted a hand and closed his eyes. Perhaps he should have accepted Clarise's offer last eve, he thought. Giselle's eyes appeared in his mind and he groaned. It was no use.

He was in hell.

The woman he wanted most in his bed was his own

wife, but he could not fathom tainting all that lush in-nocence with what he harbored inside him.

ლ   ლ   ლ

Giselle hurried across the bailey, hoping to reach her chamber to remove her wet things without running into anyone, particularly Piers. Ill at ease in her soaked bliaut, she kept her head down and scurried over the grass, ig-noring the bustle of activity around her.

"Lady Giselle," a voice said, stopping her.

When Giselle looked up, inwardly she sighed in dismay.

Saraid gazed at her with her usual disapproving ex-pression.

Giselle stiffened and met the woman's gaze. "Do you require something of me?"

"Nay." Saraid sniffed. "Not likely. 'Tis the Lady Amice who asks for you."

"Is something wrong?"

Saraid's face softened. "No. She is happily resting with the babe close. She would speak with you."

It was clear from Saraid's expression she didn't like the idea. All at once, other faces flashed across Giselle's mind, each holding that same look of censure, judging her to be lacking or worse. "Why do you dislike me?" she asked, amazed at her boldness.

When Saraid didn't immediately answer, Giselle was

tempted to duck her head and creep away, but she held fast, refusing to give in. "I have done no wrong to you."

Saraid's eyes flashed. "You are of the church."

"Aye, I was and would be again. There is naught wrong with that."

"Is there not? Was your time at Kerwick Abbey such a pleasurable experience then? Was your Abbess kind and understanding?"

"Kerwick was . . . a peaceful place. The Abbess was strict, true, but—"

"Strict? My guess is she was more than that." Saraid crossed her arms and frowned at Giselle.

Perplexed, Giselle studied the woman for a moment. Why would she care about the Abbess's behavior? "Why do you turn from God?"

"I do not turn from *God*. *He* does not impose strictures that cannot be born."

"Father Michael—"

"Is far better than most," Saraid said.

"I do not understand. The church is God's house, a sanctuary for His children."

"Sanctuary?" Saraid's mouth curled in derision. "Let me tell you about sanctuary. When I was fifteen years of age, my father ordered me to wed the Earl of Sturbridge. How foolish I was to think I would gain my own home and the devotion of my husband. The very first night of our marriage he brutally raped me and beat me for not acting the whore for him. Of course, I went to the priest."

Giselle gulped, fearing what Saraid was about to say. "And?"

Saraid's gaze turned to stone. "He told me 'twas my duty to submit to my husband, to strive to please him. So I did." She shook her head. "Nothing I did could ever please him enough. Again and again I sought the priest's aid, and again and again he told me it was my fault I had brought my husband's anger upon me. That my bruises and cuts were signs of my own sins. He even gave my husband advice on how best to punish me so I might learn how I should conduct myself."

Horror spread through Giselle's veins. How could a man of God behave in such a way? Yet, there was no doubt Saraid spoke the truth. Though she'd had nothing to do with the priest's malicious treatment of Saraid, Giselle felt the shame of it down to her soul. "I am sorry, Saraid. I . . ." She shook her head. "I never imagined a man of God could be capable of such horror in the name of the church."

"Aye, that is what your church means to me."

Impulsively, Giselle touched the other woman's hand. "I would not defend such a man. The God I know and worship would never countenance that kind of cruelty."

The hard expression in Saraid's eyes faded. "No. I have always believed Sturbridge's priest was more of the devil than God."

Giselle thought of the Bishop of Ravenswood, and gave

Saraid a wry smile. "I know what you mean. I have experienced my own brand of maltreatment at the hands of the Bishop of Ravenswood, a man highly placed in the church, yet from all I saw, completely lacking in true spirituality."

Saraid let out a sigh. "I am wrong to blame you, my lady. I know well you had naught to do with Sturbridge's priest's transgressions."

"Perhaps . . ." Giselle faltered.

"We could try to be friends," Saraid finished for her.

They exchanged a smile. "Aye," Giselle said. "I would like that."

Saraid nodded. "I, as well. But now the Lady Amice awaits."

After receiving Lady Amice's tearful thanks and admiring the babe, named Meriall, Giselle found Piers waiting for her in the great hall. With a courage Giselle was beginning to nurture, she met his gaze without allowing her anger to show.

Piers sipped ale and stared at her so closely Giselle glanced down to see if her bliaut had come unlaced. "I thought to begin your lessons," he said.

For a moment, all Giselle could think of were Olive's airy words. *Uncle Piers is most knowledgeable. He can teach you.* "Lessons?" she croaked.

His slow smile told her he was thinking of the same thing.

Giselle frowned, reminding herself it had been mere hours since he'd lain in another woman's bed.

"Riding lessons," he said.

"Oh." Giselle blinked. "Of course."

"You will need to change clothing."

Puzzled, she looked down at her attire again. She wore a simple wool bliaut, having quickly changed before seeing Amice. "Why?"

He stood and approached her. "I am going to teach you to ride as I do. Astride."

Her eyes widened. "But . . . but a lady should not ride astride."

" 'Tis safer. And many ladies do. Amice, for one."

Would it be a sin to do as he suggested? Giselle wondered. Though the sisters of Kerwick had no need to ride anywhere, the Abbess had made her opinions clear on the subject. No lady would part her legs to ride astride. Such an act invited lewd temptation. "I would be more comfortable riding aside," she told her husband.

His gaze twinkled. "Not after a few minutes. Now, I have obtained clothing from one of the young grooms." He eyed her. "It should fit well enough. I set it out in our chamber."

She gulped, but saw the wisdom of his plan. Her difficulties in riding without tumbling off the side of the horse had been what led her to seek lessons in the first place. "Very well, my lord."

"Piers," he said. "Do you need aid in changing?"

"Nay." She backed away. "I can tend to myself."

One brow lifted. "I am happy to help."

Dear Lord, what next? Giselle thought. "Nay. I shall meet you at the stable anon." She turned and fled for their chamber, hoping and silently praying he didn't follow her.

By the time Giselle clothed herself in a worn blue tunic and braies, she felt so discomfited she wasn't sure she had it in her to leave the chamber. She took a few steps around the room, marveling at how much freer she felt. At the same time, she felt oddly exposed, accustomed to loose fitting bliauts with tunics and chemises underneath.

Be brave, Giselle, she told herself. It occurred to her that if she couldn't ride she would never be able to achieve any kind of independence. Unless she persuaded Piers to take her, she could never ride all the way back to Kerwick and Sister Gertrude. The ride to Falcon's Craig had nearly done her in.

Before she could think more about all of the reasons she shouldn't go out in front of the castlefolk clad like a boy, she darted out of the chamber.

Piers waited for her in the stable holding Etain who was already saddled. When Giselle appeared, he gave her a long look, perusing her from head to toe. His approving expression lingered on the place where her breasts, always too full for her liking, strained the front of the tunic.

Giselle flushed and tried to ignore the curious stares of the grooms. "I am ready."

"Good."

He led her into a small fenced area. Giselle eyed

the horse with no small amount of trepidation. The few times she'd ridden had been on a much smaller horse.

Etain craned her head around and looked at Giselle. She patted the horse's withers, her pale coat smooth to the touch. "She is rather big," she told Piers, biting her lip.

"Etain is the best behaved horse in my stable," Piers responded as he tightened the girth. "And she is a smooth ride. You shall not have any trouble with her. Not like that beast from Hades, Angel."

Giselle had to smile at that. "How are your ribs?"

Piers gave a snort. "Aching, but 'tis not too bad." He gave her a sideways look. "Thanks to the excellent ministrations from my wife, apparently a talented healer."

"You are welcome."

He put a hand on her shoulder, his expression suddenly solemn. "Thank you for your care of Amice and the babe. If we had lost them, well," he shook his head, "my brother's heart would be forever rent in two."

"He loves her very much."

"Aye. Now, up you go," he said, holding out his hands.

Gingerly, Giselle put one foot in his cupped hands and grabbed the front of the saddle. Before she could scarcely draw a breath, she was in the air. She landed with a squawk, her legs stuck out to the sides like thin branches of a tree. *Dear Lord, what an odd sensation*, she thought as her body adjusted to sitting astride a horse for the first time in her life. Odd, but Piers was right.

He tucked her feet into the stirrups and backed away

to study her.

"This does feel more secure," she said, then squawked again when Etain began walking.

Piers caught her, and Giselle let out a breath of relief. "Move your seat a bit forward," he instructed, staring at, oh Lord, the very spot where her woman's place met the saddle.

"Wha . . . what?"

To Giselle's shock, he put his hands around her hips and scooted her forward. "Aye, that is better."

Giselle looked down at him and he winked. A strange, warm feeling started somewhere in her chest and slowly trickled down her body. *You can do this*, she told herself.

He positioned her hands on the reins. "Let your weight sink into the saddle and keep your legs relaxed," he said. "Go on and ask her to walk."

Giselle gave the horse a gentle squeeze and they were moving.

"Try to allow your body to move with her. Feel the way she rocks from side to side?"

"Aye."

"Do the same. Let her carry you. And, Giselle?"

Focused on the horse's movement, for a moment she didn't answer.

"Breathe," he said from beside her.

As they walked around the ring, she tried not to grip the horse. Etain moved with an easy, swaying walk, blowing air out of her nostrils and seemingly content to carry Giselle along.

"Whoa," Piers said.

Giselle pulled back on the reins, and Etain stopped. "What is wrong?"

He shook his head. "You are gripping with your thighs, and leaning forward too much."

"Oh." She flinched when he put his hand on her thigh.

"This should be loose. Put your calves against her side, but keep your hips open."

Giselle was so discomfited by the discussion she sent Etain off again simply to escape Piers. They walked around the ring, and Giselle focused on following Piers's instructions, breathing in and out.

"Good," Piers said. "Let me see how you do at the trot."

With that, Giselle's body froze, and she pulled at the reins. Etain stopped and dropped her head. Giselle looked at Piers, who was eyeing her with puzzlement. "You want me to go faster?" she asked.

He blinked. "You will need to if you ever want to get anywhere."

Giselle thought of all the times she'd fallen off on the way to Falcon's Craig and shuddered inside. Thankfully, she'd landed on soft grass each time, but the sensation of knowing you were falling through air from a quickly moving animal remained a frightening memory in her mind.

"What is wrong?"

"I am not sure how to do that," she finally admitted.

Piers's gaze turned thoughtful. " 'Tis much the same idea as the walk. You need to relax into the rhythm of the horse."

"Easy for you to say," she muttered.

"Are you afraid of falling off?"

"Of course I am afraid of falling off. 'Tis most uncomfortable."

He smiled. "I well know, but Etain is a good girl. She has a nice, smooth trot."

Giselle gathered up the reins and took a deep breath. He was right, of course. She needed to learn to ride at more than a walk. She pressed her legs against the side of the horse.

Etain jolted forward, and Giselle's breath left her body.

"Do not pull back on the reins," Piers called out. "Let your weight sink into the saddle."

Giselle couldn't answer. She bounced atop Etain's back so quickly she was certain it was only a matter of moments before she became unseated. *Lord preserve me*, she silently prayed over and over.

About halfway around the ring, the horse mercifully halted.

"That was not too bad, for a start," Piers commented as he walked over.

"Perhaps that is enough for today."

He shook his head. "The only way you will find your balance is to keep riding."

"I understand that, truly I do, but . . ." Her voice

trailed off and she stared at Piers, a part of her unwilling to admit just how overwhelming she found the task. *Other people ride all the time*, she reminded herself.

"Take your feet out of the stirrups," he said.

Giselle widened her eyes. Was he mad?

"Just for a moment." He put a hand on Etain's bridle. "She will not go anywhere."

Hesitantly, Giselle slipped her feet free.

"Now, let your legs hang down." He put one hand on her thigh, and Giselle flinched. Piers appeared not to notice. "Point your toes out, then in, and then down."

She complied.

He slid her foot back into the closest stirrup, then moved around to do the same on the other side. "Sit up straight."

Giselle took another deep breath and tried to sit as he instructed.

His hand moved up to her hip and Giselle froze. Warmth seeped through the fabric of her braies into her skin and she fought the urge to squirm away. What had begun as a simple lesson was quickly turning into something far more intimate, though her husband seemed completely unaware of it, thank God. "You absorb the horse's movement through your hips and your knees," he said. "If you tense your muscles, you cannot do it. That is why you bounce so much."

"I understand. I think."

"Good. Keep your body loose and try again."

Etain bent her head around and gave a soft nicker. *I can do this*, Giselle told herself as she urged the horse forward. Once more, they took off, but this time it seemed less bouncy. Before she knew it, they had made it around the entire ring.

"Much better," Piers said. "Now, let's add something."

"Not faster," Giselle said, momentarily panicked.

"Not yet. When Etain bounces you up, swing your hips up and forward, and then sit back down as softly as you can."

"What?"

He put his hands on his hips and rocked forward. "Like this."

Their gazes met and all at once Giselle felt heat rush to her face. Piers slowly smiled. Dear Lord, Giselle thought, her face flaming. His movement brought clearly to mind another activity all together, and, worse, he knew it.

She gave him a skeptical look. "Are you sure?"

"Aye. 'Twill be more comfortable for your woman's place."

If it were possible to flush more, Giselle couldn't imagine it. "I—"

"You said you wished to learn to ride," he challenged.

She lifted her chin, refusing to look at him. The knave, no doubt, was smiling in glee at provoking her. "I have not heard of such a thing."

" 'Tis my own idea. Go on."

She blew out a breath and squeezed Etain into a

trot. Giselle tried to move her hips forward, but it felt so awkward she ended up bouncing even more. She barely managed to slow Etain before sliding right over the side of the horse.

"You are popping straight up and down," Piers said. "You need to think of swinging forward."

Giselle tried again, but knew she'd failed when she cautioned a glance at Piers.

He frowned and came over. "Stand up slightly in your stirrups."

She did, though she was shaking inside in anticipation of what he might do next.

"Keep your shoulders back, and thrust your hips up and forward," he said, taking hold of her hips and rocking her.

Giselle thought she might fall off the horse in sheer mortification. "I shall try again," she said, mostly to stop him from touching her.

But instead of releasing her, he kept his hands in place and gazed up at her with a teasing light in his eyes. "I know of a very enjoyable method to practice that movement."

An image flashed into Giselle's mind before she could halt it. "You . . . you cannot be referring to . . ." She sputtered to a halt.

He winked. "Mating. Aye, I am. You could consider it another part of my teaching you to ride. A horse."

"I, uh," she swallowed and tried again. "I am not

ready for that."

"Are you sure? Last eve, I thought—"

"I was not feeling well," she quickly said. "I . . . I must have imbibed too much wine."

"Giselle, 'tis natural for a woman to feel the need of a man. And we *are* wed."

She averted her gaze. *Dear Lord, lead me not into temptation*, she silently recited. *Make of me a pure reflection of Your grace.* "Perhaps I could attempt it again with Etain."

He chuckled softly. "As you wish, my lady. For now."

Without looking at him, Giselle made herself focus on the horse and squeezed her forward yet again. Shoulders back, hips forward, she recited to herself.

"Good," Piers said. "Swing your hips a little more, as if you are seeking to touch the front of the saddle."

Giselle gritted her teeth and tried, but it was no use. She stopped and let out a sigh. "I have had enough for today."

He lifted a brow. "You need more practice. 'Tis not something to learn in a day. And you need to ease your tension," he added.

She scowled at him. " 'Tis not seemly for you to tease me so."

He shrugged, clearly unrepentant. "I think of it as encouraging your curiosity."

"I am *not* curious."

"No?" He stalked in her direction, his eyes gleaming.

"Not at all?"

Though her hands trembled, Giselle managed to say, "Nay."

"I would let you ride *me*, Giselle," he said softly. "Anytime you wish."

"I . . . I do not even understand what you are talking about." Somehow, she managed to dismount without her legs collapsing under her. When she turned, she found Piers only inches away.

"I would teach you."

Her cheeks flamed. She tried to back away, but was blocked by solid horseflesh. "Leave me be."

He swept his gaze over her. "Think about it, Giselle."

"I shall not," she said, knowing it was a lie. How could she not? Even as she admonished herself to ignore him, her imagination ran amok.

He leaned close and smiled. "Yes, you will."

She couldn't summon up a single word. He was right, and they both knew it.

Chapter XI

Giselle went straight from the stable to the chapel. If Father Michael was surprised to see her unusual attire, he had the graciousness not to show it. He came from behind the altar with a kind smile.

"Lady Giselle, what a pleasure to see you." He took her hands. "How do you fare?"

Suddenly, she wasn't sure any more than she was sure of the reason she was in the chapel. She gazed up at the gold cross and inwardly winced. "I am well, Father," she said, reluctant to confide her troubles. The priest had already made his opinions on her marriage clear.

"I must commend you on your brave aid to Lady Amice and her babe. I understand from the earl 'twas most miraculous."

Giselle couldn't help but smile at the memory. "Aye, God did, indeed, perform a miracle."

"Through you, child. Do not belittle that."

"I was fortunate to have the Lord's guidance, Father. And the experience from my days at Kerwick."

"We are all fortunate to have you with us."

"Thank you, Father."

He squeezed her hands. "Are you adjusting well to life outside of the abbey?"

Giselle gulped. "I . . . I am trying, Father. 'Tis very different."

"Ah, but also exciting, is it not? So many new things to discover." He gave her a gentle smile.

I would teach you, Piers had said. She felt her face heat once more. "Aye, that there is."

Father Michael chuckled. With a final squeeze of her hands, he said, "I am off to check in on Lady Amice and little Meriall."

After he left, Giselle knelt on the floor and stared up at the cross. Her vision blurred and instead of the lovely chapel, she saw the face of the Abbess, her gaze dark and condemning. *You must fight the taint of your blood by strict devotion to God. Born of wickedness, you must never sway from God or you shall forfeit your soul.*

Wicked. Tainted. Weak. Impure. Giselle had long lost count of the times the Abbess had called her such, followed by yet another penance to be performed.

She lowered her head, wishing she could recall more of her mother. "Forgive me, Father, for I have sinned. I . . ." she dropped her voice to a bare whisper. "I am sorely tempted, Father. And I am afraid I have become overly fond of wine. Not that I do not have cause to imbibe," she finished with a trace of defiance.

"Help me to be strong, Lord. Guide me to Your will. Grant me peace."

When she lifted her head, a shaft of sunlight caught the cross, reflecting golden light across the chapel. The heaviness in her heart lifted, and Giselle smiled.

$$\mathscr{C}\!\mathscr{S} \quad \mathscr{C}\!\mathscr{S} \quad \mathscr{C}\!\mathscr{S}$$

Giselle was about to pull on her chemise when the door to her chamber banged open. She whirled around, instinctively holding the chemise in front of her nakedness.

"Do not bother putting it on," Piers said.

Shock and fear washed over her like a frigid breeze. "What did you say?"

He shut the door and leaned against it, crossing his arms and staring at her with a hooded expression. "I am your husband, Giselle."

His gaze was so dark, it appeared black. She edged back a step. "My lord, Piers, I thought we had come to an agreement."

His lips curved. "Nay. I agreed to nothing."

"But—"

"Drop the chemise, Giselle. I would see all of you."

Giselle could scarcely draw a breath. Bare her body in the middle of the day, with the sun streaming in the open window? Dear Lord, she could not. "No."

"You deny me?" His gaze narrowed and he dropped his hands to his sides.

"Please. I cannot."

"Of course you can." He took a step forward.

In utter panic, Giselle ducked behind one of the bed curtains and pulled her chemise over her body. She barely had it over her hips when Piers swept aside the curtain. He trailed a finger down her throat, stopping at the curve of her breast.

"I have decided 'tis past time for me to claim my rights as your husband." His voice was cold, completely at odds with the heat in his gaze. "Now."

"I need more time," she whispered.

"Methinks there is not enough time in all of eternity for you to willingly come to lie with me." He flattened his hand over one breast. "I feel how quickly your heart beats, little nun. Are you thinking of how your hips will move when you are lying beneath me?"

He was so close she could feel his breath on her cheek. She closed her eyes. "No."

"I am," he said softly.

"Please do not ask this of me, my lord. Not yet. Perhaps in time—"

He barked a laugh. "How much time? A sennight? A year? More? How much time should I live as a priest? Wed to a woman I did not choose, yet denied surcease."

Giselle stiffened and flashed open her eyes. "You have not denied yourself."

"Aye, I have."

"You lie." Giselle sidled away from him. "I saw you

with that, that woman, Clarise."

"Ah, the fair Clarise. Now, there is a woman who does not hide from her pleasure."

Giselle's stomach clenched. "Then, perhaps you should seek her out."

"No. You are my wife. 'Tis your duty to see to my needs. All of them."

"You knew when you married me that I did not wish to . . . to fornicate." She looked down, unable to meet his dark gaze.

"As I recall, you offered to do so."

Inwardly, Giselle cringed. She fisted her hands in the folds of her chemise.

"Nothing to say, Giselle?"

She gritted her teeth to keep them from clattering together. She'd thought that if she had to lie with him, it would be in the dark of night, that her prayers would sustain her while he quickly finished.

"Look at me, damn you," he ordered.

Slowly, she looked up to find him right beside her.

"I want you. I ache with it," he said.

"Piers, I—"

He swallowed her protest with a kiss.

Every thought in Giselle's mind vanished beneath the onslaught of his mouth. He savored her, stroked her, and Giselle found herself helplessly responding. Dear God, she could drown in this feeling, Giselle dimly thought, twining her fingers in Piers's tunic. With a groan, he deepened the kiss, sweeping inside her mouth, sending tingling sensations over her body. He tasted of wine and temptation, and Giselle couldn't get enough of it, couldn't get close enough.

His hand moved up to cradle her head, anchoring her, kissing her so deeply he felt a part of her.

And then his hand slipped inside her chemise to cup her breast.

Giselle pressed into his hand, her breast tight and full, craving the warmth of his caress.

He flicked a finger over her nipple, and she heard herself moan. This felt so right, so perfect. She needed this. Needed him. Warmth pooled in her belly and spread downward, leaving her body aching and her legs weak.

Piers cupped Giselle's soft breast in his hand and was seized with a lust so powerful he burned with it. *She is yours for the taking.* His rod strained against his braies, and he backed Giselle up until she was against the wall.

Take her now, Eikki urged.

The image of bracing Giselle against the wall, lifting her chemise and burying himself in her took hold of him. Plunging into her mouth with his tongue, he unfastened his braies.

Now. Do it now!

Lost in the unbelievable pleasure of kissing Giselle, he barely heard. God, she was so sweet, so lush.

He put his hand on the edge of her chemise.

Rip it off.

So sweet, Piers thought, breathing in her mingled scent of lavender and awakening desire. So innocent.

She's yours. Fuck her the way you want to.

Innocent. Piers suddenly pulled away, filled with horror. Giselle's eyes were huge circles of turquoise, her lips swollen, her chemise falling off one shoulder.

She looked like a ravaged angel.

He backed away, pulling up his braies. Dear God, he'd become an animal, nearly taking his virgin wife up against the wall like she was some well-paid whore. "Giselle," he said, his voice a rasp. "I . . . I am sorry."

Unable to face the shock in her gaze another moment, he turned and fled the chamber.

❧ ❧ ❧

Giselle stood in the chamber staring at the door. She started to shake, and slid down the wall to crumple onto the floor.

What had just happened? In one moment, Piers had coldly demanded his rights, in the next set her body on fire, and finally had run away as if he were horrified by the idea of taking her.

And, God save her, with one kiss, she'd abandoned everything she'd been taught.

Now she understood why the church preached against temptation, against joining with a man for nothing but the pleasure of it. When she'd given into her body's yearnings, it had become all consuming. The heat of his huge arousal pressed against her had not brought revulsion, but a wild excitement. Nothing had mattered but touch, taste, satiating her senses.

And it had been utterly glorious.

The Abbess had been right. She did harbor wantonness in her soul.

Giselle closed her eyes and told herself to be thankful that Piers had stopped, whatever his reasoning. But a tiny voice inside her wondered if in the end he'd found her wanting. If he'd gone after Clarise, who he admitted knew about pleasure.

His expression had been one of a man awakening from a nightmare.

Giselle made herself stand, and smoothed down her chemise. She didn't understand any of it, from the time he'd entered the chamber. It was as if she dealt with two different men—one full of teasing warmth and the other harsh and frightening.

As she pulled on an undertunic and bliaut, she tried to puzzle out the mystery of her husband but failed. "Dear Lord, how have I come to this?" she asked aloud.

She'd never felt so utterly lost as she did at this moment.

Was this her penance for lacking purity in her soul? Had God turned His back on her because she had not proven herself devoted enough? Her mind spun with possibilities, none bringing any comfort.

Finally, she squared her shoulders and sucked in a

deep breath. If there was one thing she'd learned at Kerwick Abbey, it was how to move forward each day no matter how hard someone tried to beat her down.

She allowed herself a small smile as she left the chamber. Her husband had quite a ways to go before he could match the Abbess of Kerwick Abbey.

ଶ ଶ ଶ

Piers burst into Cain and Amice's chamber to find them both snuggled on their bed, smiling and cooing at their new daughter. Cain immediately broke off and stood. "Piers, by the saints, what is wrong?"

"Everything." Piers clenched and unclenched his hands.

Cain and Amice exchanged a worried look. Amice pressed a kiss to the babe's forehead and put her in a wooden cradle next to the bed. Meriall gave a big yawn and closed her eyes.

Piers took a moment to study the child, the bands around his chest loosening slightly at the precious sight.

"Tell us what ails you," Amice urged.

He gazed into her caring eyes. "I have a problem I am praying you can aid me with."

Her brow furrowed. "Is it something to do with Giselle?"

Piers looked away. "Not exactly." He sighed and slumped down onto a stool. " 'Tis my own doing."

Cain put a hand on his shoulder. "Tell us. You

239

know that Amice and I will do all we can to help."

By Saint George's sword, how he hated to admit how reckless he'd been. The image of Giselle's stricken face shifted across his mind, and more shame spilled into his gut. " 'Tis a bit of a tale."

"How can I help?" Amice asked softly.

"I thought perhaps as you can communicate with spirits, you could . . ."

"Dear God, do not tell me we have another damned wraith to deal with," Cain exclaimed.

"Not *we*, but *I*," Piers told him.

"Piers," Amice prodded. "Pray, explain."

Piers gritted his teeth. "On Parraba, there is a cave. We cleared the entrance of rubble for Lady Iosobal. She told us not to enter, but," his lips twisted, "we did not heed her advice. I ventured back into the recesses of the cave and found a miraculous chamber. Within a pool I found a gold chalice. It was so beautiful I reached down and retrieved it."

He looked up. Both Amice and Cain gazed at him with the same somber expression. They were holding hands.

"The chalice held a strange purple crystal. Curious fool that I am, I took it in my hand, and thus freed Eikki."

"Eikki?" Cain asked. "What is that?"

"Not a *that*, but a *who*. The essence, spirit, of one assuredly rightfully imprisoned in the crystal for centuries." Unable to remain still, Piers stood and paced across the floor. "A whoreson without any concern but gaining what he desires, no matter the cost to others. He is inside me."

Piers turned and faced Amice and Cain. "And he is getting stronger." He felt Eikki stir to life inside him, but managed to stamp him down.

Amice cried out and clutched Cain's hand tighter. His brother merely stared at him, his expression resolute.

"You think Amice can draw him out?" Cain asked.

"I do not know what else to do," Piers said. "He wants . . . the things he wants me to do are terrible. I am fighting him, but it is becoming more difficult. I am afraid what I might do."

"Of course, I shall try," Amice said.

Piers swallowed and allowed himself a flicker of hope. "Thank you."

"What do you know of him?" Cain asked.

"Not very much."

"What kinds of things does he urge you to do?" Amice asked.

Piers cringed. "About what you might guess. Kill. He is most insistent about . . ."

"Giselle," Cain finished, his face taut.

"Aye," Piers admitted. " 'Tis what troubles me the most."

"God's blood," Cain swore. "What a coil."

"I shall try this eve," Amice said. "In the same chamber where I summoned Muriel." She patted Piers's arm. "We shall rid you of this Eikki."

He wanted to believe her, but he had the strong feeling Eikki would not be as easy to banish as Muriel.

❧ ❧ ❧

It was dusk by the time the three gathered in the upper tower chamber. Piers watched Amice's preparations with a mix of hope and worry.

Eikki had been quiet after he'd driven Piers to nearly rape Giselle. Perhaps the spirit had expended too much energy, but Piers had the sense that Eikki simply lay in wait for his next opportunity to wreak further havoc with Piers's life.

Cain gazed at him with a solemn expression as Amice set out candles in a pattern on the floor. "Why was this cave on Parraba so special to Lady Iosobal?"

Piers shrugged, but remembered the place's odd feeling. "I am not entirely sure. Parraba is a strange place. 'Twas obvious Iosobal considered the cave important. I think it was a link to her family, to her history."

"What do you remember of it?"

"Not too much. There were strange drawings on the walls and I think there were objects on the ground, but I did not stop to study them. Veins of purple crystal ran through some of the walls, particularly in the cave where I uncovered the chalice."

Amice lit the candles and Piers saw she'd arranged them in the shape of a pentagram. He blinked with a sudden memory. "There was a pentagram etched into the stone at the entrance."

Amice frowned. "How odd."

"Aye." Piers drew in a deep breath. " 'Tis hard to describe. I felt as if I took a step back through time when I entered the cave."

Cain grunted and built up the fire. "I should have been with you."

" 'Tis not your duty to protect me, brother. Even from myself."

"I am the eldest. 'Twill always be my duty."

As Amice added herbs to a small pot hanging over the fire, Piers paced the floor. By Saint George's sword, he was afraid, and he hated it.

"I am ready, Piers."

He turned and faced his sister-in-law, clad in a snowy white bliaut, with her ancient torc around her slender neck. She appeared so calm and sure that he moved forward until he stood in the center of the pentagram with her.

The lion head terminals of the torc gleamed blood red in the firelight.

Amice took his hands. "Come to me, troubled spirit. Tell me of your woe so that I might aid you to the other side. Come to me."

Piers gazed into her eyes and felt Eikki rumble to life.

"Come to me," Amice repeated.

Pathetic, really, Eikki said in his sibilant voice. *Does she think me a mere ghost?*

"Tell me why you have come into my brother," Amice said.

Eikki laughed.

Amice sucked in a breath as she gazed into Piers's eyes. They darkened, and darkened further until they were black as night. His grip on her hands tightened, and Amice felt the first tendril of fear. No, she had to continue. Piers was depending on her. "Who are you?" she asked.

"I am Eikki," a low voice responded.

"Holy Mother of God," Cain whispered. "Amice?"

"I am all right," she told him, unable to look away from Piers. "Why have you not moved on, spirit?"

Piers's lips curved into a cold smile. "I doubt heaven would have me, my lady."

"You must release your hold on this earth. On Piers."

"Oh, I do not think so. He is proving to be most entertaining."

Amice cast about for an argument to sway him. Before, the ghosts had an earthly reason to remain, unfinished matters in their life. She'd never encountered one who believed they were destined to hell. "Heaven is open to all who repent," she finally said, repeating Father Michael's words.

She jolted as a barrage of images slammed into her mind. Death. Rape. Cruelty. Her breath came in shallow pants, and she tried to pull away.

"Nay. I believe I shall stay with Piers," he said.

And a jolt of pain shot through Amice's body. She jerked and shrieked in pain. In an instant, Cain was beside her, yanking her away from Piers and knocking his brother to the floor. He carried her outside the candles. "Are you all right?"

She shivered in his arms and held onto his shoulders tightly. "Aye."

Piers rolled over and blinked up at them. His eyes were back to brown, and he looked puzzled. "What happened?'

Amice struggled to find an explanation.

"Did I . . . he hurt you?" Piers asked as he jumped to his feet. "Amice?"

"I am well, Piers. But," she glanced at Cain. "I fear I was not able to help you."

"I sensed as much." In his mind, Eikki cackled. *You shall not be rid of me so easily.* Piers fisted his hands, anger and frustration raging inside him. "What shall I do?"

Amice gazed at him with wide eyes, but shook her head in clear dismay.

"What of the Lady Iosobal?" Cain asked, his expression reluctant but determined. "If anyone can aid you, 'twould be her. She knows her isle."

Piers sighed. "Aye. I shall send word to her, and hope her anger with me is outweighed by her sympathies as a healer."

Cain set Amice back on her feet. "From what you

have said of the woman, surely she can do something."

"I hope so." Piers walked out of the candle penta-gram. "If not . . ." He gazed helplessly at Cain.

"You are a strong man, Piers," Cain told him. "Stronger than you realize. Fight this creature."

"Believe me, Cain, I am. Every moment." Piers left the chamber, unable to stay in this place of failure an instant more. He would send a messenger to Tunvegan at once and plead for Iosobal's aid.

And pray, in the meantime, he was strong enough to hold Eikki at bay.

🦎 🦎 🦎

Giselle awoke the next morning alone but for a loudly snoring Guinevere. The covers on the other side of the bed were smooth and there was no sign of Piers. She wondered in whose bed he'd slept last night.

She clutched the bedcovers and tried to hold back the sting of tears. *I should be pleased*, she told herself. If he ignored her for other women, it was for the best. He was too much for her, she knew. Too much man, too much temptation, and too much of a mystery.

You should be content, she chided herself. *You have a fine place to live, ample food and drink, beautiful clothing, and no one reminding you over and over again that you are a tainted woman.*

Guinevere let out a snort and stretched, putting her

head on Giselle's stomach. *And you have been adopted by a dog*, Giselle reminded herself. *Your tapestry for Lady Amice is proceeding well, and you have earned the gratitude of the earl for your service to his lady.*

If only Piers hadn't kissed her, Giselle thought as she forced her body out of bed. If only it hadn't felt so . . . shockingly wondrous, so right, like she was on the verge of making an incredible discovery. For a moment, she'd let herself think perhaps she'd found someone who could care for her, hold her in strong, loving arms.

You are a fool, she told herself. *It was simple lust that drove him to kiss you, a lust that quickly died when he came to his senses and realized just who he was kissing.*

She unwrapped the cross she'd received from the Bishop and stared down at it, wishing with all her heart she could ask God why he'd put her in this situation and receive a wise answer. Guinevere snuffled against her shoulder, and Giselle leaned against the dog.

At a knock on the door, Giselle straightened. Before she could speak, Olive's bright face peered around the door. "Good morn, my lady," she greeted.

"Hello, Olive. Come in."

The child bounded into the chamber, and stopped to pat Guinevere. "What is that?" she asked, pointing at the cross.

"It is a wedding gift from the Bishop of Ravenswood."

A frown crossed Olive's face. "The same Bishop who made you leave Kerwick Abbey."

Giselle started. "How do you know about that?"

Olive shrugged and gave Giselle an impish grin. "I hear all sorts of things."

"I see."

" 'Tis very beautiful," Olive said peering at the cross. "May I hold it?"

"Of course." Giselle handed the cross to Olive, who held it up to the light, turning it around.

"Why did the Bishop send you such a fine piece?"

To remind me I am unworthy, Giselle thought, but shrugged instead of voicing the fact. " 'Twas quite a surprise," she said. That much was the truth.

Olive took a step and her leg buckled. The cross slipped from her fingers and crashed onto the floor. "Oh, no," Olive cried. "I am so sorry, my lady." She knelt on the floor. "I have broken it."

Giselle knelt next to her and picked up the cross. The back had separated, and when she picked it up, two folded sheets of vellum fell out. Puzzled, she reached for one and glanced at Olive.

The child's eyes were wide. "A secret compartment."

"So it appears." Giselle unfolded the vellum. A flowing script spilled across the page. She bent closer and tried to make out the words. She'd learned some of her letters, but the Abbess had never deemed the ability to read and write of importance enough to take Giselle from her prayers and work. "I cannot read it," she finally admitted.

"May I see it?" Olive asked. "I promise to be careful. Lady Amice taught me to read."

Giselle handed her the vellum.

Olive screwed her eyes in concentration, and studied the document. Her lips moved silently as she read.

"What does it say?" Giselle asked.

"It is a record of marriage." Olive squinted at the document. "Between Annora St. Germain and Edward de Sauvin, son of the Earl of Claybourne."

"Annora was my mother's name," Giselle said. Her heart began to beat faster.

" 'Tis signed by a priest, a Father Thomas, and dated the second day of June, in the year of our Lord Eleven Hundred and Eighty-Nine.

Giselle pointed to a blob of hard gray wax. "What is that?"

"Some kind of seal. There is a name next to it, but I cannot make it out." Olive gently set the vellum down and reached for the other sheet.

Giselle simply sat there, her heart pounding but the rest of her body numb.

Olive scooted closer. "This is *so* exciting," she said. "I shall read it to you. 'On this twelfth day of August, in the year of our Lord Eleven Hundred and Eighty-Nine, I Annora de Sauvin, born Annora St. Germain, make this record in the hope that one day the truth of what I am too ashamed to face shall be known'."

My mother, Giselle thought, and her throat closed.

249

Olive paused and looked at her in sympathy. "She writes, 'Before my husband returns to collect me, I must flee. I am with child, and I cannot bear the shame of it. It is my hope that one day, my dear husband and my father can forgive me'."

Dear God, it must be true, Giselle thought. Her mother had lain with the Bishop while she was wed to another.

"There is something more, but it is smudged. No, I see." Olive's little face turned pale.

Giselle swallowed. "What is it?"

"She . . . she writes, 'I fear Edward will never believe that Aldrik forced me, that my beloved husband will always wonder if the child I carry is his. So I must leave the only home I have ever known. I must protect my unborn babe. I must protect Giselle'."

For a moment, Giselle couldn't say a word. She could scarcely breathe. "Oh, my God."

"Who is Aldrik?"

Giselle sucked in a breath. "The Bishop of Ravenswood."

Olive's eyes went wide in horror. "We must go to Father with this."

Giselle's mind spun, and she couldn't seem to find the strength to stand. St. Germain, she thought. Her surname is St. Germain. No, de Sauvin. Somehow, she managed to stand, though her mind was dazed and her limbs felt leaden. Olive carefully set the vellum aside, and helped her dress.

Within a few minutes, Giselle followed Olive out of the chamber, clutching the sheets of vellum and the cross in her hands.

❧   ❧   ❧

Piers held a quill in his hand and stared down at the blank piece of parchment. Perhaps he should forgo the message and journey to Tunvegan to throw himself upon Iosobal's mercy, he thought, then rejected the idea. Though a part of him thought it would be a good thing to be away from Giselle, a larger part felt duty bound to remain.

But, how to explain? Just say it, he told himself, dipping the quill into a pot of black ink. *Greetings*, he wrote, and then stopped. Saints, he wasn't sure which he hated more—having to admit his stupidity or his help-lessness.

He'd been like a curious child, heedless of the possible consequences. Why he'd done so ground into him with a sharp ache of guilt. The truth was that life had always come easily to him. He had a natural talent with horses, which had brought him a reputation across the land. From the time he'd started to notice them, women had fallen into his arms without hesitation. And Cain had always been the responsible one, paving Piers's way to leading an idyllic life.

He'd never really had to fight for anything he wanted.

Perhaps Eikki was God's way of repaying him for that.

He gritted his teeth and made himself write the words. *Iosobal, I beg your forgiveness. I should never have entered your cave, and I am heartily sorry for it. Because of my reckless stupidity, the essence of a devil in the guise of a condemned Fin Man now resides within me. I pray you can aid me. He is called Eikki.*

He scrawled his name at the bottom and rolled the parchment before sealing it with warm wax.

Even with his fastest horse, it would take almost a sennight for a messenger to reach Tunvegan. He hung his head and sent up a silent prayer. *I will control the bastard*, he thought savagely. *By God, this is one fight I shall win*, he told himself. *No matter what it takes.*

Resolved, he went to seek out a messenger.

❦   ❦   ❦

Giselle and Olive found the earl in his solar, frowning at a stack of parchment.

"Father?" Olive said, as she skipped into the chamber. "We need to show you something!" She scooted around his worktable and slid onto his lap.

He smiled and ruffled her hair. "You are saving me from studying the accounts. Lady Giselle?" he asked. His gaze held an odd note of concern. "Is something wrong?"

Olive tugged at his tunic. "We found something *important*," she whispered.

Giselle set the cross on the table. "Thanks to Olive, we uncovered this," she said, holding up the sheets of vellum. With a shaking hand, she gave them over.

His brows furrowed as he read. Astonishment slowly washed over his face. "You are . . ." He shook his head and stared at her. "You knew naught of this?"

"Nay." Giselle sank onto a stool, her legs too weak to support her.

He picked up the cross and studied it.

"I dropped it, Father," Olive said. "The back broke off. For once, my clumsiness did something good."

"You are not clumsy, sweet. But you are right. 'Tis finely worked. Absent an accident, it could have hung on the wall forever without anyone knowing it held such secrets. To be sure, the Bishop of Ravenswood had no idea what it held," he murmured.

"Why . . ." Giselle swallowed, "why do you say that?"

He lifted a brow. "According to this, you—"

The door flung open and Piers walked in. At the sight of Giselle, he froze.

"Good that you are here, Piers," the earl said. "Olive and Giselle have just presented me with a bit of a mystery."

Olive's eyes brightened. "We found a hidden compartment in Giselle's cross."

Piers looked at Giselle, a question in his gaze.

She nodded, unable to do more.

The earl stood and handed the vellum to Piers. " 'Tis very interesting."

Piers sat on the edge of the table and read. When he finished, he looked at Giselle in wonder. "Do you know what this means?"

"I know my surname," Giselle answered.

"Not just that." He exchanged a glance with the earl, whose expression had turned angry.

"I do not understand," she said slowly.

"You are the daughter of Annora St. Germain." He fisted a hand. "Which also makes you the heiress to Kindlemere."

Giselle's mouth dropped open. "My mother was a . . . a lady?"

Piers nodded. "Aye. I remember hearing the story. Your grandfather, the Earl of Kindlemere, was heartbroken over his daughter's loss. He never stopped looking for her." He pointed to the circle of dried wax. "This is his seal—a dragon rising from a lake."

Giselle slowly pulled the chain she always wore from beneath her chemise. A gold ring hung from the end. "Like this," she said.

Piers took the ring in his hand. "Aye, *exactly* like this."

"Kindlemere," Giselle said, her gaze fixed to Piers's. "But that belongs to the Bishop."

"No doubt persuaded the king to award it to him, given the apparent fact there were no blood heirs remaining," the earl said.

Giselle's hand went to her throat. "But . . . he knew . . ."

Piers's gaze was cold. "Aye, he well knew who you

were. 'Tis obvious he deliberately kept that fact to himself." He barked a laugh. "He 'gifted' you with a cross that belonged to you all along."

"I cannot believe it." Giselle sprang to her feet and paced across the room. "All this time, I thought I was a simple orphan, fortunate to be able to claim Kerwick Abbey as a home." Her eyes filled with tears. "My grandfather?"

She was so distraught she didn't even flinch when Piers took her hands in his. "Dead, Giselle. I am sorry," he told her, squeezing her hands gently.

Olive jumped up and down. "You must avenge your lady's honor, Uncle Piers. Like Pendragon."

Piers's lips twitched. "Pendragon?"

"He is the hero in a story Lady Amice told me. When the evil wizard steals away the fair Sebille, Pendragon battles him in honor of his lady."

Giselle gulped and waited for her husband to tell her he was far too busy wenching to take on such a task. She sucked in a breath when he turned to look at her, his golden brown eyes dark with purpose.

"Aye. You are right, Olive. 'Tis my duty and my honor to recover your birthright, my lady."

Giselle gave him a wobbly smile. "The Bishop is a powerful, and, I have heard, ruthless man."

"I am not without my own resources, my lady."

"Uncle Piers will be your hero, Lady Giselle!" Olive cried out enthusiastically.

Amy Tolnitch

Giselle could scarce take in the notion of having a hero fight for her.

"We must petition the king on Giselle's behalf," the earl said, drumming his fingers on the table.

Piers nodded, his face set in fierce lines.

"What of Edward de Sauvin?" Giselle whispered.

Piers glanced at his brother, who shook his head. "Never heard of the man, nor of the Earl of Claybourne," the earl said, his face thoughtful.

Giselle's heart fell. For a moment, she'd allowed herself the fantasy she might have a true father out there somewhere. At the same time, she inwardly cringed. Her mother had clearly been unsure whether the man who sired her had been the Bishop or this Edward de Sauvin.

"Giselle," Piers said, squeezing her hand once more. "I shall send a man to London to make inquiries. If Edward de Sauvin yet lives, we shall find him."

Tears leaked from her eyes. "Thank you." That he would undertake her cause so earnestly stunned her. She looked around the room and saw similar expressions on Olive's and the earl's faces. Unflagging support. Anger over the Bishop's perfidy. Anger for *her*. Giselle could scarcely draw a breath she was so touched.

And then it occurred to her. If Kindlemere Castle did rightfully belong to her, then she was no longer dependent upon anyone. She gazed up into Piers's eyes and saw the same thought mirrored within.

"Let us see what transpires, my lady," he said quietly.

She nodded and pulled her hands free.

"Piers, what do you wish to do with the other information contained here?" the earl asked, his mouth turned down.

Initially, his question puzzled Giselle, and then she remembered her mother's cryptic words. In the shock of discovering her true identity, she'd momentarily forgotten. Though she admonished herself to remain calm, rage ripped through her. "That . . . whoreson ravaged my mother," she spat.

Piers blinked in obvious shock. "So it appears."

"*He* should be the one exiled from the church," she said, gritting her teeth, her mind filled with memories of her lovely mother, even dimmer memories of the small cottage in which they'd lived a solitary life. Her mother should have had so much more. *She* should have had so much more.

And it was all the fault of one deceitful man who was less in service to God than to his own avarice.

"I think, for now, we should keep that fact to ourselves," Piers said. "Hold it back until we find out the Bishop's response to Giselle's claim."

Revenge is not the way of the Lord, Giselle told herself over and over, to no avail. The need for vengeance burned in her blood. The theft of her inheritance, the concealment of her identity was one thing. The Bishop's bloated face leapt into her mind. That he, a poor excuse for a man, had taken her mother, leaving her with no choice but to flee her husband in fear and shame could not be forgiven.

" 'Tis a matter best handled discreetly," the earl agreed.

"Giselle?" Piers lifted her chin. "Are you in agreement?"

For the second time, his behavior surprised her. He was actually asking her opinion? "I do not know."

"I understand why you would wish to use this to ruin him," Piers said. " 'Tis a delicate matter, though. I would that we locate your father before revealing what we've learned of the Bishop's crimes."

"But I do not know who my father is." Tears welled in her eyes once more.

"Do you resemble the Bishop?"

She shook her head vehemently.

"Not at all? Nothing?"

"Nay! Even he said I looked exactly like my mother."

The earl coughed. "Assuming the marriage did indeed occur, you are legally the daughter of Edward de Sauvin."

Giselle stared at him. "Even if he is not my true father?"

Piers and his brother exchanged a long look. When Piers turned back to her, his gaze held a curious knowledge. "The law presumes legitimacy."

"I . . . I wish there was a way to know for certain."

"Do not give up, Lady Giselle," Olive urged. "Perhaps you shall find something in you that resembles de Sauvin."

Giselle eyed her doubtfully, but didn't want to disappoint the child. If not for Olive, she would never have discovered any of this. Along with the Bishop's calculated choice of a "gift" for her. She blew out a breath. "Mayhap."

Piers suddenly grinned, and Giselle felt the warmth of it flow through her body like a tempting sweet just out of reach. "Think on it, Giselle. At last, you know who you are."

"Aye." She smiled back at him. "I do."

"And you have my word I shall do all in my power to ensure you receive what is due you," he added.

"As will I," the earl said.

As much as Giselle wanted to pursue her birthright, to in some small way avenge her mother, the convent part of her shied away from provoking the Bishop of Ravenswood. "The Bishop will not take kindly to having his rule challenged."

"No doubt. From what I recall, Kindlemere is a wealthy estate."

Giselle bit her lip.

"You need not fear him, Giselle," Piers said. "You are under *our* protection now." His voice was so passionate Giselle could only stare at him.

"I . . . thank you. Where is Kindlemere?"

" 'Tis in the land of lakes, my lady," Olive said.

Giselle cocked her head. "How do you know that?"

" 'Tis where Lady Amice is from. She says 'tis most beautiful."

"Oh."

The earl slapped a hand against his forehead. "Of course. Thank you, Olive. Perhaps Amice knows something of matters at Kindlemere."

"Where is she?" Piers asked abruptly.

The earl rolled his eyes. "Conferring with Gifford, I believe, in his workroom."

"Come, my lady," Piers said, taking Giselle's hand. "Let us question her. Perhaps she knows something of this Edward de Sauvin."

Giselle let herself be pulled along, dimly aware of the warm strength of Piers's hand clasping hers. By the time they reached Gifford's workroom, Giselle was nearly running, holding up her skirts with the hand not gripped by Piers. At the doorway, Piers banged a knock, then opened the door.

Lady Amice sat on a stool next to Gifford, a puzzled look on her face. She glanced at Piers and Giselle, and her gaze went at once to their clasped hands. Giselle told herself to pull free, but the simple fact was that the revelations of what she'd found were so startling she found herself needing to lean on Piers's strength. Even liking the feel of his big hand around hers, she realized.

"Piers?" Lady Amice said, rising from her stool. "What is it?"

Gifford peered at Giselle. "You look a bit pale, my dear. Sit." He pulled out a stool and pressed her onto it, filling a cup and setting it before her.

Reluctantly, Giselle eased out of Piers's grip and sat.

Piers scowled. "We have just discovered the truth of Giselle's identity."

Lady Amice's eyes widened. "How?"

"Documents hidden in the cross sent by the Bishop of Ravenswood." He said the name as an epithet.

Giselle found herself incapable of speech, and took a sip of ale.

"Well, don't dawdle, boy," Gifford said. "Tell us who the girl is."

"She is the daughter of Annora St. Germain and," he paused, glancing at Giselle, "Edward de Sauvin."

"St. Germain?" Lady Amice asked, her brow furrowed. "That sounds familiar."

"The only child of the Earl of Kindlemere," Piers spat.

"Oh! Oh, my!"

"Aye. That bastard stole Giselle's inheritance from her."

Gifford squeezed Giselle's shoulder, his expression sympathetic. "Poor thing." Then he grinned. "I always sensed you were a true lady."

She managed to return his smile. "Thank you, my lord."

"What do you know of Kindlemere?" Piers asked.

Lady Amice absently rubbed her belly, now sizably smaller. "I have never been there. My father did not encourage me to travel," she continued in a sour tone. "But I do recall the Earl of Kindlemere visiting Wareham." She smiled at Giselle. "I remember him as a kind man."

Giselle tried very hard not to cry for the grandfather she'd never had the chance to know.

"Do you recall the story of his daughter's marriage?"

"She married . . . I cannot recall the man's name. And then she was gone," Lady Amice finished in a hushed tone.

"Aye, I heard that much of the story," Piers said, pacing the room. "What of her husband?"

Lady Amice shook her head. "I am sorry. I do not remember anything about him. Perhaps Rand would know more."

"Rand?" Giselle asked.

"My brother. I shall write to him, if you like."

Giselle splayed her hands on her skirt and nodded. "Please. I would know if my . . . father yet lives."

"Of course." Lady Amice looked at her with sympathy. "This must all be quite shocking for you."

"That would be the least of it, my lady." Giselle gripped the fabric of her bliaut to stop her hands from shaking. She felt the heat of Piers's hand on her shoulder and instinctively leaned into it.

"Worry not, my lady," he said. "We shall find out the remainder of your past, and persuade the king of your position."

"I fear I cannot even conceive of myself having a 'position,'" she said faintly.

Lady Amice rose. "Gifford, we shall continue this discussion anon." She gave him a sharp look. "In private."

Gifford cocked a brow and took a swig of ale. "As you wish, my dear. But, I tell you, I saw—"

"Cease." Lady Amice cast a sideways look at Giselle.

"Well," Gifford began.

The stern look in Lady Amice's eyes stopped him short.

Giselle was too caught up in her own discoveries to even care they were clearly discussing Gifford's claimed sighting of a ghost.

"Giselle, I shall write to my brother at once."

"Thank you, my lady."

"I should be about my own part in this business," Piers said. "Giselle?" He eyed her with clear concern.

"I shall be fine," she said faintly.

Gifford stuck out his flat chest. "I shall keep the girl company. Perhaps I can teach her a thing or two."

Piers quirked a grin. "Keep an eye on him, my lady. One never knows what mischief my uncle shall plunge himself into."

"Hrmph." Gifford waved a hand. "Go on, both of you. Our Giselle is safe in my hands."

As Piers and Lady Amice left, Gifford's words rang through Giselle's half-numb mind. *Our Giselle.* She shook her head, trying to puzzle through everything that had just happened. It was simply too much to take in.

"Thought he wouldn't aid you, eh?"

Giselle slowly gazed up at Gifford, who stared at her with one brow lifted. "I did not know what to expect."

"If you can reclaim Kindlemere from that thieving Bishop, you could petition for an annulment. I assume."

Giselle colored. "I suppose I could."

"Be a mistake, though."

Giselle swallowed a sip of ale, thoughts whirling though her mind too fast to comprehend.

"Likely, the king would just hand you off to one of his favorites. Some fawning sycophant, no doubt. You'd do better to stick with Piers."

"He does not want me." The words jumped out, an ugly truth Giselle had not intended to share with Gifford.

Gifford laughed. "I think you are mistaken, my lady."

A hollowness settled into Giselle's chest. "Perhaps he does, in the way he apparently wants just about any available woman." Her mouth turned down. "But he does not want me for a wife, for myself."

Gifford patted her hand. "I am not sure about that. But—"

"What?"

"Well, it is just that Piers is a complicated man. He is much more than appears on the surface."

Giselle recalled the man who'd kissed her as if he never intended to stop, and shivered. "Aye."

"Give him a chance, my lady."

Giselle stood, suddenly needing to be outside the castle walls. "I can do no less for the man who would aid me in recovering my birthright," she finally said.

Gifford gave her a contemplative look, and went back to mixing some kind of concoction in a pot.

And Giselle escaped into the morning sunshine, utterly at a loss as to what to do.

Chapter
XII

Lady Iosobal of Tunvegan Castle and the Isle of Parraba snuggled into her husband's arms and studied the note sent by Piers Veuxfort.

Her husband, Lugh MacKeir, nibbled on her ear. "What does he say?"

" 'Tis bad, Lugh. Very bad."

"A woman turned him down finally?" Lugh asked, chuckling.

"Nay." She turned and gave him a chiding look. It had no effect but to bring a grin to his face. If she were honest, she would admit she had never had any intimidating effect on Lugh MacKeir. Thank God.

"You are looking most fierce, lady wife."

"I told you not to go into my cave."

He raised a brow. "Aye, I ken you did not wish me to discover who you really were."

She let out a breath. " 'Twas more than that. That cave . . . even I do not know how many chambers it holds, nor what may be hidden inside them."

"What has this to do with Piers?"

"Read." She handed him the piece of parchment and watched the color slowly leech from Lugh's face.

"By the saints, what can be done?" Absently, he rubbed her arms. "Who is this Fin Man?"

Iosobal leaned against his broad chest, marveling yet again she had found a man so accepting of her unusual ancestry. "Some of the Fin Folk earned their fearsome reputations. Bringing storms upon unwary travelers. Kidnapping young women to keep in their hidden island homes. There is a tale of one, more powerful than most, whose rapacious appetites knew no bounds."

"And this . . . thing has possessed Piers?"

"So it seems." She shook her head. "It must be horrible for him."

"We must aid him." Lugh shot to his feet, his hands automatically reaching for his sword.

Iosobal had to smile at his typical ferocity. "Your blade will not vanquish a spirit."

Lugh scowled at her, then slowly smiled. " 'Tis my way."

"Aye, and I love you for it, but we must think of other means in this instance."

"Can you not just," he waved a hand, "make this spirit go away?"

"I am not sure. I have never tried anything like that."

"We must go to Falcon's Craig."

"Aye." Iosobal worried her lower lip.

"What plagues you, my heart? Surely the Lady of Parraba is more powerful than one old Fin Man."

She smiled. "Pray that I am."

Lugh gave her a smug look. "I've no need of prayer. I know my wife."

"We shall leave on the morrow. Einar can look after Ailie."

"She will wish to come with us, you know."

"Not this time. I would not expose her to this."

"You are worried."

"Aye. Very."

Lugh sighed. "Then, we shall leave Ailie at home where she is safe. It will probably cost me one of Argante's foals."

Iosobal smiled, though her thoughts were grim. She had an idea, but it would be dangerous. Far more dangerous than anything she'd ever done. She stared down at the note, silently cursing Piers for his reckless curiosity.

Perhaps this was God's way of forcing her to face the heritage she'd always hidden from.

"Iosobal?"

She realized Lugh was staring at her.

"I am going to parlay with our daughter."

"Good luck."

"Aye." He turned to go, then stopped and pressed a kiss to her forehead. "Are you all right?"

"Yes. I must think on this."

"We shall rid Piers of this cursed presence."

Iosobal nodded her agreement, but inside she prayed the cost would not be as high as she feared.

❦ ❦ ❦

Piers studied the missive he'd written to King John and handed it to Cain. "What think you of this?"

Cain stretched out his long legs and read. "Very well done. John cannot ignore this, no matter how much the Bishop of Ravenswood has apparently ingratiated himself with the court. And your offer to pay a fee for settling the matter will no doubt draw his attention."

"If he believes us," Piers said with a frown. "No doubt the priest at Kindlemere is long gone."

Cain rubbed his chin. "Gone from Kindlemere, but perhaps not yet dead."

Piers shot up, hope and purpose washing over him. "Burness Abbey lies not far from Kindlemere."

"Send to the Abbot."

"Aye." Piers quickly scrawled another letter.

"Has Simon left for London?"

"He leaves on the morn." Piers sighed. "I wish for Giselle's sake he learns her father lives, but I fear one of us would have heard of the man if 'twas true."

Cain leaned forward. "Piers, assuming the king acts as he should and returns the St. Germain estates to Giselle, you need not feel responsible for her."

Piers froze and stared at his brother. "Annul the

marriage, you mean."

"Aye." Cain waved a hand. "Though I shall ever be grateful to Giselle, naught has changed about the kind of woman she is. I do not wish to see you in a loveless union."

Piers opened his mouth to agree with Cain, but instead said, "I would not feel right to abandon her now."

Cain narrowed his gaze. "Do you care for the girl?"

Again, the words Piers meant to say didn't come. "When she is not going all stiff and pious on me, she is . . . I don't know. There is something about her that brings out more in me than simply the urge to mate."

"Well, that is news indeed." Cain grinned at him.

"Aye. Unfortunately, I find myself wanting Giselle as well, even without Eikki's demands."

"If you take the girl, there will be no going back."

Piers ran a hand through his hair. "I know. And I won't until I rid myself of this cursed presence."

Cain stood and clapped a hand on Piers's shoulder. "You know that I shall support you in whatever you decide to do about your marriage."

By Saint George's sword, was that a tear threatening to form in his eye? "I know. I think I should not make any decision on the matter until I know if the king will restore Giselle's birthright."

"Then you'd best keep Eikki under control." Cain looked so troubled Piers forced a light smile to his lips.

"Do not worry. I'll not let that whoreson make me

do aught I do not wish."

Cain picked up the sheets of parchment and sealed the letters closed. "I shall dispatch messengers with these."

After Cain left, Piers simply sprawled in his chair, staring at nothing. Did he care for Giselle? Could their marriage become one in truth? *Take the chance fate has handed you, and set the girl free,* he told himself. *She can turn Kindlemere Castle into a place of worship and not have to worry about being chained to a pleasure loving man possessed by the essence of evil.*

But, by God, he couldn't do it. Not yet. *You're a selfish bastard,* he told himself.

And he wondered if his vow not to claim his wife would turn out to be as fragile as the look in her eyes.

❧ ❧ ❧

Giselle sat on the sand, her legs pulled up under her, staring out over the sea. Giselle St. Germain. Giselle de Sauvin. The names rolled through her mind. Edward de Sauvin. The Earl of Kindlemere.

It struck her that she really no longer knew who she was.

Heiress? Bastard child? Novice? Nun? Wife?

As she continued looking over the endless blue water, a question popped into her mind. *Who do you want to be?*

For the first time in her life, it appeared she actually

had choices.

With that realization came another, though it was hard to bear. Even if the Abbess of Kerwick Abbey welcomed her back with open arms, she would not wish to return. Her heart ached with the loss, but she could not lie to herself. Kerwick had been a refuge, one she had not chosen.

She spilled sand through her fingers, thinking.

"Giselle?"

She looked up to find Piers standing over her. "It has been done," he said as he settled himself on the sand beside her. "Messengers are on their way to the king and to the Abbot of Burness Abbey. I have someone leaving on the morn for London."

Giselle swallowed, an image of the bishop's furious face leaping into her mind. "The Abbot of Burness Abbey? What has he to do with this?"

"Cain and I thought it was worth finding out if the priest who married your parents yet lives."

"My parents." She hung her head. "I do not even know who my father is."

"It matters not to your claim on Kindlemere, but . . . I understand your concern that you're not the legitimate offspring of your mother and her husband."

"How could you possibly understand?" She waved a hand toward the immense walls of Falcon's Craig. "You have always known who you are, where your rightful home lies. I only learned my surname today."

"Because I know that I am, in truth, illegitimate."

She looked at him in shock. "What?"

He gave her a wry smile. "Aye, though I did not know it for many years. My mother—." he broke off and shook his head. "Be glad you did not have the misfortune to meet her. She was obsessed by another man, the Earl of Holstoke. I am of his blood, not my . . . father's."

"Oh." Before she could stop herself, she put her hand on his arm. "I am sorry."

He nodded. "Other than Cain and Gifford, you are the only other person who knows."

A tingling warmth began in her belly and spread. "Thank you for telling me."

"Now you understand why your legitimacy, or lack thereof, matters naught to me."

"Aye." Giselle sucked in a breath. "Piers, if the king restores Kindlemere to me, you, well, you need not feel responsible for me. We could . . . seek an annulment." She found herself looking into his eyes, scarcely able to breathe.

"Is that what you want?" he asked softly. "I know I am not the kind of man you ever expected to marry."

Giselle smiled. "And I am just as sure I am not the kind of woman *you* expected."

"No." He smiled back at her and the warmth in her body expanded. "What say you we wait and see what transpires? Once we regain Kindlemere for you we can discuss this again."

"You sound so sure."

"You are not alone anymore, Giselle. I promise you I shall do all in my power to regain your birthright. Regardless of how it came about, now you have family. Allies."

Tears stung the back of her eyes. "I never thought to have a family."

He stood and reached down his hand. "Well, now you do. Let us go in. I feel as if my belly is knocking against my ribs."

She put her hand in his and let him lead her toward the great hall. It was so comforting she simply clasped his hand and walked.

"Perhaps we can finally persuade you to try Cook's lamb."

"I believe I shall."

His frank gaze of approval warmed her to her toes.

ॐ   ॐ   ॐ

Giselle tied off a stitch on the tapestry she was embroidering for Lady Amice. On a nearby window seat, Amice gently rocked little Meriall, who was finally succumbing to sleep.

"I never imagined one small babe could be so demanding," Amice said with a sigh.

Giselle glanced up. Amice's hair was in disarray, and her eyes were cloudy with exhaustion. "Why do you not hand her off to a nursemaid?"

Amice smiled down at Meriall. "I cannot bear to do that. She is mine."

"Is it not customary to do so?"

"Aye, but . . ." Amice smoothed a tuft of hair on Meriall's tiny head. "It means so much to me to be able to hold her. I never thought to be able to bear a child."

"Why not?"

Amice looked at her and sorrow clouded her features. "When I was younger, I . . . lost a babe. He was Cain's, but we were not wed at the time. Cain had left me to marry his mother's choice, to do his duty to his family. I was so grief stricken I . . ."

"Oh, my lady, I am so sorry. I did not know."

"Of course not. Not many know the story."

Giselle bit her lip. "Gifford told me that a ghost brought you and Cain back together." She could hardly believe she was even saying such a thing, considering it might be truth and not delusion.

"Aye." Amice gave a small laugh. "I can see you find that hard to believe."

"The existence of ghosts is something I have never contemplated, my lady."

"Please, call me Amice. And it is true. Poor Muriel refused to leave Falcon's Craig, and devoted herself to tormenting Cain so much that he sent for me."

"Ah."

Amice's face took on a dreamy expression. "Aye, It

was difficult, but Cain and I, well, it turned out neither of us ever lost feelings for the other. And Muriel eventually reunited with the spirit of Cain's ancestor, who had treated Muriel much the same as Cain did me."

Giselle's eyes widened. "That must have been fascinating."

"Aye, and rewarding. In the end, Muriel and Gerard taught both Cain and I a valuable lesson."

"What was that, my, uh, Amice."

Amice beamed a smile at her. "Why, to never run from love. To not let pride or duty blind you. To seize love with both hands and never let go for anything."

" 'Tis a sweet story," Giselle said, wondering what it would be like to find a love so powerful.

Amice covered a yawn.

"Would you like me to tend Meriall for a bit?"

"Would you mind? She should sleep for a while now."

"As should you."

"Thank you." Amice deposited the babe in Giselle's arms and stretched. "I would dearly love a nap."

"Do not worry. I am capable of holding her for a while. I shall fetch you when she begins to fuss."

Amice was gone before Giselle had settled the child in her arms. Giselle looked down at Meriall's tiny face and something in her chest unfurled. She could not stop staring at the babe, so perfect, so precious and small.

What would it be like to hold her own babe one day? she wondered.

But that would mean lying with her husband. Probably more than once. She shivered, beset by a strange tingling in her veins at the prospect.

Meriall disappeared from her vision.

Giselle was lying on her back atop a pile of furs, the chamber lit only by firelight. Naked. The fur felt deliciously soft against her skin. The strangest feelings rippled through her: anticipation, excitement, and above all, desire.

Over her loomed a man, but his features were shrouded in shadow. Big shoulders blocked the firelight as he bent over her, his skin hot.

He kissed her and she sighed in pleasure. Then his tongue was in her mouth, savoring her, stroking her. She moaned and pressed her body closer to his.

He skimmed a hand down over her breast, teasing her rigid peak, then moving down over her belly.

When he touched her center, she arched into his hand, keening her need. With each stroke, her body tightened until she was bucking against his fingers, blinded to everything but the rising sensations in her body.

His tongue stabbed into her mouth, and her body exploded, rapture seizing her and sending her over the edge of pleasure.

With a hiss, the man lifted her knees, posing her for him. She lay back on the furs, replete yet breathless with sharp expectation.

His manhood jutted from his body, big and proud.

She licked her lips, and she saw the shadow of a smile

277

on his lips.

And then he was inside her, stretching her, filling her so completely, so wondrously that she moaned yet again. The friction of him sliding in and out of her brought gasps from her throat, and the heat in her body built again.

She spiraled into the sky, screaming her release as her lover pumped into her, taking her with him.

Giselle stared down at Meriall, and wanted to scream. She wasn't sure if it was in horror or anger that the vision had ended. Who was the man? What did it mean?

She adjusted the babe in her arms, and stared out the open window. Again the question rose in her mind. What did she want to do with her life? If all went well, she could retreat to Kindlemere and live a simple existence, surround herself with prayer and the comfort of the Lord. Safe and secure from temptation. She could free Piers from a marriage he clearly did not want.

Or did he? She was no longer sure, no more than she was sure herself.

She shifted on the window seat slowly as to not disturb the babe. Her vision had left her with a tight feeling in her body. Even she knew it for what it was—frustrated desire.

She started to chastise herself, as she had so often over the years, then stopped. The Bishop and the Abbess had lied about her mother. She had not been the wicked seductress they painted, but a woman horribly violated by the Bishop. Why had he condemned her mother?

The answer came to her and she sucked in a breath. It was obvious. The Bishop could not accept that he would hunger for a woman, so naturally it must have been the woman's fault. He had poisoned the Abbess with his version of her mother's character, and of course she had believed him. Why would she not? He was a respected man of God, while she, Giselle, was simply a penniless orphan who was fortunate to have a roof over her head.

So, they had lied, made her believe something inside her was bad, so bad only a strict life in seclusion would save her.

She allowed herself a small smile, imagining the Bishop's surprise when he was confronted with her discovery.

"Now I know him for the lying thief he is," she told Meriall.

She felt as if a monstrous weight lifted from her shoulders, as if she were suddenly free and light.

Cuddling the babe close, she closed her eyes.

Perhaps . . . perhaps there was a chance for her to find a place of happiness in her life.

And perhaps, just perhaps, the very man who denounced her had inadvertently handed her that chance.

🐎 🐎 🐎

Clarise cornered Piers as he exited the training field. He was sweaty and weary from fending off Madoch's attacks, and wanted nothing more than to pour a bucket of water over his head and sit down somewhere. At the sight of her, arms crossed, her expression both smug and determined, Madoch slipped away.

She sauntered toward Piers, her crossed arms lifting her breasts so they overflowed her plain, brown bliaut. "My lord, may I speak with you?"

He sighed. "I think you should feel free to call me by my given name, Clarise."

Her face brightened, and Piers was tempted to take back the offer. "I have missed you," she said, sidling closer. She put a hand on his arm.

"I am busy these days, Clarise." Out of the corner of his eye, he spotted Giselle looking down on them from a window, and cursed under his breath.

Clarise pursed her lips. "Aye, I heard of the nun's discovery." She smiled. "Now you can send her away."

Piers gritted his teeth. "The king has not yet granted our petition."

"Surely he will." She inched closer until she pressed her body against his. "Do you not miss me, my . . . Piers?"

He glanced up in time to see Giselle duck out of sight. "Clarise, you know I enjoyed your company, but I am wed. You shall have to seek your pleasure elsewhere."

She pouted her lips. "But no man satisfies me as you do. And your . . . wife, so devoted to her prayers. Does she pray while you take her?"

Piers stepped back. " 'Tis none of your affair."

"No, she does not, does she? Because she denies you her body, denies you your rights as her husband."

A ripple of anger spread through him. *The wench is right*, Eikki hissed. *Your wife shows you no respect. She is good for little else. She has no skills, save embroidery and an endless ability to pray.*

The hell of it was that Eikki was right. Piers looked up at the window where he'd spotted Giselle, but saw nothing. She hid from him, even now, when he'd taken up her cause as his own, shown her naught but kindness and patience. "Clarise—"

"I can give you ease," she said, purring the words. "You know that. You deserve that."

He shoved her away. "Find another to lie between your legs, wench. Leave me be." He stalked past her shocked face toward the tower where Giselle no doubt was even now engaged in prayer.

🦎 🦎 🦎

After shrinking from Piers's sight, Giselle made her way to their chamber and took up her rosary. Desperate to find some sense of peace and place, she began saying the familiar prayers. They had always soothed her, connected her to a higher power, but today, all she could think about was that as she said her prayers, her husband was lying with another woman.

Why does it bother you? she asked herself. *If he takes*

his pleasure elsewhere, he shall not bother you. Still, the images that floated through her mind refused to cease.

Somehow, she had become possessive of her husband. She hated the thought of him being in another woman's arms, claiming her body the way he'd . . . Oh, dear Lord, she thought. Was Piers the man in her vision? She clenched the rosary tight. Who else could it be? Her visions were not always true, she reminded herself. Despite the dire fate she'd seen for Lady Amice and her babe, that destiny had not befallen them.

But, if not Piers, then who?

Captured by her whirling thoughts, it took her a moment to realize the door to the chamber had swung open. She glanced around and, to her shock, found her husband standing there. She clutched her rosary to her like a talisman as she stood. "I thought you would be busy with Clarise," she said, appalled at the shrewish tone of her voice.

He gave her a cold smile. "I could be. She is willing enough."

"No doubt."

He strode into the room and perched on the edge of the bed.

Giselle backed toward the window seat, apprehension unfurling in her belly. This was not the Piers who showed her humor and kindness, but the one who held coldness in his gaze.

"I have been thinking of our marriage," he said.

"Oh?" She tried to feign calm, but knew she'd failed when his expression turned knowing.

"If we remain married and Kindlemere is restored to you, it shall be our responsibility to see to the estate."

Her eyes narrowed. So, he would accept the marriage if it would gain him Kindlemere, she thought.

"What skills do you possess to manage such a large holding?"

"What?" An examination of her suitability to such a task was the last thing she expected him to say.

He gave her a patronizing look. "Have you experience in overseeing the ordering of supplies?"

She shook her head.

"Directing the cook?"

Again, she indicated no.

"Ensuring the linens are washed and changed?"

"Nay."

He continued with a long list of duties, many of which Giselle did not even understand. And none of which she had been taught to do.

Finally, he leveled her with a stare. "If I understand correctly, you cannot manage an estate nor see to its defense if I am absent. You can make tapestries, heal when needed, and, of course, pray until your knees ache with the effort." His mouth turned down. "You do not even know how to ride a horse."

Why the last stung so much, she wasn't sure. "I am improving."

He smirked. "I have yet to give you the full test. Wife."

Giselle lifted her chin, wishing her lower lip would stop trembling. "You know I have not been granted the kind of instruction that a lady of the castle would receive. I can learn."

"Can you?" He turned a lazy gaze to hers.

"I will ask Amice to instruct me in the duties of a chatelaine."

"What of the duties of a wife?"

Giselle flushed.

He stepped closer, so close that she could clearly see his eyes, dark with purpose and something else, something that sent a tremor of alarm and resentment through her. "Nay," he said. "I shall see to that instruction myself."

"Then do it," she snapped. "Or is threatening me, frightening me more enjoyable to you than the deed itself?"

"So, the little nun develops some backbone now she knows she is heiress to a large estate."

"Kindlemere has naught to do with this. I tire of your taunts. I tire of you being kind one moment, and . . . cruel the next."

Something indefinable flushed in his dark eyes.

"Perhaps 'tis a lack of womanly companionship that makes me . . . irritable."

She waved a hand at the window. "Seek out your whore. 'Twas clear she was all but begging for your attentions."

"That she was. But I find I've a taste for innocence."

Giselle stood her ground as he closed the distance between them, clutching her rosary in damp hands.

He brushed a loose strand of hair from her forehead, his gaze hard on hers.

"You will not . . ." Giselle gritted her teeth, "force me."

His gaze heated. "Nay."

Giselle opened her mouth to tell him to leave her be, but before she could utter a word, he kissed her. No, not a kiss she dimly thought, helplessly surrendering to the addictive taste and touch of him. A brand of possession.

He pulled her close and she could feel his arousal hard against her belly. Before she could stop herself, she found her fingers wound in his hair, holding him close.

When his hand skimmed over her breast, she gasped, the memory of her vision too fresh to stamp down.

Images flooded her vision.

Piers, his gaze soft and tender, looking at her as if he truly felt affection for her.

Two bodies, wound together, mating in a frenzy that bordered on violence. Sweat. Cries of passion. The slap of skin against skin.

And around them, a dark, crushing presence. Mocking laughter in the air.

Giselle jumped back and put her hand over her mouth, aghast to realize she was panting for breath.

Piers's eyes glittered like burnt amber.

"Why do you do this?" Giselle managed to sputter.

"Because I want you."

She swayed and sank onto the window seat. "Why?"

He laughed and the tension in the chamber eased. "You are a beautiful woman, Giselle."

She frowned. "Beautiful? Nay, my hair is too pale, my eyes too odd, and my body . . . is—"

"Lush."

Giselle snapped up her gaze at the reverent tone of his voice. "The body of a sinner, like Eve," she corrected.

"That sounds like a description by the Abbess," he said dryly.

"Aye." Giselle had to smile at the disgusted expression on his face.

"Believe me, there is naught at all wrong with the way you are fashioned."

Giselle's smile faded. "You *are* a something of an authority, I understand."

He lifted a brow. "I think of myself as a man who appreciates the unique flow of a woman's soft curves."

Giselle snorted, then blinked, astonished she'd made the sound. Doing such a thing at Kerwick would have earned her an immediate slap.

Instead, Piers gazed at her with a mix of curiosity and approval. "Come, my lady. 'Tis time for another riding lesson."

🐎 🐎 🐎

No wonder I am tense, Giselle thought as she struggled to find her rhythm atop Etain.

"You are gripping with your knees," Piers shouted. "Can you not feel it?"

Giselle flopped forward, and the horse thankfully stopped.

Piers eyed her with disdain. "That is an excellent way to find yourself on the ground in front of her hooves," he said.

"Perhaps I would do better if you were not hovering about, criticizing me," she snapped.

"I doubt it."

Losing control of one's temper has no place in God's grace, she told herself.

"I have an idea," Piers said, frowning.

Giselle was afraid to hear it. "What now?"

"You need to stop fighting her. Take your feet out of the stirrups."

"Why?"

He grabbed hold of Etain's bridle. "Just do it. We are only going to walk."

Giselle clasped the front of the saddle and shook her stirrups free.

"Now, sit straight and close your eyes."

"Are you mad?"

At that, he grinned. "Quite possibly, but not in this

instance." He clucked to Etain and she began walking.
"Close your eyes, Giselle."

Well, why not? she thought. *At least if I fall it will only be at a slow pace.* She closed her eyes.

"And breathe," Piers said.

What a strange sensation, she realized as she swayed along.

"Imagine your lower body is made of soft butter."

She felt her legs relax.

"Good."

After a couple of turns around the ring, Piers stopped Etain. "Take back your stirrups and try again," he told Giselle.

Giselle ached in places she refused to mention, but Piers's previous expression of disdain stuck in her mind, and she did as he said. Butter, she told herself, as she squeezed Etain forward.

"She is more interested in that servant walking by with a pile of dirty laundry than in listening to you," Piers said.

Ignoring him, Giselle kept going, dismayed to see the horse's head was indeed tilted, ears pricked, toward a young woman crossing the bailey. "Listen to me," she told Etain, but the mare just plodded along, giving no indication she'd heard a thing.

Softly, Giselle began singing her favorite hymn, a song to the Virgin Mary. When Etain's ears flickered back toward Giselle, she sang louder. She envisioned herself riding across the open grass, the sounds of music and song washing over her, and squeezed Etain into the trot. As they moved together, she sang louder yet, and by the time she brought Etain back to a walk, she realized she'd heard nothing from Piers for quite a while.

She found him standing in the center of the ring with a stupefied look on his face.

"By St. George's sword, you did it!" He was grinning at her. "Well done."

"Thank you." She rubbed Etain's withers, and whispered praise to the horse.

"You may become an adequate rider yet," he said.

His voice had changed. Giselle snapped her gaze to his. Was she imagining things or were his eyes a darker color?

"As for the rest of your abilities, well, we shall see, I suppose." With that, he turned and left her alone in the ring, sitting on a placid Etain and feeling the brief bubble of connection between her husband and her burst into nothing.

❧ ❧ ❧

The next morning, Giselle crept into the stables, savoring the quiet. It was not quite daybreak, but the dense cloud cover overhead promised a gray day. Etain stuck her nose out hoping for a treat, and Giselle offered her a ripe apple. As the horse happily munched, Angel craned his head out and fixed Giselle with a big, liquid stare.

Hesitantly, Giselle offered him the second apple. He plucked it gently from her fingertips, his soft lips brushing against her palm.

"Can I help you, my lady?" a man asked.

Giselle recognized him from the time Piers had attempted to ride Angel. "Nay. I am just exploring."

"A beautiful beast, is he not?" he asked, nodding at Angel. "A pity no one's been able to ride 'im."

"He seems so gentle," she said, stroking Angel's nose.

Michel scratched his head. "Aye, that he is, a true gentleman until some poor fool lands on his back."

"Has anyone but Piers tried to ride him?"

"Aye, a few grooms, but each time has ended in the same way, with the man eating dirt and being lucky to escape injury."

Angel nuzzled her hand. "Has any woman tried to ride him?"

"A *woman*? Oh, nay, my lady." He appeared horrified at the very idea.

A slow burn of anger wound through her. Of course, it could not be possible a mere woman could accomplish what the great horseman, Piers Veuxfort, could not. All at once, his contemptuous questions from last eve rang through her mind, ending in his pronouncement that she couldn't even ride a horse, seeming to sum up his conclusion on her lack of worth. She gazed at Angel, thinking, and the horse pushed against her arm.

"You need not stay with me, Michel. I am sure you have tasks to see to."

"Aye, my lady. There is no end to those in a stable." With a nod, he disappeared to the far end of the stable, his whistling blending with the scrape of a pitchfork.

Giselle took a deep breath and led Angel out of his stall. Glancing around her to ensure no one observed, she quickly saddled him and put on his bridle, hoping she'd remembered how to do it correctly. "Come on, boy," she whispered, patting his head.

Angel blew out a snort and meekly followed her into the fenced ring.

At which point, Giselle realized that she wore a gown. *Well, it won't matter too much if he takes off,* she told herself. *I won't be on his back long enough to worry about my attire.* "Now, boy, I need you to be good," she murmured. "I am just learning how to do this." She studied him, and he bent his head around to gaze at her. He looked relaxed, his ears twitching back and forth, his stance loose.

Before she could lose her nerve, Giselle hoisted up her skirts, put a foot in the stirrup, and swung onto Angel's back, fully expecting to be flung over the fence.

Instead, Angel let out a sigh and dropped his head.

Giselle tried to remember to breathe, and squeezed him into a walk. As Angel ambled along, she began to relax, holding the reins loosely and swaying side to side with his rocking walk. "What a good boy you are," she told him, stroking along his withers. "Good boy."

"My lady!" Michel shouted. "Get off that horse!"

She snapped a frown at him. "I am fine."

"But, but, he's a menace! Please, my lady. Get off before you get hurt."

"I am not going to get hurt." She ignored the pleading look on Michel's face and focused on her ride. *You can do this*, she told herself. *You can do this. Dear Lord, give me the strength and nerve*, she silently prayed.

"Come on, boy, trot!" She clucked at Angel and squeezed her legs. So smoothly she scarcely realized he'd done it, they were trotting along. Giselle let out a laugh, grinning like a fool as they sailed around the ring. I could ride all day on him, she thought. "Good boy!" she shouted.

And nearly fell off when she caught sight of her husband standing outside the ring. "By Saint George's sword, what the hell do you think you are doing?" he bellowed.

Angel tossed his head in annoyance.

"I am riding," Giselle yelled back. "And pray, keep your voice calm. You are plaguing Angel."

Piers's mouth dropped open. "Plaguing Angel?" he squeaked. "Do you remember nothing of my attempt to ride him?"

Giselle clucked at Angel to keep him moving and gave him a pat. "Of course I do. Just as I remember suggesting that Angel simply did not like men." She shot him a smug look. "Obviously, I was right."

Piers blinked, and then slowly smiled as he watched

them trot smoothly around the ring.

"No doubt, some *man* told you you were not good enough," Giselle muttered to Angel.

"Look at that, my lord," Michel cried.

"I see. You were right, Giselle. I should have heeded you," Piers said.

Giselle glanced at him in surprise.

"Angel is yours, lady wife."

Giselle settled Angel to a halt, eyeing her husband doubtfully. "You will give him to me? But, surely he is very valuable."

"I did pay a goodly amount of coin for him, true, but until now he's been naught but a waste of food and water." He tilted his head. "He belongs to you."

"Thank you." Giselle bent down and hugged the horse's thick neck. "Did you hear that, my sweet boy? You belong to me now."

Angel simply stood there, accepting her gesture of affection as if it were his due.

Beside Piers, Michel slowly clapped his hands. "I never woulda believed it, my lady, if I hadn't seen it with my own eyes. Just wait until I tell the rest of the men about this!" He grinned. "The nun has tamed the wild beast."

Something shifted in Giselle's chest as she dismounted. She turned to the groom, who was gleefully chuckling. "I am a nun no longer," she said.

Piers's eyes opened wide, but he said nothing, standing back to let her lead Angel back into his stall.

Chapter
XIII

That evening at supper, Giselle's ride on Angel was the talk of the castle. Piers didn't know whether to be proud of his wife or to take her aside and try to shake some sense into her. She'd surprised him yet again, his timid nun of a bride, who was turning out not to be so timid after all.

Dear God, he'd thought his heart would stop when Michel ran to tell him Giselle refused to get off that damnable beast. And then when he saw her, calmly trotting around the ring, a victorious smile on her face, a whole other feeling had taken over his heart.

"Well done, Lady Giselle," Gifford called down the table atop the dais.

"Thank you, Gifford," Giselle said softly as she sat beside Piers.

Cain slanted a look at Piers, then at Giselle. " 'Twas quite a brave thing to do, Giselle." His voice held a note of curiosity.

"Aye," Amice agreed. "I know well how to ride, but

I would not have risked climbing onto that beast."

Giselle smiled, a soft but undeniably triumphant smile. "I simply tested an idea," she said as she reached for a chunk of cheese. "I thought perhaps Angel's problems were due more to a fear of men than a truly wicked spirit."

"And so you proved," Gifford boomed, slapping his hand on the table. "Showed you, didn't she, nephew," he added with a chuckle.

Piers abruptly realized that was precisely Giselle's intent. And why. He cringed inside, remembering his harsh words denigrating her value, words more of Eikki than himself, but uttered nonetheless. "Aye, that she did," he automatically agreed, his mind dwelling yet again on what he could do to send Eikki back to whatever hell he'd been rightfully condemned to. Pray God that Iosobal would aid him.

He looked up to find Cain regarding him with an expression of concern. Piers forced his lips into a light smile and averted his gaze.

" 'Twas not my intent to . . . embarrass you, my . . . uh, Piers," Giselle said quietly, her fingers playing with the folds of her bliaut.

"Of course it was. And well-deserved."

Her gaze snapped to his, color staining her cheeks.

"I was unduly harsh with you, Giselle."

Her flush deepened, but she did not look away. "Your words were largely true. I do not possess the skills to be mistress of an estate like Kindlemere."

"A lack that is certainly not your fault."

"I tell you, I saw something," Gifford said in a loud whisper.

Amice tried to hush him, but he shook his head vehemently. Saraid put a hand on his shoulder, her expression fondly resigned.

" 'Twas in my workroom."

Piers grinned. "More likely one of those infernal substances you've got in there caused your mind to imagine things." He blinked when Giselle scooted her chair closer to his.

"Is he talking about a ghost?" she asked.

"Aye," Gifford answered. "I am, indeed."

"Gifford, please," Cain said, running a hand through his hair. "Not again."

"Why is that no one will believe me?" Gifford took a long drink of ale. "Damned bunch of narrow-minded souls." He pointed a finger at Amice. "You, of all people should heed my words."

"I believe you," Giselle said.

Piers about fell out of his chair. Even Gifford turned and stared at Giselle open-mouthed. "You do?" he asked, blinking.

"Aye."

Gifford grinned from ear to ear. "*Finally*, someone in the family with an open mind."

"I caught a glimpse of something in the chapel. No one save me was there, but . . . something assuredly was."

"Amice," Cain said, touching his wife on her arm. She shook her head.

"Well, any place this old is bound to have a few wraiths left knocking around," Piers said. " 'Tis nothing to worry about." He patted Giselle's hand.

She shot him a surprised glance. "I am not worried."

"Good girl," Gifford said.

Piers merely sat there trying to wrap his mind around the fact not only had his timid nun of a wife conquered Angel this day, but now calmly announced she'd seen a ghost without so much as a flicker of fear. He shook his head, wondering if he was not the only one possessed by another.

He continued to sit in silence and sip his wine while his wife participated in a discussion about the existence of ghosts that proved so spirited even Cain gave up trying to rein in Gifford's zeal for the subject. Of course, Giselle from time to time offered some bit of church doctrine on the matter, which Gifford genially listened to and then promptly ignored.

It struck Piers he had never observed his wife enjoying herself so much in the company of others. Was it simply that she now knew her heritage and stood to gain a measure of independence?

Or, dare he hope the rigid, pious woman he'd married was discovering there was another life for her, if she was brave enough to seek it?

He could only pray, he thought, his gaze moving to

the swell of Giselle's breasts as she responded to another volley by Gifford.

Pray hard.

❧ ❧ ❧

Aldrik, the Bishop of Ravenswood, read the missive from King John with mounting rage. He crumpled the vellum in his fist and tossed it to the floor. "Damn that bitch!" he roared.

"Interesting language for a bishop," Donninc commented from where he sat in the corner, calmly sipping the finest wine from Kindlemere's stores.

Aldrik flexed his fingers, overwhelmed by the wish it was the girl's slender neck between his hands. He sucked in a breath as Donninc retrieved the message from the floor. "How could she know?" He paced, stopping briefly to grab a cup of wine.

Donninc let out a low whistle. "You've been found out, my friend."

"I know that, damn it." Aldrik gritted his teeth. " 'Tis not to be born. Kindlemere is *mine*!" He gazed around the sumptuous solar, mentally comparing it to the one at Ravenswood Abbey. It was like comparing a chalice of wrought silver to one of chipped wood. *No*, he thought. *He would not, could not give this up.*

Donninc set the vellum down on a table and retook his seat. "Perhaps one of the sisters at Kerwick told her."

"No. I made sure none of those silly crows knew a thing, not even the Abbess." He narrowed his eyes to slits.

"I am surprised John would so quickly consider their petition."

"As am I." Aldrik barked out a bitter laugh. "Falcon's Craig may lie in the middle of nowhere, but rumour is that it is a wealthy estate. No doubt the Earl of Hawksdown eased his brother's way with coin."

"What shall you do?"

Aldrik looked at Donninc and saw the man appeared amused by the whole debacle. But that was how Donninc viewed life in general—through jaded amusement. Of course, Aldrik would be every bit as jaded as his half-brother too if, like Donninc, for years he'd been offered to numerous and varied guests of their father for their entertainment. "You were right. I should have dealt with the girl before when she was still under my control."

Donninc raised a brow.

"I can trust no one else to see to this matter."

Aldrik sat down opposite Donninc.

"What do you want me to do?" Donninc asked, taking another sip of wine.

"Kill them both. With Giselle gone and the earl's brother dead, the matter will go away. I shall assure John it was all a mistake, and the earl will have no reason to press the matter."

"Other than to avenge his brother's death."

"Ruffians abound everywhere."

Donninc's lips curved in a thin smile. "Any particular way you wish the deed to be done?"

"Nay. Use your imagination." Aldrik paused, his gaze boring into Donninc's. "As long as there is no tie back to me, I care not about your methods."

"Ah, an incentive indeed."

"Just get it done."

Donninc nodded and slipped out the door.

ॐ ॐ ॐ

"Truly, my lady, you should try it," Nona urged as she combed Giselle's hair. " 'Tis a luxury few can sample." She giggled. "The Lord and Lady seem to enjoy the bathhouse very much."

"So I gathered." Giselle had seen the structure of course, half-hidden in the depths of the gardens. She had never been brave enough to caution a closer look.

" 'Twill be just the thing to lift your spirits. Forgive me, my lady, but as of late, you seem a bit melancholy."

Giselle let out a sigh. Nona was right. Giselle felt as though she floated in a sea of waiting. Waiting to find out the king's response to their petition to return her birthright. Waiting to learn if the man she might be able to call Father yet lived.

And, if she were honest with herself, waiting to see if Piers would do more than give her heated looks, more than sleep beside her, all smooth muscles and heat, so close but never touching. Waiting to know if he intended to take the final step to making their marriage one in truth.

She shivered. "Perhaps you are right, Nona. 'Twill be a new experience."

Nona finished combing and gave Giselle's shoulder a squeeze. "And most relaxing, I imagine." The maid bustled about, gathering new clothing.

"It seems odd to be carrying clothing and such outside." Giselle swallowed, realizing that everyone she passed would no doubt guess she was on her way to bathe. "I am not sure about this—"

"Come, my lady, 'twill be fine and good. As you say, a new experience." Nona winked and pushed her gently out of the chamber. "The bathhouse is already stocked with scents and drying cloths. I shall run and have a groom make sure the water is heated."

Giselle opened her mouth to protest, but instead watched Nona scurry down the steps. She glanced down at Guinevere, who thumped her tail on the floor. "What could be the harm in it?"

The dog pushed her head against Giselle's legs.

"All right." Giselle slowly walked down the steps and out into the bailey, her shoulders squared as if she felt there was not a thing wrong with her course. She paused a handful of times, beset by uncertainty, but each time she reminded herself it was merely a bath and continued on. An image of the Abbess's horrified face crept into her mind, but she brushed it away.

Guinevere trotted beside her as they entered the gardens. Giselle let out a breath of relief to find no one about. "You'd best stay out here," she told Guinevere. The dog found a patch of sun and plopped down in the grass, letting out a snort and promptly closing her eyes.

Giselle cautiously edged the wooden door open. "Is anyone there?" she called. Her voice echoed off the stone walls.

The groom had worked quickly, Giselle thought as she took in the brace of burning candles lighting the small structure with pale gold light. She walked in and draped her clothing on a wooden bench. A cupboard sat against one wall holding stacks of folded cloth, and a line of stoppered vials stood next to the sunken area in the center.

She picked one up, took out the stopper and sniffed before smiling. Lavender, of course. Going to her knees, she swept her fingers through the water in the huge, sunken tub. It was blessedly warm. After pouring in a measure of scent, she sat back on her heels and stared into the water. Should she? Dare she?

Telling herself that Guinevere would surely bark if anyone approached, she quickly disrobed and slipped into the water. "Dear Lord, this is wondrous," she murmured as the warm, scented water covered her body up to her neck. Nona had been absolutely right—it *was* soothing.

And quite possibly the most decadent thing Giselle had ever done in her life.

She tried to muster up some reason why she should not enjoy the sensation so much, but failed utterly, the strictures she'd lived under so long refusing to come to mind. After finding a spot to lay her head on the edge, she closed her eyes and simply breathed in, feeling her limbs relax one by one until she floated free in the water.

Lost in unexpected delight, it took her a moment to realize she'd heard a sound. Her eyes flashed open, and she let out a squeak of surprise.

Her husband stood there silhouetted in the candle-light. "Giselle," he said, his voice low and smooth.

Her body immediately lost its languor, instead tensing in a wild combination of fear and excitement. "I, uh . . ."

He pulled off his boots.

Dear Lord, her throat was so dry she couldn't utter a word. Instead, she watched silently as he shed his clothing, revealing a body she'd come to know, in truth had come to crave.

But not, she realized with a hitch of her breath, as she wished to.

"You do not mind if I join you, do you?" he said, stepping into the water.

Giselle burned inside. All she could think of was the fact that only a warm shimmer of water separated them. "No."

He moved and Giselle noticed he'd brought a ewer and a cup with him. She held her breath as he filled the cup, bending down to reveal muscled buttocks and strong thighs.

Breathe, Giselle, she told herself. *It is only a bath.*

She knew she lied when he turned around.

As he walked toward her through the water, she tried to swallow, but found she couldn't. Dear Lord, the man was huge. Olive's words spilled though her mind, bringing with them a rush of heat. *She says Uncle Piers is built like a stallion, and knows very well how to use the gifts God has given him.* Now Giselle understood what she'd meant.

He sat down in the water beside her. When he looked down, he sucked in a harsh breath, and Giselle realized her breasts bobbed close to the surface. She started to bend forward, but Piers stopped her with a touch to her shoulder. "No. You are beautiful."

Giselle looked at him and saw his expression was taut, his eyes gleaming.

Carefully, he set the cup of wine on the edge of the tub, and took her chin in his hand. "I told myself I would not do this," he said. "But—"

"I want you to." Giselle couldn't believe the words had come out of her mouth.

With a groan, he pulled her onto his thighs and seized her lips in a bruising kiss. On and on it went, lips crushed together, tongues tasting, stroking, sucking. Giselle was dimly aware she sought as much as she gave, smoothing her hands over his shoulders, gripping tight.

His manhood was a hard, hot mystery pressing against her.

He pulled back his head with a soft curse and filled his hands with her breasts, his roughened fingertips brushing the tips, coaxing the hardened points into fullness. "Oh," Giselle gasped, and then gasped anew when he took one in his mouth and suckled hard.

She held onto his broad shoulders with everything she had, dissolving into need and heat as he worshipped the part of her body she'd always been ashamed of.

"You are beautiful," he said again, pressing an open-mouthed kiss to hers.

Lost in the magic of his mouth, she barely felt him ease her legs apart. Beyond caring, beyond embarrassment, she still cried out when he touched her. And touched her again, stroking circles against a part of her that instantly came to tingling life.

She panted for breath and found herself staring into his intense gaze. Dear God, it was all at once too much to bear, too exposed, but her body didn't care, seeking the touch of his fingers, her whole being shrunk to that one spot. "Piers," she gasped.

He slowly smiled. "Pleasure, Giselle. Give yourself up to it."

Surely this must be sinful, she thought, at the same time realizing she didn't care. His fingers moved faster, drawing the hot ache in her body into a sharp need, building and pulsing. She held on to his shoulders and rocked against his hand. More, she needed more.

He let out a growl and pressed inside her with his thumb.

Lights exploded behind her eyes and her body erupted. Giselle stared into Piers's gaze, absolutely spellbound by the sensations buffeting her.

For a moment, they simply gazed into each other's eyes. The water swirled around them, warm and fragrant. It was utterly still but for the labor of Giselle's breathing.

Floating in the mist of discovery, it took Giselle a moment to realize that Piers was stroking her back, at the same time edging her back onto her knees in the water.

When he lifted her atop his thighs and she came up against his manhood, her breath stopped.

He gazed at her with glittering eyes. "Pleasure, Giselle," he rumbled, and her body clenched in response.

As he drew her lips into a lingering kiss, he slid his hands down and lifted her over him. Slowly, so slowly Giselle nearly cried out to him to hurry, he lowered her, the head of his manhood slipping inside, then the hot, heavy length of him, stretching her, filling her. Dear Lord, she thought. She'd never imagined anything like this.

When he paused, she moaned.

Through gritted teeth, he said, "Your virgin barrier. By Saint George's sword, you are so tight, I . . .

Giselle wriggled and Piers briefly closed his eyes.

She knew she was missing something, but had no

idea what it was. "Piers. Teach me."

He thrust upward and Giselle cried out, a shaft of pain slicing through her. Piers simply held her close, not moving. The pain quickly slid away and Giselle wriggled again.

"You have all of me now," he said, his gaze hot on hers.

Giselle was so overwhelmed she couldn't speak.

Slowly, he began to thrust, deep strokes that seized Giselle's body in a storm of sensation. She kissed him, open mouthed, her tongue mating with his as he continued to surge inside her.

"Wrap your legs around my waist," he said with a groan. "Hurry."

When she did, he lifted her out of the water and laid her down gently on the edge of the pool, bracing his arms against the stone. "No," he said. "Gentle." A sheen of sweat shone on his forehead.

Again and again he plunged into her until Giselle thought she couldn't possibly draw a deep enough breath, couldn't possibly take any more pleasure.

But then his fingers found her again, and she realized she could. She cried out at the same time his face convulsed and he let out a long groan.

They collapsed on the stone floor, wrapped in each other, Piers making soothing noises as he stroked her arm.

Giselle told herself she should be mortified, but found her mind unable to chide her. "That was . . ." She coughed.

Piers chuckled. "Worth waiting for, I am thinking."

"Oh, yes." Giselle flushed and slid out of his arms.

He lay back, his hands behind his head, obviously at ease in his skin.

Abruptly uncomfortable, Giselle looked around for her clothes.

"You should soak in the water for a bit. 'Twill soothe you."

She was halfway to the drying cloths. He was probably right, she told herself. She slipped into the water.

Languidly, he rose. "I shall leave you to it." After pulling on his garments, he crouched beside the tub and stroked a fingertip down her cheek. "Otherwise I would be tempted to teach you a few other things this day."

Giselle was sure her face was scarlet.

He pressed a gentle kiss to her lips and left.

Giselle sank deeper into the water, telling herself to be grateful that he'd gone, but wondering with no small amount of curiosity just what he had in mind to teach her.

❧   ❧   ❧

Piers paused outside the bathhouse and collapsed onto a garden bench, his hands shaking. What the hell had he been thinking? He stared at the garden, seeing nothing, and fought for control.

Eikki had been there, just as he'd claimed, prodding, urging Piers to take Giselle with the kind of single-minded selfishness that would have left her weeping. It had taken everything Piers had to avoid succumbing to Eikki.

But you did, he reminded himself. You held on and loved Giselle the way she deserved, the way *you* wanted to.

It had not been without cost. Instead of feeling satiated and at ease, he was shaky and on edge, depleted by fighting Eikki's invasive presence.

He took deep, even breaths and prayed for Iosobal's quick arrival.

🦎 🦎 🦎

Giselle drew in the scent of the misty morning air and glanced at her husband. They rode across a rolling expanse of green, the castle far in the distance. A creek gurgled along in a dip to their left. At the edge of a forest, she spied the tawny head of a deer poking its head out.

" 'Tis a lovely day."

Piers gazed at the sky. "Aye, but I fear 'twill not last. I can smell the rain coming in."

"I do not smell anything but lush grass and wild primrose."

"You have not lived on the coast long enough yet."

She smiled at him. After the bathhouse, a wall had crumbled between them. Giselle found she was enjoying getting to know Piers very much.

"I cannot believe how well behaved that beast is for

you." Piers sounded so disgruntled Giselle had to laugh.

She stroked Angel on the withers. "He likes me."

"Aye. The creature has good taste at least."

The warmth in his gaze sent a tingle down to her toes. High overhead, a hawk flew, its shrill cry riding the winds.

"Let us trot until we reach that line of trees," Giselle said, pointing. "I need more practice."

Piers winked at her and spurred his mount forward. "I would be happy to provide it, my lady, in more comfortable surroundings."

Giselle giggled as she and Angel pursued Piers. The breeze shifted through her plaited hair as they rode up a slight incline. "I am talking about riding a *horse*," she called out, ruining the chastisement by giggling again. She focused on moving with Angel's rhythm, but he was so smooth, it was easy to do and she found her gaze roaming over the verdant countryside.

A glint of something in the trees caught her eye and she started to call to Piers.

Before she could, she watched in horror as he slid off his horse, landing in an awkward tangle on the ground. "No," she cried, kicking Angel forward.

When they reached Piers, his face was pale. "Go, Giselle. Ride for Falcon's Craig."

"But, you are injured. I—"

"Go!" he roared. "Now!"

Mired in indecision, she looked up and her blood

froze. A troop of men burst from the trees heading straight in her direction. "Oh, my God."

"Go, Giselle. Give Angel his head."

"I shall be back for you," she swore, before wheeling Angel around and kicking him hard. "Run, boy," she cried, too overwhelmed with fear to care that he burst into a gallop at her words, the ground rushing by at terrifying speed.

She glanced back to find her pursuers gaining on her, and wrapped a hand in Angel's thick mane. "Come on, Angel. Run!"

They caught her before she gained hailing distance of Falcon's Craig. Two men circled around in front of her, blocking Angel's path, while another came up beside her. He shot her a cold smile.

"What are you doing?" she demanded. "What did you do to my husband?"

The man plucked Angel's reins from her hands. "Has the little nun developed feelings for a man so quickly?" He laughed but it was not a sound of mirth. "An unfortunate thing, that."

"Let me go. I must seek help for Piers."

"I think not, Lady Giselle."

It dawned on her in deepening horror that he knew who she was.

She clenched her jaw. "Who are you? What do you want?"

"So many questions. So much spirit. The Bishop

would be impressed."

Dread gripped her in a harsh hold. "No."

The man nodded to one of his companions, and in moments she found herself face down, tied in front of her kidnapper.

"Bring the beast," the man ordered. "He'll fetch a fine bit of coin."

"Where are you taking me?" Giselle spat.

He slammed his hand against her cheek. "Shut up."

Her stomach roiling, Giselle did as he bade as they headed into the forest.

∽ ∽ ∽

Piers watched the men take Giselle, calling himself every bit a fool. He should have been more alert to their surroundings, but like a besotted simpkin, he'd been too caught up in his bride.

Fear for Giselle chilled his blood. The Bishop had to be behind this.

He had to get back to Falcon's Craig and gather help. Pain lanced through him as he struggled to a sitting position. "At least the bastard's aim was off," he told his horse, who contentedly nibbled on grass nearby.

And the mail shirt he'd worn beneath his tunic had deflected much of the arrow's bite.

He smiled grimly in the direction the men had headed. "You made a mistake when you did not stop to make sure your arrow struck true," he swore.

Pushing the pain from his mind, he crawled onto his mount's back. He kicked the horse into a gallop, gritting his teeth against the throbbing in his shoulder and praying he would not be too late to save Giselle.

🙴 🙴 🙴

Within minutes of being captured, the skies did as Piers had predicted and unleashed a torrent of rain. As she bounced along on her captor's horse, Giselle took deep breaths and focused on not heaving out the contents of her stomach.

Rain quickly soaked through her bliaut, and her hair hung in sodden tangles, soon muddied by flecks ground up by the horse's hooves.

Concern over Piers's condition overwhelmed fear for herself. She'd not seen how badly he was injured, but she had seen enough to know he'd been struck by an arrow and was bleeding profusely.

Please, dear God, save him, she prayed over and over. *I am the one who has provoked the Bishop's wrath. Please do not make Piers pay for it.*

Finally, Giselle felt the horse slow, and then mercifully stop. Someone jerked her off the animal, and she landed on her bottom on the muddy forest floor. She looked up at a cold, sharp-featured face.

"Can you build a fire?" the man grunted.

Dear heavens, was she to be subjected yet again to a criticism of her useful skills? she wondered, realizing the beginning of hysteria creeping into her mind. "No."

He snorted in obvious disgust and looked at the man still mounted. "Useless wench. Don't know what you want with her."

She cut her gaze to the other man, who laughed. He was a stranger, but something in his gaze seemed familiar.

"Open your eyes," he said.

"The Bishop ain't goin' to be happy about this," the third man said.

"My brother does not need to know everything. And he will *not* learn of this." He swung down from his horse and handed the reins to the man who'd tossed Giselle onto the ground. "Am I clear?"

Giselle looked around her, horror freezing her in place and at the same time demanding she run. She was in a dense, unfamiliar part of the forest. Trees pressed thickly in on them from all sides, and the skies were still gray though the rain had eased. She got to her knees and found a boot planted squarely in her chest, shoving her back down again.

"Oh, no," the man said. He chuckled, and Giselle's skin crawled. "You cannot outrun me."

"Who are you?"

He sat on a nearby log and gave her a sly look. "I am called Donninc."

"You are the Bishop of Ravenswood's brother?"

Humor lit his gaze. "Half-brother. Thankfully, I do not resemble him."

"Why . . . why are you doing this? My husband—"

"Is assuredly dead. Do not waste your thoughts on him."

Giselle sucked in a breath. "No. You lie."

"Do I?" He glanced over his shoulder at the other men tending the horses and starting a fire. "Hamon is an excellent archer. When he takes a shot, it's a killing blow."

"You bastard!"

He shrugged. "That I am. I am also the man who holds your fate in his hands."

Giselle curled her hands into fists and glared at him. "What do you want? I have no coin."

His laughter sent shivers down her spine. "I have plenty of coin." He fixed her with a stare that made Giselle scoot backward.

One of the men shouted, and the anxious neigh of a horse sounded through the small clearing. When Giselle's gaze snapped toward the sounds, she saw movement in the trees. For just an instant, she stared into round, yellowish eyes. Cai? Her heart leapt with hope.

The animal vanished.

"You have annoyed my brother most heartily with this claim upon Kindlemere."

Giselle stuck out her chin. "He stole it from me."

He appeared amused by her declaration. "He is most fond of the estate."

"He shall not keep it."

"Ah, but there I believe you are wrong, Giselle."

Her name sounded disturbing on his tongue. "I can prove I am Annora St. Germain's daughter."

"You do not understand. You will never have the chance."

Giselle's heart beat faster.

"Aldrik instructed me to kill you, of course." Donninc smiled. "But I cannot see the waste of so much beauty."

"You are . . . possibly my uncle," Giselle managed to get past her lips.

"I doubt Aldrik possesses the strength of seed to sire a child," he said coldly. "And clearly, you do not favor him. I understand that you very much resemble your poor departed mother."

"Who your *brother* ravished." Giselle trembled with rage.

"A family tradition, it seems."

It took a moment for his words to sink in. The moment they did, Giselle surged to her feet. "No."

He merely lifted a brow. " 'Tis your choice."

"I will not submit to you."

"Oh, you will," he said as he stood. "Sooner or later. I can be very persuasive."

She tried to run, but her limbs were so stiff Donninc easily caught her. "Let me go!" she shouted, beating against his shoulders.

Instead, he laughed. He dumped her on the ground once more. "I do hope you will not give me too much trouble." He leaned over and stroked a finger down her cheek. "I would hate to mar that silken skin."

Giselle's stomach clenched with fear.

"If you have needs to see to, now is your opportunity."

Her expression must have betrayed her intent. He wagged a finger at her. "I will give you a few feet of privacy. No more."

As much as she wanted to curse him and refuse, her body's demands would not wait. She slowly rose and headed toward the trees.

"After all, it's nothing I will not see soon."

She gritted her teeth and ignored him, accomplishing what she needed to as quickly as possible and returning to the clearing. As bad as the other men undoubtedly were, she held onto the faint hope Donninc would not forcibly take her in their presence. When she saw him watching her, she wasn't so sure.

"Good girl. Do as you're told and we will get along very well." She flinched when he brushed his hand against her cheek.

"I will never do as you bid me. You waste your time."

"Would you rather die?"

She glared at him and he chuckled. "I thought not," he said.

He dragged her over to a tree and bound her hands

behind her with a length of scratchy rope, securely fastening her to the trunk. Giselle closed her eyes and started to pray.

Chapter
XIV

Piers pounded into the bailey at Falcon's Craig at the end of his endurance. His wound had long ago turned from a biting pain to one searing down his arm, he was drenched by the rain, and his head was swimming.

He rode up to the great hall.

Someone spotted him and shouts rang out, but Piers was too focused on remaining conscious to know who it was. Arms lifted him from the horse and carried him into the hall. Through bleary eyes, he spotted Cain.

"By the saints, what happened?" his brother shouted. "Hawis, fetch Amice!"

Piers gripped Cain's tunic in his fist and took shallow breaths. "Giselle. The bastards got Giselle."

"Who? The Bishop's men?" Cain guessed.

"Do not know, but who else could it be? We have to go after her!"

Cain's face darkened. "*I* shall. As soon as we see to you."

Piers tried to tell him they could not wait, but he lost his battle with consciousness and closed his eyes.

∂ঙ্গ ∂ঙ্গ ∂ঙ্গ

Padruig was in the process of polishing his sword, an activity he found particularly soothing, when he heard Cai's distinctive scratch at the door. When he opened it, the wolf bounded in, his ears up. He gave a short whuffing sound, and then howled.

Puzzled, Padruig smoothed his hand over Cai's fur, looking for an injury.

Cai batted him on the arm with a paw and whuffed again.

"What is it, boy?"

The wolf ran to the door and then back to Padruig, before sitting on his haunches and tilting his head.

"Is someone out there?" Padruig picked up his sword and peered out the door, but saw nothing but a red squirrel scampering up a tree.

Cai gave what sounded suspiciously like a snort of disgust and ran to the upper level of Padruig's home.

More and more perplexed, Padruig heard the wolf rummaging through things. When Cai ran down the stairs, understanding dawned. He carried a piece of Giselle's wimple in his teeth. The wolf set it down at Padruig's feet and whuffed again.

"Giselle is in trouble."

Cai trotted to the door and looked back.

"Aye, I ken." Grimly, Padruig fastened on his sword and packed on a few daggers just in case. "Lead on," he told the wolf.

Nose to the ground, Cai led him into the forest.

☿ ☿ ☿

As afternoon shaded into night, Giselle sat on the wet ground trying not to shiver and blanking her face of the mix of anger and fear pressing down on her. Earlier, she'd refused the scraps of dried meat one of the men had tossed her way and the offer of a skin of ale from a smirking Donninc. Her belly cramped with hunger, and her mouth was dry as sun-baked sand, but she could not bring herself to accept a thing from her captors.

Shadows lengthened while the men drank from their skins, conversing in low tones. From time to time, one of them would gaze her way. The speculative anticipation in their eyes suffused her body in cold dread. Donninc was the worst, his smug expression telling her he fully expected her to yield to him, whether by choice or by force.

Filthy whoreson, she thought, momentarily shocked at her choice of words, even unspoken. The description fit, however. Dear Lord, the man could be her uncle, and he didn't care at all.

Taking advantage of the fact she was far enough from

the fire to be cloaked in shadows, she worked at freeing her hands, tugging at the ropes until her wrists ached. Still she worked, praying for a small slip, something to help her get free and run once the men fell asleep.

"Are you cold, Giselle?" Donninc called over.

She glared at him. "Nay."

He laughed. "If you would like to move closer to the fire, I am sure we can make some . . . arrangement."

Share his blankets, he meant. "I would rather perish from cold," she said clearly. And meant it.

Not so much as a flicker of annoyance crossed his face. It was as if the man was crafted of cool steel, brushing off her insults and accusations as of too little importance to matter.

"Would have thought the wench learned her place in that abbey," one of Donninc's companions commented. Giselle had privately named him The Frog. His features were thick and coarse, his lips wide and full, his cunning eyes large and slightly protruding.

"Aldrik clearly allowed the Abbess to coddle her overmuch," Donninc responded.

Giselle wanted to laugh aloud. Coddle? If life in the service of the Abbess amounted to coddling, she would hate to . . . Her thought process halted when Donninc caught her gaze. She swallowed as best she could and resumed tugging at the ropes.

"Expect you'll take care the wench learns other-wise," the third man said slyly. Hatchet, she had named him, with his sharp, thin face and narrow, flat gaze. Next to Donninc, he scared her the most, eyeing her with blatant lust.

"I shall enjoy it," Donninc told him and smiled at Giselle.

The rope slipped a tiny bit, and she swallowed the denial she wanted to shout. The last thing she needed was to provoke him enough that he came over and noticed what she was doing. Between the pain in her wrists and the slippery feel of the rope, she was pretty sure he would see her blood on the rope if he cared to look. Instead, she closed her eyes and pretended to sleep, all the while working on loosening her bonds and listening to the men, waiting for them to sleep.

In the firelight, she'd seen Donninc's dagger. The man was so arrogant he left it sitting on a rock next to the fire.

She wanted that knife with a ferocity that shocked her. Not that she would know what to do with it. The very fact she could envision herself wielding it at all was horrifying enough.

Forgive me, Lord, she silently prayed. *I know not what is becoming of me. All I do know is that I cannot become that man's* . . . Her mind shied away from the word but it rang in her skull all the same. Whore. That was what he intended, he'd made no secret of it.

Lord, please aid me, she prayed and nearly gasped when she felt a section of the rope slip free. She stilled, listening closely to the sounds around her, peering toward the men under half-closed eyelids.

Two bundled shapes lay next to the fire. Snores rumbled from the men. Where was the third? she wondered, biting her lip. And which one was he?

Remaining still, she waited and watched until a shape lumbered back into the clearing. Hatchet. She felt his gaze upon her and barely suppressed a whimper of trepidation. The sound of boots shuffling though wet leaves came to her ears.

"You are not asleep," his voice whispered next to her ear.

Her eyes flashed open to find his only inches away. She pressed her back against the tree bark. "Stay away from me."

"And let Donninc sample the goods first?" He smiled, revealing a mouth of rotten and broken teeth. The stench of his breath made her gag. "I am thinking I'll break you in first."

She spit in his face.

In an instant, his arm was around her neck, cutting off her breath. "Bitch," he said softly. "You'll pay for that." He ran a hand down the front of her bliaut and twisted her nipple through the fabric. "Aye, you'll pay."

Giselle pulled at the ropes with all her strength. *Lord, aid me, please aid me*, she said to herself over and over. And then it happened.

Hatchet was so absorbed with pushing up her skirts

he never noticed she was free. Drawing a deep breath, she shut away all thoughts but survival and grabbed his dagger from his belt.

His last expression before she plunged it into his throat was astonishment.

Gasping for air, Giselle pushed him off her, and ran.

🦎 🦎 🦎

Cain paced the hall while Amice and Hawis tended Piers's wound. Though his brother had yet to wake, the wound did not appear as bad as they'd feared, Piers's mail preventing the arrow head from going in all way. "Thank God he had the sense to wear mail," Cain said.

"I do display a bit of sense on occasion," Piers remarked in a dry tone.

Relief thudded through Cain at the sound of his brother's voice.

"Should have taken a couple of the men too," Gifford told him sternly.

Piers's face darkened. "Aye, I know."

Cain watched as Amice pressed a poultice to Piers's chest and bound it into place with a length of linen. Piers was pale, but he pushed himself into a sitting position. "Give me some of that ale," he told Gifford.

For once, their uncle relinquished his jug without protest.

"Where were you when you were attacked?" Cain

asked him.

"About two or three leagues east of the castle." He moved again and winced, stopping to take a drink. "I will show you."

"Nay," Amice cried. "You cannot. You will reopen the wound."

Piers stared at her, his jaw clenched tight.

"She is right, Piers," Cain said. "I will find the place."

When his brother looked at him, his gaze was so bleak Cain's fury doubled. "The bastards took Giselle into the forest."

Cain nodded. "Did you recognize them? Anything about them at all?"

"Nay. They wore no colors."

"How many?"

"Three. I did see that much."

Cain put a hand on Piers's shoulder, sensing his shame at not protecting Giselle. "I shall find her."

"If it is indeed the Bishop behind this, he means to kill us both."

"He shall fail."

"What if—"

Amice shushed him.

Cain pressed a kiss on Amice's lips. "Take care of him until I return." He gave Piers a sharp look. "You will do as my lady bids. I vow I shall not return without Giselle."

Piers blew out a breath. "See if you can bring back one of the bastards alive. I would know who threatens us."

"If I can." Cain gestured to Rauf, a member of his garrison. "Gather ten of your men." He smiled thinly. "We are going hunting."

❧   ❧   ❧

Padruig crept through the forest, following Cai closely and listening for any sounds out of the ordinary. After the hard rain, the sky had cleared and moonlight sifted through the trees.

Cai loped along, pausing from time to time to scent the air, his long body taut with focus. Suddenly, the wolf stopped and lifted his head. In a moment Padruig heard it too, the sound of feet crushing leaves and twigs. He drew his sword and moved behind a wide oak tree.

A figure burst into sight, running without any effort to quiet its passage.

Before Padruig could try to stop him, Cai raced toward the person and uttered a short bark. To Padruig's shock, the figure dropped to his knees and put its arms around the wolf.

A sliver of moonlight glinted off pale hair, and Padruig realized the figure was Giselle. He rushed over and put his hand on her shoulder. She was crying, broken sounds that tore at his heart. "Giselle. 'Tis Padruig."

"Help. Please, help me."

Padruig removed his hand and realized it was wet. The coppery scent of fresh blood filled his nose. "Are you hurt?"

"Nay."

"Are you being pursued?"

"I . . . I am not sure."

"Can you walk?"

She sobbed in response.

"Come." He sheathed his sword and slung her into his arms. "Cai shall warn me if others approach. You can tell me what happened once we are safe."

She burrowed into his chest like a wounded bird seeking solace.

He moved quickly toward his dwelling, his senses alert for sounds of pursuit.

"You seem to making a habit of rescuing me," she said, her voice breaking.

"This time you appeared to be rescuing yourself."

At that, she fell silent and didn't say another word until they reached his home.

෴ ෴ ෴

Giselle couldn't seem to stop shaking, though Padruig's solid warmth cradled her and Cai stayed close as they moved through the trees. Dear Lord, she had killed a man. She closed her eyes tight, but the image of his face swam in her vision, blood pouring from his neck, his eyes wide in shock.

It wasn't until she heard the thump of a heavy door

that she opened her eyes. She felt her life playing itself over as Padruig gently deposited her on a stool and built up the fire. Cai sat on the floor next to her, his strangely knowing gaze fixed on her face.

"Drink this," Padruig said, pressing a cup into her hand.

She took a sip, and warmed wine trickled down her throat.

Padruig took the other stool. "You are safe now, Giselle."

"Thank you." She gazed into his calm eyes and let out a breath. Then she glanced down at her clothing and began shaking all over again. Her bliaut was soaked with blood. She moaned and closed her eyes.

"Giselle," Padruig's voice said close. "You are safe."

Dimly, she felt him unlace her bliaut, then her undertunic and lift them off. She'd opened her eyes, but a murky fog pressed down on her, trapping her limbs and blurring her thoughts. He ran a damp cloth over her face and arms, carefully cleaning each hand. Blindly, she reached out and found Cai's thick fur.

Within a few minutes, she found herself enveloped in one of Padruig's tunics. He tied a length of leather around her waist and sent her a faint smile. " 'Twill do for now."

"Please . . . Burn my clothes."

He nodded and gathered up the soiled garments, rolling them into a ball and taking them away.

Giselle stared into the flames and forced herself to calm. *It is over now*, she told herself.

"What happened?" Padruig asked.

With a cry, Giselle jumped up. "Piers! We must find Piers!"

" 'Tis full dark out."

She shook her head. "You do not understand. They shot him. They took me away. He was bleeding. He told me to run, and I did, but Angel wasn't fast enough and they caught me." She pressed a hand to her mouth but failed to stifle a sob.

Padruig held up a hand. "Slower, Giselle. Who?"

"The Bishop of Ravenswood's brother and two others," she spat. "Filthy whoresons," she added, fisting her hands.

"I thought the Bishop wanted naught to do with you."

"He didn't until I found out he'd lied to me, that he'd stolen my birthright from me."

Padruig nodded and stood. "What of the men?"

She rocked back on her heels, but managed to remain upright, digging her nails into her palms. "They . . . the brother meant to . . ." She flushed and met Padruig's angry gaze. "One tried to . . ." she gulped and stopped.

"I ken." Padruig calmly slid a dagger into his boot.

"I . . . killed him, Padruig," she whispered. "With his own dagger while the others slept." She didn't even realize she was crying until she felt him wipe her cheeks with the sleeve of his tunic. He held her close, rubbing her back as if she were a child.

"You did what you had to, Giselle. 'Tis no an easy thing, I ken."

"His face, he . . ."

"Earned his fate."

Giselle let out a breath. She would pray for the man's soul nonetheless.

"About your husband."

She stepped back. "We must find him."

"Aye. Cai," he called to the wolf. "Come." The wolf trotted to Padruig's side and followed them into the night.

ॐ ॐ ॐ

Piers awoke dripping with sweat, the edge of a nightmare slowly fading from his mind. Giselle, he thought and sat up in bed. His shoulder hurt enough that he gritted his teeth, but he stood and drew on a fresh tunic. Thankfully, his chamber was empty of a nursemaid to try to push him back into bed.

He threw open the window shutters to find it was nearly daybreak. Streamers of orange and gold spread across the heavens, lightening the gray sky. The shore was absent birdcalls, the only sound the soft rush of the waves against the sand.

His chest tightened as he made his way out of the chamber. No matter what anyone said, if Cain had not returned with Giselle, he was going after her himself.

When he entered the great hall, his mouth dropped open. He swayed on his feet, so overcome with relief he felt lightheaded. "Giselle," he croaked.

Her gaze shot to him, and she leapt up with a cry. In an instant, Piers found his arms full of his wife, her fingers touching his face, her mouth curved in a broad smile.

"I wanted to check on you, but Amice persuaded me to let you rest," Giselle said.

Piers slung an arm around her shoulder and made his way to the dais, where his brother sat, ringed by Amice, Father Michael, Gifford, Saraid, and . . . he blinked. "Padruig?"

The big man nodded. " 'Tis good to see you up and walking. Giselle was most worried for you."

Piers took a seat, shaking his head. "It appears I owe you thanks once again for rescuing Giselle. What happened?"

For a moment, no one spoke.

Padruig took a long drink of ale. " 'Tis Giselle's story."

Piers gazed at Giselle, who was staring down at her lap. "Giselle?"

She blew out a breath and lifted her gaze to his. "I . . . escaped."

Piers took her hand and felt the tremor beneath her skin. He also felt the pad of a bandage around her wrist and scowled. "The men were from the Bishop?"

"Aye." She frowned. "One was his half-brother, a man called Donninc."

"How did you manage to get away?"

The silence at the table grew heavier.

"They tied me to a tree, but they did not do a very good job of it. I suppose they did not expect I would be brave enough to try anything."

"Fools," Piers said, squeezing her hand.

She gave him a tremulous smile. "One of the men tried to . . . I loosened the ropes and stabbed him. Then I ran." She reached for a cup, but her hand was shaking so badly she knocked it over. "Padruig and Cai found me."

Piers gazed at her. He could read between her words enough to guess one of the bastards had tried to rape her. Anger surged in his belly. Anger and shame that he'd failed to protect her. "Well done, my lady. Well done." He pulled her close, and stroked her hair. "I am sorry I was not of more use to you."

She leaned into him, and her body relaxed with a long shudder.

"Bastard should pay for this," Gifford spat, slamming his cup down on the table. "Seizing an innocent woman, attacking Piers. 'Tis unpardonable! And by a man of God, no less."

"I do not believe the Bishop of Ravenswood can rightfully claim to be a man of God," Father Michael commented.

Piers shook with the strength of his fury. "Would the coward show his face at Falcon's Craig. I would enjoy sending him to meet his God." *He sent men to attack our woman*, Eikki growled. *Kill him*. For once Piers agreed with him.

"You cannot go after him, Piers," Cain said as if he'd read Piers's mind. "Not openly. The man is too allied with the king."

"Donninc told me the Bishop had ordered him to kill me," Giselle shouted, startling Piers so much he let go of her.

"You should stay within the castle until the matter of Kindlemere is resolved," Padruig told her. "I will remain as well."

Though the implication he could not protect his own wife rankled, reason won out and he gave Padruig a nod. "Another pair of eyes and a good sword arm would be welcome. Who is Cai?"

"Cai is Padruig's wolf," Giselle told him.

Piers blinked. "A wolf?"

Giselle smiled. "Aye. He is the one who found me."

Padruig nodded. "Aye, and led me to you."

"Well," Piers said. "Imagine that."

"I shall send word to the king of this perfidy," Cain said, his expression grim. "I suspect any relation of the Bishop's is cunning enough to absent himself. It will be Giselle's word against the Bishop's."

"What of Piers?" Giselle asked. "He was attacked as well."

"He is not able to identify the men," Cain said.

Piers put a hand on her shoulder. "Padruig is right. Stay close until the king grants our petition. Once Kindlemere is decreed yours, the Bishop will have nothing to gain by harming you."

Giselle looked at him, her eyes bright and shiny.

"Other than his hatred of me." She sucked in a breath. "I believe you are right, though. He is too cunning and protective of his position to risk losing it all." She covered a yawn with her slender hand.

" 'Tis time for you to rest," Piers told her.

"I am weary." She rose. "Do you need me to tend to your shoulder?"

He smiled at her. "Nay. Amice did a tolerable job."

His sister-in-law gave a huff from the other end of the table. "I shall send Nona to you, Giselle," she said.

Piers watched her leave, his heart heavy in his chest. By Saint George's sword, how close he'd come to losing her. He was tempted to follow her to their chamber, but told himself to leave her be.

Gifford chuckled. "Look at him, my dove," he said to Saraid. "Every bit as besotted as I predicted he would be."

Piers turned back to find all of them smiling at him with knowing expressions. He rolled his eyes and took a sip of wine. "I was concerned for Giselle, of course. She *is* my wife."

No one's expression changed. Even Padruig's usually impassive face held more than a hint of mirth.

Piers tried to frown but found himself unequal to the task. "Well, hell," he finally said and applied himself to food and drink.

❧ ❧ ❧

Instead of immediately seeking refuge in slumber, Giselle drew out her rosary, smoothing her fingertips over the golden agate. She curled into a spot on the window seat and gazed out over the sea. Guinevere padded in and thumped down onto the floor with a snort.

Well done, Piers had said, upon hearing she'd killed a man. Well done. The stones tumbled through her fingers.

What had she become? What had happened to the rules that had governed her life for so long?

One: Your only purpose is to serve God. As she threaded the rosary through her hand, she thought perhaps that was not her *only* purpose after all. The highest one, true, but surely God did not expect her to forsake living at the same time.

Two: Unless necessary for a task or in prayer, your voice shall remain silent. That may be so in the Abbey, but not at Falcon's Craig where the halls rang incessantly with talk and laughter.

Three: Idleness is a sin. She tilted her face toward the weak sun. No, she'd not been idle exactly, but at the moment idleness held a great deal of appeal.

Four: Your body must be a pure reflection of God's grace. Are not all of God's children a reflection of His grace? As to the pure part, well, she'd lost that, and if she were being honest with herself, it happened at the moment she'd first laid eyes on Piers.

Five: Honor God by imbibing simple food and drink. Somehow, she didn't think good wine, lamb in a garlic and saffron sauce, and apple tarts qualified as simple. She sighed.

Six: To flaunt your body is an offense against God. She thought back to the bathhouse, and shivered. The way Piers had looked at her, his brown eyes darkening as he stared at her breasts had made her feel such warmth in her belly she knew if that was flaunting her body she would do it all over again.

Seven: To covet possessions is against God's will. She stared down at her finely woven, blue bliaut, and then looked around the chamber, the wide bed piled with soft covers, the carved trunks against the walls. The comforts were far from her mean cell at the Abbey, and she was glad of it.

Eight: Hard work is a tribute to God's greatness. Well, she hadn't toiled as she'd done at the Abbey, but she had not been completely idle either.

Nine: The only purpose of fornication is to bear children. She looked down at Guinevere and flushed. An image of Piers's face at their wedding supper sprang into her mind. *They lied,* he'd said, with that beguiling grin of his. Heat flooded her face as her mind traveled once more back to the bathhouse. "I have definitely strayed from that rule," she told Guinevere, who responded by thumping her tail.

Ten: Obey and submit to those in authority. Number ten was sounding more and more to her as a way for the Abbess to ensure Giselle did whatever the Abbess directed.

Eleven: Displays of emotion are coarse and vulgar. She'd displayed more emotion in the last month than she had in the past fourteen years of her life. "And it feels good," she said defiantly.

Twelve: You must resist temptation, for it is the work of the devil. On that one, she saw nothing but Piers, gloriously naked, reaching for her, touching her. Her husband was one temptation she feared she'd lost the ability or interest in resisting.

And she had killed. In her own defense, to be sure, but killed nonetheless. She swallowed thickly, remembering the look of shock in Hatchet's narrow eyes, the blood pumping from his throat. She drew in a shaky breath and said a prayer for the man's soul.

"I did what I had to do," she said aloud, and stretched out on the bed. Guinevere jumped up and settled in next to her, laying her furry head on Giselle's stomach. Giselle hugged the dog close and shut her eyes, praying she could shut out all of the thoughts and doubts swirling in her mind.

But as she drifted in that hazy state between sleep and wakefulness, another place slowly crept into her mind.

A high-backed, heavily carved chair, the top of a man's head coming into view. He sat in a vast solar, lit by a crackling fire and candles along the curved walls. The chamber smelled of woodsmoke and the vinegary scent of sweat.

"I can still see your face," the man's voice whispered to no one. "Still smell the scent of roses on your smooth skin, still remember your smile. Oh, yes, that smile. Taunting me, tempting me."

The man stood and strode across the solar, picking up a silver chalice. He turned it so that it caught the firelight. "You were the only one who ever guessed my secret. Beautiful, bewitching Annora, with eyes far too perceptive." He cracked out a bitter laugh and tilted his head back, drinking from the chalice.

"You knew, yet you sought me out that night. Sought my counsel." He flung the chalice against the wall.

"And like Adam, I was unable to resist the temptation." He dropped to his knees and sobbed.

Chapter
XV

"Y ou cannot be serious," Aldrik said slowly, punctuating each word with a slam of his fist against the table. A jug toppled to the rush floor, but he ignored it, glaring at the pathetic lump of humanity before him.

"There weren't nothin' we could do, your grace. Somebody must have helped the wench get away."

Aldrik fisted his hand. "Why was she still alive?"

The simpkin shifted on his feet.

"I see." Aldrik's gut clenched at the realization of Donninc's weakness. "He thought to enjoy the girl first."

"She *is* a comely bit of a thing," the man said defensively.

"So, Donninc kept her alive until he could get her somewhere to enjoy her. Why was no one watching to make sure she didn't have the chance to run?"

"Tom had the first watch, your grace. We found him with his own dagger in his throat."

"Convenient. Where is my brother?"

When the man's gaze slid away, Aldrik knew Donninc had gone into hiding. Most likely, this quivering minion had no idea where.

Confirming his suspicion, the man shrugged. "I do not know, your grace. He sent me to deliver the news to you. That's all I know."

"What of the husband?"

"Got to be dead. My shot was true. We all saw the man fall."

"Well, that is something at least." Aldrik picked up a cup and twirled it in his hands. "I see I shall have to take care of this matter myself." He allowed himself a thin smile. "Fortunately, I was smart enough not to depend on Donninc to accomplish the task to my satisfaction." He waved a hand. "Get out."

The man sidled to the door.

"One more thing. If you happen to see Donninc, tell him not to bother coming back. I have no use for fools and liars."

After Donninc's man left, Aldrik let out a growl of frustration. A simple task he'd set his brother to accomplish. It should have been easily done.

How he hated the girl. Hated the weakness she represented, hated her face, so much like her dam's.

It would have been so easy to rid himself of her when she was at Kerwick. An accident on the stairs, a random attack by an unknown intruder, just the right amount of nightshade in her food? Yes, he'd thought of all those things each time he laid eyes on her.

Well, he still had a few weapons in his arsenal. While he would have liked to see the girl dead, banished and forgotten would have to suffice.

Either way, he would never give up Kindlemere.

ক্ক ক্ক ক্ক

Iosobal sat in her solar at Parraba surrounded by books, so frustrated even the sight of her beloved husband carrying honey cakes and sweet wine did not lighten her mood. Lugh sat down next to her and shoved some of the books aside to make room for the platter, ewer, and cups.

"I cannot find anything about Eikki." She waved at hand at the tomes in disgust. "No reference to him, let alone how he became imprisoned in the crystal."

Lugh rubbed his chin. "What of the cave? Are there more books there?"

She blinked and smiled. "Mayhap." She snuggled close to him and laid her head against his firm shoulder. He put his arm around her and dropped a kiss on her forehead. "How did I gain the good fortune to have a man so wise?"

His chest moved beneath her cheek in a low chuckle. "Well, it was good fortune indeed. And luckily, I was aware of my great appeal enough to persist against your frightened efforts to push me away."

"Arrogant man."

"A lesser man would have fled the first time you leveled him with your Lady of Parraba look."

"My what?" She laughed and gazed up at his face.

His green eyes twinkled down at her. "The one where you lift your chin and gaze at a person as if they are naught but a worthless insect unworthy of a moment of your time."

"Oh." Iosobal flushed, knowing he was right.

"Of course, with my great wisdom, I quickly grasped that 'twas a defensive guise."

She smoothed her fingers over the fine wool of his green tunic. "I would agree with you, but I fear 'twould only fuel your arrogance."

"Every time I look at you I am humbled, my lady wife."

His solemn tone brought tears to her eyes. " 'Tis I who should be humbled."

Lugh gave a snort. "Enough of the love talk, wench. What say you we partake of a honey cake and a sip of wine before exploring your cave?"

"A fine idea."

ベ ベ ベ

It took Giselle only a few days to feel very much like a prisoner, albeit a well-treated one. Her chamber was the only place she wasn't watched. If she was in the solar working on Amice's tapestry, either Amice or a maid would be sure to show up with apparently nothing to do but engage in idle chatter. If she went to the garden, a guard was sure to follow, hovering at a discreet distance that somehow managed to annoy her more than if he'd simply walked with her. Michel, the stable groom, had taken to following her about the stables like a lost puppy looking for its dam. Her attempts to ride Angel, who had thankfully found his way back to Falcon's Craig, were so closely scrutinized she eventually gave up and just came to brush him and deliver a treat.

And Piers had turned into an aloof, brooding man she barely recognized. Each night, she retired and left a candle burning, waiting for him. Each night, the candle burned down and he did not come.

The only conclusion she could come to was that he so regretted consummating their marriage he could not even bear to lie in the same bed with her.

On the morn of the fourth day, she stopped by the kitchen to grab a chunk of bread and stomped toward the training field. She'd had Nona plait her hair in one long braid and put on the clothes she'd taken to wearing for riding.

If she was to have a husband who wanted nothing to do with her and the responsibility of Kindlemere, she decided she'd better learn something about defending herself.

As she neared the training field, she spotted Padruig engaged with a member of the garrison. Both men leapt and swung across the trampled grass, the clank of metal filling the morning air.

Giselle gnawed on her bread and watched.

Padruig must have spotted her, because he held up a hand to halt his opponent. Breathing heavily, he approached her with a grin. "Good morn, Giselle."

She swallowed the bread, wishing she'd had the foresight to bring a skin of wine. "Good morn, Padruig."

He wiped his forehead with the sleeve of his blue tunic. The morning sun threw his scars into sharp relief against the tanned skin of his face, but his blue eyes shone bright and clear.

"I have a boon to ask you," she said.

"I will not take you outside the castle walls, my lady. 'Tis not safe."

"Nay, 'tis not that. I wish you to teach me."

His brow furrowed. "Teach you?"

"Aye. How to fight. How to defend myself."

His grin slowly widened. "The nun has decided to become a warrior?" His gentle tone took the sting out of the words.

She put a hand on his thick forearm. "I cannot always depend on you to save me, friend."

"What of your husband? 'Tis his duty to see to your welfare."

Giselle bit her lip. "Mayhap, but I wish to possess some skills myself. I was fortunate, Padruig. Fortunate that foul man was too interested in what he found

345

beneath my skirts to pay attention to anything else, and fortunate the dagger found its mark. I do not want to depend on good fortune."

He eyed her closely. "Is there aught amiss, Giselle?"

The urge to crumble into tears and lean on his strength and understanding was overwhelming, but at some point during the restless nights awaiting her husband, Giselle had determined to nourish her independence. She gave Padruig a weak smile. "Much is amiss, as you know. My future depends on the whim of an unpredictable king."

"You shall have a home, regardless of the king's decision."

"I shall have a place to live, true." Her smile faded. "I am not sure I shall ever have a home."

Their gazes met, and he nodded. "I understand, my lady. I shall teach you." He set aside his sword, and handed her a dagger. " 'Tis the best weapon for you. A sword would be too heavy and cumbersome."

She stared down at the dagger in her hand and fought back a wave of revulsion, seeing a dark spurt of blood instead of the pale silver of the blade.

"As you know," he began quietly, "when you strike, you strike to kill."

Though her body trembled with the step she was about to take, Giselle made herself remember the expression on her captors' faces, Donninc's smug certainty he would use her body as he saw fit, the leers on the other men's faces; she made herself remember the terrible feeling of helplessness. She lifted her gaze to Padruig's. "Aye."

And her training began.

Cain was deep in thought trying to decide whether to commission a sapphire or opal necklace for Amice to mark Meriall's birth when Gifford burst into his solar, toting his usual jug of ale and aquiver with his typical exuberance.

"Cain! Cease languishing about and come see this."

"I am not languishing," Cain said without looking up from studying the drawing of the necklace's design. "I am about a very important matter."

Gifford peered over his shoulder. "Ah, a gift for the lovely Amice. Good idea, boy. That wife of yours deserves to be showered with jewels for putting up with you."

"As you can see, I am working on just that. I am thinking perhaps a combination of—"

"Think on it later. You have to see something."

"Has one of your experiments wreaked vast destruction?"

Gifford drew himself up and smoothed down his flyaway white hair. "Of course not. I am most careful."

"Is Falcon's Craig under attack?"

"If it were, I surely would not be standing here calmly discoursing with you. I would be seeking my sword."

"Gifford."

His uncle grinned. "Our girl is out on the training field."

At that, Cain started to pay attention. "Giselle?"

"The same. Come on now."

"Where is Piers?" Cain asked as he stood.

Gifford waved a dismissive hand. "Damn fool took off early on that beast of his. Galloping across the countryside, no doubt."

Cain frowned as he followed Gifford out the door. With each day that went by without word from Iosobal, Piers grew more distant, more on edge. He had tried to talk to his brother a score of times, but Piers had evaded Cain's questions, insisting he would be fine.

Cain was beginning to doubt it, and that scared the hell out of him.

"That brother of yours is a troubled man," Gifford commented as they walked across the bailey. "Hasn't been right ever since we left Parraba. And now he neglects his bride." He said the last with such disgust Cain had to smile.

"Perhaps you could offer him instruction."

"Tried. Boy's as thick-headed as someone else I know." Gifford halted and grabbed Cain's arm. "Look."

Across the flattened grass Giselle stood facing Padruig, holding a dagger and obviously listening intently to something Padruig was saying. Suddenly, she lunged, the blade flashing.

Padruig ducked the thrust, and took her wrist, showing her some adjustment in the way she held the dagger.

"Girl's not going to be caught defenseless again," Gifford said proudly.

"So it seems." Cain studied the two for a moment. "I am not sure what is more strange—the fact Piers's convent bred wife is learning to fight with a dagger or the fact her instructor is a scarred Scot with no past."

Gifford tipped some ale in his mouth. "Giselle is not the same girl who arrived at Falcon's Craig."

"Nay. Thank God."

"Padruig, though, he is a puzzle." Gifford eyed him over his jug. "Have you learned aught of him?"

Padruig had taken to lingering with Cain after supper while Amice settled Meriall and took some time to herself, but the man was far from loquacious about his background. "Not as much as I would like. He hails from the Highlands, but is vague on specifically where."

"Denies a clan as well. Odd, that."

"Aye. There is a story there, no doubt."

"Mayhap he did something to be banished from his clan and does not want to speak of it."

Cain studied the patient way Padruig dealt with Giselle and shook his head. "He does not seem the type of man to be guilty of such a deed."

"Perhaps it was not his fault. Perhaps another set things in motion that Padruig was powerless to prevent," a faint voice murmured, though no one else stood close by. At least, no one of flesh and blood.

Gifford's eyes bulged and he choked on his ale. He whipped his head back and forth. "Did you hear that?" he whispered.

Cain let out a groan. "Unfortunately, yes."

"I *knew* there was another one! Damned wraiths cannot let us be."

"Well, at least this one does not appear to mean us harm," Cain remarked dryly.

"I must speak with Amice at once." Gifford toddled off, taking frequent pulls from his jug and cursing to himself.

Cain turned to watch Padruig and Giselle parry. The girl had a natural fluidity about her. And Padruig was clearly a seasoned warrior. He reminded Cain of Lugh MacKeir. That was it, he decided. When Lugh arrived with Iosobal, he would put him on the mystery of Padruig.

If Iosobal arrived.

      ॐ   ॐ   ॐ

The king's messenger arrived that afternoon, an officious hanger-on by the name of Lionel Walmesley, who Cain had met several years ago when the man was no more than a purveyor of herbal "cures" to members of the court.

"He says he bears news from King John," Nyle, Cain's seneschal, said, standing in the doorway to Cain's solar, where Cain had retreated to once more ponder the right combination of jewels to adorn Amice's lovely neck.

Cain turned the pieces of parchment bearing the necklace design over and stood. "Find Piers and Giselle. I will greet our guest in the hall." He paused on his way out. "You might as well inform Gifford. He will be most unhappy if we leave him out of things."

Nyle chuckled. "As you say, my lord."

Cain found Lionel seated at the high table in the great hall, imbibing wine and staring covetously around him. As Cain walked across the rush-strewn floor, he saw Lionel leer at one of the serving maids, who, Cain was please to see, lowered her gaze and hastened her step. "Walmesley," he said. "Welcome to Falcon's Craig."

Lionel stood, a deferential expression pasted on his face which Cain was certain was patently false. "Lord Veuxfort. What a pleasure it is to see you once again."

Suppressing a grimace, Cain gestured for the man to sit back down. "I understand you bring news from King John."

"Aye."

"Regarding our petition on behalf of Lady Giselle?"

"The same." Lionel removed a sealed fold of vellum from a pouch and set it on the table.

Cain did not pick up the vellum. "My brother and his wife should be joining us anon." He was about to offer Lionel food when he saw a servant hustling in their direction with a platter heaped high. Clearly, Lionel had lost no time ordering to his own comforts.

"How does our honorable king fare?" Cain asked, though in truth he could have cared less.

Lionel shrugged and stuffed a large piece of cheese into his mouth, washing it down with wine. "Glorious as always. England shall never see a finer ruler than John."

Fortunately, Cain was saved from having to come up with an appropriate response by Amice's arrival. After exchanging greetings and, in Cain's mind, an undue amount of fawning compliments from Walmesley to his wife, Piers and Giselle came into the hall, quickly followed by Gifford and an obviously curious Saraid.

Walmesley's eyes widened at the sight of Giselle, currently clad in a pale blue bliaut. Her face was pale as whitewash, and she clung to Piers's arm. Though Cain much preferred Amice's dark elegance, he had to admit Giselle had an ethereal beauty that appealed to a man on an elemental level. He could not blame Walmesley for staring.

"You are from John?" Piers asked, nearly barking the question.

"Aye." Walmesley nodded to Giselle and Piers. "The king bade me tell you he has given your petition much thought." He gestured toward the vellum.

Giselle stared at it as if it contained venomous snakes.

"Piers," Cain said, handing him the vellum. "Let us discover our good king's decision."

Piers had to fiercely concentrate to keep his hands from shaking as he broke the royal seal. He'd not realized until this moment just how much it mattered to him to reclaim Giselle's birthright for her, to defeat the Bishop of Ravenswood if only by vellum and ink rather than the sword he would have favored.

He sensed Gifford creeping up to crane his head over Piers's shoulder, and felt Giselle's stark gaze on him.

Quickly, he skimmed through the greetings and expressions of surprise over the news of Giselle's true parentage. He halted near the bottom of the sheet, his heart thumping.

"Kindlemere is yours," he told Giselle. "He has granted our petition."

If Giselle had not been holding onto Piers's arm, she would have fallen. He eased her onto a stool and poured her a cup of wine.

Gifford let out a shout and twirled Saraid in the air.

"I am . . . amazed," Giselle said, staring at the vellum. "He believed us."

"The evidence was incontrovertible, my lady," Walmesley said, a cunning gleam in his eye. "Clearly, the Bishop of Ravenswood was in error."

Piers put a hand on Giselle's shoulder in warning. He sent her a look that told her to let it go.

"Has the Bishop been informed?" Cain asked.

Walmesley nodded, this time with a satisfied smile that told Piers he was no ally of the Bishop of Ravenswood.

"Hah!" Gifford exclaimed. "A celebration is in order. Hawis!" he bellowed, looking around the hall. He pulled

Saraid along behind him. "Hawis!"

"I have been instructed to carry the grant fee with me on my return."

Giselle looked up, obviously perplexed. "Grant fee?"

"It will be taken care of, as I stated in my prior missive to the king," Piers said. He squeezed Giselle's shoulder. "Do not concern yourself with that."

"But . . . but you have to pay to get back what should have been mine in the first place?" She sounded so indignant Piers found himself smiling.

" 'Tis simply the way of things."

"What is the fee?"

When Piers did not answer, she gave Walmesley such a fierce stare the man's mouth dropped open. "What is the fee?" she demanded.

"I, uh, fifty thousand shillings, my lady."

"Nay." Giselle jumped up, her gaze on Piers. " 'Tis a fortune. I cannot let you pay this."

"Of course I shall pay it, and gladly." Piers was dimly aware he was shouting. "You are my wife. 'Tis my duty and my honor to do so."

Giselle slumped back onto the stool, shaking her head as if life had suddenly become too confusing.

Piers knew exactly how she felt.

❧   ❧   ❧

Giselle strolled along the sand, Guinevere keeping pace

with her. Though a guard followed at a distance, Giselle was too mired in her own thoughts to care. Asides, she carried a dagger now, she thought with an inward thump of shock.

She felt so adrift she wasn't even sure where to start sorting out the bewildering morass her life had become.

One by one, recent events tumbled through her mind. The Abbess and the Bishop throwing her out of Kerwick Abbey, their patent scorn wrapping her in misery. Nearly being ravaged not once, but twice. Her marriage to Piers. The incredible sweetness of an act she'd vowed never to do. How foolish she'd been. How ignorant of life. And now, of all things she turned out to be not the baseborn orphan she'd been led to believe, but a titled woman with an estate.

She sank down upon the sand and put her hand on Guinevere's fur.

In the process of all that had befallen her, she'd broken just about every one of her rules and at this moment couldn't seem to care.

Idly, she sifted the cool sand through her fingers and gazed out over the sea.

The peace of the endless blue expanse washed over her, distilling her thoughts. Over all of the changes, all of her new experiences, everything that had occurred since that rainy day at Kerwick, one naked fact pealed through her mind.

There could be no annulment now. She was as

bound to Piers as he was to her.

Why her heart leapt at the realization she refused to ponder.

Giselle sat in the great hall that eve, determined to quell her doubts and uncertainties to revel in the satisfying news she would take back what the Bishop of Ravenswood stole from her. She smiled at the group of musicians playing on the left side of the hall, tapping her foot to the rhythm of the psaltery.

Masses of candles dispelled the shadows, and the fine silk of her deep blue bliaut felt rich beneath her fingers. Servants moved between the tables, dispensing ale and wine with a free hand, and the hum of a hundred conversations surrounded her.

It seemed to Giselle everyone was smiling.

Father Michel leaned near her. "I have not had the chance to tell you how pleased I am for you."

"Thank you, Father. It has all been quite a shock. I have to keep reminding myself to believe it."

The priest's eyes twinkled. "Your husband is proving to be a bit more of a man than you initially anticipated, I imagine."

"Aye." Giselle glanced around the hall, looking for him. She spied him walking in with Gifford and Saraid. He was laughing at something Gifford said, and the sight of him struck her like a bolt of fire to her belly.

How beautiful he is, she thought. He'd clearly come from a bath, his tawny hair still damp. An emerald colored tunic cloaked his broad shoulders and his face was alight with mirth. Many of the women's eyes followed him as he strode toward the dais, but Giselle realized with a shiver that he looked only at her.

Dear Lord, she thought. *How did it come to be that this beautiful, strong, loyal man is mine? Mine.* The very word sent a tremor of excitement through her.

"My lady," he said when he reached her side. His gaze slid over her. "You look most lovely this eve."

"Thank you."

The earl stood and the hall quieted. "I offer a toast this night," he called out. "To achieving what is right and defeating those who would threaten it." He lifted his cup and people called out cheers.

He drank deeply, sat, and gazed at Giselle with approval.

She lifted her cup. "My thanks to you for your support, my lord."

"You are family. No thanks are needed."

Her eyes burned as she took a sip of wine. Blinking, she turned to Piers. "And my thanks to you as well. I cannot convey to you the depth of my gratitude."

Piers leaned close and winked. "Oh, I can think of a way you can."

Giselle flushed, but inside her body warmed.

The rest of the supper passed in a haze. Giselle was sure she ate, drank, and conversed with those seated around her, but the heat of her husband's thigh pressed close to hers, his velvety voice, his smiles occupied all of her thoughts.

By the time he suggested they retire, her body felt like a tightly stretched bowstring.

When she thought of Piers's odd behavior of the past weeks, she decided it must have been the strain of awaiting the king's decision. Though she was still having difficulty accepting the idea, he seemed to genuinely consider the Bishop's theft of her identity and birthright as his personal battle to wage.

She'd made no secret of her early impressions of him. He probably feared that if the king ruled against them, she would perceive it as proof her first opinion was correct.

"What are you thinking?" he asked, breaking into her thoughts.

They were partway across the bailey. Torches cast wavering light at intervals, but it was dark and still save for occasional shouts by guards patrolling the walls. Giselle took a deep breath of the night air, fresh with a faint scent of woodsmoke.

Piers took her hand in his calloused palm. "Is aught amiss?"

"Nay. I suppose I am simply having trouble adjusting to the idea Kindlemere is ours. I wonder what it is like."

"I wonder what kind of stables it possesses."

Giselle laughed.

"Come, my lady."

"Are you terribly weary?"

He led her into their chamber, and turned with a mischievous smile. "Nay."

Giselle looked around her. Fat candles burned along one wall, while a fire sparked golden light. Upon a table near the bed sat a ewer and a pair of cups.

Piers put his hands around her waist. "I thought a private celebration was in order."

"Oh." Giselle licked her lips, suddenly shy. As many times as she'd revisited their time in the bathhouse, it still seemed like a dream to her, like something that had happened to someone else.

"Would you care for some wine?"

"Yes," she said softly when he released her and poured. She took the cup and perched on the window seat.

Piers sat beside her and simply stared.

Giselle was so nervous she could barely bring the cup to her lips without spilling the contents.

"Turn around," Piers said.

She blinked.

"I want to brush out your hair."

Her heart thumping, she shifted around so her back was to him.

"After your eyes, your hair was the first thing I noticed about you," he murmured as he uncoiled the plaits. "I thought at the time it was like wind-tossed silver."

A shiver rippled down her back.

He smoothed his fingers through the weight of her hair and drew a brush through it, smoothing out the tangles. "You looked like an angel," he said, pressing a soft kiss to the side of her neck.

Giselle just leaned back, lulled by the steady pull of the brush through her hair, the sonorous sound of Piers's voice making her feel beautiful beyond measure.

"I did not want a wife." He chuckled. "Particularly an angelic one." He continued brushing her hair and pressed a kiss to her temple.

Giselle simply sighed and sipped her wine.

"And, of course, you stared at me as if you'd suddenly swallowed something rancid." He nibbled on her ear.

"Mmm. I was in shock over finding myself here." With a start, Giselle realized Piers had unlaced her bliaut and undertunic. She jumped when he smoothed a hand over her breast, covered only by her thin linen chemise.

"But there was something about you, even then," he murmured, stroking a finger over her nipple.

A part of her wanted to squeak in protest, but his touch felt so wondrously good Giselle stamped it down.

"And that was before I knew you possessed the most perfect breasts God has surely ever fashioned."

Giselle tried to catch a breath and failed.

He lifted and turned her so she knelt facing him, his gaze so hungry Giselle shivered. Shocked at her boldness, she took his face in her hands and pressed her mouth to his.

With a groan, he hauled her atop his lap and plundered her mouth, his tongue stabbing deep at the same time his hands roamed over her body.

Giselle closed her eyes and gave herself up to the tempest of sensation.

She clutched his shoulders as he kissed her throat, her neck, and then drew the tip of her breast into his mouth through her chemise. Buffeted by spirals of heat, her eyes flashed open when she felt his fingers stroke the entrance to her body. His burning gaze consumed her.

Giselle let out a cry. "Piers."

He slowly smiled and flicked a finger over her skin.

The bowstring snapped. Her body clenched down and erupted.

"So beautiful in your pleasure," he whispered. The expression on his face was reverent.

Awash in the power of her release, Giselle forgot to be embarrassed.

He picked her up and laid her on the bed, slowly stripping her clothes, his gaze so frankly appreciative Giselle simply let him. In moments, his own clothing joined hers on the floor.

Dear Lord, he *is the beautiful one*, Giselle thought as he joined her on the bed, his warm hardness pressing along the length of her. When he nudged her thighs apart, she trembled with anticipation.

Then he kissed her, a tender claiming that spread

warmth through her body. "Open for me, Giselle," he said, and she did, gasping when he slid his thick length into her.

He rose up on his elbows, and began to move, thrusting almost gently, rocking her. She stared into his eyes, her entire being transfixed by him, feeling as if he'd crept into her very soul.

His features grew taut, and Giselle began to meet his thrusts, arching her body off the bed.

"Dear God," he rasped.

Pleasure built in her, a growing fire she couldn't control, didn't want to control. "Piers. More."

She saw relief spill over his face before he lifted her hips and took them both into rapture.

Afterward, Giselle felt absolutely boneless. And absolutely sated. She snuggled against Piers's hard chest and let out a sigh.

"Turn over," he said, his voice holding an edge.

Giselle blinked at him. "What?"

"Turn over and get up on your knees."

"What? Why?" She glanced down and sucked in a breath at the sight of his manhood jutting up against his belly.

He smiled. It was not his smile of moments ago, but one that sent a chill of foreboding down her spine. "Just do as I tell you." He flipped her onto her stomach and spread her legs.

Giselle tried to turn around but he held her down.

"What are you doing?"

"Taking you as I wish." His voice was so cold Giselle couldn't believe this was the same man who'd just brought her to such exquisite bliss.

She cried out when he slapped her buttocks. "Get on your knees."

"Are you mad? I am not—" Her voice broke off in shock when he yanked her to the side of the bed so her legs hung over the side. His fingers dug into her thighs.

"Or not," he said. "I can just as easily take you this way."

No, she thought. *Not like this*. She twisted around and stared at him. His eyes were like burning embers in his face, dark and fathomless. "Nay."

His lips twisted. "You are my wife. Your duty is to obey me, to ensure my needs are satisfied." He bent down and cupped her chin. "All of them."

She glared at him though inside she shook with fear. "Who are you?" she asked slowly.

"Your master."

"No. My husband, aye, but not my master."

" 'Tis the same."

"No!" She pushed away and fell onto the floor, scooting back against the side of the bed. *Something is wrong*, she told herself. *Very wrong*. Her vision played over and over in her mind as she stared at a man with cold eyes and a cruel twist to his mouth.

"Come now, little nun. You belong to me."

"I shall not submit to such . . . depravity," she hissed.

He chuckled. "Oh, we have not even started with that. And what difference does it make how I bury my rod inside your hot, damp body. You shall still enjoy it. You cannot hide that from me."

Giselle was so appalled at his crudity she could scarcely draw a breath. "No. Who are you? 'Tis as if you are two men. Even your eyes," she said pointing. "Who are you?" she shouted.

He seized her wrist in an iron grip and hauled her to her feet. "Bend over," he hissed.

Tears filled Giselle's eyes, but she glared back at him. "No, Piers."

At the sound of his name, his body heaved in a great shudder and he closed his eyes. When he opened them, they were golden brown once more. And filled with such bleak pain Giselle's heart turned over, desperate to hear his explanation but at the same time terrified at what she might discover.

"Dear God, I am sorry, Giselle," he rasped, striding across the room to fill a cup with wine, which he drained in one long swallow.

Curiosity overcame her fear, and she pulled a sheet over her nakedness. "What is this? You love me with such tenderness, and then . . . then you become a cold stranger."

He refilled his cup, and slowly turned. "That is because I *am* two men."

"That is impossible." She sank onto the window seat.

"It should be."

"I do not understand."

"No, of course not. How could you?" He drew on braies and sat on the edge of the bed cradling his cup. "But you deserve to know. To know what a reckless fool your husband has been."

Giselle stared wordlessly at him while he told her an incredible story. At the end, he bowed his head. "I should never have touched you, should have sent you away from this, but I was too selfish. Now you are bound to the demon I have become."

On wobbly legs, Giselle rose and sat beside him, placing her hand over his. "Not a demon. A man faced with a test from God, a challenge to your faith and honor. One I am certain you shall win."

He lifted his gaze, clearly stunned by her words.

"I shall aid you as I can."

"You . . . Kindlemere is yours now, or soon shall be. I release you from any bond to me. You can make a new life there."

"I shall not abandon you in this dark hour."

"Giselle . . ." He shook his head. "I know not how to rid myself of this curse I have wrought. Amice tried and failed. I . . . Eikki would have harmed her if Cain had not been there."

"God does not burden us with more that we can surmount."

"Do you truly believe that?" The hint of hope in his voice tore at her heart.

She stood and retrieved a cup of wine, suddenly parched. "I do, with every bit of my heart and soul." She laughed, but it was a broken sound. "Do you have any idea how I felt when the Abbess and the Bishop threw me out of Kerwick?"

He gave her a measured look. "They tore you from the only life you had known."

"Aye. From everything I knew. All that made me feel safe. *Everyone* I knew."

"Was there someone in particular?" he guessed.

"Sister Gertrude. She was a mother to me." Giselle scowled. "They did not even let me speak to her before they tossed me atop a horse and dragged me away."

"I am sorry, Giselle. If you would like to see her, I shall take you to Kerwick."

Tears filled her eyes. "I would like that." She gazed out the window. "When I arrived here, I was terrified, utterly lost, convinced that for my sins God had turned His back on me."

"What sins?"

She shrugged. "The Abbess always told me my soul was tainted."

"Old bitch," he swore.

"I realize she was merely repeating the Bishop's words." She turned back to Piers. "And now, well, I have gained a family, and a husband who cared enough to fight for me, things I never had and never thought to have."

He rose and took her hands in his. "I am afraid, Giselle. Afraid Eikki shall overcome me again and I will hurt you."

"I am not," she said, surprised to find she meant it. "You will not allow it."

His face crinkled in a smile. "You have much faith in me."

"Aye. And you must have faith in yourself. 'Tis what will save you."

Chapter XVI

The next morning, Cain sat in his solar, enduring Gifford's prolonged advice on Amice's necklace when he felt a cool draft of air cross his face. He looked up, expecting to see someone entering the chamber, but the door remained closed. With an inward shrug, he said, "Gifford, I have decided upon opals. They possess a fire inside that reminds me of Amice."

"Fine choice, Veuxfort," a man's voice said.

Gifford let out a screech as Cain leapt up, his hand going to his sword.

Lugh MacKeir gazed back at him with a huge grin on his face. To his side stood the most unusual looking woman Cain had ever seen. Her purple eyes stared back at him with a trace of amusement, as if she knew very well the effect of her appearance.

"MacKeir!" Gifford shouted. "Nearly scared me into losing my jug, man." He clapped Lugh on the shoulder, then took the woman's hand. "And Lady Iosobal, as lovely as ever. 'Tis wondrous to see you again."

The woman smiled indulgently at Gifford as he pressed a fervent kiss to her hand.

Cain was so relieved to see them he felt like shouting himself. He nodded to Lugh, then walked to Lady Iosobal, palms outstretched. "Thank you for coming, my lady."

Her gaze became solemn. "I shall do what I can," she said, placing her hands in his.

At the contact, Cain felt tendrils of warmth spread into his palms. He glanced at The MacKeir, who was still grinning like the besotted fool he undoubtedly was.

"By Saint George's sword, we shall have to have another feast," Gifford announced, then narrowed his gaze. "What do you mean, my lady?"

"He does not know?" Iosobal asked.

"Know what?" Gifford demanded, his mouth drawn into tight outrage.

Cain sighed. " 'Tis Piers's story to tell, Gifford."

"Knew that boy was hiding something," Gifford grumbled as he headed out of the solar. He paused at the door, his eyes softening as he looked at Iosobal. " 'Tis indeed well to see you both, no matter the circumstances."

"And you, old man," The MacKeir said.

"May be old, but I've still got my wits about me." The door slammed behind him.

Iosobal laughed. "I have missed him."

"Aye. He does add a bit of color to life," Cain said. "You must be weary from your travels. Let me find

Hawis to see you to a chamber."

The MacKeir laid a hand on Cain's arm. "We are not fatigued. And I would see this fair bairn Amice has been gracious enough to give you."

Cain felt his own besotted grin spill over his face. "She is a perfect beauty. Just like her mother. But . . . you have traveled far."

Iosobal coughed.

The MacKeir leaned close. " 'Tis one of the advantages of being wed to a woman of indescribable beauty as well as other talents. It took us only moments."

Cain's jaw sagged, and he looked from The MacKeir to Iosobal then back again.

"You look a bit pale, Veuxfort," The MacKeir said, clearly enjoying Cain's shock. "Perhaps we should find this Hawis and procure some wine before seeking your lady out."

"Aye." Cain shook his head. "Imagine that," he said as he led them from the solar. He tried, but found it impossible to do so. Magic, he thought with an inward cringe. Still, as they made their way toward the great hall, he reminded himself Iosobal's magic was quite possibly the only way to save Piers.

Eventually, after setting Hawis to fetching wine and a mountain of food to tide The MacKeir over until supper, they settled into Amice's solar.

"She is indeed a comely lass," The MacKeir proclaimed upon seeing Meriall. "As is her mother." He pressed a kiss to Amice's mouth, and Cain frowned. "I would like to make known my lady wife, Iosobal," he added, pulling Iosobal to his side.

Amice smiled. "I am so pleased to meet you. Piers and Gifford have told us much of you and your beautiful island."

"Parraba is a special place. Perhaps you and Lord Veuxfort shall come and visit it one day."

"I should like that. And Lugh," Amice said, "how fares Ailie?"

"Thank the saints and Iosobal, she is well. Near to driving me mad with her antics, though."

"Hmm, some justice in that," Cain commented.

"Hawis!" The MacKeir bellowed as the door opened, revealing the woman with a trio of servants behind her. "You are just in time. I am fair to starving."

Hawis directed the servants to setting about platters of cold meat, cheese, bread and an assortment of smoked fish. She set a jug on a table near to The MacKeir and smiled. "Do you require aught else?" she asked, directing her question to Cain.

"Have someone find Piers and tell him he is needed in Amice's solar."

She nodded and herded the servants out.

🐎   🐎   🐎

"You should have told me," Gifford said, frowning at Piers. "I knew something was amiss after you went into that accursed cave."

"He did not tell me either, until just last eve," Giselle told him

Piers held up his hands. "I thought to be rid of this ... thing afore I would have to admit my stupidity. And, Gifford, you were so enraptured with Saraid I did not wish to bother you with my problem."

Gifford tapped his foot and ran a hand through the white filament of his hair. "It would not have been a bother. You are my kin." He stared hard at Piers.

But not a legitimate one, Giselle thought, her heart aching anew for Piers.

"Iosobal is here," Gifford said.

"What?" Piers shouted. "Why did you not tell me at once?" He shot off from the stables.

Giselle had to run to keep up with him. "Who is Iosobal?" she said on a breath.

Gifford jogged beside her. "The Lady of Parraba."

His words held a wealth of meaning, but Giselle had no time to question him further. Within moments, they burst into Amice's solar en masse.

Giselle stopped short as Piers rushed to a strange woman. The woman was striking, with long dark hair and eyes of a purple color Giselle had never seen. She gazed for a moment at Giselle, and Giselle was struck with the thought that the woman's appearance was the least of her differences.

"Lady Iosobal," Piers said. "Thank you for coming.

MacKeir," he added, nodding to a huge man with black hair and piercing green eyes.

The man called MacKeir set down a jug and walked over to Giselle. He was so massive Giselle had the urge to flatten herself against the wall, but instead she made herself take a step forward and smile.

"Ah, you must be Piers's new bride," he said with a gleam in his eye.

"Uh . . . aye. I am Giselle."

He winked. "Piers, by the saints, you have found yourself an angel."

Giselle flushed when he took her fingers in his.

"I am Lugh MacKeir, my lady, Laird of Tunvegan, and the luckiest man in the world to call Lady Iosobal my wife."

Before Giselle could respond, he was pulling her across the solar, his meaty grip giving her no chance to refuse.

"Lady Giselle," Iosobal said in a melodic voice. "I am pleased to see that Piers has found his match."

The sense that Iosobal was something more than simply another woman grew in Giselle's chest when she smiled in greeting.

"Well?" Gifford barked. "Are you going to help him?"

Giselle flinched at his loud tone, but Iosobal merely turned to Gifford with a cool look. "That is why I am here."

"What can you do?" Giselle found herself asking,

almost afraid to hear the answer.

The MacKeir slung an arm around his wife's shoulder. "Iosobal is a great healer."

"But . . . Piers is not injured." Giselle frowned.

"Giselle," Piers said, taking her arm. "Perhaps it would be better if you—"

"She must stay," Iosobal interrupted.

Giselle looked back and forth between Piers and Iosobal. "I do not understand."

"I think you do," Iosobal said softly.

Thick silence blanketed the chamber. Giselle stared at Iosobal, but felt every eye upon her. "I . . . I know naught of expelling spirits," she finally said.

"Eikki is more than that."

Piers looked at Giselle's face, white as bone, and felt Eikki stir to life. *You think to defeat me with one of my blood?* he hissed. *Even she does not understand all that I am.*

We shall defeat you, Piers thought.

Even if you could deduce a way to be rid of me, it will be too late. Giselle will be mine.

No, Piers thought. *She shall never be yours. Never. I will kill myself afore I shall allow that to happen.*

Eikki chuckled. *Brave words, but death is forever.* He laughed again. *Or, at least, that is what I have been told.*

"Piers?" Iosobal was staring at him intently. "Are you well?"

He blinked. "Nay. This bastard increasingly bedevils me."

She took his hands, and heat spread up through his arms. Concentration narrowed her features, and the heat spread into his chest.

"Iosobal," Lugh said, putting a hand on her shoulder.

" 'Tis all right, love," she whispered.

For a moment, lightness flooded Piers, and he felt free of Eikki. He held his breath. Could it be this easy after all?

And then Iosobal stumbled back, and ice replaced the warmth in Piers's veins.

She gazed at him thoughtfully, then glanced at Lugh.

"What happened?" Cain asked, his expression revealing he'd already guessed.

"I have contemplated long and hard on this matter," Iosobal said slowly. "This," she gestured with her hand, "merely confirmed my thoughts."

Dear God, please do not let her tell me there is nothing she can do, Piers silently prayed.

"I cannot simply dispel him from your body," she told Piers. "I am sorry, but I feared such would be the case."

"What . . . what can you do?" Piers's mouth was so dry he could barely speak.

"Kill you."

Chapter
XVII

G iselle realized she had fainted when she looked up at Piers's face from the floor. For a moment, she merely stared at him. "No," she said, finding Iosobal. "You cannot mean that."

Piers lifted her into his arms and she clung to him.

"Let me explain," Iosobal said, accepting a cup from her husband.

A loud banging at the door interrupted her. "My lord?" a man's voice shouted. "My lord, we have a visitor."

"Damned poor timing," Gifford commented.

"It always is," Cain muttered as he opened the door.

Nyle stood outside. "I am sorry to disturb you, my lord."

"Who is it? Has Walmesley returned for more coin?"

"Nay, my lord." Nyle drew in a breath, glancing at Giselle who stood unsteadily on her feet. " 'Tis the Bishop of Ravenswood. He demands to speak with you at once."

Giselle let out a high cry, and swayed against Piers.

"Faith, my lady," he whispered in her ear.

Cain frowned. "To me?"

"Aye. He and his men await you in the hall."

"Who is this man?" The MacKeir demanded.

"The whoreson who ravaged Giselle's mother, hid Giselle in a convent, and helped himself to the estate she is entitled to by birth," Piers told him.

The MacKeir let out a hiss. "And he dares to show his face here? Why?"

"Good question, MacKeir," Cain said.

"Is . . ." Giselle swallowed, "is there a man called Donninc with him? Tall and lean, with pale gray eyes?"

"I saw no one resembling that description, my lady."

Piers growled low in his throat. "If there is, he shall not live to draw another breath."

The MacKeir shook his head. " 'Tis a good thing we have come, my love. Clearly, my aid is needed as well as yours."

Giselle's trepidation eased when The MacKeir puffed out his chest, put his hand on the pommel of his sword, and took Iosobal by the hand. "Let us see to this knave."

"I look forward to it," the earl said, and led the way.

꧁   ꧁   ꧁

The Bishop sat on a chair before the huge fireplace in the hall, his men gathered around him. All but the bishop were well-armed.

At their approach, he slowly rose, and his reptilian gaze flickered over Giselle.

Piers wanted to rip out the man's throat with his bare hands. He kept tight hold of Giselle and halted beside Cain. "You are not welcome here," Piers snarled.

The Bishop glanced at him, then away as if Piers were no more than a mildly annoying insect fluttering about his face. "My business is with the earl."

Cain placed his hand on his sword in a pointed gesture. The MacKeir moved up on his other side. "As my brother stated, you are not welcome at Falcon's Craig. State your business and be gone."

"No offer of refreshments? No comfortable place to rest before we undertake our journey?"

"Nay. And your men shall await you in the bailey," Cain said, crossing his arms. "Nyle?"

"Aye, my lord."

"See to it. Have Rauf keep a close eye on them."

The Bishop's mouth turned down. "I should have expected nothing more from a place on the edge of nowhere. Go." He gestured to his men.

"Is Ravenswood not close to the Welsh border? I understand the abbey has fallen into disrepair," Piers said. "You are no doubt anxious to retire there to rebuild."

The look of abject hatred the Bishop sent him brought joy to Piers's heart.

"This matter of Kindlemere has all been most unfortunate," the Bishop said, fixing Cain with a smug stare.

"I imagine it is indeed *unfortunate* to find your thievery exposed," Cain responded calmly. "Nonetheless, there it is."

"Kindlemere is mine."

"Not any more," Giselle spat. Piers looked at her and wanted to cheer. She held up her chin in defiance, her eyes blazing in anger. No longer a timid nun, he thought with approval.

The Bishop took a step forward, his face mottled with color, his hand half-raised. In a heartbeat, the hiss of three swords leaving their scabbards rent the air. "You would strike a man of God?" he asked, disdain tightening his thick features.

Piers forgot to respond, he was so shocked to see his wife holding a dagger in her hand.

"You do not deserve the title," Giselle said coldly.

"But, my dear, that is exactly who I am. An honorable man of God, devoted to the church and its teachings."

"State your business and be gone," Cain told him. "I tire of this game."

"Hmm, but it has everything to do with you. Or, more exactly, with your wife, who I understand recently delivered you a daughter."

A hard, cold seed of doubt stole into Piers's chest. He glanced at Amice, who held Meriall in her arms, her face pale.

"Aye, your wife, who is a *witch*," the Bishop spat.

Amice recoiled, but Iosobal caught her. The MacKeir moved to stand beside them, exchanging a knowing glance with his wife. "Wait," Piers heard him say.

Cain laughed. "You jest. You came all the way to Falcon's Craig to make such a ridiculous accusation?"

" 'Tis not ridiculous." The Bishop withdrew a sheaf of vellum from a pouch tied to his belt. "I have signed statements from two witnesses. Both say that *she*," he pointed a finger, "consorts with spirits."

"Would you like me to slay him for you, Amice?" The MacKeir asked in a casual tone. " 'Twould be a simple task."

"The pleasure should be mine," Piers snapped.

Cain held out his hand for the vellum.

With a look of triumph, the Bishop handed over the sheets.

Giselle was trembling so violently her fingers dug into Piers's arm where she clutched him. She glanced back at Amice but found her attention drawn to Iosobal, who fairly shimmered with fury. Iosobal took a step forward, but her husband held her back, murmuring something to her.

As if Padruig had his own brand of the sight, Giselle sensed his solid presence behind her.

Cain read over the two statements, then walked over to the fire and tossed them into the flames. "My wife is no witch," he said quietly.

"Burning those shall not take away my proof."

"Proof?" Cain raised a brow. "You shall never prove the Countess of Hawksdown is a witch. And consorting with spirits? If you dare to make such a claim, I will ensure you are treated as the madman you are."

The Bishop glared at him, then shifted his malevolent gaze to Giselle. "You are not worthy of an estate such as Kindlemere," he roared. "Daughter of a whore!" He advanced on her, and Giselle tried to remember to hold her dagger the way Padruig had taught her. "You are a *nothing*. Less than nothing. A weak girl whose soul is beyond redemption."

"Nay! And you are a lying whoreson," another man's voice shouted.

Giselle whipped her head around to the source of the voice. A man of middle years strode across the hall, his craggy features set into lines of pure rage, his eyes glittering with menace.

His turquoise eyes were identical to hers.

"It is no surprise you would stoop to threatening innocent women to pursue your craven goals," he barked.

The Bishop drew himself up and cast the man a disdainful look. "Who are you to cast such aspersions upon me?"

The man came to a halt and sent Giselle such a tender look her legs nearly buckled. "I am the Earl of Claybourne."

When the Bishop said nothing, the Earl of Claybourne continued, "I have just come from the king. It is only in honor of my wife's memory that you shall not be exposed for all of your crimes."

"I committed no—"

"Liar!" Giselle shouted, unable to listen to another word. "You *forced* my mother. Because of *you*, we lived without any of the comforts she knew. Because of *you*, my mother died without her family around her. Because of *you*, I did not even know who I was!"

"No—"

With a snarl, Giselle lunged, but Piers caught her in an iron grip. "Nay, my lady."

Giselle sucked in a breath and glared at the Bishop, whose face was white with shock. "Get out," she said, her voice every bit as cold as his had been that day at Kerwick Abbey. "Crawl back to Ravenswood, and pray the king leaves you even that."

For a moment, their gazes clashed, then the Bishop lowered his in defeat. Giselle could not resist a smile. "Nyle?"

"Aye, my lady."

"Will you do me the service of throwing this piece of refuse from the castle?"

Nyle's face split into a wide grin. "With pleasure." He seized hold of the Bishop's arm and dragged him from the hall.

"Too bad it is not raining," Giselle said.

Piers laughed and lifted her up, twirling her in the air before kissing her soundly.

"Hawis!" The MacKeir bellowed.

"Already on the way, laird," the older woman shouted, herding servants bearing the platters of food and jugs of drink.

When Giselle could breathe again, she turned her gaze to the Earl of Claybourne.

He held out his arms, tears in his eyes. "My child."

She threw herself into his arms.

❦   ❦   ❦

Piers stared into Giselle's horrified gaze, and realized he had no memory of what had transpired since they retired to their chamber. When he looked at her, really looked at her, nausea burned in his gut.

"Dear God," he whispered. She stared back at him, her hair in wild tangle around her face, her chemise rent down the front, and her mouth swollen. "What . . . what happened?" He took a step in her direction, but she backed away. At the same time, Piers realized he was naked. And powerfully aroused.

"Did I hurt you?" he finally managed to ask.

Her eyes were huge, pale jewels in her white face. She shook her head, the movement jerky. "Nay, not really."

Piers drew on a pair of braies, wincing when the fabric rubbed against his skin. "What happened?"

"You do not know?"

"Giselle, please." His gaze fastened on the tear in

her chemise, and raw fury erupted in his veins. *Eikki, you bastard*, he swore inwardly.

"You . . . I do not even know how to say it. 'Twas as if you became *him*. Your eyes, your voice, everything was different." She pointed to a mound of fabric on the floor. "You tore off your clothes. And then . . . then you began ripping my own."

Ignoring her expression of distrust, he gathered her in his arms. "Giselle, it was not me, you must know that."

She drew in a long, shuddering breath. "I do know, but 'twas so frightening."

"Go to Kindlemere. Leave on the morn. I shall send a score of men with you to ensure your safety."

"No." Giselle twined her fingers in his hair. "I shall stay."

He drew back and gazed at her, pain searing his eyes. "Do you not understand? I do not remember any of it! That bastard took control of me."

"I understand. I saw it all."

"Then you see you *must* go."

She smoothed a hand over his shoulder. "You stopped. Piers, you stopped him."

Frustration and fear ate at his gut. "This time. What of the next?"

"Iosobal—"

"Has a plan, aye, but . . ." He dropped his arms and walked to the window to gaze out at the star-filled night sky. "Will it succeed?"

"If not, we shall find another way." She stood beside him. "Look before you. Listen to the pounding of the sea. All of this is God's gift to us. *He* is where true power lies, not with a long dead and cursed man."

"Your faith humbles me."

"My faith sustains me. And it is why I know you shall banish Eikki for good."

"You should go. Leave me."

"I cannot."

He smiled at the fierceness in her voice. "My little nun has become a warrior."

She smiled back at him. "Aye, that I have, and I tell you it feels very good inside."

His angel, he thought, staring down at her, ethereal in the light of the stars and the moon. "I do not deserve you, Giselle. I never did."

"Well then, you shall have to work on that."

"I am not sure I possess the raw material. Go to Kindlemere. Make a new life for yourself."

"Cease. I am not going anywhere." She pulled at his hand. "Come to bed. In the morn, we shall see what we can do to dispatch Eikki to the hell where he belongs."

Exhausted, he let her tug him into bed. Once there, he gathered her in his arms and closed his eyes, his mind full of prayers and the desperate hope that a God he'd never paid sufficient homage to would hear him.

Giselle's eyes snapped open. The chamber was still and dark, the fire burned to embers. She listened for sound, but heard nothing.

Go back to sleep, she told herself, absorbing Pier's warmth. She closed her eyes, but sleep did not come. Breathing deeply, she pressed closer to Piers.

Sleep. Sleep. Sleep.

Shadows gradually parted, revealing a man lying on the floor, a woman crouched beside him. A heavy herbal scent hung in the air. Beyond the two, others stood in the shadows. Waiting.

Piers turned his head to someone just out of sight. His gaze was cloudy, the sound of his shallow breathing audible.

Iosobal knelt next to him, her palms on his chest, her face drawn into fierce focus.

Around them, a deep purple mist grew and swelled.

"Do something!" a voice cried. Giselle's voice.

No one answered her.

Piers writhed on the floor, his skin taut over the bones of his face. Tears spilled down Iosobal's cheeks as the mist thickened and grew colder.

"No!" a voice shrieked.

And Piers let out a long sigh, his eyes abruptly lifeless.

Giselle lay in bed staring at nothing for the remainder of the night, the cold dread of what she'd seen spreading across her limbs. The image of Piers's vacant gaze would not leave her.

He had died. And she had watched it happen.

Dear Lord, if you show me the future, why can you not show me how to change it?

❧ ❧ ❧

Lugh sat back in his chair and studied the man called Padruig. Other than sleeping servants, they were the only two left in the hall. "I am told you are most skilled with a sword."

"Aye." Padruig looked at him, his blue gaze wary.

"Perhaps you will indulge me in a bit of sword play on the morrow."

"Of course, laird."

"These Veuxforts cannot offer a mon good sport. Not Highlanders." Lugh leaned forward. "Like us."

"I left the Highlands long ago."

"Why?"

Padruig looked away. "I can still remember the crisp air of a fall morn, the sweet scent of heather on the spring air, the bracing chill of the loch."

"Which loch?"

"There are many, as you well know."

Lugh growled under his breath. "There is something familiar about you, Padruig." He tapped his fingers on the table. "Your clan?"

"I have no clan."

No clan, the man said. It was unthinkable. Lugh

slowly turned Padruig's words over in his mind. "You forsook your clan," he finally said. "And hide away here in the forests of England."

Padruig stood. " 'Tis my own business, laird."

"Had to be a lass involved."

At that, Padruig sent him a grim smile. "Is there not always?"

"I can use a skilled man at Tunvegan."

For a moment, a spark of utter yearning lit in Padruig's gaze, but then he shook his head. "My thanks for the offer, laird, but I shall never return to the Highlands."

Lugh frowned. "But—"

"There is naught for me there anymore." He nodded. "I shall bid good eve to you."

Lugh watched as Padruig left the hall, his stride long and assured, his shoulders broad and squared. *That is no simple clansman*, Lugh thought. He grinned and took a sip of wine. *Reminds me a bit of myself.*

Which would make Padruig the laird. Laird of a clan he'd abandoned. Lugh tried to envision ever doing so, and failed.

Still, the man had rendered aid to Lady Giselle. More than once, it seemed.

Lugh tossed back the last of his wine and left to seek out his wife. Perhaps Iosobal could divine the man's story. He smiled when he thought of the woman his wife had become. It was all he could do to restrain her from striking the odious Bishop down where he stood.

He was more than fair tempted to do the same himself.

Bad business, that. And Piers, wed to a lass who'd spent most of her life under the control of a convent. He laughed as he climbed the steps to their chamber, then sobered when he considered the dilemma Piers found himself in.

Though Iosobal refused to admit it, even to him, Lugh could tell she was concerned. Nay, more than concerned. His wife was afraid.

Chapter
XVIII

Piers stared at Iosobal, wishing he'd misheard her, but realizing with cold certainty he had not.

She gazed back at him, her purple eyes filled with a disturbing blend of apprehension and compassion. " 'Tis the only way," she said softly.

"Nay," Giselle cried, catching at his arm. "You must not do this!"

"Giselle—"

"Nay!"

"I have to try, Giselle." And he did, he knew it in his soul. Knew it when he looked at Giselle, wild-eyed and fearful for his safety. Knew it when he'd come back to himself last eve to see Giselle gazing at him in horror.

"You cannot. Piers, I must speak to you about this."

"You may speak plainly. I have no secrets from my family." He cracked out a bitter laugh. "Not anymore."

Giselle looked around the solar and licked her lips. Her shoulders slumped, but she soon straightened them and lifted her chin. "I . . . sometimes I see things."

When no one disputed her, Piers saw her blink in surprise. He put his hand over hers. "What did you see?"

Anguish cloaked her lovely face. "I saw you die. Piers, I saw you die."

"Well, that is the idea," he told her.

"No. You *died*, Piers. Lady Iosobal was crying." She shook her head, tears streaming down her cheeks. "You cannot do this."

"I cannot live with Eikki. Can you?"

"There must be another way," she insisted. "Lady Iosobal? Surely, there is something else . . ."

Iosobal's grave expression gave Giselle the answer. With a high cry, Giselle turned back to Piers. "Do not do this! You will die!"

As he gazed into Giselle's eyes, another truth smacked into his mind, leaving a twisted mass of warmth and dread. By Saint George's sword, he'd fallen in love with his little nun.

Nay, he told himself. It could not be. He'd grown fond of her true, but . . . love?

Yet there it was.

He would not destroy her by allowing Eikki to remain within him. Last night had taught him he was no longer able to control the bastard. How long would it be before Eikki took over more and more, subjecting Giselle to his depraved desires, his need to dominate? Not long enough.

"Piers," Iosobal said. " 'Tis your decision. I can make

no promises."

"Do it," he told her, ignoring Giselle's gasp of distress. "As soon as possible."

Cain put a hand on his shoulder. "Are you sure?"

"Aye." Piers looked down at Giselle and managed to smile. "I am sure."

"Come to the east tower at dusk. I shall be prepared by then," Iosobal said.

Piers nodded. "As shall I."

🏇 🏇 🏇

Giselle knelt in the chapel and clutched her rosary. Though she appreciated his counsel, she was glad Father Michael had gone to the village. She needed to be alone with God.

She gazed at the gold cross atop the altar, but saw only Piers's face, ravaged by poison, the look in his eyes when he finally realized he was going to die.

"God, please aid me. Help me find a way to save him."

A pool of blue light from the window overhead shifted across the floor.

After she'd fled the solar where Iosobal had delivered her plan, The MacKeir had sought her out. Believe in Iosobal, he'd told her. She is the most powerful healer I have ever known. He'd gone on to tell her stories, the first how Iosobal had saved his daughter.

With magic.

Giselle wanted to believe, but despite the Abbess's frequent exhortations that magic was of evil, Giselle had never really accepted its existence at all.

There *was* something odd about Iosobal, however. And The MacKeir did not appear to be the kind of man to give in to delusions.

Still . . . Giselle bent her head to pray. *God, please deliver us from this evil.* She shivered, remembering the man Piers had turned into the night before.

Eikki was evil. She had no doubt of that now. If Piers had not regained control . . . She clutched her rosary tighter, her body trembling. She would have been at the harsh mercy of a condemned being, one who had gazed at her from Piers's face with the kind of hunger that had made her skin turn cold.

Go to Kindlemere, Piers had said. As much as Giselle wanted to flee this madness, she could not leave him. That realization surprised her more than anything.

She gazed up at the window, the blues, yellows, and reds of the glass spilling colored light into the chapel. Have faith, she told herself.

Calm settled into her, and she stopped shaking.

Faith. Have faith.

      ❧   ❧   ❧

Piers looked around the east tower chamber, and the import of what he was about to do took hold. Earlier, someone had pulled some stools into the empty chamber, lit a fire, and opened the windows to the cool night air.

Gifford shot him an anxious glance.

"Do not worry, uncle."

"How can I not worry?" Gifford's white hair, never smooth, floated around his face like a cloud. "You are placing your life in peril."

"My life is already in peril."

The door opened to reveal Cain. Behind him was Father Michael.

"Father Michael," Piers said slowly. "What do you do here?"

The priest put his hands on Piers's shoulders. "Your brother told me everything."

"You must think me mad."

"Nay. Reckless and brave. Not mad."

Iosobal stood by the window, her gaze upon the priest. The MacKeir flanked her, his arm around her waist. "Father, I am no sure you should be here," The MacKeir said, frowning at Cain. " 'Tis more than prayer we are about this eve."

Father Michael nodded. "Aye, so I understand. To my mind, 'tis all God's work."

Giselle stepped forward. "To mine as well, Father."

"Well," Piers said, his throat suddenly tight. "Then let us be about it."

You are a fool, Eilikti growled. *This woman's magic is nothing to one such as me.*

Go to hell, Piers told him.

Never.

Iosobal set the golden chalice on the floor. Piers made his feet move forward to look. Nestled within, just as when he first saw it, lay the purple crystal.

"Are you ready?" Iosobal asked.

"Aye." Piers pulled Giselle to him and held her close. He felt her body shaking and she clutched his tunic in both hands. He tilted her chin up and took her lips in a long, lingering kiss that left shadows in her eyes. "Pray for me," he told her.

She blinked. "Always."

Iosobal handed him a cup. "Drink."

He drained the cup.

🦎 🦎 🦎

Giselle put her hand over her mouth to stifle a cry when Piers collapsed to the floor, Cain catching him just in time to lower him gently.

Iosobal rushed forward and knelt beside him. Her vision, Giselle thought. It was exactly like her vision.

Dread cramped her belly, but she couldn't look away.

"It is taking effect," Iosobal said calmly.

Piers's gaze caught Giselle's and held. His face was pale, his brown eyes fixed on hers. Eyes that abruptly turned black.

"You shall not defeat me," he snarled.

Somehow, Giselle found courage and held the gaze of the one she knew was Eikki. "We shall," she said. "Leave my husband alone."

Though Piers's breathing was shallow, the being inside him laughed. "Nay. You shall be mine, Giselle. Mine to do with as I please."

"Dear Lord," Cain gasped.

Iosobal put her hands on Piers's chest. A faint, then opaque glow of white spread from her fingertips.

Piers's body jerked, his eyes shifting back and forth from brown to black.

Around the chalice, purple mist rose, just as Giselle had foreseen it. Cold mist that spread through the chamber.

"Iosobal?" The MacKeir asked.

"Eikki fights me," she said, her voice shaky.

Father Michael dropped to his knees and began to murmur prayers.

No, Giselle thought as she watched.

As much as the white glow from Iosobal spread, the purple mist swelled to meet it.

Piers's breathing turned to rough rasps, and his legs twitched.

"Nay!" Iosobal shouted. "Begone!" Her eyes glowed with fierce determination, but Giselle could see the truth in them.

It was not enough.

"Iosobal!" Cain shouted. "Do something!"

"I am trying. Eikki is taking Piers with him, though

Piers is fighting him."

Dear God, no, Giselle prayed. *God, aid us. Help him.* Tears streamed down her face, her gaze still locked with Piers's.

"Giselle," Iosobal said. "Aid me."

Giselle looked at her in shock. "Me? But, how? I have no magic."

"Aye, you do. The greatest magic of all."

"I do not understand." She sank onto the floor across from Iosobal.

" 'Tis love, Giselle. *That* is true magic."

Father Michael caught her gaze and nodded. His words streamed through Giselle's mind. *What do you think is the most important of God's teachings? 'Tis love.*

"Join with me," Iosobal urged. " 'Tis the only way to save him."

Love? Giselle stared down at Piers. His eyes cleared to golden brown, burning with determination. "But I don't . . ."

"Giselle," he rasped.

She gazed into his eyes, and then up at Iosobal, who eyed her with a knowing expression. Dear Lord, Iosobal was right. The realization crashed through Giselle like a searing bolt of lightning. Love. Sucking in a long breath, she slowly put her hands atop Iosobal's and closed her eyes.

Warmth shot up her arms and through her body. Images crashed into her mind's eye. Piers grinning at her. The fierce, yet tender expression on his face when he loved her. Teaching her how to ride while teasing her. Challenging her beliefs. Standing by her when she discovered the Bishop's perfidy.

Aye, love, she thought, and felt a surge of pure power unwind in the chamber. She opened her eyes.

Bright, white light lit the room, pulsed with power and magic. Iosobal was chanting something, but Giselle could not hear her over the pounding of her heart. Piers's eyes were shut, but she could feel the even rhythm of his heartbeat beneath their clasped hands.

"No!" a voice cried. Eikki's voice. Giselle flinched with the rage of it, but held onto Iosobal.

Light flashed and filled the chamber, blinding Giselle.

"Nooooooooo!" Eikki's voice howled, fading at the end.

When Giselle could see again, Iosobal lay slumped in her husband's arms, her face wan with fatigue. Her heart in her throat, Giselle looked down, terrified she would find Piers's eyes closed in final surrender.

Instead, he grinned and sat up.

"Piers? Eikki?" Giselle stammered.

"Gone."

"Oh, thank God." For a moment Giselle couldn't speak as tears erupted once more. "I was so afraid you would . . ."

"Die," Piers finished. His grin faded. "'Twas a close thing."

"Too damned close," Gifford said in a shaky voice, before taking a long drink from his jug of ale.

Giselle put her palm against Pier's cheek. "How do you feel?"

"Free."

"Give me some of that ale, Gifford," Cain ordered, his own voice none too steady.

Giselle's lips quirked as Gifford handed over the jug, obviously too shaken to guard his brew.

Piers put his hand over Giselle's. "Thank you. You have given me an incredible gift."

She knew he was not talking about her aiding Iosobal, but the reason she was able to do so. Abruptly ill at ease, she lowered her gaze. He knew she loved him. She waited for him to tell her he was fond of her, but that it would better if she lived at Kindlemere without him.

"Giselle," he said quietly.

She swallowed and forced herself to lift her gaze.

"I love you too. More than I ever imagined possible."

" 'Bout damn time!" Gifford shouted.

Between her tears, Giselle started laughing as her husband caught her in his arms and kissed her until her head swam.

❧ ❧ ❧

"You look so much like your mother," the Earl of Clay-bourne said. "I did love her, you know."

Giselle stood in the bailey, with Piers at her side, trying but utterly failing to keep her tears at bay.

Her father took her hands. "I am pleased to see you have found a good man to take care of you." He turned to Piers. "I cannot tell you what it means to me to have found my child." He gave a bittersweet smile. "And to know the fate of my wife."

"I wish she would have trusted in you," Giselle said softly.

"As do I." He studied her for a moment. "But I understand. Your mother was . . . was like a bright, beautiful light. I was not the only man to seek her hand. Truth be told, I was jealous of the attention she received, though I never saw that bastard's interest in her."

"I think . . ." Giselle gulped, trying to force the words out. "I think she died of a broken heart. My memories have faded with time, but I can still see her staring out across the hills with a sad look on her face. She would never talk to me about her past."

He squeezed her hands. "If ever you have need of me, I shall be there."

"Please come and visit us at Kindlemere," Piers said, sliding a hand around her waist. "You and Giselle have many years of catching up to do."

"I shall." He pressed a kiss to Giselle's forehead. "Be well, my child."

"Must you leave so soon?"

"Aye. I have obligations that will not wait. Send

word to me when you are settled at Kindlemere. I promise I shall come."

Giselle nodded.

"Treat her well," her father told Piers.

"I shall treat her as the precious jewel she is," her husband vowed. "Every moment."

" 'Tis all a father can ask." With a final smile, he walked away.

Giselle leaned into Piers, and sighed. "Every moment, you say?"

Piers held her close and nibbled at her ear. "Aye. What say you I start right now?"

"Hmm. Do you perhaps bear a gift for me?"

"Some women might consider it such."

She slapped at his drifting hands. "I was thinking of another sort of gift. Perhaps a new rosary?"

He turned her in his arms, his eyes twinkling. "I shall buy you all the rosaries you want. You can adorn the walls of Kindlemere with them, if you wish."

She put her palm against his cheek. "I was jesting. The one I have will suffice. But," she said, leading him back toward the hall, "I do have a boon to ask."

"Ask away, my jewel."

"Will you attend mass with me?" She stopped and gave him a somber look. "I can never give up my devotion to God."

"I would not ask you to. I shall be honored to attend mass with you." He smiled. "I have much to give thanks for these days."

She returned his smile. "So you do, indeed."

The door to the great hall flew open and Gifford's voice bellowed out across the bailey. "Piers!"

Piers groaned. "What now?"

"Piers!" his uncle shouted again. "Get in here."

Giselle followed Piers into the great hall, and stopped short. But for Gifford, muttering something about seeking out a sword, everyone stood motionless, varied expressions of shock on each face.

When Giselle saw what they were staring at, she swayed on her feet and grabbed for Piers's arm.

Something shimmered in the air in front of Padruig, something faintly resembling the form of a woman.

Padruig's face could have been carved of stone, but for his blazing gaze.

"Ye canna run forever from your destiny." The shimmer expanded, and then faded bit by bit until nothing was left.

For a long moment, no one spoke. "Well, that was interesting," The MacKeir finally said, resheathing his sword. Beside him, Iosobal stood with a curious expression on her face.

"Damned spirits," Gifford groused. "Amice, we have need of you again."

Lady Amice shook her head. "She is gone."

Gifford peered around the hall. "Are you sure?"

"Aye." Giselle saw Amice exchange a confused glance

with the earl.

"What happened?" Piers asked.

"Another damned ghost showed up, that is what happened," Gifford answered. "I told you there was one about." Saraid handed him a cup of ale.

Giselle let go of Piers and approached Padruig. She touched his arm, and he flinched, as if he'd been sleeping, or so dazed he was unaware of anyone else's presence. "Padruig?"

"I must go," he said, his voice nearly a whisper.

"To where?"

"Home, of course."

She narrowed her gaze. "I shall walk with you out to the bailey."

"You need not."

"I want to."

He nodded, and gave his farewells to the rest of the group. Giselle was afraid Piers would insist on accompanying her, but with a glance, he understood her wish to speak to Padruig alone.

As they walked to the stables, Giselle put her hand on Padruig's arm once more, and pulled him to a stop. "I never believed in ghosts."

"I am no sure I do yet."

"But that . . . it . . . she spoke to you. What did she mean about your destiny?"

He smiled and took her hands. "Giselle, do not worry for me. You have a new life ahead of you now.

Treasure that. Live."

She bit her lip. "Padruig, you have helped me in the past. Let me help you now."

For a moment, such torment filled his gaze that Giselle caught her lip between her teeth. "You cannot aid me, lass. 'Tis my path to walk alone."

"But, Padruig, I—"

"Nay, lass. Wish me Godspeed and be happy." He pulled free, and walked away, turning once to offer her a final smile.

Giselle watched him go, her heart heavy with questions, wishing he would trust her enough, but knowing it was not in his nature to do so. *I have no clan.* His words came back to her.

And suddenly, the bailey disappeared.

Fires lit the black night, a patchwork of gold strewn across the countryside. The pounding of hooves rumbled the ground, the labored breathing of horses audible in the air. A man shouted, his voice carried away by the bitter wind.

A broken body lay in a circle of firelight, a tangle of dark hair cradling a young, ashen cheek. Blood soaked her gown and spread into a pool beneath her body. One arm lay outstretched, as if in death she sought to reach something. Or someone.

A howl of disbelief, of fierce agony rent the air.

Smoke billowed and clouded the scene, clearing to reveal another. A man faced away, his golden hair spilling down his back, his broad shoulders rigid, his feet planted in a wide stance. *Padruig.* Pain and guilt cloaked him like living shadows of what once was.

His sword caught the sunlight and gleamed like a ribbon of firelit water. A sword washed in blood.

Before him stood an older man, his hair a shock of red, his gaze wide, filled with both relief and wariness. Though his tunic was torn and bloodstained, he slowly smiled.

"Welcome home, laird" he said, and bowed in obeisance. "Welcome home to Castle MacCoinneach."

Giselle smiled and returned to the hall.

Epilogue

P iers led a blindfolded Giselle through the long corridors of Kindlemere Castle. She held tightly to his hand, flushing at the twittering of servants when they passed. When she stumbled, she reached up to remove the blindfold, but Piers's hand stopped her.

" 'Tis a surprise," he told her. "Behave."

He led her up steps, but Giselle was so disoriented she couldn't tell where they were going. Finally, he stopped and she heard the sound of a door opening. " 'Tis a wedding gift," he said, and swept off her blindfold.

Giselle looked around the chamber in wonderment. Thick rush mats covered the plank floor and tapestries hung on the walls, closing out the drafts of air. A fire burnt merrily in a corner fireplace, turning the chamber into a cocoon of warmth.

She walked toward the center of the chamber and trailed a hand through the warm water. Blue tile lined the tub, easily big enough for two.

"Do you like it?" Piers asked.

She wound her arms around his neck and kissed him. "Mmm, yes. Would you like to join me?"

"I thought you would never ask."

Within moments, she found herself nestled in Piers's arms, leaning against his broad chest and swishing her feet through the water. " 'Tis very decadent."

"I surely hope so."

She laughed, and turned in his arms. "This is exactly what I envisioned the first time you asked me what I thought of Cain's request for an indoor bathing chamber."

His brows lifted. "At the same time you were praying to God to deliver you from the dire fate of marrying me?"

"Aye." She sighed and traced a pattern on his chest. "I think even then He knew I did not mean it."

Piers chuckled, drew her close, and nuzzled her hair. "You certainly had me convinced."

"How foolish I must have seemed to you."

"Nay. Innocent and naïve, perhaps. Misguided for certain. Not foolish." He stroked his fingers down her arms, and over her belly. "Courageous, yes. And, of course, I wanted you in my bed from the very first moment."

"Only in your bed?" she teased.

His eyes flared. "I think 'tis time for the second part of my wedding gift."

Giselle smiled as her husband proceeded to love her with a passion that left her heart so full it could not hold more love for him. Afterward, when she lay sprawled across his lap, savoring the quiet and the soothing warmth of the water, it struck her that the last remnant of her rules had gone from her mind and heart.

Perhaps it was time to make some new rules, she mused. *Number One: Let not pride or duty blind you, but seize love with both hands and never let go.* Aye, now *that* was a fine rule to live by.

Abruptly her vision filled with the image of her mother. She stood bathed in a soft glow of gold, her beautiful face so real that Giselle felt as if she could reach out and touch her skin. Her mother smiled, nodded in approval, and slowly faded away.

And Giselle's heart finally soared free.

Chapter 1

Wareham Castle, Cumberland, 1196

"Please come to Falcon's Craig," the note read. "I am in need of your unique services. I own Villa Delphino on the Italian coast. It is yours if you will aid me." Amice de Monceaux read the Earl of Hawksdown's boldly scrawled letter for the second time and crushed the vellum in her fist.

Then she started shaking. How could Cain ask this of her? Tempt her with the one thing he knew she had always dreamt of ever since her brother told her stories of the sun-drenched land. And why did he own the villa? That was her dream.

Her stomach churned with memories, too many, too clear even now. After five years, she could still feel Cain's arms around her. And could still hear his calm voice saying, "I am betrothed," before he walked away.

The door to her chamber opened slowly. "Amice, dear? Are you in here?"

"Aye, Mother." Amice stuffed the vellum under her mattress and crossed the rush-covered floor to take her mother's arm.

Lady Eleanora pulled free and paced across the chamber, her pale fingers fluttering like butterflies in a meadow. "I cannot find Beornwynne's Kiss. Your father, the whoreson, must have hidden it again."

Amice took a deep breath, no longer startled by her mother's language. And, truth be told, she accurately described her late father. "Mother, the necklace is right here." She opened a trunk and lifted out a carved box, placing it in her mother's hands. " 'Tis safe, as always."

Her mother sat on the stone ledge in front of the window slit and opened the box. She gathered up the heavy gold and amethyst necklace in her gnarled fingers.

Amice laid a hand on her mother's shoulder and felt bones, as if she held a tiny bird beneath her palm. "Would you like to go sit in the garden, Mother?"

Her mother's brow furrowed, and she tilted her head to stare at Amice. "Where is Isolda? I told her to get my blue gown ready for the feast tonight."

"Mother, Isolda died last year." Amice kept her voice even, though she wanted to scream at the loss of the vibrant person who had been her mother and friend.

Blinking quickly, her mother looked around the chamber, as if she expected Isolda to pop out from behind the bed at any moment. "Aye, of course." She gave a small laugh. "I was confused for a moment. Poor Isolda. How I miss her."

Amice squeezed her mother's shoulder and took a deep breath. "Come with me outside. 'Tis a beautiful day."

"What were we talking about?"

"Beornwynne's Kiss."

"Of course. I . . . forgot." Her mother dropped the necklace, grabbed Amice's hands and squeezed tight. Too tight. Amice felt her mother's frail body tremble.

"Mother," she began.

Her mother's gaze clouded. "Beornwynne's Kiss will protect me, see me safe across the river when I die."

"And you have it."

When her mother looked up at her, her gaze was far away. "Is this it?" she asked, her lips trembling.

Amice stared down at the top of her mother's head, the strands of silver hair mixed with white, and her heart splintered. "Mother, all is well."

Her mother patted Amice on the hand and rose. She wobbled and caught herself for a moment with her hand on the seat, waving Amice away with the other. "I believe I shall go down to the kitchen and see if Cook has prepared any meat pies."

" 'Tis a good idea." Amice watched her mother's departure with a heavy heart, the knowledge that she was dying an aching lump in her belly.

The' only reason Amice remained at Wareham was to care for her mother. And by Michaelmas, her brother, the Earl of Wareham, would be wed to a woman who made it clear Wareham would have only one mistress.

Soon, she would have no place.

She closed her eyes and envisioned soft sand, a sparkling blue sea, and golden sunlight. Yes, there she could find peace. Take what Cain offers, her inner voice urged. Take it and flee to warmth and beauty.

How simple it sounded, but in her heart she knew it would take every scrap of strength and pride she possessed. Five years ago Cain Veuxfort had nearly destroyed her. Had taken her heart into the palm of his hand and then crushed it in his uncaring fist.

Her mouth curved in a wry smile. Now, it appeared he had a troublesome ghost who would not leave him alone. He needed her, the Spirit Goddess. She would be a fool not to take everything she could gain from Cain Veuxfort. Aye, he would give her what he offered and more.

And she would be free.

❧   ❧   ❧

Cain strode into his solar, wiping sweat from his forehead. He unbuckled his sword belt and poured a cup of ale, which he downed in one long swallow.

"Any survivors, my lord?" his seneschal, Nyle, asked.

"Geoffrey is improving, but he still swings like a maid." He sat and leaned his sword against the wall. "How are the figures, Nyle?"

Nyle rubbed his eyes and looked at the columns of numbers running down the parchment. "Good."

"Well done. What do you think of—"

The door to his solar suddenly crashed open. "There you are!" His Uncle Gifford blew in, closely followed by Cain's brother, Piers. Gifford carried a jug with him and spared not a glance for Nyle.

Gifford and Piers came to an abrupt halt in front of Cain. His uncle gazed at him with twinkling eyes. "Is the . . ." his voice dropped, "Spirit Goddess coming?"

Cain gave him a stern look. "I am attending to important matters here. And that . . . title is supposed to be secret."

Gifford snorted.

Piers waved a hand in dismissal. "You are always attending to important matters."

Gifford took a swig from the jug, plopped it down on an empty space on the table, and sat on the remaining stool. "Well, answer my question. Is she coming?"

"Aye. Lady Amice shall arrive soon."

"Ha! Wonderful news. Go on now, Nyle. We need to speak to the lord about something truly weighty."

"Some might judge keeping a roof over our heads and food on the table of concern," Cain suggested.

"Pah. Time enough for that later. Now, we want to know about our guest."

Giving up, he nodded to Nyle. "Go. When these two release me, I shall send for you."

Nyle's lips twitched. "Good luck, my lord."

He exited quickly, and Piers grabbed the vacated stool. His brother drummed his fingers on his thigh and gazed at Cain expectantly. "When will she be here?"

"I do not know exactly."

Gifford rubbed his hands together. "We shall put her in the rose chamber. It has a lovely view of the ocean and, of course, the garden. We want her to feel welcome."

"Gifford, the only reason she is coming is to get rid of that damned ghost," Cain reminded them. God knew, he reminded himself of that fact twenty times a day.

Piers elbowed Gifford, who reluctantly handed over the jug. "Wonder what the girl looks like."

"Visited Wareham once," Gifford commented. "Cannot say I remember the girl. Her father, though." He shook his head. "A brute of a man."

Cain's own memory surfaced and he nodded. "Aye, that he was."

His uncle peered around the solar and lowered his voice to a near whisper. "Got to be a sad case, what with not marrying and engaging in this ghost business." He blinked at Cain and snatched back the jug.

"Amice de Monceaux is the most comely woman I

have ever seen." At the flash of suspicion in Piers's eyes, Cain realized his slip.

Piers leaned forward and there was a brief tussle between his uncle and him for the jug. "Give it to me, you old sot."

"I brought the jug. Get your own."

Cain watched them go back and forth and shook his head, wondering how his life had gotten so out of control. All the scene needed now to make it complete was an appearance from the ghost of Falcon's Craig. "Enough," he barked.

The two looked back at him like guilty boys caught stealing custard tarts from the kitchen. "Sorry, Cain," Piers said with a sheepish grin.

Gifford coughed. "So, how well do you know the wench?"

For a moment, Cain could not answer. It was a simple question, but impossible to answer. Did he know her? He had thought so once, but he was not sure he ever truly had. And knowing was far too mild a term to describe his tangled feelings for Amice. "She is a lady, not a wench. And when I fostered at Chasteney, Amice was there as well."

Piers took a pull from the jug and glanced sideways at Gifford. "Uncle, I sense a tale here. What do you think?"

Gifford settled back and crossed his thin legs. "My boy, I believe you may be correct." He stared at Cain. "Well?"

Cain was beginning to feel besieged. "As I said, Amice was at Chasteney the same time I was."

"And? Did you bed her?"

He fought a flush. His uncle was never one to hold

his tongue. Had he bedded her? Oh, aye, though rarely in a bed. Five years had not dimmed his memory one bit. Or his guilt. Heat puddled in his stomach and raced down to his groin. He shifted on his chair and gave Gifford a stern look. "I am not answering that question."

"What does she look like?" Piers asked with a gleam in his eyes.

"You shall not try to add Amice to your collection of women." Piers was the kind of man women fought over. His boyish good looks and lighthearted view toward life drew women in like the tide to shore.

"Why not?"

Cain just looked at him.

"Ah, so that is the way of it. Brown, blonde, or red?"

Making a vain attempt to smooth down his white hair, Gifford noted, "I prefer red on a woman, myself."

"Brown, blonde, or red what?" Cain asked.

Gifford slapped a hand on the table. "Hair, of course."

Cain rolled his eyes. "Dark brown hair."

His brother leaned forward. "And? What else?"

For a moment, he let himself remember. "Big dark eyes. Tall, slender, with the longest legs I have ever seen on a woman."

Piers stared for a moment, then said, "Damn. Are you sure I—?"

"Aye."

Gifford started cackling and reached for the jug. "You just answered my question."

Well, hell. Cain shrugged.

Piers made a pass at the jug, but Gifford clutched it tight. Turning back to Cain, he asked, "What happened?"

He drew a mantle over his expression. "You know what happened. Mother saw fit to tell me I had been betrothed to Luce. Honor demanded I marry her." He silenced Piers's protest with a raised hand. "It was my duty as the earl. To keep both of you in home and," he paused, "ample drink."

Gifford gave another snort and passed the jug to Piers. "Luce. Naught but a twisted bit of fluff. Why Ismena liked her is beyond me. God rest both their souls, of course."

"Mother liked Cain's wife because she could deliver Styrling Castle," Piers reminded him. "And enough coin to pay the King's amercement."

"Not right," Gifford muttered.

Cain rubbed the back of his neck. He refused to think of his late wife, let alone discuss her. "None of it matters now. Luce is dead. As is whatever Amice and I might have shared." How he managed to utter the last with such certainty he could not fathom.

Piers's gaze narrowed. "Some things have a habit of lingering."

"Like that demented wraith who keeps mucking up my experiments," Gifford groused.

"Which is why Amice is coming here. She shall rid us of the ghost for good."

Gifford popped up and started toward the door. "I shall make sure Hawis gets the chamber ready."

"I have already spoken to her, Uncle."

Half turning, his uncle said, "I had better make sure." Opening the door, he muttered to himself between swigs from his jug.

Piers gazed at Cain and lifted a brow. "I have always wondered why you bought Villa Delphino."

Cain gritted his teeth. "I like Italy."

"Hmm. But you have only visited once."

"I am busy." He kept his gaze blank. It would only encourage Piers to learn the truth, that the villa reminded him of what could have been. He had seen Amice everywhere at Villa Delphino, imagined her in every room. It took only once to convince him he should never have bought the place, never tried to keep a memory alive.

"You have been alone too long, Brother."

"I like being alone."

"A man alone shall forfeit the sweetness of life."

Cain scowled. "More of your nonsense."

"You have an obligation."

Heirs, he meant. "Why don't you legitimize one of yours?"

Piers shook his head. "I am too careful to sire bastards. And you are the earl."

Cain stood and placed his hands atop the old, scarred table. "I married once. 'Twas a farce."

"Not all women are as corrupt as Luce. Perhaps, this Amice—"

"Nay!" He shook his head, mentally crushing an unruly surge of hope at the thought. "Nay, Piers. Put it from your mind."

"Very well." His brother's expression said the topic was far from forgotten. "I shall be in the stable. Pleasance is nearly ready to foal."

"Good." Cain watched his brother depart, and he dropped back into his chair, burying his face in his hands.

What had possessed him to send for Amice de Monceaux?

Just as he gave in to the thought, his inkpot went sailing into the air, landing with a wet plop on top of Nyle's carefully written accounts. As he watched the black ink drip across the parchment, he knew he had no choice.

Amice would rid him of the ghost. He would happily give up Villa Delphino and return to his life. Naught more. He was the Earl of Hawksdown now, not a young man swept away by beautiful eyes, a sweet mouth, and the body of a goddess. I am strong, he reminded himself.

"I am in control," he said aloud.

The inkpot rose from the parchment and did a little twirl in the air.

Cain grabbed up his sword and strode out of the solar.

❧   ❧   ❧

The next morning, Amice and her companion, Laila, were mounted in the bailey bidding farewell to Amice's brother, Rand, when a shout rang out.

"Who is it?" Rand called up to one of the guards.

A bellow rolled in from outside the castle, and Amice cringed. She knew that voice. Lugh MacKeir of Tunvegen, Highland laird and frequent visitor to Wareham.

Rand started laughing at the expression on her face.

"Rand, please. I must go."

Her brother looked up at the guard and ordered, "Raise the portcullis. 'Tis a friend."

With a heavy, grinding sound, the iron portcullis slowly lifted, and a huge, roan destrier pounded into the bailey, blowing air from its nostrils. The MacKeir easily balanced atop the beast, clad in his green and black plaid and an impressive collection of blades. Behind him rode a troop of his Highlanders, all nearly as massively built and armed as if they approached the greatest battle of their lives.

The MacKeir came to a halt and gave her a graceful bow. "Lady Amice, you are even lovelier than last I saw you."

"Thank you, my lord." She smiled in what she hoped conveyed a cool distance.

He gestured with an arm like a tree trunk. "Is she not the most beautiful woman you have ever seen, men?"

Caught between the temptation to blush or laugh, she watched as ten battle-hardened Highlanders all bobbed heads in unison, chorusing, "Aye." One of the men shouted out, "Make a fine bride for you," and she wanted to press her heels to her horse and flee.

"I have decided 'tis time, my treasure." The MacKeir glanced down at Rand and nodded an acknowledgment.

"Time for what?" And why in the world was he calling her his treasure? She frowned down at her brother, but Rand just stood there grinning.

"Why, to claim my bride, of course." The MacKeir's smile broadened, and he inched his mount closer to hers. He seized one of her hands in a meaty grip. "Your wait is over. The MacKeir has come for you at last."

She stared at him in astonishment. He clearly expected her gratitude. True, she was well past marriageable age, but still. "What . . . what are you talking about?"

Before he could answer, Rand loudly cleared his throat. "Chief MacKeir, I do not recall having an agreement for Amice."

"Details, my friend. I shall agree to whatever you require for the privilege of possessing this rare jewel."

She tried to pull her hand free but it was like trying to escape a lion's paw. "Rand?"

"Chief MacKeir, Lugh, please come into the hall and share a cup. You must be thirsty from your travel."

With a last squeeze, The MacKeir released her hand and leapt from his horse. "Fine idea, my lord." He clapped Rand on the back. Luckily, her brother was a big man himself, or he would be sprawling on the ground from the force of the blow. Of course, during his long friendship with Lugh MacKeir, Rand had learned to brace himself. "Come, Amice," The MacKeir said as he held out his hand to her.

"Unfortunately, I cannot, Chief MacKeir. I am leaving."

Heavy black brows furrowed into a single line. "Leaving? But 'tis too soon, my precious. My men and I need to remain overnight and rest our horses."

She sighed. "Not with you. I must journey to Falcon's Craig."

"Nay. I forbid it." His forest green eyes flashed with possession. "My bride stays with me."

The whole conversation was so ridiculous, she was tempted to laugh. But she knew Lugh MacKeir well enough to clamp the urge. She had always thought of him as a gentle giant, but underneath dwelled a formidable Highland chief. She forced herself to smile politely. "I am not your bride, my lord."

He waved a hand. "Merely a matter of time. Do not worry, Amice. You shall be mine."

"I am not worried."

Obviously, he understood her response as assent and shot her an approving nod. "Let us discuss this in the hall. I have a powerful thirst on me, and I would look upon you."

"Chief MacKeir, did you not hear me? I must leave. Now."

He took a step toward her, his expression hardening.

Rand grabbed his arm and whispered something to him. As Amice watched, The MacKeir allowed Rand to pull him a small distance away and the two men held a soft, but clearly heated discussion, punctuated by several sharp looks in her direction from Chief MacKeir.

Finally, he stared at her brother and slowly tipped his head.

Amice looked at Rand, but his expression told her nothing. The warriors flanking The MacKeir stepped forward as he returned to her side.

Swallowing thickly, she waited for him to speak.

"You may journey to Falcon's Craig." He scowled. "Though I like it not, your brother convinces me 'tis important to you."

"Thank you, my lord."

"But when you return, I shall be here, ready to take you to Tunvegen where you belong."

Tunvegen, deep in the Highlands, far from anything or anyone familiar. Far from a villa perched over the warm sea. She gripped the reins tight. "Has my brother agreed to this?"

"Nay. But he will. As soon as we come to terms." He stepped closer and before she could get out an objection, swept her down to the ground.

She peered up at him, all at once aware of just how big he was. Normally, she was nearly as tall as a man, but next to The MacKeir she felt almost fragile.

"You are mine, Amice."

She opened her mouth to protest but found it plundered by another. And plundered it was, his firm lips capturing hers, tasting her, stroking her tongue, and sweeping through her mouth with gentle force.

He broke the kiss and cocked a brow. " 'Tis only the beginning, my flower." He puffed out his broad chest. "The MacKeir shall make you cry with joy."

Her jaw dropped. Dear God, how was she to escape this wild Scot? A journey to Falcon's Craig suddenly did not seem long enough. Before her bewildered eyes, Chief MacKeir and his men trooped into the great hall with Rand, talking and laughing like the greatest of friends. Surely, Rand would not give her to this big bear of a man. He knew her heart's desire, supported it in fact.

"Come, Amice," Laila said. "We should go before your Chief MacKeir changes his mind."

Amice was on her horse and outside the gatehouse faster than she had ever been in her life. Surrounded by her guards, she spurred her mount to a gallop and never looked back.

ISBN#1932815260
ISBN#9781932815269
Jewel Imprint: Amethyst
US $6.99 / CDN $9.99
Paranormal Romance
Available Now
www.amytolnitch.com

A Lost Touch of Paradise

Amy Tolnitch

For the first time in his life, Lugh MacKeir, Laird of Tunvegan, finds himself in a battle he cannot win. His precious daughter is dying of the same illness that claimed his wife.

The Isle of Parraba is a whispered legend, a place rumored to be ruled by a sorceress, an isle no one can reach. Yet, legend speaks of a powerful healer as well. Lugh MacKeir, desperate, determines to find Parraba and face its mysterious ruler.

Iosobal is the Lady of Parraba, mystical and magical, a woman apart from the world around her. Drawn to something familiar in Lugh's child, however, she reluctantly agrees to help her in exchange for Lugh clearing the blocked entrance to a very special cave.

But the child's illness defies Iosobal's skill, and Lugh's task proves more of a challenge than he anticipated. In the end, the secret to saving Lugh's daughter lies in Iosobal's ability to open her heart to a brash warrior who has invaded her tranquil sanctuary. She must find the courage to end her isolation, and the wise innocence of a child must lead them all to A LOST TOUCH OF PARADISE.

ISBN#193281566X
ISBN#9781932815665
Jewel Imprint: Amethyst
US $6.99 / CDN $9.99
Available Now
www.amytolnitch.com

For more information
about other great titles from
Medallion Press, visit

www.medallionpress.com